THE RECKONING

M.K. Easley

CONTENTS

THE RECKONING

By M.K. Easley

*Shoutout to my beta squad. I never could have done this without
your time, effort, enthusiasm, patience, and humor.*

CHAPTER 1

Tristan Wallace did her best to ignore the whispers as she walked down the hall. For the last three years, it had been the same thing -- *freak, weirdo, witch* -- no matter where she went in Jamestown Academy, the whispers followed her. Of course, it had all been started by Emmeline Strandquest on the first day of ninth grade when, upon taking one look at Tristan, she had declared that evil walked among them.

Though presented that way, this was nothing new for Emmeline or for Tristan, as Emmeline had been proclaiming the same thing since the two had been classmates at Diamondback Elementary; the difference with high school, however, was the larger audience Emmeline was able to hold captive, and with her shiny, bouncy hair the color of blackberries, wide green eyes, and peachy pink skin, Emmeline was the quintessential, drop-dead gorgeous popular girl who captivated with ease. She had, as far as Tristan could remember, strolled into kindergarten with an air of old-world confidence that had followed her all the way through to high school, causing countless classmates to trail behind in the hopes she'd turn her attention their way.

As a casual observer, it was a mystery to Tristan how someone so rotten on the inside could accumulate such a desperate mass following, but Tristan supposed she was likely only in a position to make that observation due her personal rule, backed by her parents, to befriend none of her classmates. This was an easy enough feat, considering most of the kids in the small, small town of Lavelle, Louisiana fell into two categories -- Emmeline worshippers or outcasts. The kids in the middle of the road mostly ignored Tristan, not wanting to become targets of Emmeline and her cronies themselves, though Tristan had surface acquaintanceships with a few of them, mostly as a result of school projects or shared home-rooms.

This area was one in which she totally differed from her twin siblings, Olivia and Evander, who were sixteen and in the eleventh grade. Both of them were among the most popu-lar in their class, and more than once, much to Tristan's ex-treme annoyance, it had taken their friends by surprise to learn that Tristan, seventeen and a senior, was their sister. It wasn't that the younger Wallaces weren't also strange, just a little bit different in a hard to identify way, but they were both as beautiful and outgoing as it came, so their peers took their offbeat vibe as nothing more than a twin personality quirk. Tristan, while also striking with her long, wheat-col-ored hair and expressive dark eyes, had accepted long ago that she couldn't hold a candle to her fair ginger siblings in any manner.

"You're wrong." A cheerful voice piped up from beside Tristan, and she jumped, turning to find Olivia had appeared seemingly out of nowhere.

"What?"

"You're crazy smart and you can be funny, usually when you're not trying to be, and you're thoughtful and gor-geous. You don't need to compete with me and Ev, but you'd be a tough contender if you did."

"Oceana," Tristan hissed, gripping her sister's arm. "What did I tell you about reading my thoughts?"

"What did I tell you back?" Olivia asked, shaking her off, her gray eyes narrowing. "I usually can't; sometimes you just come through as loud as day. And don't call me Oceana here, *Trinity*."

The thing was, Emmeline wasn't *entirely* off-base with her accusations. Tristan wasn't a witch -- anyone with good sense knew witches weren't real and never had been, even predating the Salem trials -- but she and her family *were* part of an exclusive, underground community whose essential belief was that, through the practice and the act of worshipping the universe and its elements, the mind could be enlightened to supernatural heights. It certainly seemed to be true for Olivia, who, outside of Jamestown Academy, went by her elemental name, Oceana. She'd been picking up on people's thoughts since she was a child, and had become nearly effortless at what she called "tuning in". Recently, she'd begun to experiment with *influencing* people's thoughts, to get them to change their minds and do or say what she wanted while making them think it was their idea, at which it seemed she'd be proficient as well. Evander, who went by Ember outside of school, shared her ability to read thoughts, though his focus was more on the desire for extraordinary physical strength. Tristan, better known as Trinity to her family and community, at a young age had learned she could move things with the power of her mind alone.

As she grew up, however, Tristan withdrew from her practice, unsure that completing high school and marrying into the community was the path she wanted to take. It was the path she'd been prepped for her entire life -- her parents were even close with the family of the boy, Canton Crenshaw, who went by Celes, with whom they had decided Tristan would settle down. Unlike some of the more devoted community members, however, Sasha, who went by Sol, and Urien, who went by Umbris, had made it clear that they would not force their children into any particular way of life. Nevertheless, it was this prepping that had prompted Sol and Umbris to encourage Tristan not to make friends with her classmates -- as the oldest child in the family, the expectations placed upon her were different than those of her younger siblings, and it would be easier for Tristan to blend into the community if she didn't also have to manage relationships with oblivious outsiders. This had always suited Tristan fine; though having no friends could get lonely, her classmates were generally a bunch of fools, so she didn't feel like she was missing out on too much.

The bell rang just as Tristan and Olivia parted ways, and Tristan took her seat near the back in her A.P. Literature and Composition class. Though the school year had only recently started, this class had quickly become Tristan's favorite. The work was challenging, the teacher was laid back, and there was no Emmeline Strandquest. There was, unfortunately, Tara LeBlanc, one of Emmeline's best friends, but her seat was far enough away from Tristan that no problems typically arose.

"OK, so since we've been doing this now for about six weeks, what better time to assign your senior project?" Ms. Allona West clapped her hands together, grinning at the students. She ignored the groans and kept talking. "It will be a partner project, due at the end of the year, and I am assigning your partners now so you can get used to the idea and take your time working through the material. I'm also assigning them now because this is your senior year and you are going to be slammed harder than ever before, and since I'm nice I don't want to add much to your pressure."

Tristan's stomach began to hurt. Group projects had historically not gone well for her, and she hadn't expected an English class to be the type that called for a joint assignment. She glanced over at Tara, the idea of being partnered with her worse than nearly anything else Tristan could imagine happening within the bonds of this class.

"Your senior project will consist of five elements. A paper, a project, a portfolio, community service, and a presentation. Before you ask, *Ms. West, what does community service have to do with our senior project?* The answer is everything. Community service is the fastest and easiest way to establish a network within the community you will be unleashed upon at graduation. Since the goal of your senior year is to prepare you to get out there and into the early stages of what will become your eventual career, you will find that networking will be a common theme in all of your classes, and with good reason."

The class murmured amongst themselves, and Tristan's stomach clenched harder. This project was quickly turning into a scenario from her school-related nightmares.

"I know it sounds overwhelming. I'm overwhelmed listening to myself, if I'm being honest with you, and I don't envy your position. Jamestown Academy is one of the top-tiered schools in the state, as I'm sure you've heard *ad nauseam,* but they didn't buy that reputation. The curriculum you're staring down this year is challenging, but it's not insurmountable, even if it will feel that way at times. You're in this class because you're smart, and by now you've hopefully learned some kind of time management and or study skills, so you'll probably do OK. I hope, anyway, because I don't want to see any of you roaming these halls next year. I won't even look at you, I swear it. Don't test me; trust me."

Ms. West waited for the students to settle before heading to her desk and picking up a sheet of paper.

"OK, as painlessly as possible, here we go."

Tristan didn't usually think anything of her last name, until it came to situations where alphabetical order was required. On the plus side, the odds that she'd be paired with someone at her end of the alphabet were slim, so she'd hopefully be put out of her misery sooner rather than later.

"Beckett Benson, your partner is Tristan Wallace."

Snickers, whispers. Tristan ignored them, looking across the room to where Beckett sat, a few desks ahead of Tara. He was part of the popular crowd, had even dated Emmeline Strand-quest in sophomore year, but was one of the few popular kids who left Tristan alone; there were better classmates with whom she could have been paired, but there were also far worse. Beckett looked over at Tristan, his sharp, blue-green eyes meeting hers. She expected to see some kind of revulsion, some indication that, along with the few meat-head friends he had in the class, he'd be groaning or other-wise expressing displeasure at being paired with her. It was a surprise, then, that he looked almost... *friendly?* Tristan frowned, turning back to her notebook. She didn't know a great deal about Beckett Benson other than his dumb name -- he'd joined Jamestown Academy in tenth grade, so there was no elementary school history between them, but he'd assimilated quickly into the jock/cheerleader crowd, prob-ably because he was, as most of the girls and some of the boys whispered, *hot.* Tristan glanced over again to find he was still looking at her, observing her like she was a specimen beneath a microscope. She stared back at him, trying to see him objectively instead of in the context of his friends. His build was bordering on stocky -- he was shorter than most of his football teammates, but layered with compact muscle -- his light brown hair was stylishly messy, and his square jawline could probably cut glass if given the chance. Those eyes, though, a brilliant greenish blue like the waters in the Caribbean, were by far his best feature; they were genuinely beautiful in color.

"I hope you're going to take holy water to your meet-ings with Tristan, Beckett," Tara said, leaning forward, not bothering to lower her voice. She and the people around her laughed, but Beckett just shot her a withering look before turning back to the front of the class. An awkward silence fell over that side of the room.

Tristan raised her eyebrows. She hadn't expected him to defend her, of course, but she also hadn't expected him to shut Tara down with a look. Frowning for a second time, Tristan looked up at Ms. West, who had finished doling out the assignments and had started to talk about their senior project once again.

***

"Tristan!"

Tristan turned to find Beckett coming towards her once class had dismissed. She waited by a bank of lockers, moving out of the flow of students so he could catch up with her.

"Hi," Beckett said, stopping in front of her and sounding a little out of breath.

"Hi," Tristan replied cautiously, appraising him with wary eyes. They were nearly the same height -- Beckett had less than three inches on her.

Beckett stared at her for a moment before nodding and smiling.

"I wanted to see when you wanted to get together to discuss our project."

Tristan opened her mouth to respond, when another voice spoke directly behind her.

"Oh my God protect me, get *away* from my locker before you put some weird voodoo curse on it."

Tristan stepped aside to find Emmeline looking at her the way one would look at something nasty on the bottom of their shoe. She was flanked as always by Tara, as well as Hattie Guillory, Bailey Jones, Eloise Brach, and Georgiana Luker, her closest and most vicious friends.

"Oh, hi Beckett," Emmeline said suddenly, though Tristan knew she hadn't just noticed him. Her voice sweetened to a sickening cadence, and Tristan had to work hard not to roll her eyes.

"Emmeline. Tara, Hattie, Bailey, Eloise, Georgiana." Beckett nodded at all of them, a wry expression on his face, but turned back to address Tristan. "Bell's gonna go off in a few. Let's start walking, we can discuss it on the way."

Not sparing Emmeline one more look, Tristan walked off with Beckett, knowing the other girl was fuming. She hid a smile behind her hand.

"Anyway, when works for you to get together about our project?"

"I'm free pretty much any day after school."

"Friday?"

"Including Friday."

Beckett smiled, a half-grin that showed off one dimple.

"Where do you want to meet?"

"The library would probably be best. You know, since that's where the research materials are," Tristan said dryly.

"No." Beckett shook his head, and Tristan raised her eyebrows in surprise. "No, I can't stay in school when I'm not supposed to be here. I won't be able to think to get anything done. It's like a weird claustrophobia."

Tristan squinted, cocking her head at Beckett, who appeared to be serious.

"You... don't use the library here? What do you do for research projects?"

"I use the internet, from the comfort of my own home."

"But what about group projects?"

Beckett grinned.

"I use the internet, from the comfort of my own home, with my partner or partners. Have you ever used the internet?"

"Yes I've used the internet," Tristan shot back, giving him the same kind of withering look he'd given Tara in English class. "I guess I just prefer the library."

"Not me. So should I come to your house, or should you come to mine?"

"Uh, no," Tristan said immediately, shaking her head. "No, neither. Why don't we just meet at the lake, since that's outside but still close enough to the building in case we need to access the dreaded library for something?"

"Fine by me." Beckett grinned again. "See you by the lake after school on Friday."

He strolled away, and Tristan watched him go, as mystified as she'd been when he'd been standing beside her. She figured it could be that she was out of practice when it came to socialization, but she was pretty sure that was one of the strangest conversations she'd ever had.

***

For the remainder of the week, Beckett tried unsuccessfully to not stare at Tristan every chance he got. She'd always been a mystery to him, but in their nearly three years of schooling he'd never gotten an opportunity to talk to her; if he was being honest, however, he also hadn't *created* any opportunities because he found her somewhat intimidating -- it was hard to remain unbiased when you heard the same rumors about the Wallaces on repeat day after day, and while Beckett Benson did not believe in the supernatural, he preferred to remain curious at a safe distance.

More than the murmurs that surrounded her and her family, though, Beckett always felt just slightly disquieted after he saw Tristan. He didn't see her *too* often around the Academy, just by the nature of the company he kept, but whenever he did see her, whenever she'd look right at him, he'd suddenly feel like the ground beneath his feet had turned to sand. She was attractive by all standards, but what intrigued and unsettled Beckett was her eyes -- they were not just dark, they were piceous, like a completely starless sky, and they seemed bottomless, like they drew in the light from around her, which only served to make them darker.

It had come as a surprise to Beckett, then, that talking to Tristan had been a perfectly normal experience; he was ashamed to admit that the stories he'd heard whispered about her and her family -- about midnight rituals and animal sacrifice -- had set him up with the expectation that she wouldn't be like every other teenager that surrounded him. In their brief conversation, he'd been even more surprised that she'd shown a hint of humor in both her responses and the way she'd looked at him about wanting to avoid the library. From what he could tell from their interaction and just having classes alongside her through the years, she was smart and serious about her studies, and could not have been less interested in the "typical" high school experience of extracurriculars, football games, weekend parties, and summer night meetups -- AKA, everything he participated in regularly. In short, she was fascinating to Beckett, and he felt like he'd hit the lottery when he'd been assigned as her partner on their AP Lit senior project.

After the last bell on Friday afternoon, Beckett removed his burgundy blazer, burgundy and gray striped tie, rolled up the sleeves of his white dress shirt, and slung his backpack over one shoulder. After confirming with his football buddy, Jason Dalton, that he'd be at the party being thrown by Matteo Cosgrove that evening, Beckett made his way to the lake, which sat adjacent to the Academy, in the opposite direction of the football field. The school had installed wooden benches intermittently around the lake's perimeter, which was also dotted with trees and flowering bushes. Beckett sat on the first bench he came across, his back to the Academy, and he waited.

Only a few minutes had passed when he sensed Tristan coming rather than heard her. It was an odd experience, one he hadn't had before, and he turned to see Tristan, still a good distance away, looking surprised that he'd spotted her. As quickly as the surprise had registered, however, her face settled into its usual neutral mask. Once Tristan had reached him, she dropped her backpack on the bench beside Beckett and sat, pulling out a black binder. Her hair lifted away from her shoulders in the gentle October breeze that blew across the lake, the golden brown strands catching the late afternoon light, glowing like they'd caught fire.

"OK," Tristan began, flipping through the pages of notes she'd handwritten, oblivious to Beckett's observation. "So our first task is to pick a subject that we're going to build our project around. We should pick something that points toward an eventual career that can also have community service incorporated into it. My first thought would be an English teacher or tutor, but I feel like everyone is going to pick that. What do you think?"

Beckett stared at her, his eyebrows raised.

"What?" Tristan asked, somewhat defensively.

"Sorry, I just didn't expect that we were gonna be jumping in with both feet here."

Tristan gave him the same look she'd given him when he'd mentioned not using the school's library, the one where she appeared to be trying to suss out whether he was serious, stupid, or messing with her.

"Isn't that why we're here?"

"It is." Beckett grinned. "I just didn't realize it would be all business and no small talk."

"I don't small talk," Tristan said shortly, briefly shaking her head as she looked back at her notes. "I was also think--"

"But small talk is, like, the cornerstone of human interaction."

Tristan looked up at Beckett again, very clearly trying to hold her temper.

"And our senior project is, like, the cornerstone of us graduating."

Beckett was full-on smiling now, which made Tristan want to hit him across the face with her binder.

"You don't want to be my friend, Tristan?"

Tristan ignored the weird little feeling that jumped up in her stomach when Beckett said her name. His eyes had casually skimmed over her face as he spoke, and Tristan could feel heat creeping up her neck.

"I am not here to make friends. I am here to study, and

to get good grades, and to graduate, and, with luck, to get out of Lavelle. I've made pretty good progress on that goal so far, and I'm definitely not changing course now. Especially not for you."

"Especially not for me? Ouch," Beckett said mildly, his gaze still friendly. "You don't even know me, but OK. Today I'll accept your rejection. I have to warn you, though, it's gonna be tough for you to not be friends with me. I am pretty charming."

"Clearly," Tristan said, her voice ice cold. Her eyes flickered over him in a way Beckett assumed was supposed to be acrimonious, but all it did was add fuel to his fire. Before she looked away, Beckett could have sworn he saw the very, very faintest quirk of her lips, but when he looked again, she was stone-faced.

"We can choose any topic, as far as I know," Beckett said, pulling out his own notebook and opening it. "It doesn't have to be related specifically to English. I agree most people are probably gonna go the easy route of English teacher and maybe tutor, but I kind of like both ideas. What if we did ESL teacher or tutor?"

Tristan pressed a pen against her lips, thinking, and Beckett looked away across the lake. He did want to be friends with her, did believe she would eventually come around, and didn't want to scare her off by staring at her mouth like a creep, even if it was a very kissable mouth.

"I like it," Tristan said finally, nodding and looking surprised. "Lots of avenues for exploration and community service. So do we go teacher or tutor?"

"Let's go teacher. Not that tutoring is not something you can make a career of, but there is more credentialing involved with teaching. The community service aspect will be built right in if we can land tutoring jobs here or in the next town over, too, so I guess we do get to incorporate both after all."

Tristan nodded again.

"OK. So should we meet here on Fridays and bring whatever we've gathered throughout the week? We'll touch base and sort through the materials, see what overlaps and what we can fit together?"

"Fine by me."

Tristan stood, shouldering her backpack.

"By me, too. I'll see you Monday then, Beckett."

"See you Monday."

Beckett watched Tristan go, wondering what it would be like if she'd hung around, wanted to spend time with him for more than just a school project. He realized, as she disappeared around the building toward the parking lot, that he was kind of crushing on Tristan Wallace, which was both surprising and not surprising, considering how captivated he'd always been by her. Telling himself that his crush was in vain for multiple reasons, not the least of which was Tristan's clear dislike for him and the fact that they'd both be graduating and going their separate ways come June, Beckett slowly gathered his things. He laughed to himself as he headed towards the parking lot to his car -- he'd never listened to his own good advice, and he wasn't going to start now.

***

"Trinity?" Sol's voice floated up the stairs later that night, and Tristan poked her head out of her bedroom.

"Yes?"

"Dinner."

Tristan made her way downstairs, into the formal dining room where her parents were already seated, ready to eat. Olivia and Evander were nowhere to be found, as usual.

"Hi honey," Sol greeted, sweeping her long, pale blonde hair behind the shoulders of her red cardigan.

"Mom, Dad," Tristan greeted, sitting to the right of where Umbris was seated at the head of the table.

"How was school?" Umbris asked, as they began to eat. His dark eyes, Tristan's eyes, studied her face, and Tristan arched an eyebrow.

"Really?"

"What?" Umbris asked innocently, raising a wine glass to his lips.

"Trying to read me without even waiting for my answer? School was the same as it is every other day."

"You met up with the Benson kid after class, we saw," Umbris commented, and Tristan glared at her parents.

"You were spying on me? Seriously?"

"You're never late coming home. We got worried. We weren't spying, honey." Sol's voice was maddeningly calm, always was. Tristan could not think of a single time in her entire life that Sol's timbre had risen above soothing, almost musical.

"You could have, I don't know, called me? Like normal parents would?"

"Why would we call you when we could just check in on you?" Sol asked, and Tristan thought about throwing her dinner plate across the room, just to get a reaction.

"That won't be necessary," Umbris said calmly, and Tristan groaned.

"Oh my gods. Where are Oceana and Ember? Why do I have to sit through this alone?"

"Some party. Matteo something or other. Cosmo? Cogden?"

"Cosgrove. Really?" Tristan asked, wrinkling her nose.

"They seemed to be under the impression that everyone would be there," Sol replied, her slate colored eyes studying Tristan over the rim of her water glass.

"Everyone? Unlikely. All of the insufferable popular juniors and seniors? Probably. It will always be a mystery to me why Oceana and Ember waste their time on those people."

"Well, they're not like you," Sol said, setting her glass down silently. She smiled serenely at Tristan. "How is our scholar doing so far in the year?"

"Fine. The course load is hefty, but it's nothing I can't handle."

"You've always had a mind for information," Umbris nodded, looking proud. "You'll be an asset to the community once you're free from high school."

Tristan looked down at her plate, pushing food around with her fork. She concentrated on sealing off her thoughts, which was the extent of how she used any ability she had these days; this topic was one she preferred to avoid with her parents. Her growing sense of panic over leaving Jamestown Academy just to do nothing but marry off and start breeding was all the evidence she needed that the life Sol and

Umbris led was not the life for her. Over the summer, she'd applied to several colleges, near and far, and she dreaded the responses starting to come in. She knew that Sol and Umbris would ultimately support whatever she chose, but Umbris, at least, made it clear what his preference for her was, and she hated the idea of letting him down.

"Speaking of the community," Sol said, just as Umbris opened his mouth to speak again. "Next Saturday night is the monthly gathering. You know this, but I expect you'll be there, along with Oceana and Ember."

"Of course," Tristan nodded.

"We'll also expect you three to stick around here and retire early on Friday night. You'll need to get as much sleep as you can."

"I know," Tristan said, finishing her dinner.

"I know you know," Sol replied. "What you don't know is that this month's gathering is in a new place -- the Crenshaws have offered to meet up with us when we get there. I understand Celes is looking forward to seeing you again."

Tristan forced a smile, but said nothing.

"He really is very nice," Sol said, looking carefully at Tristan.

"Yes, he is. May I be excused?"

Umbris nodded, exchanging a look with Sol. When Tristan had disappeared up the stairs, Sol spoke.

"She's unsettled."

"She's sealed her thoughts, too."

"I guess we should have expected this sooner or later,"

Sol sighed. "I thought we'd get lucky since we made it this far."

"Do you think it has to do with the Benson kid?"

"It could. It could have to do with a lot of things."

Sol was almost certain she knew what it was, at least in part. She was an expert at reading nonverbal cues, but she didn't have to be an expert to notice the slight slump of Trinity's shoulders, or the tense lines that developed around her mouth whenever they brought up her future in the community. Sol and Umbris expected Trinity to immerse herself in the community, to build a life there, as that was what they and their ancestors had done before her.

From birth, children of community members were granted a place that held for them until they graduated high school; after graduation, they'd be taken in by the network of neighbors around Louisiana and offered opportunities in their preferred field of work, relocating based on where they'd be hired. The females were still expected to marry and reproduce young, but the law requiring it had been abolished years ago. Most families in the community gave their children no choice but to walk their predetermined path, but Sol had told Umbris long ago that it was something she would never force upon her children, and that if he wanted there to be a *their* children, he would agree. It was her only condition before she'd consent to marry him, and Umbris had complied.

As a teenager, Sol had suffered the grisly, public death of her sister, Adara, after Adara had rebelled and tried to sever ties with the life, as part of the community, that their father, Orion, had chosen for them. Orion had been ruthless, and Adara had been made into an example, and it was a trauma Sol had carried with her ever since. She'd never shared the details with Umbris -- who had not been there for the execution due to caring for his dying mother -- and planned to keep it that way. Should Umbris try to go back on the vow he'd made to her, however, she'd find the strength to speak of it.

CHAPTER 2

Tristan opened her bedroom window and leaned on the broad sill, her knees on the long bench that ran below, watching as the small bit of sun that was still visible through the trees sank beneath the horizon. The comforting sounds of her backyard filled her bedroom, and the sky slowly changed from blue-gray, to fiery red-orange, and, eventually, to dusky purple. Halloween was in six days, and the evenings were slowly starting to cool down, though the days were still blazing hot. She rested her chin in her hand, trying and failing to keep her thoughts from wandering to Beckett.

There was something unsettling about him that went deeper than his declaration that he'd accept the rejection of his friendship *today*. She knew he'd meant well, could tell that his intentions were good, so it wasn't an unease over the idea of future interactions with him. More than feeling unsettled, it rattled Tristan that she couldn't identify what exactly it was about him that was making her feel the way she felt when she thought about him. *You don't want to be my friend, Tristan?* He'd drawled, and Tristan's stomach swooped again at how her name had sounded leaving his mouth. It had sounded... intimate. Familiar on a level she'd never experienced with anyone, let alone Beckett Benson. The week between their project assignment and their meeting at the lake, Tristan had noticed Beckett staring at her as they passed in the hallway, or when he should have been paying attention in class. For not the first time, she cursed the fact that she did not have Olivia's ability to read thoughts; sure, Tristan could pick up on someone's *vibe,* but that did her no good when what she really wanted to know was what they were thinking to themselves when they thought no one could hear. More frustrating still was that Beckett hadn't even pretended he wasn't looking at her when Tristan had stared back at him pointedly -- he'd just smiled and turned his attention back where it belonged.

A deer entered the yard below, and Tristan watched it idly. She spent most weekend nights contentedly cocooned in her bedroom, studying or reading or watching TV, oblivious to whatever her peers, including her siblings, were up to. She didn't have any social media accounts, didn't care to give Emmeline and her crew one more avenue through which to harass her, and she didn't usually feel like she was missing anything for it. Until now. Now, in the privacy of her room, with her thoughts sealed from her parents, she let herself wonder what Beckett was doing, if he was thinking of her too or if he'd left her and any thought of her at school.

Tristan focused on the deer's neck, where the tawny fur changed to white, staring until her vision began to blur at the edges. The doe lifted her head, sensing something in the air had changed, and stood stock still, her satellite ears twitching.

Tristan closed her eyes. Blackness swirled in her mind, forming a funnel of energy that quickly produced an image of a handsome face with a pair of vibrant eyes and a confident smirk. Suddenly, the eyes looked right at her, slamming the energy back towards her so hard that Tristan gasped, opening her eyes and grabbing the windowsill so she wouldn't tumble backwards. The deer ran off like a shot into the wooded area beyond the yard.

***

"Beckett!" A voice boomed right next to his ear, and Beckett blinked, turning his head to find Jason not two inches from his face, his hands cupped around his mouth. The noise of the party roared back to life, and Beckett almost winced at how loud it was.

"Dude, where were you?" Jason asked, hitting his shoulder.

"I don't know," Beckett responded truthfully, trying to shake off the dazed feeling that had settled over him. "Did I fall asleep?"

"Do you sleep with your eyes open?" Jason asked. He held his red plastic cup out in front of him, shaking his head and widening his eyes. "Am I too drunk, or are you not drunk enough?"

Beckett forced a laugh, standing up.

"It's me. I'm gonna get a drink, I'll be back."

Beckett made his way to the kitchen, trying to figure out what had happened. One minute he'd been shooting the shit with his football teammates, and the next... The next? A noise had distracted him, a low-pitched whistling like a wind tunnel was in the next room. He'd focused on it, trying to hear better, but the harder he listened the fainter it'd become. And then he'd seen something -- a deer? And then he'd seen Tristan, her hair long and loose, her eyes burning as black as ember. It was almost like a vision, but she'd been more alive, like if he'd reached out he would have been able to touch her, to feel her skin against his hands. He probably should have felt scared, nothing like this ever having happened to him before, but in the moment he'd been unable to do anything but stare. Beckett had sought Tristan's gaze with his own, but as soon as their eyes had locked, Jason had interrupted. What the *hell* had that been?

Someone bumped into him, and Beckett snapped back to attention, reaching out to steady the small figure.

"Sorry--"

"--Oops, my bad!" Olivia Wallace looked up at him, her strange gray eyes flickering with recognition.

"You OK?" Beckett asked, and Olivia nodded.

"I'm fine. Yourself?"

"Fine. Hey, you're Tristan's sister, right?"

"Right. Why do you ask?" Olivia looked at him suspiciously.

"No reason. She was assigned to be my senior project partner in English class, that's all."

Olivia's shoulders relaxed.

"Sorry. I get defensive when people ask me about her, I guess."

"Such a good sister." Emmeline spoke from behind Beckett, sidling up next to him before he could reply.

Olivia raised her eyebrows briefly, but said nothing to Emmeline.

"Can I do something for you, Emmeline?" Beckett asked, looking at the hand she'd snaked around his arm.

"Why don't you come upstairs with me and I'll tell you all the things you can do for me?"

"OK, see you around Beckett," Olivia said, beating a hasty retreat as Emmeline started to pull him out of the kitchen.

"Alright, I am not drunk enough and you're too drunk

for this," Beckett said, peeling Emmeline's hand off of his arm once they got into the hallway by the stairs. "Why don't you go find the girls?"

"But I want you, not them." Emmeline pressed up against Beckett, pinning him against the wall. Her red dress was short, low-cut, and skintight, her lipstick the exact shade of the fabric.

"I wore this for you," Emmeline told him, her lips inching closer to his. "We had such a good time together, didn't we Beckett? We can do that again."

Beckett was sure any mortal man would be tempted by Emmeline. He was completely over her and was still having a hard time remembering why that was in that moment.

"Ah, sorry." Evander Wallace turned the corner and then immediately turned back around.

That broke the spell. Beckett eased Emmeline away from him and ran a hand through his hair.

"I don't think so, sorry Emmeline."

"No, *you'll* be sorry," Emmeline said, her face flushing. She began to stomp off, then stopped, turning back to Beckett, who'd gone back into the kitchen. "And this better not have anything to do with that witch Tristan. I see the way you've been looking at her!"

"I promise it has nothing to do with her and everything to do with you," Beckett said dryly, and Tyler Daniels, another footballer who was fixing himself a drink, whooped.

"Shut up, Tyler!" Emmeline yelled, once again stomping away.

"Somethin' goin' on with Tristan Wallace, bro?" Tyler

asked, grinning cheekily at Beckett as he drawled in his direction. Tyler's accent always seemed to increase three-fold when he was drinking. "Didn't think you were into the blood-drinkin', howlin' at the moon types. That's what she is, you know. One-a them *Twilight* vampires."

"Tyler?" A sweet voice spoke from the other side of the kitchen, and Beckett and Tyler looked over to see Olivia leaning against the door jamb. "Did you know the very definition of an idiot is someone who treats unsubstantiated rumor as fact?"

"Olivia." Tyler put his hand to his chest as he sauntered over to her. "You're callin' me an idiot? I'm wounded. I thought what we had was special."

Tyler knuckled Olivia under the chin, knowing she'd had a crush on him for a long time, and Olivia fought off a grin. What Beckett wasn't sure if she knew was that Tyler also had a long-standing crush on her.

"I was just teasin' my buddy Beckett, I promise," Tyler said earnestly. "I meant no offense to you and yours."

"Keep my sister's name out of your mouth, *teasin'* or not," Olivia told him, looking up at him with wide eyes. She walked her fingers up his arm, her voice still sweet as can be. "Or you'll never, ever get a chance with me."

Olivia leaned in, whispering something in Tyler's ear before smirking and strolling away. Tyler stared after her, dumbfounded, and Beckett grinned into his cup, rejoining the party.

***

"How was the party last night?" Tristan asked Olivia and Evander late the next morning at breakfast.

Evander, who was staring dumbly at his plate, merely

grunted, while Olivia arched a perfect eyebrow.

"It was fine. Kind of lame, kind of not, same as usual."

Tristan nodded, trying to play it casual.

"Sounds about right. Who was there?"

Olivia just stared at her.

"What?"

"Are you seriously asking me about a party thrown by one of your classmates?"

"Yes, why? Is there some rule that says I can't?"

"No," Olivia said slowly. "It's just, you usually deliver some kind of sarcastic commentary on how you think it went and never bother to listen to a fact-check, you know, since you're better than all of us and all."

"Oh my gods, fine, forget it," Tristan snapped, just as Sol and Umbris entered the dining room. "I don't care; you're right."

She gathered her plate and utensils and left the table in a huff, and Olivia looked around for the hidden cameras.

"Have I gone crazy?" Olivia asked Evander, bumping his elbow. "She never cares about these parties, right?"

Evander just grunted.

Tristan flopped back on her bed, absentmindedly looking at the model of the solar system that hung above her bed. She really *didn't* care about the party, wasn't sure why she'd asked. Well, that was a lie. At the time, she really just wanted to know about Beckett, but the moment had quickly passed. Beckett was interfering in too many of her thoughts, and if she wasn't careful, she'd make a fool of herself because of it. Besides, how pathetic was it that she was practically obsess-

ing over him after two brief interactions? The downsides of shunning the typical high school experience continued to reveal themselves.

A knock on her door. Tristan looked over to see Olivia standing in the doorway, twirling a long strand of copper hair around her finger. She was still in her pajamas -- slim black sweatpants and a faded T-shirt -- and she looked much younger than her sixteen years. In fact, if Tristan squinted just a little, she could see Olivia at various ages standing just the same way in just the same spot.

"Can I come in?"

"The door was open," Tristan replied, and Olivia crossed the room, sinking down onto Tristan's bed. Tristan shifted over to make some room.

"I didn't mean anything by what I said," Olivia said, observing Tristan with her owl-like eyes. "I mean... I wasn't wrong, was I?"

Tristan laughed in spite of herself. "No, you weren't wrong."

"The party really was the same as they always are. Loud music, loud people getting drunk, hookups, breakups, the usual."

"You better not have been hooking up," Tristan said, raising her eyebrows.

Olivia rolled her eyes, but blushed just slightly. "Of course I wasn't."

"Hmm," Tristan said, still eyeballing her.

"Don't even!" Olivia very suddenly became unreadable, and Tristan grinned.

"If you can seal, I can seal." Olivia crossed her arms.

"You know I can't read your thoughts anyway," Tristan said. "Thank the gods."

"Ha ha," Olivia said, stretching her legs out.

"So who broke up last night?"

"Christie Dobell and Davison Hench, again. No surprise there. Oh but ew, I think Beckett Benson and Emmeline Strandquest hooked up again."

"What?" Tristan pushed herself up on her elbows, trying to keep her expression neutral.

Olivia nodded, wrinkling her nose.

"Yeah. She took him upstairs with her I think, if they even made it up there -- I didn't stick around to find out." Olivia mock shuddered, and Tristan lowered her head back down onto her pillow.

Olivia chattered on about the party, but Tristan had stopped listening. Beckett and Emmeline, hooking up? Why now? Why at all?

"I'm gonna go get a shower," Olivia said finally, oblivious to how Tristan had been ignoring her.

"OK. I'll be here."

Olivia left and Tristan resumed staring at the solar system, trying to get her thoughts in some kind of order. She was irrationally bothered by the idea of Beckett and Emmeline, but mostly she was worried about what it would mean for her senior project if their hookups turned into round two of a relationship. She laid there, lost in thought, until she noticed that the solar system had begun to move. It spun in a slow circle, gradually picking up speed. Tristan pushed up onto one elbow, frowning. She was not doing that... was she? A whir filled the air as the mobile spun so fast, it was merely a blur. As suddenly as it had started, it stopped, and Tristan jumped off of her bed, her heart pounding.

She hurried down the hall and knocked on Olivia's door. Olivia opened it, her hair half blown dry, and Tristan pushed past her, pacing back and forth.

"What's wrong?"

"My solar system was spinning. Is something bad coming?"

"What?" Olivia frowned.

"My model of the solar system, above my bed. It was spinning, Oceana. I didn't do it."

"What way?" Olivia's face was grave. "What way was it spinning?"

"Clockwise, I think? Yes, clockwise."

Olivia blew out a breath, relief flooding her features.

"An omen would have been counterclockwise. You're coming up on your crash, that's all."

"What?"

"Your crash, before the gathering? You know, when you get a burst of pure energy and it signals that in five days you're going to crash? It usually coincides with the gathering. Trinity? Does this..." Olivia trailed off, looking curiously at Tristan. "Does this not happen to you?"

Tristan shook her head, as confused as Olivia.

"I get tired around gathering time, but I've never had an energy burst and I've never had a crash. It happens to you every month?"

Olivia nodded. "Yes. But I use my abilities. You don't. Have you been, recently?"

Tristan shook her head again. "I haven't."

"Well then you're unsettled. Is that why you sealed?"

"I... maybe."

Olivia nodded. "You're unsettled. That's why it happened. OK, sit down. You need to know what to expect now with the crash. Ugh, suckage -- it'll be Halloween for you. You'll spend the drive to the gathering sleeping, most likely, since you won't feel better until you get there and get your energy infusion; make sure you tell Mom and Dad you need to ride with us. I think they think you were finally going to try driving yourself this month."

Tristan sat apprehensively on the edge of Olivia's bed.

"OK. So the crash is like..." Olivia thought for a moment. "It's like the most tired you've ever been, times one hundred, plus the worst flu you've ever had, times fifty. You won't feel sick necessarily, like your stomach won't be bothering you or anything, but you'll feel like you're half-dead and you'll look it, too. And it's hard to think. So, so hard. It's like this fog settles in your brain and you don't have the energy to clear it. Me and Ember are gonna have to drive you to and from school, unless you stay home."

"I can't. I have two pretty big tests that day. Oh gods, am I going to fail?" Tristan's eyes widened in horror, but Olivia shook her head.

"All of your knowledge will be there, you're just going to have a hard time accessing it. I know you don't like to use your abilities, but if you can remember how to transfer energy, you can borrow some from your classmates to help you cut a path through the brain fog."

"Oceana, you know we don't bring our abilities to

school with us," Tristan said seriously. "That's like, the only rule. We don't use them there."

"There are exceptions to every rule, Trinity, and besides, it's just borrowing energy. There will be plenty to go around; you're not going to harm anyone."

"I don't like this."

"Well, look at it this way," Olivia said, shrugging. "At least you won't be bored at the gathering this month."

"I don't get *bored*," Tristan said, but she couldn't come up with an alternative descriptor. She just didn't usually get much out of the gathering -- she didn't use her abilities and didn't practice regularly, and the residual energy in the air that she picked up was nice but not necessary. Most months she ended up people-watching instead of participating, or going for a walk with Celes once he'd gotten his infusion. It'd been years since she'd gotten an energy infusion herself, something else to prepare for, but the memories she had were pleasant enough.

"Mom and I are heading into town today, do you want to come?" Olivia asked, pulling a mustard yellow cardigan on over her floaty, dark green dress.

"No thanks."

"You're too young to be a shut-in, Trinity," Olivia said disapprovingly.

"I'm going to walk down to the river," Tristan replied. "I can avoid people *and* get out of the house. Win-win."

Olivia put on a pair of chunky heeled brown booties, shaking her head.

"Suit yourself."

Tristan followed her out of her bedroom and went back into

her own, gathering her toiletries for her own shower. When she'd finished, she braided her wet hair and dressed in her favorite pair of skinny jeans and a plain white v-neck shirt. Tristan slipped into her black canvas sneakers, sprayed herself with bug spray, and then made her way downstairs.

"I'm going for a walk!" Tristan called, not waiting for a response.

She left through the back door, stepping into the sprawling yard that backed right up to the woods. The house she and her family occupied sat dead in the middle of three acres of land -- a long, winding driveway stretched before it, and a long, lush yard stretched behind. The house itself was fairly unremarkable, at least as far as Tristan was concerned. It was a Tudor style home like others in Lavelle, just large enough for their family of five, and, when looked at with an object-ive eye, charming in a fairytale kind of way. Unfortunately, the general oddness of The Wallaces that most people in Lavelle picked up on, helped along by Emmeline's smear campaign, made it seem like something out of a more sinis-ter fairytale -- like perhaps just in the basement were Hansel and Gretel, waiting to be rescued or otherwise devoured.

In spite of that, or maybe because of it, the family saw a ton of Halloween traffic, and fairly frequently found local kids creeping around their property after dark. Umbris and Sol were always gracious towards the trespassers, but the younger Wallaces could never manage to pass up an op-portunity to put on a little show -- after all, it was what the creeping kids had come for. The last group had been treated to Tristan backlighting Olivia with a green light while Evander had blasted a thunder effects track through his phone's Bluetooth speakers. Olivia had cackled into the perfectly windy night, having donned a long black cape, and the siblings had laughed for hours after the kids had run off screaming.

Smiling to herself, Tristan entered the woods, the trees offering a welcome respite from the beating sun, which had decided to come out from behind the clouds as she'd crossed the yard. She felt herself relaxing as she walked, not realizing until that moment how tense she'd been. She unsealed her thoughts and breathed in the heady scent of the fall foliage. For not the first time, she wished she lived somewhere that experienced *real* autumn -- turning leaves, biting mornings, chilled evenings. It was one of the reasons she was hoping for an acceptance letter from a college, any college far North, if not her dream choice of the prestigious Ward Livingston University, perched on the Chelsea River right on the edge of Boston, Massachusetts. Time seemed to crawl in Lavelle, Louisiana, but Tristan knew it couldn't be that way every-where.

After walking a while through the peaceful woods, Tristan came upon a part of the Mississippi that wound its way through Lavelle. The woods leading to that particular area were terribly overgrown and buggy, which meant there was never anyone there -- which made it a perfect, undisturbed thinking spot for Tristan. She sat on the grassy riverbank, taking off her sneakers and digging her toes into the soft soil. She tilted her face up to the sun, closing her eyes, and she evened her breathing, letting the rays recharge her soul. It was tiring, sealing her thoughts, and it didn't help that she felt guilty doing it. Being able to sit here and let go was exactly what she needed to re-center herself.

***

Over in his neck of the woods, Beckett climbed out of his bedroom window, dropping down to the roof below, where he stretched out on his back. Inside the house, his par-ents were fighting again. Something about money this time, though Beckett was sure they'd fight about anything they could. He stared up at the sky, wondering how long his parents would stay together once he'd left for college. The sun beat down on his face and he closed his eyes, becoming pleasantly drowsy. The voices in his house faded until all he could hear was nature, as though he'd stepped back in time. There was something comforting about lying in the sun, something soul-cleansing, which was why this little piece of roof was his favorite spot in Lavelle. It was completely unshaded, completely undisturbed, and perfect for thinking.

CHAPTER 3

Tristan and Evander drove to school together on Monday. Usually, Evander and Olivia carpooled, but Olivia's crash had come that morning; she had chosen to stay home in order for Sol to administer a mini-infusion, which would hold Olivia over until the gathering.

"What a way to wake up this morning, huh?" Evander asked as they drove, referring to their entire household being awakened by Olivia groaning like she was on death's doorstep.

"I know; Oceana totally shattered my zen after my walk in the woods yesterday. She said she crashes every month, but I swear I've never heard her making the noises she was making this morning. I know I wouldn't have missed it before."

"Because she hasn't. She thought her crash was coming tomorrow, since she and I usually end up on the same schedule, so she had no time to prepare."

"How do you prepare? Apparently I'm in for my first on Thursday."

"Ah, Halloween? Suckage."

Tristan smiled.

"Oceana said the same thing. You guys know I'm not crazy about Halloween though, right? And it's not like I have plans."

"What do you mean?" Evander asked, looking surprised. "Every year you're out front or inside jumping out at anyone who approaches. You don't enjoy that?"

"Not really," Tristan admitted. "I do it because I know you all get a kick out of it, and, OK, sometimes if someone I don't like comes up it's fun to scare them, but otherwise... not really."

"Well you've fooled me then," Evander said, looking out the window. "I mean, you painted yourself silver last year. That's dedication from someone who doesn't enjoy it."

Tristan laughed.

"So how do I prepare for this crash?"

Evander shook his head.

"There's no real way to prepare. Nothing you can do will make it any better. Oceana's version of prepared is to know it's coming and to brace herself, that's all."

"So yours is tomorrow? It's gonna be quite the week for Mom and Dad."

"I don't need their help. I just stay in my room and sleep or watch TV. It's not so bad, though getting through the rest of the week is gonna be brutal; those mini-infusions barely do anything for me. What's your plan for Thursday?"

"I have to go to school, I have two fairly important tests that day. Mom did say I can stay home Friday, though -- Oceana told her that my crash is coming this week, too, when they went into the city this weekend."

Evander laughed, and Tristan looked over at him.

"What?"

"Good luck with the tests. You'll be exhausted just

getting dressed for school, never mind having to actually use your brain for something useful."

"Oceana said I can borrow energy to make it through. She claims it doesn't break any of our rules since no one is being harmed and there will be plenty to spare in school."

Evander nodded, looking impressed.

"That's actually not a bad idea. I wish she'd shared that with me."

Tristan laughed again and pulled into the school's parking lot. Evander jumped out, bidding her goodbye and going to meet up with some of his friends from the football team. Tristan watched him go, wondering how strange it must look to their classmates for Evander and Olivia to be so well-liked and popular while Tristan was... not. It was strange to *her,* and she didn't care nearly as much about appearances as the people she was forced to see on a daily basis.

Tristan pulled her backpack out of the backseat and headed towards the Academy, ending up trailing Emmeline and her crew by a few feet. The unpleasant reminder that Emmeline and Beckett had gotten back together sprang into Tristan's mind, and she had to work not to groan.

"...Just don't know what his problem is..." Emmeline's voice floated back to Tristan, and she picked up her pace just slightly, her curiosity piqued.

"...Accused him of being into Tristan, but I *know* he's not that dumb..."

Tristan told herself to hang back. All it would take was one cronie catching her out of her peripheral vision, and they'd turn on her like a pack of hungry dogs. Still, she continued to creep forward.

"No, Eloise, I don't know," Emmeline snapped, and

Tristan was sorry she'd missed Eloise's question. "But I'm not worried, and I'm not giving up. I saw the way he looked at me. And I know what I felt when I had him up against the wall."

The group laughed, and Tristan slowed her step. So Emmeline and Beckett were *not* back together, but Emmeline was trying. The sun broke through the clouds overhead, and Tristan looked up, smiling. For now, her senior project was safe. *For now, Beckett Benson is single,* a little voice in her head whispered, which she promptly ignored.

***

Tristan had just closed her locker, her arms full, when Emmeline elbowed her hard, sending her books and papers flying everywhere.

"Oh my gosh, oops!" Emmeline put her hand to her mouth in mock surprise, her eyes wide. "I didn't even see you there! You forgot to make yourself un-invisible this morning!"

The other kids in the hallway laughed, and Emmeline shot Tristan a malicious grin before continuing on her way. Shaking her head, Tristan gathered her things, her face burning.

"Need help with those?" A familiar voice asked, as Tristan attempted to restack her books in her arms.

She looked up from where she knelt, right into the face of Beckett Benson, and her stomach flipped just a little.

"No. I'm fine."

Beckett retrieved her last two notebooks from where they'd landed after skidding down the hall, waiting until she stood before placing them gently atop the pile.

"Thanks," Tristan muttered, blowing a strand of hair

out of her face.

"I can help you carry them if you tell me where you're going," Beckett said, eyeing the pile.

"I said no thank you," Tristan snapped, and Beckett held up his hands, backing up a few steps.

"OK, OK. Just offering." Beckett looked like he wanted to say something else, but decided against it. "I'll see you around, Tristan."

Tristan shook her head as he walked away, turning on her heel and stalking off to class. He'd said her name that too-familiar way again, which made her think of Emmeline commenting earlier that she'd known what she'd felt when she'd pinned Beckett against the wall. Tristan's face flushed again, and she immediately forced those thoughts out of her head. If she was going to get through senior year with Beckett as her project partner, she was going to have to keep him at a distance, both outwardly and in. Fantasizing, even tangentially, about what it might feel like to be pressed up against Beckett Benson could lead nowhere but straight into trouble.

Tristan took her seat in Chemistry, ignoring the way Emmeline snickered in her direction. She pulled out her notebook and opened it, keeping her gaze on the teacher, Mr. Waterston, who looked like what you'd get if you put trousers, a dress shirt, and a bowtie on a bowling pin. He was a tall, bespectacled, white-haired chemistry enthusiast who walked with a heavy limp and positively beamed whenever he got into his teaching groove. Tristan was not a huge fan of the subject, but she appreciated Mr. Waterston's passion, which made her want to do well in his class.

"Mr. Waterston?" Emmeline raised her hand when Mr. Waterston had taken a moment to drink from the bottle of water he kept on his desk.

"Yes Miss Strandquest?"

"Talking about energy changes and endo- and exo-thermic reactions has got me wondering. Is it possible, scientifically, for a human to ever change its form?"

The class began to murmur, and Mr. Waterston cocked his head, furrowing his brow.

"Sorry, I'm not clear on what you're asking. Are you asking if a human can undergo an endo- or exothermic reaction? Like spontaneous combustion?"

"I'm asking..." Emmeline trailed off, tapping her finger against her lips, then smiled brightly, starting again. "OK. Let's say you have a human, right, who shuts themselves in their house all the time, doing all manner of ungodly who knows what kinds of things, real weird things, and who has been seen on the rare occasion they leave the house practically worshipping the sun and the moon? Could it be that they're, I don't know, some kinda shapeshifter? Some kinda... *witch?* Do those things exist in God's created nature, or do they come straight here from Hell?"

Tristan could feel her classmates staring at her, could see them laughing behind their hands and nudging each other.

"Ms. Strandquest, I have no idea what you're talking about, and if I wanted you to waste my time, I'd ask you to talk to me about fashion. Settle!" Mr. Waterston raised his voice over the class's laughter, and Tristan glared at Emmeline, who'd twisted around in her seat to leer at her. "Let's move on."

Tristan ducked out of class as soon as the bell rang, successfully avoiding another Emmeline run-in. Her next two classes were Emmeline-free, and she'd take her lunch, as usual, in the library instead of the cafeteria. Her first class after lunch was with Emmeline, but that would be it for the rest of the day. If she was diligent, she could make it through with minimal contact; for whatever reason, Emmeline had more of a target on Tristan's back than usual that day.

Tristan's diligence paid off, and it was with a sigh of relief that she stopped by her locker before English, her last class of the day before free period. In a repeat of that morning, she'd just closed her locker door when Emmeline shoved her books out of her hands once again, sending them flying down the hall.

"What the hell is your problem?" Tristan snarled, balling her hands into fists.

"You are." Emmeline came right up to Tristan, their noses practically touching. "A little advice, Tristan? The next time you wanna eavesdrop on one of my conversations, *don't*. Witch."

Tristan was late for English, muttering an apology to Ms. West as she rushed into class, taking her seat without looking at anyone. She opened her notebook and bent her head, feeling Beckett's eyes on her. It took most of the class for her racing heart to calm, for the fire to leave her cheeks. She was angry at Emmeline, yes, but more angry at herself, not just for getting caught, but for eavesdropping at all.

After class, she heard Beckett calling her name, but she fled down the hall away from him, heading back to the library for her free period. She couldn't keep thinking Beckett was different; even if he didn't torment her the way Emmeline and her friends did, he didn't defend her, either. It was dangerous to think anything more of him than her project partner, to think of him in any capacity outside of that, and she'd do well to remember it.

Beckett watched Tristan practically run down the hall away from him, disappearing around the corner to her next class. He didn't know why she was avoiding him, didn't know what he could have possibly done when he hadn't seen her since that morning. Had she been that offended by his offering to help carry her books? She'd been hostile, Beckett had picked up on that right away, but it didn't make sense that she'd avoid him over their encounter.

"Dude, you gotta stop staring at Tristan Wallace. It's getting weird." Jason stopped beside Beckett, looking slightly alarmed as he followed Beckett's gaze down the hall. "What's your deal? People are starting to talk. You know that girl's a freak, and so is her family. I don't know who decided Olivia and Evander get a pass, but it wasn't me, so I just keep my mouth shut and go along with it. But they're freaky, too. Slightly less freaky, but freaky."

"She's my partner for our English project. And she's really not weird. You ever talk to her?"

Jason looked outright horrified by Beckett's question and, though Beckett knew it wasn't nice, he laughed.

"Listen, Emmeline Strandquest is thirstin' after you in a bad way. Most guys in this school would kill to be in your position. And I'm pretty sure Emmeline would kill most girls who tried to take her position, but she's hot, so she'd probably get away with it. Anyway, I know you guys broke up a while back, but don't overthink it, man. Snatch that fine piece of ass back up before she moves on for good."

Beckett laughed again, shaking his head as he and Jason made their way down the hallway towards the back entrance of the school.

"Nah, man. Been there, done that, don't wanna do it again. But listen, I told you. Tristan is my project partner;

we're not even friends. I didn't realize I was staring at her."

"Whatever you say. Just don't wanna get here one morning and discover you were dragged off for a ritual sacrifice because you got too close to the Wallaces." Jason grinned, pushing open the back doors and bellowing at Tyler across campus on the football field. Tyler bellowed back.

"For believing in God, y'all sure are superstitious in this town," Beckett said, shaking his head, and Jason nodded his head in agreement.

Football practice that day was brutal, but Beckett was extremely impressed with Evander Wallace. Though he was slight of build, he was an absolute beast on the field, and Beckett knew that if he played that way in their upcoming game, they'd crush the competition. He approached Evander after practice, as they all crossed the field back to the Academy.

"Hey man, great playing today."

Evander surveyed him with cool gray eyes, identical to Olivia's.

"Thanks."

"You been training off the field or something?"

"Or something," Evander smirked.

Privately, Beckett sort of agreed with Jason's assessment about the twins. There was definitely something as offbeat about them as there was about Tristan, but the twins also gave off an ultra-cool vibe that Beckett knew most of the popular crowd secretly wished they could attain for themselves. Beckett was older than the twins, yet even he felt like a dweeb next to Evander Wallace.

"Good talk," Beckett clapped Evander on the shoulder,

then jogged off to catch up with Tyler and another teammate, Henry Aspern.

Evander took the opportunity to read Beckett as he walked off. He was different than the other guys, that much Evander knew, but Evander had overheard some things that made him wary of Beckett's proximity to Tristan -- or his desired proximity, anyway. That part came through loud and clear to Evander; Beckett was interested in Tristan, whether or not he'd admit it aloud.

Evander focused, waiting for the snapshot in his mind to develop. Beckett's general aura was good, which was promising. His intentions, even his deepest, most secret intentions, were solidly in the positive realm. His overall color was quite a lovely shade of dark blue, which indicated that he was true of heart. It was the band of yellow, acting as an outline around the blue, that Evander knew contained the desire for popularity, the hesitation to upset the status quo, the struggle to do what he knew was right if it meant putting him in a bad spot with his friends. Though beyond normal for kids their age, it was the presence of that yellow outline that Evander worried about, in the context of Tristan.

Once in the locker room, Evander quickly showered and dressed, going to meet Tristan at her car. She was sitting in the driver's seat reading when he got there.

"Finally," Tristan said, starting the car, and Evander looked at her in surprise.

"Wow, what's up? Your aura is almost completely red right now."

"Nothing," Tristan muttered, peeling out of the parking lot. Evander knew she was going to seal, so he quickly concentrated, getting a glimpse of laughing faces and Emmeline Strandquest looking like the cat who'd caught the canary before he hit a wall.

"Rough day?"

Tristan snorted, but said nothing.

Evander left her alone, and, when they arrived home, Tristan went straight to her room, where she stayed until the next morning.

***

School the next day was slightly better than the day before. Emmeline made a couple of snide remarks in the halls and in class, but otherwise let her be. Beckett did not attempt to talk to Tristan when he saw her in the morning, which was fine by her.

At lunch, Tristan got in the food line with her tray, looking around the vast cafeteria for an open, unobtrusive seat while she waited her turn. Olivia was seated in the thicket of her junior and senior friends, laughing at something Tyler Daniels had just said.

"Hey there," Beckett spoke from behind Tristan, and she turned, surprised to see him.

"Hi."

"Know what you're getting?" Beckett gestured with his tray to the buffet behind the glass divider.

"Oh, no, not yet."

Beckett nodded. "Me either. I'm thinkin' tacos, though, you know, since it's Tuesday."

Tristan just stared at him.

"Taco Tuesday? No?"

She shook her head.

"Huh. Well, it's a thing. And you can't go wrong with tacos any day of the week, in my opinion."

Tristan scrunched her mouth to one side, in an effort, Beckett knew, to not smile.

"Have you had a chance to do any research for our project?" Beckett asked her, and Tristan nodded.

"I have. That reminds me, though, that I can't meet you on Friday. I won't be here."

"Oh," Beckett looked surprised. "OK, no problem. Goin' somewhere?"

"Yes," Tristan lied.

"How about Thursday then?"

Tristan looked like she was struggling with something, internally.

"Ah, um, sure. Thursday after last class."

It was her turn for food.

"I'll take the tacos."

Beckett saw Tristan look at him from the corner of her eye, and, as she turned to walk to the cashier, a quick smile passed over her face. Beckett smiled after her, joining her at the register.

"You wanna sit together?" Beckett asked, paying for his lunch.

Tristan's pretty eyes widened briefly, then a cool expression took over her features.

"No. I'll see you around, Beckett."

And then she was gone, making her way swiftly to a table by

one of the massive cafeteria windows, which overlooked the sweeping Academy grounds.

Beckett went to sit with his friends, and Emmeline, who never missed a thing, immediately latched onto him.

"You feelin' OK, Beckett?"

"Fine, why?"

"I saw you talkin' to Tristan over there, wanted to make sure she didn't put some kind of curse on you."

"Curses aren't a thing, Emmeline, and neither are witches. Don't you get tired of this?"

The lunch table quieted. Emmeline straightened her shoulders, sweeping her hair back.

"Curses and witches, demons, evil, they do so exist. They don't come from God, but they walk right alongside us. If I've said it once, I've said it a hundred times, Beckett -- you only got here in tenth grade, we've *always* gone to school with Tristan. I'm not talking just to talk."

"I don't know, it seems you *do* a lot of talking just to talk, Emmeline. Do you have proof of what you claim?"

"Just look at her," Emmeline pointed across the cafeteria. "Don't tell me you don't know there's something weird about her. Have you seen her eyes? I'm not even sure she has pupils; they're the devil's eyes. More than once I've seen something sinister in them, and I've rushed home to pray until I felt like something had stopped looking over my shoulder."

Beckett just looked at Emmeline, not knowing what to say. It wasn't that she made a compelling argument -- "just look at her" was problematic in many ways -- but Emmeline appeared to genuinely believe what she was saying, and, looking around the table, Beckett could see his friends believed her, too. He looked down at his lunch.

"Beckett," Emmeline laid a gentle hand on his arm. "You're a nice guy, and it's not surprising that you'd want to be nice to Tristan because she's your project partner, but listen to me. To us. You need to steer clear of her. The twins are weird too, but harmless -- I honestly think Tristan is holding her whole family hostage, in a way, which would make anyone weird. I'm telling you this because I care about you, not because I have ulterior motives."

Beckett scrubbed a hand over his face.

"Can I eat my lunch, please?"

"Oh, of course!" Emmeline smiled, finally releasing his arm, and turned to talk to Hattie.

Beckett looked at Jason, who raised his eyebrows as if to say *I told you so,* and then he looked over at Tristan, still sitting alone by the window. As Beckett turned back to his lunch, he saw Olivia staring at him from the table across from him. Her expression was unreadable, but Beckett somehow knew she was angry. He was sure she'd witnessed the whole conversation with Emmeline, witnessed how he'd said nothing and, just like every other good little minion in Emmeline's army, fell in line and took her at her word because it was easier than arguing.

Appetite gone, Beckett stood, leaving the table with his tray.

"Beckett? Beckett! Where are you going?" Emmeline called after him, but Beckett ignored her, dumping his lunch in the trash and leaving the cafeteria.

CHAPTER 4

On Wednesday, Tristan was called to the library early in the morning to help assist with shelf organization, which she genuinely loved, and not just because it got her out of morning classes. As far as she was concerned, the library was her safe space; it was cavernous and quiet, and, even if Emmeline or her friends did show up, the librarian, Miss Lewis, suffered no fools and no unnecessary talking.

Tristan wove her hair into a braid and got to work, the morning flying by. The organization was tedious, but it gave her much-needed focus, so that by the time she went to the cafeteria to grab lunch, she was feeling much less anxious than she'd been the previous day.

"Hey."

"Hey," Tristan looked up from her food, surprised to see Olivia and Evander standing beside her table in the cafeteria. "What's up? Are you guys OK?"

"Fine. Are *you* OK?" Olivia asked in return.

"Fine," Tristan said slowly. "Why?"

Olivia fidgeted for a moment, her gray eyes casually surveying the cafeteria in an effort to make sure no one was eavesdropping. Her skin was paler than usual, her whole demeanor more subdued, and Tristan knew she was still feeling the effects of Monday's crash. Evander looked much the same from his crash yesterday, and remained silent while Olivia led the conversation. Olivia nodded at him and Evander left, Tristan frowning as he went. She sat down beside Tristan and spoke in a low voice.

"I have a bad feeling."

"What do you mean?" Tristan's stomach clenched.

"I don't know. It's just out of reach, but it's there." Olivia wanted to say more, but was hesitating, assessing Tristan instead.

"You know I hate when you do that," Tristan said. "Just tell me the rest. Is it about me?"

"I don't know," Olivia said again. "It might be. I think it's originating from Emmeline, so probably? But I can't tell yet. I just know something strange is going on, and it's no good."

"Oh," Tristan's shoulders relaxed. "Well that won't be anything new. Whatever it is, I can handle it, O. I'm not afraid of her."

Olivia opened her mouth, but the bell rang just then.

"We'll talk later. I have to go get my books."

"Take it easy, OK? I can tell you're still feeling off."

Olivia nodded.

"I'll see you after school."

**

The rest of the day passed without incident. Ms. West had everyone break into partner groups during English, to work on their project, and Beckett seemed as subdued as Olivia had at lunch. Tristan looked at him curiously a few times, but he just looked back at her with an expression she couldn't decipher.

They were nearing the end of class when Beckett finally spoke of something other than their project.

"Any Halloween plans?"

"No."

"Not even giving out candy? Isn't your house one of Lavelle's most popular trick or treating spots? I seem to remember that your family usually goes all out. Didn't you wear silver body paint last year?"

Tristan blushed, and Beckett grinned.

"Oh yeah, don't think I forgot about that."

She'd been a weeping angel statue last year, and, while she had been painted head to toe, she'd also been wearing clothing. Very little clothing, but still.

"Believe it or not, I'm not really a Halloween fan." Tristan told him.

"So no silver body paint this year?" Beckett asked, and Tristan looked at him exasperatedly.

"No."

Beckett grinned at her again. "I'm just teasing. I like teasing you."

"You and everyone else in our class," Tristan shot back, before she could stop herself. As she watched, Beckett's face fell. He nodded slowly before looking back down at his work, picking up a pen to resume writing.

Tristan looked skyward. She didn't want Beckett as a friend, not really, but she also didn't harbor any ill-will towards him; lumping him in with their classmates when he really wasn't like them was not fair of her.

"I'm sorry. I didn't m--"

"No, don't," Beckett interrupted, his expression grave as he looked up at her once again. *"I'm* sorry. For a lot of things, but right now, for teasing you. I know we're not friends, you don't know me like that, so I know it sounded like more of the same. I won't do it again."

He became preoccupied with the papers spread across his desk, then, and Tristan stared at him, taken aback. What did he mean, he was sorry for a lot of things? What things?

When Beckett didn't look up again, Tristan got back to work herself, shaking her head just slightly. Something strange was definitely going on.

CHAPTER 5

The next morning, Tristan's alarm went off at its usual time. She reached for her phone, but her arm would not move. Opening her eyes, which felt as though they'd been glued shut while she slept, Tristan groaned. Her whole body felt as though it weighed a ton and weighed nothing at the same time. Her alarm continued to chirp cheerfully, and she reached for her phone again, straining to lift her limb from the bed. With great effort, she grabbed it, taking a rest before lifting it to swipe the alarm off of the screen. She closed her eyes, unable to remember ever in her life feeling so exhausted. Her bedroom door opened and Olivia came in, eyeing her apprehensively.

"Trinity?"

Tristan opened her eyes again, her head flopping over on the pillow.

"Still think you're going to school today?" Olivia asked, folding her arms over her chest.

"I have to," Tristan said, her voice heavy with fatigue. "I told you. Two tests. Help me up."

Olivia pulled her into a sitting position, and Tristan took a deep breath, swinging her legs out of bed. She paused, closing her eyes once again.

"This is pathetic," Olivia commented, and Tristan slowly lifted her head, glaring at her sister.

Olivia sighed, shaking her head.

"OK. You're going to have to take some of my energy."

"No. You have none to spare."

"True." Olivia thought for a moment, then walked to Tristan's door and called for Sol.

Sol appeared a few minutes later.

"Good morning girls. Trinity, are you OK?"

"She's crashing. She's never crashed before, did you know that?" Olivia asked, and Sol shook her head.

"I'm not sure how that's possible."

"She doesn't use her abilities much, Mom. She hasn't in like, ten years or something."

"More like six or seven." Tristan corrected.

"And crashes don't usually start until puberty, so that explains that." Sol nodded. "OK, just relax, Trinity, and I'll go get your mini-infusion ready."

"She's going to school. Or she thinks she is." Olivia raised her eyebrows at Sol.

"I am. I have two big tests today." Tristan ran her hand over her face.

"Can she borrow some of your energy, Mom? Just enough to help her get ready for school? Once she's there, she can borrow from everyone else."

Sol thought for a moment, studying Tristan's face. Her eldest looked as awful as one could expect to look during a crash -- white as a sheet, eyes squinted against the all-consuming exhaustion, body sagging under the same weight -- but her jaw was set, and Sol knew no amount of arguing would keep her home that day. Nodding, she approached Tristan, laying a gentle hand on her shoulder. She closed her eyes, and within moments Tristan began to perk up a bit.

"There." Sol stepped back. "It's not as good as a mini-infusion, but it should get you through."

Tristan still felt like she weighed about a thousand pounds, still felt like she could lie down and easily go back to sleep for a week straight, but she no longer felt as though the most basic of tasks were impossible. She stood, assuring Olivia and Sol that she was OK, and slowly made her way to the bathroom.

Everything took extra long that morning. Tristan had to take a rest after brushing her teeth, after brushing her hair, after getting dressed. She laid, eyes closed, in the backseat of her own car as Evander drove the three of them to school, an indignity she wouldn't soon get over. When they arrived, she waved Olivia and Evander ahead of her, looking at the distance between the car and the Academy, wondering if not staying home was a monumental mistake. Moving as though she'd been pushed down the stairs the night before, Tristan made her way to her locker, enduring more staring than usual on the way.

"Are you gonna blow chunks? You look like you're gonna blow chunks." An underclassman gave her a wide berth as she crept by, and Tristan just scowled at him.

She reached her locker, resting her forehead against the cool metal and closing her eyes. Her knees felt weak, and her hand shook as she reached for the combination lock, spinning the dial from memory. It was another few minutes she didn't have before she was able to open the door and pull out her books, and, when she had closed the door and turned around, she found Emmeline, Georgiana, Eloise, and Tara staring at her from across the hallway.

"Wow. You look shittier than usual today," Emmeline said, looking Tristan up and down. "I didn't even know that was possible. Is this some kinda Halloween performance art, or have you not gotten to feed on the blood of the innocent recently?"

Tristan was not going to engage. It was never worth it, she knew that, but when her energy had disappeared so had her tolerance for Emmeline Strandquest, so she whispered something unintelligible.

"What was that?" Emmeline asked, leaning forward.

Tristan moved close enough to Emmeline to make her uncomfortable, which she knew because Emmeline blinked her spangled eyelashes -- which matched the sparkly cat-eared headband she wore -- several times in quick succession, her nose wrinkling.

"I said, I think I'm coming down with the flu." Tristan coughed for effect, not covering her mouth, and Emmeline and her friends shrieked, scattering away in a flurry of glittery, animal-eared headbands and overwhelmingly floral perfume.

"I swear to God, you are going to be so sorry if I get sick!" Emmeline yelled, practically running towards the bathrooms, covering her nose and mouth.

Tristan laughed to herself, continuing on to homeroom.

Word spread quickly that Tristan was ill and coughing on everyone who got close to her, so she got to enjoy a rare day of being completely avoided at all costs. A few times she was accused of faking, of putting on a show because it was Halloween, but even those people steered clear of her, just in case. Additionally, a couple of her teachers, upon seeing her, requested she sit in the back so as not to infect anyone else.

As Olivia had instructed, Tristan borrowed energy from her classmates, not needing to touch anyone since the air was so charged, and made it through her morning Economics test just fine.

Not hungry, Tristan opted to go outside for lunch, sitting on the bench she and Beckett had occupied by the lake. She leaned her head back, letting the sun warm her face, though it didn't feel nearly as comforting as it usually did.

"She's here!" A voice called nearby, and Tristan cracked one eye open, slowly turning her head to see Beckett heading towards her.

"Hey." Beckett stood directly in her sunlight, and Tristan squinted up at him, annoyed. "Olivia and Evander are looking for you. What's going on? Some kids swear you're doing a Halloween act, but Emmeline was crying earlier that you have the flu and you coughed on her. Are you OK?"

"She's fine. Thanks for helping us look," Evander said, approaching. His tone made it clear that he expected Beckett to leave, so, with a final curious look at Tristan, Beckett reluctantly did just that.

"How are you holding up?" Olivia asked, sitting beside Tristan while Evander watched Beckett to make sure he really was going back up to the school.

"Oh, you know," Tristan said, but she was too tired to say more.

"Yeah, we know."

The three of them sat on the bench in silence, and Tristan relaxed, thankful for their presence. This crash was by far the most challenging and strange thing she'd encountered in recent memory; she certainly felt sick, understanding now why Olivia had been groaning like she was dying on Monday morning, but she didn't *feel* sick. It was impossible to put into words, because it didn't make sense to feel sick without feeling sick, but Tristan decided Olivia had done a good job of describing it. It wasn't just exhaustion, either -- it was so far beyond that Tristan decided she'd be able to turn cartwheels the next time she did feel that tired. She, appropriately, felt as though she'd lost all but the very basic energy required to survive, like a strong enough breeze would carry her away, or at least knock her over. She felt withered and one hundred years old, and an earlier glance in the mirror had confirmed that she was hunched over and a shade of white not usually found in humans, so she looked it, too. It was fitting that this had happened on Halloween, really, and Tristan suspected she'd hear from Beckett in the coming days that for someone who didn't have plans for the holiday, she'd sure seemed to devote herself to the celebration.

Lunch ended too soon, and Olivia and Evander helped Tristan up. She brushed them off, irritated.

"I'm not your grandmother; I'm fine."

"You actually really do look like grandma though, right now, just a little less wrinkly," Olivia said thoughtfully, and Evander snorted.

"Sister of the year," Tristan muttered, and Olivia grinned, squeezing her hand and bounding off after Evander, leaving Tristan to her own devices.

By the time English class rolled around, Tristan thought she was actually going to die. Just close her eyes, put her head on her desk, and never wake up again. Unfortunately, her second and final big test was in this class, so, while she did close her eyes, it was to again borrow some energy from her classmates. When she opened them, she saw Beckett looking over at her, his brow knit in concern. Ms. West stopped at her desk, hesitating before she put the test paper down.

"Are you OK?"

Tristan nodded.

"Fine."

"Are you sure? I can hold this for you until tomorrow, if you think you need to go to the nurse."

"I'm not going to be here tomorrow," Tristan said, then quickly clarified. "At school."

"Hey Ms. West!" Jason Dalton, a big lughead of a thing and, inexplicably, one of Beckett's close friends, protested loudly. "How come you never hold tests for me?"

"Because you do the bare minimum, Mr. Dalton, and I'm not even sure how you got into this class," Ms. West said unflinchingly, to the hoots and hollers of her students, not even bothering to look in Jason's direction.

"I'm fine," Tristan said again, holding out her hand for the test.

"If you take this and you fail, I can't let you take it again. Do you want me to hold this until Monday? Last chance."

"I'm not going to fail!" Tristan said haughtily, offended, and Ms. West smiled.

"There's Tristan. OK. Godspeed."

Tristan closed her eyes and took a deep breath, then turned her test paper over. She just had to make it through this, and then she could go sit in her car until Olivia and Evander had finished their classes.

***

Beckett told himself not to follow Tristan. He had to be

at football practice, and he didn't want her to think he was stalking her. Still, he was worried. She looked awful, like something traumatic had happened to her, or like she'd come down with an intractable illness, and it was actually hard to watch her shuffle through the halls like she was seventy instead of seventeen. If she hadn't looked around to see him coming when he'd found her on the bench at lunch, he would have thought she'd died right there by the lake.

At first, he'd thought the gossip that she was pulling some elaborate Halloween stunt was probably true -- even though she'd said she had no plans and was no fan of Halloween, he'd gone to her house with his friend group every year for the last three, and he saw with his own eyes how into it she got alongside her family. As the day had gone on, however, Beckett realized the gossip was wrong. Tristan was legitimately suffering, and it shook him to see her that way.

He hemmed and hawed at the back door of the school, watching football practice begin without him, torn between minding his own business, which he was sure Tristan would prefer, and going to check on her. It suddenly occurred to him that she might have attempted to drive home, which was what propelled him through the Academy and out into the parking lot to look for her car. His sense of alarm increased when he didn't immediately spot the unassuming black Nissan, which in no way stood out amongst the many, many other black cars in the lot. He pulled out his phone to -- to what? He didn't have Tristan's number, or Olivia or Evander's, for that matter, and there was no one else he could call without them refusing to help or telling him to forget it and to get to football practice.

Beckett surveyed the lot one more time, more slowly, and blew out a long breath when he noticed her car on the far right end, parked beneath a tree with low-hanging branches. He approached the vehicle as the final bell rang faintly in the Academy behind him, and stopped in front of the open driver's side window, taking a moment to look at Tristan, who had her head against the seat headrest, her eyes closed. Her skin was impossibly, unnaturally white -- Beckett didn't think a living human could be so pale -- and she was just as still.

"I'm not dead." Tristan spoke suddenly, and Beckett jumped.

Tristan opened her eyes, still not moving as she looked at him.

"What do you want?"

"I wanted to make sure you're OK. I take it we're not meeting today."

"I'm fine. Do you know how many times I've said that today? And you're right, we have to reschedule."

"Can you blame anyone for worrying?"

Tristan snorted.

"Worrying. More like being terrified they're going to catch some exotic virus that will make them look like this."

"Well..." Beckett gave an exaggerated shrug, rocking back and forth on the balls of his feet.

"I'm not sick," Tristan said, closing her eyes.

"So this is a Halloween stunt?"

"No."

"So--"

"Go away, Beckett."

"I'm just trying to understand."

"I'm just trying to sit here in peace."

"You have Emmeline and her friends thinking they're going to come down with the flu in the next few days."

That got the faintest of smirks out of Tristan, and Beckett smiled.

"Shou--"

"Tristan?"

Beckett turned to see Olivia and Evander approaching in a hurry, looking less than thrilled to see him.

"Beckett, what are you doing?" Olivia asked, looking between him and Tristan.

"Bothering me," Tristan said, at the same time as Beckett said, "Checking on Tristan."

"We told you she's fine," Evander said, his voice lilting like he was asking a question and giving an answer at the same time.

"I told him that too," Tristan piped up, and Beckett thought it figured that she'd suddenly become chatty.

"She--"

"She is," Olivia interrupted, smiling at him sweetly. "It's just that time of the month."

"Olivia," Tristan groaned, and Beckett backed up a couple of steps, flustered.

"You're not gonna let her drive, right?" Beckett asked Olivia, looking dubiously at Tristan.

"Right. We got this, Beckett." Evander answered for Olivia, tapping the side of the car as he spoke. "In the back, sis. O is going to drop me back at the field."

Tristan, with obvious effort, turned in her seat, practically oozing into the back of the car. She laid down and threw an arm over her eyes, muttering about Evander being lazy, and Olivia smiled again at Beckett.

"See you tomorrow, Beckett."

"You'll see me tonight, probably," Beckett replied. "You guys always do such a good job with Halloween, I wouldn't miss it."

"See you tonight then." Olivia got into the car and so did Evander, not bothering to say goodbye to Beckett.

The trio drove off and Beckett watched them go. Olivia had been lying about Tristan, but Beckett figured it was what he deserved. Her personal business was none of his, and he'd had no right to pry. He trekked back to football practice, apologizing to Coach Dunne for being late. Coach Dunne didn't want to hear it, and sent Beckett off to run laps for the remainder of the practice, which Beckett assumed was supposed to be a punishment, but was something he actually preferred over practice that day. He was distracted, and distraction meant a higher risk for injury, and running helped clear his head anyway. Besides, using practice to press Evander for more information would be just as risky as running drills distracted -- Beckett knew Olivia would crack long before Evander would, and Olivia would never crack.

Giving up for the time being on the mystery of Tristan Wallace, Beckett instead thought about her smirk when he'd mentioned Emmeline's meltdown. He couldn't remember ever seeing Tristan smile outright, and the realization made him want it more than he'd wanted anything recently. He respected her need for space and her odd rule of no friendships, but he didn't have to be someone's friend to make them smile. A new goal in mind, Beckett took the last few laps with ease, before hitting the locker room shower and heading home.

***

Tristan and Olivia arrived home to a flurry of activity. Sol and Umbris, along with their two housekeepers, Ivan and Ruby, had spent the day preparing the grounds and the house for Halloween, and their work looked, as usual, incredible. Their annual display was not something the people of Lavelle deserved, in Tristan's opinion, but Sol and Umbris insisted they did it for themselves as much as anyone else. Halloween was genuinely their favorite holiday.

This year's theme was a haunted dollhouse, and no detail had been spared. The normally white exterior of the house had been sprayed with what Tristan hoped was a washable black substance, giving it a rundown, rotten appearance. The flowers and bushes had been sprayed with the same substance, and the windows had all been covered with solid black contact paper, making the entire scene look like someone had isolated the house against the vibrant greenery and turned it grayscale. On their way up the drive, Tristan and her siblings had seen Ivan stringing thick, faux cobwebs along the bushes that lined the road. Entering the house, they found that heavy black drapes had been hung, and all family photos had been replaced with framed photos of skeletons in period garb. The living room fireplace was going, the bulbs in the dining room chandelier had been swapped out for black light bulbs, and more thick cobweb adorned its ornate spirals. On various surfaces, doll heads were repurposed as planters, and all of the area rugs had been rolled up and put away. Tristan entered the living room and gasped -- along the far wall were four life-sized dolls who'd been dressed in typical doll clothes and had their hair and faces done in exaggerated doll makeup. They were positioned in different ways, but all wore the same look of terror, and for a moment Tristan had thought they were real humans. This was not helped by the soundtrack of creepy, tinkering music box music Sol and Umbris already had going.

"I hate these!" Tristan yelled, and behind her Umbris laughed.

"They're great, aren't they? I've had them for years, can't even remember where I got them, and they were the first thing I thought of when we decided to do this theme this year."

"They're freaking terrifying," Tristan said, turning away.

"You better go get ready."

"Dad, seriously? All I want to do is go to bed and sleep until it's time to leave for the gathering."

"Let Oceana help you get ready. You can sit out front and hold the candy bowl -- you won't even have to try to look creepy, since you already do."

"Gee, thanks," Tristan said sarcastically, trudging up the stairs.

Tristan took off her uniform and put on a pair of black leggings and a black tank top. She didn't know what Oceana had in mind for her, so she laid on her bed and decided to take a nap while she waited. An indeterminable amount of time later, Tristan thought she heard her name. She opened her eyes and promptly screamed -- leaning over her was a ghost.

"Trinity, Trinity, it's me!" Olivia waved her hands, her voice panicky. "It's Oceana!"

"Gods, Oceana!" Tristan shouted, pushing herself into a sitting position. She put her face in her hands, concentrating on getting her heart rate back down into a normal range.

"I'm sorry! I tried calling you from the doorway, but you were out like a light!"

Tristan looked at Oceana, who wore an ashy blonde wig with blunt bangs and long pigtails. Her face, neck, and arms were painted white, and sinister arched eyebrows had been drawn onto her face in thin black lines. Her lips were crimson, the lipstick bleeding out past the corners for maximum creepiness, garish pink blush had been applied to her cheeks, and her eyes were ringed in black. She wore a short-sleeved, short black velvet dress with a white lacy bib and a mock turtleneck, white tights, and shiny black patent Mary Janes.

"Gods," Tristan said again, and Olivia grinned.

"That good, huh?"

Tristan shook her head.

"What do you have for me?"

An hour later, Tristan stood in front of her mirror, not quite recognizing herself. Olivia, who was extremely talented with makeup and costuming, had completely transformed Tristan into a life-sized doll that rivaled the ones in the living room in creepiness. Olivia had forgone the white paint since Tristan didn't need it, and smudged black around Tristan's eyes and downward from the corners of her mouth, which she'd also painted over to make it appear sewn shut. She'd dressed Tristan in a white, Victorian style dress, with a high neck, puffed three-quarter sleeves, and sweeping hemline, white tights and ratty white ballet shoes, and she'd given Tristan a pair of contact lenses that changed her eyes into a cloudy, translucent blue. Olivia had also produced a black wig with fat ringlets, the top part of which was pulled back into a bouffant and secured with a white bow. For the finishing touch, Olivia ripped Tristan's dress in various places and smudged black makeup all over it. When she'd finished, she stepped back, admiring her handiwork.

"Oceana, holy shit," Tristan said, and Olivia smiled. "Where did you even get all of this stuff?"

"I've collected it in pieces over the years." Olivia waved her hand. "You know I do those makeup tutorials for YouTube and Instagram, so I have a ton of it, but this costume stuff I picked up at some local thrift stores over the last couple of months, after Dad told me what this year's theme was going to be. That reminds me, can I take your picture for my Insta? I won't say who you are."

Tristan nodded, and Olivia positioned her by the window, turning her to and fro until the lighting was just right. She took a series of photos, up close and at a distance, and after a few minutes gave Tristan a satisfied nod. A knock sounded on Tristan's door just then, and she looked over, jumping when she saw Evander standing in full costume in the doorway. He wore a black and white pinstriped suit with the arms torn off, a white shirt, red bowtie, shiny black shoes, and his hair had been shellacked to the heavens in a 50s, James Dean style that was actually making a comeback outside of Halloween. Olivia had clearly worked her magic on him, too, using her makeup to make his eyes look like huge, round white balls, and like his mouth was open in a black perma-gape.

"You are so talented. How did I not know this?" Tristan asked, and Olivia just shrugged. "Did you do Mom and Dad, too?"

Olivia nodded, and Tristan hurried as fast as her exhausted bones would allow downstairs to see them. Olivia had not disappointed here, either, having transformed Umbris and Sol into fantastically creepy ventriloquist dummies. They clapped when they saw all of their children ready to get the night started, and patiently allowed Olivia to take photos of them, as well. When she'd finished, Umbris began directing the children to their posts -- Evander took his place in the dining room, where the table had been set with a silver candelabra with black candles, and all manner of plates and bowls of disgusting looking substances, Olivia took the living room with the dolls Tristan still wasn't sure wouldn't come to life and turn their house into a real haunted dollhouse, and Umbris and Sol took the kitchen, which you had to pass through to get out the back door. It was the usual path the Wallaces set up for their haunted houses, and this year Tristan got to take the porch again. Before she went out, Olivia called for their attention.

"Guys, I'm gonna change the vibe, OK, to make it even creepier in here? You're all gonna feel really uneasy for a minute, so I'm sorry, but just remember it's me doing it and it'll pass quick."

Sure enough, moments later a feeling of extreme unease descended upon Tristan, but, just as quickly as it had come, it subsided. Though she maintained that she was not a fan of Halloween, Tristan found herself wishing she didn't feel so terrible, so she could play along with even half as much enthusiasm as her family. Instead, she sat down in a weather-beaten white rocking chair that had just appeared on the porch that day, folding her hands in her lap and trying to keep her head cocked to one side. Last minute, Umbris and Sol had decided to keep the candy in the kitchen with them, instructing Tristan that all she had to do was act as creepy as possible while their visitors streamed into the house. Ivan and Ruby were in charge of leading the trick-or-treaters up the driveway, and just as night fell, they began to arrive in droves.

***

To say the night was a success was an understatement. Had

Tristan been feeling better, she probably would have been delighted by the screams that poured from the house every few minutes. For her part, she'd decided instead to sit stock-still, following the trick-or-treaters with her creepy eyes only. When Emmeline and her crew had arrived, the nerve, she'd been tempted to jump up and attack her, but Tristan refrained, instead glaring at her as hard as she could manage. Emmeline, dressed predictably as an angel who wore barely any clothing, was surrounded on all sides by her friends and looked scared out of her mind, which gave Tristan a small thrill of satisfaction.

Tristan didn't see Beckett in the first group of meatheads that had gone in, so she assumed he was in the next. Sure enough, a few minutes later, a group of guys dressed as Marvel characters stepped up onto the porch. Iron Man and Spider-Man both wore masks, so she didn't know who they were, but Tyler Daniels was dressed as Captain America, Henry Aspern as the Incredible Hulk, Jason Dalton as Thor, and, finally, Beckett as Loki.

"Look, it's Tristan in her natural form," Jason joked, but Tristan did not break character, continuing to stare at him lifelessly. He held up his costume's Mjölnir, and, in a terrible imitation of Thor, declared, "I am Thor, son of Odin!"

"Move it along, Thor!" Ivan called from the driveway, and Jason rolled his eyes, approaching the front door.

Beckett moved into Tristan's line of vision and, damn him, he was wearing the hell out of his Loki costume. The armor covering his shoulders, from which his cape flowed, accented the broadness of his shoulders, the black leather costume hugged his body from chest to toe, and he somehow even made the ridiculous horned helmet, long black wig, and tall, black leather boots look not quite so ridiculous. Beckett looked over at her, his lips curving into a small smile as he surveyed her from head to toe. Tristan kept a straight face, but was beyond thankful that the porch was too dark for Beckett to see the way he'd made her blush. Too soon, he disappeared into the house, and Tristan told herself to knock it off.

The next group went inside and, while another waited on the porch, a guy she recognized from the junior class decided it would be a good idea to touch her.

"Look, a doll." Theo, Tristan was pretty sure his name was, stepped forward, leaning right down into her face. "Creepy as fuuuuck."

His friends laughed, but Tristan started to get nervous about the way he was looking at her, combined with the alcohol on his breath. He hadn't backed up, was still right up in her face, and the only thing keeping him from being totally intimidating were the bushy black eyebrows he'd glued on as part of his pirate costume.

"Does it move?" Theo poked her shoulder, hard, and Tristan gritted her teeth.

"Feels pretty real." Theo poked her again and, before Tristan could react, he'd picked her up by the waist. "Let's see--"

"Get off of me!" Tristan yelled, but Theo was apparently part giant, and he suspended her in the air easily, laughing with his friends as he shook her. Tristan tried to go stiff, but her head flopped around lazily.

"It talks!"

"Put me down you psycho!" Tristan yelled again, too weak to put up a good fight, though she gripped his hands, trying anyway. She saw Ivan struggling to get through the crowd that had formed, which wasn't an easy task considering how many people had queued up by the steps.

"Hey!" Beckett ran up onto the porch from the side and grabbed Tristan away from Theo, setting her down gently before turning back to the laughing pirate.

Beckett grabbed Theo by the front of his shirt, and though Theo had several inches and probably a good thirty pounds on Beckett, Beckett yanked him forward until their noses were practically touching.

"Keep your fucking hands to yourself."

"Or what?" Theo sneered.

"Or I'll break them."

Theo tried to pull away, laughing derisively, but Beckett held him fast, and for the first time Theo looked something close to nervous.

"Try me."

"Come on! What's the hold up?" Someone in the very back of the line yelled, and Beckett released Theo, shoving him away.

Theo stumbled backwards, glaring at Beckett and Tristan. Wisely, he said nothing else, entering the house with his friends, who were imploring him to get away from Beckett. Ivan finally reached Tristan, who had sunk back into the rocking chair, and placed his hand gently on her arm.

"Are you OK?"

"I'm fine. You better get back out there," Tristan assured him, then hesitated, looking at Beckett's back. "Can you just keep the next group off of the porch for a minute?"

Ivan nodded, straightening up. He inclined his head at Beckett. "Thank you."

Beckett nodded, then turned to Tristan, dropping to one knee and pulling off his helmet and wig. He looked her over, wishing she wasn't wearing costume contacts so he could see what was going on in her eyes.

"Are you hurt?"

"I'm fine. Thank you for intervening. I didn't think you were still here."

"We just got out and were coming up the side when I heard you yell."

Tristan nodded.

"You'd better get back to your friends."

"You're sure you're OK? You don't look a lot better than you did this afternoon."

"I'll be fine." Tristan hesitated. "I like your costume, by the way."

Beckett grinned.

"I like yours, too, even though it's gonna give me nightmares tonight."

Tristan held back another smile, and after a few beats, Beckett nodded at her, rising to his feet.

"I'll see you Monday, Tristan."

"See you Monday, Beckett."

He walked off, putting his helmet back on, and Tristan resumed her role. The rest of the night went smoothly, thankfully, and when the last group had left the house, Ivan and Ruby closed the gates at the end of the driveway.

Tristan went inside, blinking until she had adjusted to the regular lighting of the house, which was harsh on her eyes that had grown accustomed to the dark.

"Well, that was a success, huh?" Sol smiled, and everyone nodded in agreement.

"Except for Trinity's attack, yes," Ivan nodded, and the smiles immediately disappeared from everyone's faces.

"What attack?" Evander asked, and Tristan shook her head.

"I'm fine. It was nothing."

"A pirate got handsy," Ivan said, as though Tristan had said nothing at all. "Picked her right up out of that chair like it was nothing and gave her a shake. Loki came to her rescue."

"Loki?" Olivia frowned, and then her face lit with recognition. "Oh, Beckett?"

"How convenient that he just happened to be there," Evander said darkly, and Tristan cocked her head.

"What are you implying?"

"Just seems suspect that the night was fine before and after Beckett, but *during* was when someone decided to be an ass to you. Who did it? Who put their hands on you?"

"He's a junior, I think his name is Theo? He was gigantic."

"Theo Fitelson?" Evander's eyes widened, and Tristan shrugged.

"Isn't he on the football team?" Olivia asked, and Evander nodded, his jaw working.

"What's his deal?" Tristan asked. "He reeked of alcohol, for what that's worth."

"That's his deal. Alcohol and we think steroids, though Coach hasn't been able to pin anything down about it." Evander flexed his hands. "He might finally on Monday, though."

"Ember," Umbris said warningly. "You know the rules."

"Still think Beckett put him up to it?" Tristan asked, and Evander shook his head.

"Nah. I believe he did that all on his own. I thought you were going to say it was Jason Dalton or Tyler Daniels or something."

"Tyler wouldn't have!" Olivia blurted, then looked embarrassed.

"We'll talk about that later," Sol said, pointing to Olivia. "For now, Trinity, are you OK?"

"I'm fine. I *was* fine. It caught me off-guard is all, and since I'm pretty weak, I couldn't fight him off."

Sol squeezed her shoulder.

"Why don't you go shower and get yourself to bed? We won't disturb you until it's time to leave for the gathering on Saturday; since you never crash and aren't used to it, we'll call you out of school tomorrow."

Tristan nodded gratefully.

"Use coconut oil to get your makeup off," Olivia told her, and Tristan nodded again.

She went upstairs, doing as Olivia said, and then showered before putting on her coziest pajamas and dragging herself into bed. Tristan closed her eyes, wanting to sleep, but instead her brain decided to relive the incident with Theo and

Beckett on the porch. Particularly, the part of the incident where Beckett had taken her out of Theo's arms and set her down as though she really was a doll that could have broken. His grip had been firm and, though Tristan was almost as tall as him, he'd lifted her with ease. His eyes had been blazing with anger, but he'd looked at Tristan kindly in the seconds before he'd gone after Theo, and then he'd looked at her with a warmth that made her tingle when they'd been alone on the porch afterwards. The whole incident really had not been a huge deal -- Tristan knew Theo would have put her back down within moments -- but she appreciated having been rescued by a superhero all the same.

Grinning to herself while she pulled the blanket up under her chin, Tristan rolled onto her side and drifted off to sleep.

CHAPTER 6

School on Friday was buzzing with Halloween chatter; nearly everyone had gone by The Wallace's house, and it was all anyone could talk about. Theo Fitelson was absent, which Beckett knew because he'd looked for him. The additional absence of Tristan was particularly conspicuous, considering everyone talked about her and their family all day.

"I hated it," Emmeline said, predictably, at lunch. She shot a look at the next table, where Olivia sat chatting with a group of her junior friends, and lowered her voice. "I had the worst feeling as soon as we got there, and I didn't feel better until I got back into town. And did you see those people dolls in the living room? I'm still trying to decide if I should call the police. They looked way too real."

"It was disturbing." Eloise nodded. "Not even good scary, just disturbing."

"It was awesome, if you ignore what family it was," Jason said. "Though it gets a lot creepier if you don't ignore it, so does that actually make it more awesome?"

"Olivia was the hottest haunted doll I've ever seen," Tyler commented, a wistful look on his face as he turned to stare at the still-oblivious object of his affection, and Emmeline pulled a face of her own.

"I'm gonna pray for you, Tyler," Emmeline said, and Tyler laughed.

"Don't you ever get tired of being so uptight, Emmy?"

"Don't call me that, first of all, and no, second of all."

"I heard you got into it with Theo Fitelson, Beckett," Tara said slyly, and all eyes were suddenly on him.

"I don't know that I'd call it that."

"Rumor has it Theo was drunk and gripped up Tristan, and Beckett here swooped in to save the day," Hattie told the table at large.

"We were walking back around the house when I saw him pick her up, yeah. It was ridiculous, what kind of psycho does that?" Beckett looked at Tyler and Henry, who nodded in agreement.

"I also heard you threatened to break his hands," Georgiana said, resting her chin in her hand, and Beckett wondered if he was under a coordinated attack.

"Did I?" Beckett asked mildly, eating his lunch. He could feel Emmeline watching him, but for once, she said nothing.

***

Tristan slept like the dead all through Thursday night and well into Friday afternoon, when Sol gently shook her awake so she could use the bathroom. Tristan did, promptly going right back to sleep afterwards.

Around midnight on Friday night, Sol administered a mini-infusion to Trinity while she slept, brushing her hair out of her face. She studied her daughter's features, relaxed in a way they usually weren't when she was awake. For not the first time, Sol wondered if discouraging Trinity from making meaningful connections at school had turned her into something she wouldn't be otherwise. She was a good girl, there was no question about that, and she had a voracious appetite for learning that her big brain took in and processed in a way Sol had only ever dreamed of being able to do when she herself had been in school. That was important, but it was also important for Trinity to feel secure in her social environment, and that was the area that made Sol worry. She knew Trinity struggled with her peers, that between the general oddness all of the Wallaces gave off and Trinity's self-imposed solitude, Trinity was often a target for the insecure popular kids who had to tear others down in order to feel any kind of positive emotion.

This dynamic also put Oceana and Ember in an awkward position, Sol knew, as they tried to navigate high school while finding a balance between being in with the in-crowd and protecting their sister from those very same people. While she knew better than anyone that high school was merely a blip on the radar of life, Sol couldn't help but feel she and Umbris, despite their intentions, had made a pretty major misstep with Trinity, especially now that it looked like she would not be joining the community when she graduated. That was a conversation Sol needed to have with her soon -- she didn't know if Trinity realized the kind of sacrifice that came with turning her back on the community, couldn't let her make her decision without being fully informed. Sol also needed to talk to Umbris, but preferred Trinity approach him first, as she knew Umbris would respect that much more than Sol speaking to him on her behalf.

Trinity sighed in her sleep, one corner of her mouth lifting in a half-smile, and Sol was overcome with curiosity about what she was dreaming. For as much as she hung around the house, Sol knew very little about the inner workings of Trinity's mind, knowing she preferred to seal her thoughts, which was a privacy Sol and Umbris respected. Sol told herself to walk away, to continue respecting that privacy, but Trinity was out cold and would never know if Sol took a peek into her subconscious.

Slightly ashamed of herself, Sol placed a gentle hand on Trinity's forehead, closing her eyes. She was suddenly at Jamestown Academy, standing in front of a bench, upon which sat Trinity and Beckett Benson, dressed in plainclothes. They were turned in towards each other, and when the breeze blew a strand of hair across Trinity's face, Beckett reached over and tucked it behind her ear. Trinity smiled at him, and Beckett smiled back at her, his thumb stroking her cheek.

Sol opened her eyes and removed her hand, wanting to leave whatever came next to Trinity only.

So Trinity had a crush on Beckett Benson. Sol was surprised, though perhaps she shouldn't have been -- from everything she'd heard around town about the Benson family, it seemed that Beckett, at least, matched Trinity in kindness, intelligence, and maturity. It came as a surprise to the townspeople, considering how tumultuous the relationship between Ray and Gabriella Benson was rumored to be, but Sol knew more than anyone how a person could flourish and even thrive in spite of their bloodline.

***

Tristan awoke sometime on Saturday, sitting up in bed with relative ease. She felt much better than she had on Thursday, though still not one hundred percent. Stretching, her stomach growled, and she reached for her phone. Eleven A.M. She got out of bed and wandered downstairs, finding it empty. The stillness of the house meant the rest of her family was still sleeping, in preparation for tonight's gathering.

Tristan entered the kitchen, opening the fridge and staring inside, trying to clear the lingering fog in her brain to no avail. While sleep had done her a world of good, she'd had vivid, sometimes bizarre, sometimes incredible dreams that left her feeling mentally exhausted. As Tristan reached for a yogurt, she noticed a small bruise encircling a pinprick in the crook of her elbow. Sol must have done a mini-infusion while Tristan had been sleeping, which explained why she was feeling better-ish.

Tristan perched on a stool at the kitchen's island, eating her yogurt and a handful of almonds, thinking about the dreams she had. She couldn't quite remember anything in detail, but she'd definitely dreamt about Beckett in his Loki costume, which had her face going red for reasons she refused to explore. Standing, Tristan threw away her trash, washed her spoon, and went back upstairs, getting back into bed. She'd sleep for a few more hours, and then it would be time to pack up and head out to who knows where for this month's gathering. A nervous chill ran through Tristan -- she was growing increasingly uncomfortable at these things, knowing she planned on deflecting from the community sooner rather than later -- but she closed her eyes, choosing not to stress about it until she had to.

CHAPTER 7

For as long as Tristan could remember, the monthly gathering had been held up North, in different secluded areas within a ten mile radius of New Orleans. The reason for this, as she'd always understood it, was that New Orleans is an energy hotbed, and that energy flows outward in all directions, gets picked up by the gulf winds, and carried into the fringe bayous where the community would safely gather. That the location had abruptly changed this month was a shock, and more concerning still was that no one seemed to have any information about *why* it had changed.

Nevertheless, once dusk had fallen, The Wallaces piled into Umbris and Sol's sleek black SUV, heading South on Route 23. Tristan had only traveled South a few times, and not very far -- Lavelle itself was far enough down so that it already bordered the towns that were unincorporated, and beyond those towns it was just marshland and more marshland. They drove for so long that Tristan started to get nervous that they would drive right off the Earth; the only comfort was Olivia tracking their route on her phone's map in real time.

At long last, they came to the end of Route 23, and Umbris went right down a dirt road. After a while, they passed a large white sign for a marina, and Olivia promptly zoomed in on the map of the area.

"Whoa," Olivia said. "Look at this."

She showed Tristan the map, which indicated that the road

they were on would dead end at an enormous, nearly perfect circle of geography, a series of marshland and canals and, right in the middle, Tristan suspected, an undisturbed island that would serve as their gathering place.

Tristan had just started to ask how they were going to get to the meeting spot, when Umbris took a sharp left, driving through a small lot that ended abruptly at the water line. He killed the engine and the five of them emerged from the car, Tristan and her siblings unable to see anything in the black of the night that had fallen. Sol and Umbris, who had spent their lives fully immersed in the community and therefore had abilities that even their children didn't know the extent of, could see just fine.

"Here come Dune and Thera," Umbris said. "Celes and Sanguin are not with them."

Tristan let out a silent breath of relief. It wasn't that she didn't like Celes, he was fine, she just needed to prepare to see him. He, like both sets of parents, was under the impression that Tristan had been marked for him, and as a result was just slightly more intense than Tristan preferred. Sanguin was his older sister. Tristan was pretty sure she'd heard Sanguin speak maybe twice, maybe, in all of the years they'd known the Crenshaws.

"Umbris, Sol." Dune Crenshaw greeted them warmly, holding out his hand as he and his wife, Thera, seemed to materialize out of the dark just a few feet away.

"Trinity, Oceana, Ember, it's good to see you again." Dune nodded at them, and they returned his greeting politely.

"If you want to follow us, the boat is down the bank a little ways. We will take it out to the island."

As she followed behind Umbris and Sol, Tristan's ears

pricked when she heard Sol ask Thera about the location change.

"Any idea at all?"

Thera shook her head slightly.

"We have only heard rumors, nothing has been confirmed."

"We haven't heard anything at all," Sol replied.

"Well, we have the benefit of living in New Orleans, of course," Thera said, and Sol nodded, waiting for her to continue. "Again, this is rumor, but what we heard more than once was that someone saw the last gathering. Someone who should not have seen us."

"A commoner?" Sol asked, surprised, and Thera nodded.

"More than one. Three campers looking for a desolate spot to set up camp. No word on what happened to them, once they were discovered in turn, but you know what usually happens."

Tristan suppressed a shiver. She knew there was a fringe group of guards in the community who felt it was their duty to *take care of* commoners who accidentally discovered them -- felt that if word was ever taken back to common society about what they'd seen, that it had the potential to spread too quickly, to result in a misunderstanding and subsequent witch hunt and the endangerment of the community that had thrived for over one thousand years. This was a group Umbris and Sol kept their family far away from, but the knowledge of their existence was chilling enough on its own.

The group reached the boat, a little thing that Tristan doubted would carry all of them safely across the bayou and back, and Olivia grasped her hand as they started to move. It was standing room only in the dinghy, and the only hand-hold was a wooden beam in the center with a lantern on top. Tristan looked at her sister through the eerie yellowish glow, whose expression she was sure matched hers -- nervous.

"You look great," Olivia whispered. "Out to impress Celes tonight?"

"No," Tristan said immediately, looking down at her outfit. She'd gone with the required all black, of course -- black knee-high boots, black skinny jeans, black v-necked sweater, and last minute had decided on a black velvet choker as a finishing touch. Hanging from the choker was a tiny silver triquetra with paralleled double lines -- a trinity knot. It had been a sixteenth birthday present from her parents, and they'd given her a matching ring, which she'd left at home that night. She'd decided not to straighten her hair, as it had sounded like too much effort, so it waved softly past her shoulders.

"You look great, too, as usual," Tristan told Olivia, smiling. "Very Audrey Hepburn."

Olivia had opted for a pair of skinny black ankle pants, shiny patent loafers, and a black turtleneck. Her copper hair hung long and straight nearly to her waist, and she'd given herself a killer smoky eye and bright red lip.

"*You do too, Ember,*" Evander said in a high-pitched voice, and Tristan laughed.

"You do, you're right."

Ember rolled his eyes, plucking at his black t-shirt which he'd paired with black jeans and black boots. He always looked effortlessly cool and his attitude matched, but Tristan knew that in reality Evander was fairly meticulous about his appearance.

"So Trinity, how is school going?" Thera asked, turning to look at her as the boat neared the opposite shoreline.

"It's going well," Tristan replied. "Busy, and the course load is heavy, but I like the challenge."

"Is it even challenging for you, though?" Olivia commented. "You're so smart, sometimes I think you should be teaching the teachers."

Tristan blushed.

"It is challenging. I'm not that smart."

Olivia and Evander groaned in unison, and Thera laughed. The boat bumped softly onto the bank, and the group fell silent once again. Dune led the way, through the thick trees and bramble, walking for what felt like at least an hour.

"No service," Olivia muttered, behind Tristan, and Tristan turned her head only to speak out the side of her mouth as Olivia switched her phone off.

"Of course there's no service, have you looked around? Who are you trying to get ahold of, anyway? Everyone is here, and you know you can't contact anyone back in Lavelle."

"No one," Olivia snipped, a little too quickly, and Tristan raised her eyebrows but let it drop.

Just as Tristan's feet started to hurt, her whole body tired, the trees opened to a massive clearing, around the perimeter of which many narrow, black silk tents had been erected. At the far end of the clearing a decent fire was going, and people absolutely swarmed the area.

"Ah, Celes, there you are!" Dune called, and Tristan took a deep breath, readying herself.

"Dad." Celes nodded, but his gaze instantly went to Tristan. "Trinity."

The way he said her name reminded Tristan of the way Beckett said her common name, but with hardly a fraction of the impact.

"Hi Celes," Tristan said, and her family, the traitors, continued on, leaving her alone with him.

"It's nice to see you again. You look great."

Tristan studied Celes's face, trying to see him objectively. He was handsome, there was no denying that; in fact, Tristan could see the girls she went to school with falling all over themselves if they ever met Celes. He was nineteen, soon to be twenty, having graduated from his New Orleans high school two years earlier, but he looked much older, most likely due to how tall and well-muscled he was. His black hair was long, touching his shoulders, which were exposed beneath his sleeveless black button down, and his eyes were a pale, greenish hazel -- almost yellowish, even, like a cat's eyes. Tristan also knew he was smart, at least as smart as her, if not smarter, which was part of why he'd been chosen for her. Even though he was nineteen, he was the definition of the expression *still waters run deep,* and Tristan felt confident that if she joined the community and started a life with him, it would be a life of stability and quiet thoughtfulness. On paper, he was ideal. Applied, Tristan didn't just want a life of stability. What about adventure? What about taking risks and being spontaneous and finding out what sparked passion and then pursuing that thing? Celes would be a wonderful husband to someone *like* Tristan -- who, comparatively, was in a constant state of being unsettled and who longed for nothing more than to be a normal, common girl -- but how could she say that out loud? And who would she say it to first, if she ever found the courage?

"It's nice to see you too," Tristan replied, before her silence became awkward. "Where's Sanguin?"

"She's around here somewhere. Shall we walk?" Celes asked, gesturing behind him, and Tristan nodded.

She could feel his eyes on her as they walked, but she knew he wouldn't be silent for long. It was one of the things Tristan genuinely liked about Celes -- he left nothing to mystery.

"You're sealed."

Tristan nodded. She glanced up at him.

"Trying to read me, Celes?"

"No, I wouldn't do that. It's just obvious."

Tristan was sure it was. Sealing was not forbidden, but it was not exactly a welcoming thing to do, and Tristan was running a small risk of admonishment by sealing in the community. From experience, she also knew that sealing gave off a slight iciness that could be felt by anyone standing within close proximity, though it didn't seem to bother Celes.

"Do you know why the gathering was moved to here this month?" Tristan asked. "I thought we were going to drive right off into the Gulf."

Celes smiled.

"Seemed like it. No, I don't know. I've only heard rumors, but you can never trust a rumor."

Tristan nodded.

"Stop." Celes held out his hand and Tristan walked into his arm, not expecting the road block. She looked up at him, noticing he'd tensed all over.

"What's wrong?"

"Unseal. Now."

"Ce--"

"Unseal, Trinity."

Swallowing nervously, Tristan unsealed, feeling incredibly vulnerable. She prayed quickly and fervently that all thoughts of Beckett Benson stayed away tonight, as that was the very, very last thing she needed anyone picking up on.

Moments later, Tristan heard a group of footfalls approaching from behind. Celes gently pulled her out of the way by the elbow and, as Tristan watched, one of the community's Elders, Pele Dumont, passed by with a small entourage. Just as she'd gotten past Tristan and Celes, Pele looked over at Tristan, her violet eyes meeting hers. A small sensation of shock ran up Tristan's spine, and she shook it off, not breaking eye contact with the Elder. Celes had saved Tristan from a public scene, but of course Pele knew that Tristan had been sealed only moments before. She arched an eyebrow at Tristan and continued onward, towards the fire. Tristan and Celes exchanged a look.

"Thanks," Tristan said, and Celes nodded.

"C's, line up." A voice resonated across the clearing, and Celes turned to Tristan.

"I'll find you after my infusion."

And then he was gone, disappearing into the crowd presumably to meet up with his family, who would join an infusion line at one of the tents. Tristan continued walking, looking for her own family. A few people greeted her as she went, but most looked at her with near disdain. It was well known that Tristan, daughter of Umbris Wallace, did not use her abilities, which, again, was not forbidden, but was definitely frowned upon.

Eventually, Tristan found the rest of the Wallaces standing with another family, a family whose bloodline in the community stretched back to its foundation, The Telarie de Maragons. They were old money and they looked it -- no matter how put-together Tristan ever was, she felt like an absolute schlub beside the daughters, Mora, Monse, and Mortua. Their parents, Terminus and Noxis Telarie de Maragon, were intimidating on a level Tristan had never experienced prior to meeting them, and she did not understand why Umbris and Sol had to strike up a conversation with them of all the people at the gathering.

Monse gave Tristan a look as sharp as her cheekbones, her white-blonde curls brushing her face as she turned her head, and Tristan remembered too late that she'd unsealed. Tristan gave her a nervous smile and a nod.

"Monse. Mortua, Mora, nice to see you again."

Monse just raised an eyebrow, and the other sisters greeted her coolly. Tristan looked at Olivia, who took her hand and laced her fingers through Tristan's, squeezing. Tristan didn't need to use any special ability to know Olivia was as on edge as she.

"Where's Ember?" Tristan asked quietly, sealing once again, and Olivia shrugged.

"I haven't seen him since we got here. He was heading for Aeris Abernathy last I saw."

Tristan nodded. Ember and Aeris had struck up a friendship within the last year, but Tristan suspected Ember, at least, wanted to be more than her friend. Aeris was a petite, plucky redhead and the total opposite of what Tristan would have ever expected Ember to be into, but she guessed attraction was funny that way.

"Hi Oceana." A voice behind the girls spoke, and they turned to see Hydran O'Quinn standing a foot or so away, a somewhat shy smile on his face. Hydran was Olivia's age, but with a round, pleasant face that made him look younger. His hair was brown and shaved close, his eyes also brown. He'd had a crush on Olivia since they were kids.

"Oh, hi Hydran," Oceana replied, smiling.

"Hi Trinity," Hydran greeted, and Tristan greeted him in return.

Tristan watched Olivia interact with Hydran, knowing, even if he didn't, that Olivia's heart wasn't into their exchange. For the first time, it occurred to Tristan that she and Olivia may be more alike than she'd realized, and she wondered who it was in Olivia's life that was distracting her, if anyone, or if it was just that she'd also realized community life would not be for her. While the community expectation was always placed heavily on the oldest child, the younger children did not escape altogether.

To simplify, the expectations of joining the community operated sort of like a monarchy -- each family had an heir and a spare, or several spares, as the case may be, and so the expectations were highest and firmest for the eldest, and still in place but not as rigid for the subsequent children. While Umbris and Sol guided their children's lives with the intent of them eventually joining the community, Olivia and Evander would not have mates chosen for them the way Tristan had. They would also be granted the opportunity to graduate and either go on to college or on to establish careers, settling into those roles before setting out to find a mate, if that's what they wanted, and they would be free to move about the country while they did. Tristan would be heavily persuaded to stay in Louisiana, leaving only if Celes's career took them out of state. The whole thing was antiquated, and

Tristan longed for a day where the old rules were abolished and new, progressive rules took their place. She felt beyond fortunate that Sol and Umbris would not force her to do anything she didn't want to do, as she knew there were some families -- the Telarie de Maragons, for example -- who did not give any of their children a choice in the matter.

Letter by letter, everyone was called to line up for their infusions. Tristan, who usually sat them out because she didn't need them, fidgeted nervously behind Evander.

"Would you chill out?" Evander finally said, turning around. "You're getting your mud all over me."

"What?"

"Your aura. It's muddy. Chill out."

Tristan took a deep breath, trying to get ahold of her anxiety. She looked around the clearing, catching Celes's eye. He looked much better than he had when she'd first seen him -- more vibrant, healthier, sharp. She felt a flash of attraction, which completely caught her off-guard, and which she immediately shut down. She could not start this, not now, not when graduation would be here in the blink of an eye and she broke the hearts of everyone around her.

"Oceana." Evander leaned around Tristan to look at his twin. "Can you do something about Trinity? She's making *me* anxious because she won't calm down."

Tristan shot Evander a dirty look. Olivia looked her over, nodding slowly.

"Do you mind?"

Tristan shook her head. Anything to make her stomach stop hurting. Olivia placed her palm square in the middle of Tristan's back, and Tristan felt a delightful warmth flowing into her. Her heart rate slowed, her mind calmed, and she was able to take several good deep breaths. She twisted around, marveling at Olivia.

"I didn't know you could do this."

"I *just* realized I could. Like, *just,* as in within the last couple of weeks."

"You're a healer like Mom," Tristan said in awe, and Olivia beamed at the compliment.

"Thank you," Evander said without turning around, and Tristan sighed contentedly.

Olivia had removed her hand, but the effects lasted. Tristan watched calmly as Evander disappeared into the tent ahead of her, and, when it was her turn, she didn't hesitate to enter herself. The inside of the small tent was as sparse as could be; it contained one cognac colored easy chair, one wooden chair, upon which sat Glacis Colquitt -- who was a daughter of one of the Elders, Azure -- one IV pole and related equipment, and a jet black, metallic cooler, which Tristan knew contained the infusion bags.

"Trinity," Glacis greeted, looking surprised to see her. "I'm surprised to see you."

"I'm surprised to be in here," Tristan replied, sitting down in the squashy chair.

"Do you remember how this goes?" Glacis asked, as she pulled a vinyl pouch out of the cooler. Inside was a clear, shimmering liquid.

"No, but I have been in the hospital before, in New Orleans, and I've been given IV fluids. It's basically the same thing, right?"

"Right." Glacis smiled, hanging the bag and preparing the needle she'd place in Tristan's arm.

Tristan sat back, staring at the tent flap. She'd always done much better with needles if she didn't watch them pierce her skin, and she knew this would be no exception. There *was* an exception, however, in the form of the total lack of sensation when Glacis placed the IV. Tristan wished there was a way for that to happen in the common community.

"Close your eyes," Glacis instructed, and Tristan obeyed. "Try to clear your mind if you can. It will go much quicker if you're totally open."

Tristan doubted that would ever happen, here or anywhere else. Her mind did not believe in sitting idle, and no amount of influence, supernatural or not, could change that.

"Trinity. Try to clear your mind." Glacis spoke softly but firmly, so Tristan gave it an actual effort.

She failed, of course, but the infusion went quickly enough, and when Glacis had removed the needle -- also a sensation-free experience -- Tristan jumped to her feet. She felt better than she had in at least a week, if not more, and she smiled at Glacis, who smiled in turn.

"Thank you."

"I hope to see you again next month, Trinity."

Tristan left the tent, finding Celes waiting for her. He smiled, and Tristan smiled back at him, noticing that his eyes lingered on her choker.

"Shall we walk while we wait for the rest to finish?" Celes asked, and Tristan nodded.

They headed away from the clearing, which was something they did each month -- they liked to explore the area where they'd gathered, Celes always bringing two small flashlights so they could see where they were going.

"So I guess you've started using your abilities again, since you got the infusion this month?" Celes asked, and Tristan bit her lip.

"Not exactly."

Celes nodded.

"It's because you've been sealing."

"Olivia said it's because I've been unsettled."

Celes shook his head.

"Did you crash?"

"Yes, on Halloween."

"It's because you've been sealing. Being unsettled will drain you, but long-term sealing will crash you."

Tristan was surprised; even Sol had alluded to her crashing because she'd been unsettled.

"A lot of people mix them up," Celes said, though Tristan had said nothing aloud.

"So is it going to happen every month now?"

Celes shook his head again.

"It builds. If you keep sealed, you'll crash again in a few months. The infusion will hold it off a bit, and not sealing so much will, too. If you keep doing what you're doing, you're probably looking at crashing again around February or March."

Tristan took that in before changing the subject.

"How is your ability coming along?" Tristan asked, and Celes stopped walking.

He looked at Tristan, his eyes twinkling, and then looked at the landscape ahead of them.

"Turn off your light."

Tristan did as he instructed, waiting. Gradually, the night around them grew lighter and lighter, so everything came into focus as though it were the middle of the day. Celes lifted his chin, and the landscape in front of him and Tristan began to twist soundlessly. Around it went, until they were staring at the night sky directly in front of them, the forest suspended above them.

"Celes," Tristan breathed, looking at him. "You did it."

Celes lowered his chin and everything returned to normal. He looked satisfied, but was shaking his head again.

"I didn't. I've perfected a mirage, not an actual manipulation."

"Well you could have fooled me!" Tristan exclaimed. "That was amazing!"

"Thanks." Celes looked touched.

Tristan switched her flashlight back on.

"Should we keep going?"

Celes hesitated, but then nodded, and they resumed walking. As they walked, they chatted about school and the last gathering, and before long the sounds of the current gathering had faded.

"I think we sh--" Tristan started, but a branch cracked nearby and she froze, grabbing Celes's forearm. She felt him tense up, and they fell silent, listening, the air around them electrified. There was definitely someone there, or some-ones, so now it was a matter of who made the first move.

"What business have you here?" A deep voice finally growled, and Tristan looked up at Celes.

"We're here for the gathering." Celes said in a clear voice.

The woods around them suddenly lit up, and Tristan gasped. They were surrounded on all sides by at least fifty black cloaked figures, each one holding a torch. *This* was the fringe group -- the guards -- who hunted unsuspecting commoners.

"Your names."

Tristan couldn't figure out who was speaking, couldn't get any air into her lungs to answer them.

"Celes Crenshaw, son of Dune and Thera, brother of Sanguin."

"And you?"

Tristan was gripped with fear, unable to speak.

"She's Trin--"

"She needs to answer for herself."

Celes took her hand, squeezing it until she looked at him. He nodded at her, and Tristan heard him in her head. *I won't let anything happen to you.*

"T-Trinity Wallace," Tristan began.

"Louder."

"Trinity Wallace, daughter of Umbris and Sol, sister of O-Oceana and Ember." Gods help her, she'd almost given Olivia's common name.

"Prove yourselves and you may return to the gathering."

"What?!" Tristan and Celes cried in unison.

"Prove yourselves and you may return to the gathering."

Tristan was in full-blown panic mode by now. It had been seven years, at least, since she'd used her ability, and she knew it wouldn't come back easily enough to work with her in this scenario.

"I don't think that will be necessary," Celes said, turning around slowly. "Commoners would have no reason to know our true names or those of our families, and you can easily verify who we are just by reading us."

"Prove yourselves and you may return to the gathering." The voice said it more slowly this time, as though Tristan and Celes were stupid.

Oceana, Tristan squeezed her eyes shut, hoping this would be one of those times she'd pop into Olivia's head unexpectedly. *Celes and I are in trouble. We're somewhere around three miles west of the gathering. Bring Mom or Dad, and hurry.*

"Show them," Tristan told Celes, seeing no way out of this.

"But you--"

"I'll think of something," Tristan said, but her only plan was to hope Olivia had heard her and stay alive until help came.

Celes lifted his hands and separated them, which also, with a deafening crack and bone-rattling vibration, separated the landscape. A chasm opened up, and around them the cloaked crusaders cried out in fear. Celes quickly brought his hands back together and the landscape returned to normal in an instant, causing a murmur to ripple through the group.

"Sufficient. Now the girl."

"I can't."

"Trinity," Celes said sharply.

Tristan looked at him sadly, shrugging. What else could she do? She had to hope being honest would pay off.

The group began to murmur again, and they closed in on Tristan and Celes.

"You can't?"

"I haven't used my ability since I was ten, seven years ago. I can kind of read people, on a basic level, and I can transfer energy, but that's about the extent of what I can do these days."

One of the guards stepped forward, Tristan assumed the one who'd been talking all along. She was surprised to see he looked to be about Umbris's age, tall and thin with light hair and a serious face, his appearance not at all matching the cadence of his voice. He looked at Celes with sharp, dark eyes.

"Have you brought a common girl to the gathering, trying to pass her off as one of ours?"

"No!" Tristan said immediately, unsealing. It wouldn't matter -- she couldn't do anything unsealed that she could do sealed -- but it at least made her feel like she was making an effort.

"Silence." The man looked at Tristan in a way that quieted her. He turned back to Celes. "Have you?"

"No," Celes practically growled. "She told you who she is."

"Yet she claims to have no ability. You can go. She cannot."

Tristan looked at Celes, trying not to panic. He planted his feet, taking Tristan's hand once again.

"I'm not going anywhere without Trinity."

"Cute."

Before Tristan could even blink, Celes had been ripped away from her, out of sight, and her arms were pulled roughly behind her back.

"Celes!"

"Trinity!" Celes yelled from somewhere in the distance.

"You will tell us how that boy was able to sneak you into this gathering," The leader said, circling around to stand in front of her.

"He didn't sneak me anywhere. He and I have told you who I am."

"Who you claim to be. A seventeen year old girl who cannot do anything but the most basic, lazy tasks that require next to no effort or practice."

"That's right." Tristan was getting mad now, and she jerked her body, but the person holding her just squeezed her arms tighter.

"If you are who you say, why do you have no ability to show? Why don't you practice your craft? Answer me!"

Tristan closed her eyes as the leader gripped her shoulders, shaking her. *Because I'm not joining the community!* Tristan thought, but how could she say that out loud? She wasn't ready, and it wasn't his damn business!

Suddenly, Tristan could have sworn she heard Beckett say her name. She went still, tilting her head.

"What's she doing?" Someone nearby whispered.

Tristan drew in energy from the guards and cast around her mind's eye, the energy forming into the familiar black funnel which then produced an image of Beckett, lying on what she assumed was his bed, shirtless and staring into space. Tristan watched him, enraptured, for several long beats before very suddenly remembering where she was and what was happening. Her face flaming as brightly as the torches the guards held, Tristan sealed.

"Let her go."

Tristan opened her eyes as the hands on her released their hold. The leader was looking at her with the oddest expression on his face, perhaps unsure what to make of what they'd both just seen.

"She sealed. A commoner cannot do that."

"Entros Janek, this is Umbris Wallace." Umbris's voice suddenly boomed across the field, making everyone jump. "Release my daughter immediately."

Tristan, though she'd very lamely managed to rescue herself, nevertheless sagged with relief as she turned to see Umbris, Olivia, and Celes booking it towards her. In no time they'd reached her, and Umbris dealt with the guards while Celes cupped her face and ran his hands down her arms, checking to see if she was OK. Olivia flitted around nervously behind him, and Tristan reached for her hand after she'd hugged Celes, assuring them both she was fine. She sealed again, paranoid Olivia or Celes would see what had transpired, would see what Entros had seen.

"I heard you," Olivia said immediately. "But I couldn't find Mom or Dad right away, and by the time I found Dad and we rushed out here, Celes was on his way to get us. He told us what happened."

Tristan listened to Olivia and Celes's nervous chatter, but she also listened for Umbris's interaction with the lead guard, Entros, wondering if Entros would tell Umbris what he'd seen. It wouldn't mean anything to the guard, not really, even though Beckett was clearly a commoner, and it would only be embarrassing for Tristan for Umbris to know, probably... but that was a lot of uncertainty. Tristan held her breath in the hope Entros would not find it worth mentioning, but then, with a sickening start, she exhaled raggedly -- it had just occurred to her that Entros more than likely would have heard her thoughts about deflecting, right before she'd connected with Beckett. Her stomach rolled with nausea; if he had, which of course he had, there was no way he'd keep that to himself.

Entros stepped around Umbris to address Tristan, and Celes moved in front of her, blocking her.

"Celes, it's OK," Tristan said, and he moved, but he kept his eyes locked on the guard.

"I am sorry for the misunderstanding," Entros said genuinely. The odd expression he'd worn earlier passed over his face, settling instead in his eyes. "It was suspicious that you couldn't prove yourself, but I was clearly in the wrong."

Tristan nodded, and Umbris exchanged a nod of his own with Entros, who, Tristan noted with equal parts relief and surprise, hadn't sold her out after all. Tristan looked quizzically at Entros, full of questions that would only press her luck to ask, but Umbris put his hand on her back, guiding her away from the guards.

"Dad--"

"Trinity, Celes. In the future, do me a favor and don't wander so far?" Umbris asked, not needing Tristan's apology.

The familiar black tents came into view as Tristan and Celes, and even Olivia though she never left the clearing, nodded their agreement.

"Entros was doing his job, whether or not we agree with it," Umbris told Tristan, who understood as much. "But he won't bother you again."

"Thanks Dad."

Umbris patted Tristan's shoulder and walked off, Olivia going with him after squeezing Tristan's hand one last time. Tristan looked up at Celes.

"And to think, the night has barely started."

Celes laughed, and they re-entered the clearing, which had been transformed into a black sea of large, soft sitting pillows. The gathering was just about to begin.

"Trinity." Celes stopped her. "I'm sorry. I told you I wouldn't let anything happen to you, and I failed."

"Nothing did happen to me. Plus, the guards are some of the most powerful in the community, so there was really nothing either of us could do regardless."

"How did you end up proving yourself?"

"Oh..." Tristan hesitated. "I sealed. That was enough, since they know commoners can't do that."

"Quick thinking," Celes nodded, and Tristan laughed nervously. If only he knew.

They continued on, finding their families together, and took their spots on the pillows, waiting for the gathering to officially begin.

The gathering followed the same agenda each month -- infusions were first, followed by the welcoming, during which one of the Elders would give a small speech thanking everyone for coming as though attendance wasn't mandatory, worship, news, a closing speech, and departure. The welcoming usually began around midnight, and the departure usually occurred around five or six A.M. Tristan could not remember a time there had ever been a deviation from that schedule.

This month's gathering was no different from the others, until worship had finished. During worshipping, the community jointly communed with nature, raising their arms and lifting their faces to the stars, unfolding from the soul in order to attain enlightenment, which was something that took years of practice to perfect. While Tristan did not use her abilities and had long ago given up on the idea that she'd ever achieve full enlightenment, she did enjoy giving her soul a workout and getting her chakras in some semblance of order. She always felt cleansed afterwards, settled after long periods of feeling unsettled.

Tristan was basking in that very feeling when the Elder who had delivered the welcoming speech, Vitalis Wylde, once again called for everyone's attention.

"At this time, I'd like to have Pele take over the remainder of this month's gathering," Vitalis said, and a murmur rolled through the crowd. Pele only spoke when major change was afoot, and it rarely signaled good news.

Pele rose from her place in the line of cloaked Elders seated behind Vitalis, exchanging a solemn nod with him as they traded places.

"I know you've been wondering why our location for the gathering changed this month, and so abruptly. I apologize for the lack of communication, which was intentional, but I'm sure frustrating nonetheless. I know there have been rumors, which we expected, and I am here to lay those to rest.

Many years ago, one of our Elders fell quite ill, and his prognosis was not good. He had to withdraw from the Elder committee, from the community even, to focus on a recovery that was not guaranteed."

Beside Tristan, Sol had gone completely still. Tristan looked at her curiously.

"It is with great pleasure that I share with you tonight, however, that our fellow Elder has recovered enough to rejoin our community. He's been recuperating in a haven not far from here, and was still too weakened to travel North to our usual place. When he asked if we could accommodate him, we were thrilled to do just that. On our honor, the committee and I deeply apologize once again for the secrecy, and for the false stories of wandering commoners finding our usual spot that you may have heard. Now, if you please, join me in welcoming back a pillar of our community and revered Elder, Orion Beltremieux."

More murmuring, a smattering of claps. Tristan looked at Sol, who was now gripping Umbris's hand, and then at her siblings, who also seemed to be piecing things together. Beltremieux was Sol's maiden name, and growing up Tristan and her siblings had heard next to nothing about their grandparents -- just that their grandmother had died when Sol was a child, and she was estranged from her father. In a strange case of juxtaposition, Tristan and her siblings had also grown up hearing about the Elder Orion, who was of the old school and had, for a brief time, led a reign of terror that had caused multiple deaths within the community, which was highly unusual. When he'd disappeared, before Tristan was born, the rumor was that he'd been ousted, and that had remained the rumor through the years. Until now.

A sudden wind swept over the crowd, and from the whispering trees behind the line of Elders emerged yet another cloaked figure. He moved slowly, heavily reliant on a sleek, coal black cane, but there was no mistaking he was extremely powerful -- not just anyone's abilities could influence the actual elements the community worshipped.

Orion stopped beside Pele and looked out over the crowd. When he spoke, his voice was both deep and papery, almost ancient in a way, and Tristan felt a chill of dread run down her spine.

"Thank you for the warm welcome. I understand much has changed in my absence, and I look forward to becoming reacquainted with the community in the coming months."

Orion nodded and walked back the way he'd come, and Tristan wasn't sure she'd ever witnessed anything more bizarre at one of these things.

"Let's go. We're going, now." Sol nudged Tristan, who nodded, and the five of them stood, which had the Crenshaws standing as well.

"I guess we're going," Tristan said to Celes, watching Sol hastily say goodbye and walk away, not waiting for anyone.

"I'll see you next month," Celes nodded, then caught Tristan's hand before she left. "Trinity, stay safe."

Tristan frowned. "What?"

Before Celes could elaborate, Umbris ushered Tristan away, and they hurried to catch up with Sol and the twins.

"Mom?" Olivia asked, but Sol shook her head.

"Not here."

It wasn't until they had reached the car and were on their way back to Route 23 that any of them spoke again.

"Mom. Orion... Is he our grandfather?" Evander was the one to go there, and Olivia and Tristan exchanged glances with him, hardly daring to breathe.

"He is my father, but he is certainly no grandfather of yours, and it's going to stay that way for as long as I can help it."

Silence again fell over the Wallaces. Tristan had many questions, but she knew Sol was shaken, so now was not the time. Forcing herself to put it out of her mind for the time being, Tristan closed her eyes just as the sun broke over the horizon. They had a whole month before they even needed to think about Orion and what his return would mean for the future.

CHAPTER 8

Tristan rarely felt this way, but after her Halloween crash, her run-in with Theo, her disorienting twenty-four plus hours of sleep, all that had gone down at the gathering, and the somber tension in her house on Sunday, she was glad to return to school on Monday morning.

The halls were buzzing with discussions of various parties that weekend, most notably one that had been held at Tyler Daniels's house, which, from what Tristan gathered, had gotten a little out of control. Indeed, Tyler was oddly subdued, and the only time Tristan saw him smile at all was when he was talking to Olivia at lunch.

As Tristan watched, Tyler got up from the lunch table and walked off, and Olivia looked after him, the longing on her face plain. Tristan looked away, feeling as though she'd intruded on a private moment that Olivia would be mortified to know she'd seen. Still, it had enforced Tristan's suspicion that Olivia's recent secretive behavior was likely a result of her involvement, whatever it was, with Tyler.

On her perusal of the cafeteria, Tristan caught Beckett's eye and, in clarity so sharp it was as though she'd actually been there, she recalled the vision she'd had of him on Saturday night. Beckett smiled at her, and Tristan gave him a very brief one of her own before she looked back down at the book she'd been reading; she could feel her face warming, and hoped fervently he wasn't still looking at her.

What had happened on Saturday night was somewhat of a

mystery to her. She hadn't been the one to initiate telepathic contact with Beckett -- she'd just closed her eyes because she'd had no idea how she'd get out of the grips of Entros and his squad. Tristan figured it was possible that she'd stress signaled, having been so scared and under pressure, but she wasn't totally sure that was the case. Hearing Beckett say her name so clearly had caught her completely off-guard, and made her think of the night of Matteo Cosgrove's party, when Beckett's eyes had found hers in her mind and she'd nearly been blown backwards by meeting up against his energy. Nausea washed over Tristan again as she remembered how she'd recklessly, stupidly let Entros in on her most closely held secret, wondering how she'd survive the anxiety of knowing that at any moment the Elders could come calling for her if Entros changed his mind and tipped them off.

The bell rang, startling her, and Tristan gathered her things. On the way out of the cafeteria, Beckett sidled up beside her.

"Can you meet after school today, since you couldn't last week?"

"Oh," Tristan said, surprised. "I actually can't; I have an interview for a barista position at Rise and Grind."

Rise and Grind was a trendy little café in what passed for downtown Lavelle. It had opened two years prior, and for the first year really struggled to get off the ground. Business had picked up dramatically in the second year, however, and now the shop was a Lavellean hot spot.

"Oh, well good luck," Beckett said, looking surprised himself. "How about tomorrow?"

"Tomorrow works." Tristan confirmed with a nod, and the pair fell into an awkward silence.

"How was your weekend?" Beckett asked finally.

"It was fine," Tristan replied. Then, "How was yours?"

"Same as always. What did you do?"

"Went out of town. I have to get to class; I'll see you around, OK?" Tristan walked off quickly, cursing herself for the ungraceful exit, but she had to hold firm on her rule -- if she wasn't careful, one conversation would lead to two, and then more, and then she and Beckett would be friends and she'd be opened up to a whole new world of crap from his other friends.

Still, guilt nagged at her as she sped to her locker. Beckett had stepped in between her and Theo on Halloween night, which had been a kind thing to do, and Tristan regretted missing the opportunity to thank him again for running interference. She sighed, pulling her afternoon books from her locker and heading to her next class. Why did not making friends have to be so complicated?

***

Tristan was walking to her car after school, chatting with Olivia, when Beckett called her name. They both turned to see Beckett jogging towards them, holding a small black notebook that Tristan immediately recognized as her school agenda.

"You left this in English class," Beckett said, stopping in front of them and holding the book out to Tristan.

"Thank you," Tristan said gratefully, taking the book. "I must have been distracted; I had no idea."

"It was under your seat. I had to go back into class to ask Ms. West a question and I saw it."

"Thanks again; this is pretty much my bible."

Beckett nodded, his eyes lingering on Tristan for a moment

before giving her and Olivia a faint smile.

"Well, I'll let you two go. Football practice calls."

"See you tomorrow," Tristan said, nodding.

"See you tomorrow, Tristan. Olivia."

Beckett jogged off the way he came, and Tristan watched him go for a moment before resuming walking with Olivia, who was looking at her sideways.

"What?"

"Nothing."

"Something."

"Nothing!"

Tristan shrugged, and they got into her car. Olivia had driven with her this morning, which Tristan suspected was due to her still being rattled by the weekend's events. She and Olivia and Evander had sat in the backyard for a while on Sunday, comparing what little knowledge they had of the Elder Orion. The consensus had been that he was as ruthless as Tristan had thought she recalled, and in particular had taken no mercy on deflectors from the community in his heyday. Though Tristan had not yet admitted aloud that she was planning to go her own way after graduation, Olivia and Evander had made especially worried faces at her when they'd had that discussion. She wasn't trying to hide from her siblings, knew it would be of no use to even try, but she wasn't ready to talk about it, and she appreciated that they did not press her for information.

"Oceana," Tristan said on the drive home, her voice measured. "Either stop staring at me, or tell me why you're staring at me before I strangle you."

"Well, to my surprise Beckett came through loud and

clear to me back there, and just so you know he's starting to wonder if he should back off because he thinks you don't like him at all. But you actually *do* have the hots for Beckett Benson, don't you? I can see it on your face."

Tristan jerked the wheel, and Olivia clutched the car's grab handle, her eyes going wide as they narrowly missed an oncoming car.

"Trinity, Gods!"

"What kind of question is that?" Tristan demanded, her face flushing as she course corrected the car.

"A valid one, but not one worth killing us over!" Olivia yelled, and Tristan shot her a dirty look.

Tristan took the turn into their driveway a little hard, and Olivia let out a growl of frustration as she gripped the car's inside door handle. Both girls slammed their doors as they got out, glaring at each other as they stormed into the house.

"What's all the noise about?" Sol asked, appearing from the kitchen.

"Oceana is being a brat, as usual," Tristan said, and Olivia protested loudly.

"Asking you if you have a crush is not being a brat!" Olivia looked at Sol. "She's just bajiggity because I think she's into Beckett Benson the way he's into her."

"Ba-what?" Sol asked, but Tristan cut her off.

"Oh please, you don't know what you're talking about!"

"Which part?" Olivia challenged, crossing her arms. "Because I'm definitely right about Beckett, and if you'd ever unseal I bet I'd be right about you, too!"

"Beckett does not have a crush on me, and I do not have one on him. We barely talk outside of our project. End of story!" Tristan's face was red; she knew Olivia wasn't lying, had no reason to lie, and it was a little too much to process right then.

"Yes he does," Olivia said smugly. "And his intentions are good, surprisingly, but like I told you, he's starting to pick up on the chilly vibe you're working so hard to give off, and he's having doubts. Not that I blame him!"

"Enough, Oceana," said Sol, looking carefully at Tristan, who was clearly in some kind of distress.

"Thank you," Tristan said fiercely. "I have to go get ready for my interview, I don't have time for this."

She stomped up the stairs to her bedroom, and Sol looked at Olivia.

"I wish you hadn't done that."

"What?"

"She's unsettled enough as it is; I'm afraid she's getting close to her breaking point, mentally. You don't need to antagonize her."

"I wasn't--" Olivia started, but she was interrupted by the ringing of the house phone.

Tristan reappeared a few minutes later, dressed in her skinny black pants and a black v-neck t-shirt. She sailed past Olivia and out the door, not sparing her a glance.

"I have to go up to the school," Sol said, looking harried as she came back into the room. "Your brother got into a fight at football practice."

"Is he OK?" Olivia asked immediately, and Sol nodded.

"I shouldn't say he got into a fight. Apparently he elbowed Theo Fitelson in the nose, twice, and they think it's broken. Ember is fine." Sol sighed. "Will you be OK until I get back?"

"Mom, really? I'm sixteen. Yes."

Sol kissed her head and left, and Olivia closed her eyes, connecting with Evander to see if he'd let her see what had happened. Evander allowed it, and, as Olivia watched, Theo strolled up behind Evander at football practice while Evander waited to toss the ball to one of his teammates.

"Halloween was fun, huh man?"

Evander ignored him.

"Your family always goes all out, and your sisters never disappoint. Even Tristan was kind of hot in a scary way again this year. I feel like she and I really had a moment there, too. Do you think she'd go out with me?"

Olivia saw Beckett look sharply at Evander and Theo, which was when Evander drew back his arm to throw the ball, his elbow smashing right into Theo's nose.

"What the fuck!" Theo yelled, as Evander jerked his arm one more time and Theo's nose made a nauseating crunching sound.

A whistle blew and Theo lunged for Evander, who easily sidestepped him, looking as unaffected as ever.

"You broke my fucking nose!" Theo yelled, as a bunch of the team got between the two of them.

Olivia opened her eyes. Theo had deserved it, and Evander had not broken any of their rules, but the Dean, Isabella LeFebvre, would come down hard on him. Jamestown Academy had a zero tolerance policy for violence.

Worth it, Evander said in response to her thoughts, and Olivia laughed, shaking her head.

CHAPTER 9

Joe Riser, the owner/manager of Rise and Grind, a New York transplant who wanted you to know it, hired Tristan on the spot. He was a no-nonsense fast talker with a short temper, but he read OK to Tristan. He instructed her to start over the coming weekend, and to wear "something like what [she was] currently wearing". He'd provide an apron and a hat. She'd train on Saturday under Ellie Williams, who'd graduated from Jamestown Academy the year before, and then she'd fly solo, under Ellie's watchful eye, on Sunday morning.

Tristan was nervous, but not about the job itself -- her eidetic memory would work in her favor as far as how to create orders -- she was nervous about the customer interaction, something she'd never been good at, and she was nervous that this job was the first step in her declining her expected path in the community. Her plan was to sock away her paychecks, paltry though they'd be, so she'd have some little nest egg of her own when she went off to college; she didn't expect that Umbris and Sol would cut her off completely, but she also didn't want to take any chances.

Tristan arrived home at the same time as Sol and Evander, whose faces were grim.

"What's going on?" Tristan asked.

"Your brother here is suspended from school for the rest of the week," Sol said, eyeballing Evander. "He broke Theo Fitelson's nose at football practice today."

"Ember," Tristan said, looking regretful.

"It was an accident," Evander said, but there was a satisfied gleam in his eye that told Tristan all she needed to know.

Dinner that night was a strained affair. Tristan was still miffed at Olivia, who was practically mute, she was sulking so much, and Umbris was livid that Evander had gotten himself suspended. Sol, as she'd been since the gathering, was also quiet, and visibly stressed.

"You know better, Ember," Umbris said, his brows knit tightly over his dark eyes. "I know you know better. I can't believe you'd pull a stunt like this."

"You can't believe I'd pull a stunt?" Evander asked, in disbelief. "What about the stunt Theo pulled on Trinity? What about him gloating about it to me like he had any right to put his hands on her?"

"I'm not his father," Umbris boomed. "Of course it wasn't OK for him to do what he did to Trinity and then taunt you, but you know our family is already something of a target in this town, which requires us to fly under the radar as much as possible. The only credit I'll give you is that you didn't use your abilities at school, but that's not worth much!"

"Dad, please." Tristan spoke up, and Umbris looked at her, his face like thunder. "If Ember hadn't done it today, maybe I would have done it tomorrow. Maybe Oceana would have done it on Wednesday. We know how we're supposed to act, but sometimes we make mistakes, especially when it comes to each other. Ember made a mistake today and he's paying for it now. He's not just suspended this week; he's suspended from the last three football games of the year, too, and he has detention for a month. Dean LeFebvre came down hard on him."

Umbris went to respond, but Sol spoke instead.

"Trinity is right," Sol said, her voice tired. "Ember is well aware of the consequences for this, at school and here at home. He got an earful from the Dean and an earful from me on the way home. He is going to become well-acquainted with this house and all that needs to be done around here in the coming months."

Umbris looked at Sol, still frowning, but he kept silent. It was very rare for Sol to do anything but passively agree with how Umbris saw fit to lead his family, another thing Tristan didn't think she'd ever be OK with, should she join the community. Additionally, it was also something that had always mystified Tristan -- while Sol was soft-spoken and generally very even-keeled, she was extremely strong of spirit, and she never backed down from doing what was right or fair. It was hard sometimes to reconcile the mother Tristan knew with the wife she appeared to be to Umbris.

Thankfully, dinner ended soon after that, and the kids were dismissed from the dining room. Umbris requested Olivia close the pocket doors behind them as they left, and she did, lingering for a moment with her ear pressed to the wood.

"Nice try," Umbris called dryly, and Olivia rolled her eyes, walking away.

Tristan went out to the backyard, lying down on the grass in order to stare up at the sky. Shortly, Olivia joined her, plopping down beside her, and Evander came after her, taking Tristan's other side. The three of them sat in comfortable silence, lost in their own thoughts, listening to the song of the Autumn evening until it grew dark. The downside to being supernaturally intuitive was when the balance was off with one in the home, the balance was off with all in the home, and currently, almost everyone in the home was off-balance.

Evander flicked his wrist, and the firepit across the yard came to life. This surprised Tristan, but she supposed it shouldn't have -- Olivia and Evander were picking up new abilities daily, it seemed, which was the way it went for most normal teenagers of the community. Practice made perfect, after all, and the twins seemed to genuinely enjoy achieving new levels of ability. It was another thing Tristan could not relate to, another thing that made her feel isolated even in the presence of her own siblings. She unsealed, sitting up, and Olivia put her arm around her. Tristan gave her a sad smile.

"I'm sorry about earlier," Olivia said quietly. "I didn't know you have been having a hard time lately, and I didn't mean to make it harder for you."

"It's OK. I'm sorry I've been snapping at you lately. Both of you."

"Thanks for going to bat for me with Dad," Evander said, giving Tristan a rare smile. "I was dreading what was coming, since he seemed to still be in the warm-up phase."

Tristan nodded.

"It gets old."

Olivia and Evander nodded as well, and the trio lapsed back into silence for a few minutes. Evander had just taken a breath to speak again, when a branch cracked at the far end of their yard. Tristan tensed, memories of Saturday night flooding back, and Olivia and Evander sat up straight. Moments later, a deer appeared, and the three of them breathed a collective sigh of relief. This broke the melancholy that had settled around them, and they laughed, which made the doe look over at them as though they'd offended her.

"I better go in," Tristan said, standing and stretching. "I have an essay to finish and a quiz to study for, on top of everything else I have to do to get ready for tomorrow."

She said goodnight to Olivia and Evander, heading up to the house. As she approached, she saw Umbris move away from the kitchen window, and Tristan wondered what he and Sol had been discussing in the dining room. As it turned out, she wouldn't have to wait long to find out.

"Trinity." Umbris called to her from the living room as she approached the stairs, and Tristan changed tack, finding him sitting on the couch, alone. The fireplace was going, the only light in the room.

"Sit, please."

Dread in her stomach, Tristan sat on the overstuffed armchair across from the couch. She sealed, unsure what was coming.

"What's up?"

"Mom told me about your argument with Oceana."

"Oh," Tristan said, relieved. She waved her hand. "It's fine; it was dumb. We're good."

"I saw. I'm glad."

Tristan waited, raising her eyebrows just slightly.

"Trinity. You know that in the extremely unlikely event you were to decide not to join the community after graduation, your Mom and I would not force you to change your mind."

Tristan's heart leapt into her throat, choking her. She nodded.

"But since that *is* extremely unlikely, you know

that... relationships... with commoners, are ill-advised? You know they can't come into the community, and besides that, of course, Celes has been chosen for you."

Tristan's heart crashed into her stomach. Of course Umbris was clueless. Why wouldn't he be?

"Dad--"

"You've done us proud these four years at Jamestown, keeping your head down and focusing on your studies and not letting your peers distract you. I would hate to see you undo all of your hard work now that you're in your senior year, especially over a boy. I shouldn't have to tell you this, but you need to keep Beckett Benson at a distance, Trinity."

Tristan's face went red. There were so many things she wanted to say, so many knee-jerk reactions she had to stop herself from having, opening a can of worms that could never be closed.

"I don't know what you're talking about," Tristan said finally, her voice stiff. "Like I told Oceana, Beckett is just my senior project partner, but frankly I'm a little offended that you think I'd trash my academic career over a silly crush, which doesn't even exist. Education is and always has been, and always *will be,* more important to me than anything else. But *if* I were ever to develop a crush on a boy, which would be perfectly normal for someone my age, by the way, I am beyond capable of maintaining more than one thing at a time. I shouldn't have to tell you this, Dad."

The room -- nay, the whole house, maybe even the whole universe -- was dead silent. Slightly out of breath, she didn't wait for Umbris to recover from his shock and respond; Tristan strode out of the room and up the stairs to her bedroom with bravado she didn't feel, closing her door and then throwing herself face down on her bed.

A few minutes later, there was a knock on her door.

"Go away!" Tristan groaned loudly, and whomever had knocked complied.

Eventually, Tristan sat up, pulling her backpack up onto her bed with her. She grabbed her laptop from her nightstand and got to work on her essay, lamenting that it wouldn't write itself. It took much longer than she expected to get through, as several times she found herself staring into space, her mind wandering.

There were too many thoughts for Tristan to even begin to organize, too many from both worlds she had a foot in, and she closed her eyes, squeezing the bridge of her nose. She closed her laptop and shoved it away, deciding to finish her essay in the library at lunch the next day.

Tristan tossed and turned that night, her usually comfortable bed feeling as hard and as lumpy as a boulder. Every time she fell asleep, her subconscious plunged her into scenario after scenario of her telling her family she was turning her back on the community, most of which ended with them shunning her and her struggling to survive as a common girl. A few ended with her public hanging, or hands grabbing her from behind and snapping her neck. Just before sunrise, Tristan had the most realistic dream out of all of them -- she and her family were at the gathering, but Beckett was there too, badly beaten and bleeding profusely, restrained by Entros and the other guards. Orion, the mysterious cloaked Elder with the ancient voice, was calling for Beckett's execution. Tristan had just thrown herself in front of Beckett in a futile attempt to protect him when her alarm went off. She jumped awake, breathing hard.

***

Tristan met Beckett after school at what she'd started to

refer to as "their bench", in her head. She was late, having spent her free period in the library, which caused her to lose track of time.

"Sorry," Tristan said, flustered, as she sat down, pulling her backpack onto her lap.

"No worries," Beckett said, glancing at her before looking back out over the lake.

Was Tristan imagining it, or did he not seem as happy to see her as he usually did?

"I--," Tristan fumbled with her notebook, dropping it on the ground. Papers scattered, and she made a noise of frustration. She grabbed at them, and Beckett jumped up to help.

Tristan's hand closed over a paper and Beckett's closed over hers. She froze, looking at him, and Beckett looked back at her, his eyes meeting hers with an intensity that made her stomach tremble. His gaze dropped briefly to her mouth, and the air between them grew charged as Tristan watched him watched her. His hand was warm on hers, and Tristan looked at it, wanting to keep the image in her memory. Finally, she looked away, and Beckett released her, chuckling awkwardly as he ran his hand through his hair.

"Sorry," Tristan said again, and Beckett stifled a laugh as she gathered her notebook and papers to her chest and sat back down on the bench.

"It's OK. Stop apologizing."

"Sor--" Tristan stopped herself, scrunching up her nose, and Beckett did laugh then.

"Hey, how did your interview go yesterday?"

"It went well, thanks. I start Saturday morning."

"Congratulations," Beckett said, and Tristan thanked

him.

"You know, Rise and Grind is my favorite coffee shop," Beckett told her, and Tristan knew he was lying.

"Really? You have a favorite coffee shop?"

"Mmhm," Beckett nodded. "Rise and Grind. I'm there every weekend practically."

"Interesting." Tristan eyeballed him, amused. "What's your favorite menu item?"

"The uh, the um, the coffee. Plain coffee. I'm not fancy." Beckett rubbed the back of his neck, then gave her a sheepish smile.

Tristan laughed then, a rich, surprisingly throaty sound, and Beckett just marveled. She was beautiful, and suddenly the biggest regret of his life was that he hadn't made her laugh before now. Beckett smiled at her, and Tristan shook her head, smiling to herself as she looked down at her notebook.

**

"Freak news alert," Hattie said, approaching Emmeline, who stood at the bathroom sinks, fluffing her hair in the mirror.

Hattie leaned her butt against the counter, and Emmeline looked at her with a mixture of annoyance and disinterest.

"Our favorite witch was just getting chummy with Beckett out by the lake."

"What?" Emmeline asked, looking sharply at Hattie. "Chummy how?"

"She dropped her shit everywhere and he helped her pick it up, and they reached for the same paper at the same time and had a moment. It was just like those cheesy teen romances you're always making me suffer through on Netflix."

"What happened after that?" Emmeline asked icily.

"They were laughing together on the bench, looking awfully cozy for just project partners."

Emmeline's expression cooled, and she resumed fussing with her hair.

"I'm not worried."

"You're not?" Hattie said, sounding like she didn't believe her.

"Nope."

"You're planning something, aren't you?"

Emmeline just smiled.

***

By the time Tristan showed up for her seven A.M. shift at Rise and Grind on Saturday morning, she was a bundle of nerves. Olivia had balked at her early start time, but Tristan, who often got up at six-thirty regardless of whether or not they had school, didn't mind. Starting at seven meant she'd be finished by three-thirty, and, while it wasn't like she had plans anyway, she still felt like that left her with a good chunk of the day for herself.

Taking a deep breath, Tristan entered the coffee shop, finding only a few customers milling about. The building was small and low-slung, but the inside -- all white brick walls, pale gray hardwood floors, and white tables and chairs -- was clean and cheerful, and smelled incredible. There was also a striking black mural of the New York City skyline on the wall behind the counter, upon which was written the cafe's menu.

Rise and Grind was located at the end of a small strip of shops, which included a thrift store, a dollar store, a fabric store, and a delicatessen, and bordered a spacious parking lot. Across the street and up a ways began another strip of shops, which were also flanked at the far end by a parking lot. This pattern repeated for several blocks, including a library and a movie theatre, combining to make a zig-zag pattern of a downtown, which, in Tristan's opinion, was really the only interesting thing about it. Lavelle was a small town, but totally lacking in the charm that steady, healthy revenue afforded other small towns elsewhere in the States, which tended to look like they'd been transplanted directly from romantic comedies and onto their permanent landscapes.

"Hey," Ellie said, looking up as Tristan approached the counter. "If you go through that door in the back and turn right, you'll be able to get back here behind the counter. Clock in, put your things down, and I'll give you the tour."

Tristan did as she was told, and Ellie finished up the drink she was making, handing it off to the waiting customer.

"There's a lull right now, so I'll show you around real quick." Ellie started with the equipment behind the counter, briefly explaining what each piece did, then moved onto the dessert case, which housed a variety of traditional and specialty items. She led Tristan into the back, which was basically the kitchen. She pointed to a door against the far right wall.

"In there is the cooking equipment for our allergy-friendly food. Most of that type is prepackaged, Joe comes in on Sundays and makes it all for the week, but once in a while we'll get a hot food order that will need to be cooked, like a breakfast sandwich or something. I'll handle those for now, but just know that when your time comes, there are specific precautions you'll need to take before you even go into that room, like washing your hands up to your elbows, putting on a smock, taking off your hat, and putting booties over your shoes."

At Tristan's surprised face, Ellie elaborated. "Joe has a nephew who's extremely allergic to nuts, like fatally allergic, so he takes the issue of cross-contamination very seriously."

"I see."

"That's pretty much it. We have a short order cook, Amos, who is here most days. If he's not, one of us will have to run the grill. He's here today, just stepped out for a minute. Our menu is mostly drinks, but we do offer some hot food, and then of course the baked goods. If you'll follow me out front, we'll get started on learning you the menu."

Overall, Tristan would call her first day a success. She mainly watched Ellie, though sometime after noon Ellie had her make the drinks while she watched. Tristan, as she suspected, created the beverages with ease from memory, and Ellie leaned against the counter, looking flabbergasted.

"I've literally never met anyone who picks things up as fast as you do."

"I have a photographic memory," Tristan explained, shrugging.

"You have an *eidetic* memory," Ellie corrected. "Which I didn't think was actually a thing outside of sci-fi movies."

Tristan laughed, and Ellie looked at her thoughtfully.

"I don't really remember you too much from Jamestown. Who do you run with?"

Ellie had graduated Jamestown the year before, going on to

pursue a degree in digital arts. Tristan didn't remember too much about her, either -- just that she'd been relatively quiet and studious, and had very much kept to her artsy friend group.

"No one," Tristan replied truthfully, feeling a little awkward. "I'm sort of a loner."

"I thought so. I remember your sister and brother, twins right? They were pretty popular, even as freshmen and sophomores. I always liked your brother."

Tristan raised her eyebrows, and Ellie's cheeks turned faintly pink.

"I mean, like, I thought he was funny. The lunch table I used to sit at was right by the one he used to sit at, and there was a lot of interaction between our groups."

Tristan nodded politely, not really sure what to say to that. Thankfully, a customer entered the shop then, saving the conversation from getting any more awkward.

Tristan left Rise and Grind that day with a smile on her face. She'd been anxious over nothing, really -- the customers were fine, the job was easy enough, and Ellie seemed like she'd be very easy to work alongside.

She arrived home to an empty house and showered, the smells of the coffee shop clinging to her hair and skin. When she was finished, she took her backpack out into the yard and sat down at the spacious patio table, spreading out her schoolwork. It was a beautiful day, and Tristan never could pass up an opportunity to sit in the sun. She opened a playlist on her phone and, as she worked, she sang along, feeling happier than she had in awhile.

CHAPTER 10

Beckett held out for three whole weeks before dropping by Rise and Grind to see Tristan, which he thought showed good restraint, considering he'd almost shown up every day since she'd been hired. He rode his bike over on a Sunday morning, entering the shop to find nearly all of the tables occupied, one by Georgiana Luker and her family. Beckett nodded at her after she'd waved to him, wondering how she managed to look normal after all the drinking she'd done at the party they'd both been to the night before, then stepped up to the counter.

"One sec," Tristan said, not yet having seen him. She finished the drink she was making and placed it and a straw on the opposite counter, then looked over, her eyes going round when she saw Beckett. "Beckett, hi."

"Morning," Beckett greeted, as Tristan approached. His eyes crinkled at the corners. "I like your hat."

Tristan touched the black baseball cap, emblazoned with Rise and Grind in white, self-consciously.

"Thanks. What can I get you?"

Beckett scanned the menu, which he realized he could have been doing earlier, instead of staring at Tristan. She waited patiently, watching him, and Beckett had to force himself to focus on the wall behind her. There was a song playing in the café about how if something was meant to be it would be, and all he really wanted to do was watch Tristan watch him.

"Let's go with the Milky Way," Beckett said finally, settling on a chocolate caramel coffee drink. "Iced."

"A solid choice. Though I thought you were a plain coffee guy." Tristan's lips twitched as she wrote his name on his cup.

"I usually am," Beckett played along, paying for his drink. "But today feels like a good day to switch it up."

Tristan shook her head, smiling, and gestured with his cup.

"I'll meet you at the other end."

Beckett moved down to wait, and a few minutes later Tristan handed him his drink.

"There you go."

"Thank you. So are you liking it here so far?"

"I am," Tristan nodded, checking to be sure no customers were waiting.

"It seems like it. I think I even saw you smile over there, but I don't know, it mighta been a mirage." Beckett sipped his drink and grinned at her.

Tristan feigned outrage. "Smiled? You must be mistaken. I don't do that."

"I saw what I saw," Beckett said, and Tristan laughed, rolling her eyes.

"I like smiling Tristan. I like laughing Tristan even better," Beckett told her, looking at her in a way that made her breath catch a little.

"What about confused Tristan?" Tristan asked, pulling a face. "Or just saw a spider in the bathtub Tristan?"

Beckett laughed. "Those too. I even like angry Tristan, and

I've never seen her, but I reckon I'd also like Tristan doing Shakespeare in the park."

Tristan acted out the emotions Beckett mentioned, adding a few of their own, until they were both cracking up.

"Safe to say I like all Tristans," Beckett said, his gaze lingering on hers until she'd looked away, blushing. He glanced toward the shop door. "Looks like you're gonna have to get back to work. I'll see you at school tomorrow."

"See you tomorrow." Tristan watched him go, waving to someone as he left. It was then that Tristan realized Georgiana and her family were still in the shop, and their table had a clear view of where Tristan was standing, which meant Georgiana, who never missed anything, had probably watched the entire interaction between Tristan and Beckett. This also meant, of course, that Georgiana would be reporting what she'd seen to Emmeline immediately.

Tristan went to greet the new wave of customers, as well as Ellie, who sailed through the door in a rush of hellos and apologies that she was so late, putting any thought of Georgiana and Emmeline out of Tristan's mind.

***

"Morning Tristan," Beckett greeted the next day, as they passed each other on the way to homeroom.

Jason, who was walking beside him, looked at Beckett in surprise, but made no comment.

"Morning Beckett," Tristan replied, returning his smile as she kept going. She'd seen him coming, had watched his eyes crinkle up as they often did when he saw her, and Tristan had told herself to be cool. She was reasonably proud of her effort, though she knew she'd probably smiled at him like a goon; their encounter the day before was still fresh in her mind, and Beckett's words had been the first thing she'd recalled when she'd woken up that morning. *Safe to say I like all Tristans*, he'd drawled. Gods help her, it was safe to say she liked all Becketts.

Tristan was about to enter homeroom when Emmeline stepped in front of her in a suffocating cloud of perfume, blocking her way.

"Did you hear the good news?"

Tristan backed up a step, just looking at her.

"Beckett and I are back together. Officially."

"What?"

"That's right, Saturday night at Jason Dalton's early Thanksgiving party. Why else do you think Beckett was in such a good mood yesterday morning when you saw him? You didn't think it was because of you, did you?" Emmeline looked over her pityingly.

"Ms. Strandquest, get out of my doorway and to your own homeroom, please," Mr. Johnson, Tristan's teacher, called from his desk.

Emmeline, smirking, moved out of the doorway, and Tristan shook her head, going into the classroom and taking her seat. So it had finally happened. Beckett and Emmeline had officially gotten back together.

Tristan told herself to pay attention to morning announcements, to not be bothered by what she'd known was inevitable anyway, but it was no use. She was having feelings about the bomb Emmeline had dropped -- feelings she didn't care to explore, but feelings all the same.

It just didn't make sense. Beckett seemed so... so... so *normal*, and so *nice*, compared to the company he kept. He was smart and thoughtful and observant, from everything Tristan had witnessed since she'd started paying attention, and really Emmeline's opposite in every way. Was being with the hot popular girl really more important than anything else? She was disappointed, Tristan realized, above everything else. She had thought more of Beckett, which had obviously been a mistake.

The more Tristan thought about it, the more annoyed she became, both at the situation and at Beckett flirting with her even though he'd gotten back with Emmeline. His ego had probably been inflated to max capacity yesterday morning, coming off a night with Emmeline, and that thought tainted the whole memory of Tristan's interaction with him.

By lunchtime that day, Tristan was well and truly disgusted. Skipping the cafeteria, as usual, she went to the library in a huff, eating her lunch in the microfilm viewing room and then losing herself in shelf organization. She had a hard time focusing in Psychology that afternoon, but she lucked out that all class was that day was watching the remainder of the movie *Memento* and taking notes. In English class, she ignored Beckett completely, which Tristan knew was immature, but until she could sort her thoughts, that's how it was going to be.

Tuesday was much the same, Tristan avoiding Beckett as much as possible, to his clear consternation. On Wednesday, Beckett finally caught up to her after English class.

"Uh, hey," Beckett said from behind her, and Tristan closed her locker, turning to look at him expectantly.

"I wanted to see if you wanted to get together after school today since we're out for Thanksgiving now until Monday."

"No thanks. I think we'll be fine to wait until next week."

"What's going on?" Beckett asked her, his eyes flickering over her face. "You've been acting weird since Monday."

"I'm sure if you asked your friends, they'd tell you I've been acting weird for a lot longer than that."

Beckett frowned. "OK. I'm still confused. Does this have to do with Sunday?"

"I have to go." Tristan turned away from him.

"Tristan, wait."

Beckett waited until she looked at him again.

"Talk to me. I thought we were starting to get along, I--"

"And I told you, and I don't know how many times I can tell you, that we're not friends and we're not going to be, Beckett." Tristan shook her head. "I'll see you Monday. Have a nice holiday."

And then she was gone, leaving Beckett more confused than ever and, frankly, kind of pissed.

***

Tristan's alarm went off at six A.M. on Thanksgiving morning, and she reluctantly got up, dragging herself into the shower. A half hour later, she slipped quietly downstairs and grabbed her bag and her keys, closing the door with a soft click behind her as she left the house.

Tristan drove into downtown Lavelle, to a large, unassuming beige building. She parked in the back and entered through the gray steel doors, down a hall and into a spacious, industrial kitchen.

"Good morning Tristan!" Susan Whitaker, the head of the soup kitchen, greeted. "You're here early."

"I signed up to do breakfast and lunch today," Tristan replied. "So I figured I'd come help set up."

"Well we certainly appreciate it." Susan lifted a gray plastic bin of dish- and silverware, handing it off to Tristan.

"It smells great already, Dolores!" Tristan called to one of the cooks, Dolores Hebert, who laughed and waved.

Tristan bumped open the door of the kitchen with her hip, coming face to face with Beckett, which nearly caused her to drop the bin she was holding.

Beckett grabbed the bin on a "whoa", steadying it until Tristan could restore her grip.

"Mornin'," Beckett greeted, the plaid button down he wore perfectly matching his eyes. He smelled good, so good, like the woods after a rainstorm, and Tristan did her best to ignore it.

"What are you doing here?" Tristan asked, trying to get her heart rate back to normal.

"Volunteering, like I do every year," Beckett replied, looking at her like he was trying to figure out what her problem was.

"Every year?" Tristan echoed.

"Every year," Beckett confirmed, rocking back on his heels. He pointed across the room. "I stood right at the other end of that table from you last year."

Tristan vaguely remembered. She nodded.

"Excuse me."

Beckett moved out of her way, going into the kitchen, and Tristan began setting the round tables. Beckett and the other volunteers who'd started to show up began carrying trays of food out to the long, rectangular table that ran along one side of the room. Before long, the room began to fill up with people in need.

As the morning went on, Beckett moved down the line, coming to stand beside Tristan.

"I'm surprised you're here alone," Tristan said coolly, not looking at him. "No Emmeline?"

"Emmeline?" Beckett snorted. "No. She wouldn't be caught dead here."

Tristan looked at him disgustedly, and Beckett cocked his head at her.

"Are you ready to tell me what exactly your problem is?" Beckett asked in a low voice. He scooped eggs onto a woman's plate and smiled at her, waiting until Tristan had offered her home fries before looking over at Tristan.

Tristan's jaw worked, and Beckett could tell she was trying to decide whether or not she wanted to respond. They served three more people before she did.

"Fine." Tristan also kept her voice low as she turned to look at him. "I don't get you. You're smart, and you seem like a good enough person. I mean, the company you keep is questionable so you could be different around people you're comfortable with, but you know, you seem OK. And you speak up when you see someone being mistreated, and you come here to volunteer on Thanksgiving, and *none* of that jibes in my mind with why on *Earth* you would date Emmeline Strandquest."

"Hey now," Beckett said, looking offended. "This isn't

fair. I didn't know you in sophomore year so I can't bring up any of your transgressions, but you can bring up mine?"

"Sophomore year? What? I'm talking about now! This year!" Tristan gestured wildly with her spoon, sending bits of home fries flying.

"This year?" Beckett frowned almost comically, following a home fry that landed in Tristan's hair, and they had to break to serve a few more people. "I have no idea what you're talking about."

"Emmeline told me on Monday morning that you and her got back together, at some party last Saturday."

Beckett's eyebrows disappeared into his hair.

"She *what?* And you believed her?"

Tristan stared at him dumbly.

Beckett shook his head in disbelief. "Emmeline and I did not get back together. Every party we're both at goes the same way: she tries to get me back, I turn her down. Saturday was no exception, but now I know why she was trying extra hard all week at school with me, too."

Tristan still said nothing, feeling like the biggest fool. That was OK, however, because Beckett was not done talking.

"I can't believe you believed her. I mean, she and I broke up over a year ago. I'm a whole year older, and wiser, and my brain is a whole year bigger."

"Well I didn't think you were thinking with your head brain," Tristan finally said, immediately regretting it. Beckett's eyes went wide and so did Tristan's. She looked away stiffly as Beckett began to laugh, and was grateful that a handful of people chose then to get in line.

"You know, I thought you were smart, but now I'm

worried that you think penises have brains," Beckett whispered, between the last and next people he was serving.

"Shut up," Tristan hissed, and Beckett started laughing all over again. He plucked the food out of her hair, and Tristan finally cracked a smile, which led to her laughing quietly with her hand covering her mouth.

"Look, can we just call a truce, or whatever?" Beckett asked, his face earnest. "I know you don't want to be friends, so I'm not suggesting we have sleepovers and braid each other's hair, but like, we can say hi around school, yeah? Walk to class together if we're going the same way? Sit together at 1--"

"No," Tristan said immediately, and Beckett put his hands up in surrender.

"OK, OK. But the other stuff?"

"Fine." Tristan nodded after mulling it over a moment.

"Fine." Beckett smiled at her, and Tristan smiled back at him, tucking her hair behind her ear before looking away.

As breakfast came to an end and everyone began clearing the tables to switch over to the lunch rush, Tyler, Jason, Bailey, and Hattie showed up. Tristan's stomach clenched as she watched them greet Beckett, who was still in the dining area, from the kitchen door.

"Tristan?" Susan asked, and Tristan turned away from the porthole window. "Can you grab a bin and start setting the tables?"

"Ah, actually, I was wondering if I could maybe help out in here? If you need it?" Tristan asked awkwardly.

"I'll take her!" Dolores called, before Susan could respond.

Tristan smiled gratefully, scurrying around Susan to go help Dolores. Dolores put her to work chopping vegetables for the soup she was making, and Tristan happily complied. They got to chatting about school and Tristan's plans for the holidays (staying home), for prom (not going), and for after graduation (oh gods).

Beckett noticed Tristan had not come back into the dining room after the last bin of dishes she'd taken into the kitchen. Offering to go grab more silverware, he entered the kitchen, seeing her across the room with Dolores Hebert, one of the longtime soup kitchen chefs. They were chatting and laughing as they worked, and Tristan looked relaxed and happy. Beckett watched her for a few beats, not usually getting the opportunity to see her like this, and their conversation drifted his way.

"...Ward Livingston University, up in Boston, is my dream school, but I'm sure I'm not going to get in..."

"...Love to become a researcher, if not for authors then maybe in the science field, but for authors would be number one... a very small pool though... I'd probably have better luck going freelance but..."

"...Major in Linguistics, I guess, and go from there. I haven't thought about..."

"Beckett?" Susan asked, coming up beside Beckett, who was leaning his hip against the counter holding the dishware bins, forgetting to pretend to look busy.

"Sorry," Beckett jumped, grabbing a handful of silverware out of the bin. "Just came to get more silverware."

Susan nodded, looking at him suspiciously, and Beckett smiled, leaving the kitchen. So Tristan was dreaming of an acceptance to Ward Livingston University, which was Beckett's longshot choice as well. What were the odds? He'd more or less settled himself on the idea of Tulane University in New Orleans, which was a fine school, but if he could have his pick, Ward Livingston was what he'd had his eye on since his freshman year of high school. Beckett was having a little trouble believing that he and Tristan had the same ambition -- in fact, he was starting to feel like the way their lives continued to intertwine in even seemingly random ways meant there was a connection between them that was a bit outside the realm of what was typical for two regular people.

Beckett set the tables, lost in thought, then brought himself back to attention as he went to resume his station at the serving table. Bailey stood to his immediate left, and Tristan finally came back out to stand to his right, giving him a small smile as she did. Beckett saw Bailey nudge Hattie, who laughed, and he looked over at them exasperatedly.

The lunch rush was busier than the breakfast rush, not affording Tristan and Beckett much of an opportunity to chat. Instead, Beckett enjoyed watching Tristan interact with the diners, a warmth he wasn't accustomed to seeing from her drawing him in. Her generosity and chattiness were infectious, and Beckett found himself interacting with the diners in much the same manner, to Tristan's delight. Bailey and Hattie threw a couple of looks his way, but even they loosened up incrementally, and Tyler and Jason were their usual outgoing selves. The vibe in the room was a good one, a happy one, and Beckett had never before enjoyed a volunteer shift so much.

When the last diners were fed and everything was cleaned up, Beckett hung around, waiting for Tristan. He waved Jason and Tyler on, ignored the looks Bailey and Hattie were giving him, and grinned when Tristan came out of the kitchen, looking surprised to see him.

"What are you still doing here?"

"I was waiting for you."

"Why?"

Beckett looked at her sideways as they headed out of the dining room and towards the back doors, and Tristan gave him a sheepish smile.

"Let me try again. Thanks for waiting, but you didn't have to; I drove here."

"No problem. I waited because I wanted to say thank you."

"For what?" Tristan asked, puzzled.

"For today. For organizing this. I know you're the one who put up the volunteer sheets around the Academy. I'm just sorry more people didn't show up."

"Oh." Tristan waved her hand. They exited the building, directly into the pouring rain.

"Gonna be a fun bike ride home," Beckett observed, and Tristan squinted at him through the downpour.

"You rode your bike here? Do you not watch the news?"

"I don't; I'm not a senior citizen," Beckett replied, laughing.

"Hilarious. OK, put your bike in the trunk. I'll drive you home."

Tristan unlocked her car and got inside while Beckett maneuvered his bike into the trunk. He got in the passenger side a minute later, soaked.

"Thank you for not making me bike home in that,"

Beckett said, pushing his wet hair back off of his face.

"You're welcome. Where to?"

Beckett directed her to his house, which was closer to their school than Tristan had realized.

"So what made you start volunteering at the soup kitchen?" Beckett asked as they drove.

"I ran into Dolores a few times at the grocery store, and one of those times she mentioned it and how they're always in need of volunteers. I went the next week and I've been going ever since. I try to make it at least once a month. What about you?"

"My Paw-Paw was homeless, back in Alabama where I used to live. He was a veteran and lost everything, and he refused to move in with us or my Aunt and Uncle, so he lived on the street until he died. The local food kitchen took such good care of him, I never forgot it. I figured it's the least I can do, but I don't go enough." Beckett shrugged.

"I'm so sorry, Beckett." Tristan said genuinely, and Beckett shrugged his broad shoulders.

"Was what it was. I'm right up there, 3054."

Tristan pulled up to the curb. The house was situated on a small, tree-lined road, an unassuming white clapboard that backed up to a wooded area, just like Tristan's. Beckett stared up at the house for a moment, and his dread was palpable. He blew out a breath and then turned to Tristan, unbuckling his seatbelt.

"Thanks again for the ride. Have a good dinner, OK? I'll see you Monday."

"You too. Thanks Beckett."

Tristan wanted to say more, but what? *Stay? Come have din-*

ner with my family instead? Why are you dreading going inside your own house?

Beckett closed the door, retrieving his bike and running it up the side of his house, disappearing into the heavy downpour. Tristan pulled a face and shifted the car into drive. It was none of her business, but Beckett's vibe had totally changed when they'd pulled onto his street, and she was so curious as to why that'd been.

***

Tristan arrived home to a warm house that smelled amazing. She closed the front door behind her, her stomach already growling, and Olivia, who was walking by, greeted her.

"Hey, how'd it go?"

"Really well," Tristan replied, smiling.

"Good." Olivia eyeballed her. "Anything exciting happen?"

Tristan laughed.

"I was handing out meals, O."

"Yeah, it's just that you're mostly bright green and yellow right now, which I mean I guess that could be from volunteering, but..." Olivia squinted at her, and Tristan rolled her eyes.

"When did you start reading auras? I thought that was Ember's thing."

"He's been teaching me." Olivia shrugged. "It's kinda boring, honestly, but I'm definitely interested in yours right now since you usually sit around dark bluish gray."

"Yellow," Tristan recited from memory. "The color of happiness and optimism. Green, the color of compassion and altruism. Gee, what a mystery."

"Orange," Evander said, walking up behind Olivia and pointing. "The color of sexual energy."

"Now you're making things up," Tristan said, and Evander shook his head.

"Am not. It's lurking there in the back."

"There is no back!" Tristan said, as Evander walked off towards the kitchen.

"Hmm," Olivia said, but thankfully let it go.

Tristan, shaking her head, went to the kitchen as well and greeted her parents, who, along with Ivan and Ruby, were preparing their Thanksgiving feast.

"Trinity!" Sol exclaimed, elbow deep in the turkey. "I didn't think you were coming home. Do me a favor and make the stuffing?"

"Ever?" Tristan asked, grinning. She pushed up her sleeves and washed her hands, getting ready to pitch in.

Umbris escaped the kitchen in which Tristan was sure he thought was a stealthy manner, which it wasn't, and Sol mock glared at his retreating back. "I see you!"

"You're very happy," Sol observed, smiling at Tristan as Umbris's laughter floated back towards the kitchen. "Good day?"

Tristan nodded.

"You know I always feel the best when I get to help people."

"Indeed," Sol replied thoughtfully, but said nothing else.

"Oh, I forgot to tell you, I have an early shift at Rise and Grind tomorrow," Tristan said as she worked. "I have to be there by five. I just didn't want you to worry when you noticed I wasn't here."

"Noted. Five until when?"

"One-thirty."

"I think Oceana and I are going to go up to New Orleans, if you'd like to join us. We might meet up with the Crenshaws."

"Oh, I don't know. Since when do you go out instead of planning the layout and pulling out the decorations for Yule?"

Sol shrugged. "There's time for both."

"Well our usual tradition happens to be one of my favorites, so I think I'll stay here while you turncoats go to the city."

Sol chuckled, and Tristan smiled, reaching for another piece of bread.

"Trinity is totally crushing on him, isn't she?" Olivia said to Evander, as they lounged in the living room.

"Who?"

Olivia gave him a look. She held up her phone, showing him a selfie Bailey had taken at the soup kitchen with Hattie. In the corner, Beckett was making a face at the camera. Olivia zoomed in on him.

"Beckett Benson."

"Oh. Duh."

"Bad idea jeans," Olivia shook her head.

"Beckett's OK," Evander said, flipping through the channels on the TV.

"It's not Beckett I'm worried about necessarily, it's what kind of shit Trinity will catch when word gets out. Which word will get out, because this is Lavelle."

Evander scoffed, and Olivia rolled her eyes again.

"I'm serious, Ember. I have a bad feeling."

"You always have a bad feeling. It's fine. Trinity would die before she admitted out loud that she likes him, so I'm sure she'll be fine."

"I don't always have a bad feeling," Olivia huffed, but Evander ignored her.

"Bad feeling about what?" Umbris asked, entering the room.

"I don't know!" Olivia wailed in frustration. "That's the problem! I just know it involves Trinity."

Umbris surveyed her, and Olivia knew he was trying to suss out if she was serious or just being dramatic.

"Dad, ignore her," Evander said, not bothering to look away from the TV. "She doesn't have any details and she's been saying this all month and nothing has happened. Nothing is going to happen. We all go to school together; we have been and will be keeping an eye on Trinity."

"You're *so* annoying," Olivia said, and Evander made a face at her. "When do you get to start going out again? Do you think you'll be any less miserable when you're done being grounded, or is this just who you are as a person now?"

"OK, OK," Umbris interjected, before the twins escalated into a shouting match. "Ember, go help Ruby set the table. Oceana, go help Ivan in the front yard."

The twins left, mumbling to themselves, and Umbris shook his head, settling into his chair by the fireplace.

***

Dinner was ready by five o'clock, and the Wallaces, joined by Ivan and Ruby, gathered around the long dining room table. As tradition dictated, they each went around the table saying what they were thankful for before digging in.

The food was plentiful and delicious, and the atmosphere was warm and content. A few times, Tristan wondered about Beckett and how his holiday was going, but then she'd be drawn back into conversation. Dessert -- pies of all different flavors -- was brought out after the main course, and by the time the plates had been cleared, everyone had a stomach ache.

"Why do we do this to ourselves every year?" Evander groaned, and everyone groaned back in agreement.

"As soon as I can move, I'm going for a walk. Anyone who wants to come is invited!" Olivia chirped, and Tristan and Evander nodded.

Once they'd had a chance to digest, the siblings went out the front door and down the long driveway, no particular destination in mind. They closed the gates behind them and started up the road, and that was when Olivia finally spoke.

"So the gathering is coming up, next weekend."

"Already?" Tristan asked, surprised. "Where did November go?"

"Already," Olivia replied. "I tried talking to Mom about Orion, but she completely shut me down. Ember, I know you're going to make fun of me for this, but I have a really bad feeling about him, and I don't think it's fair that we should be kept in the dark."

"I'm not going to make fun of you," Evander said, sounding slightly defensive. "He gives me a bad feeling, too."

"Me too," Tristan said, nodding.

"I've been thinking, and I have a plan. Trinity, do you think you could get information out of Celes? Like do you think he'd agree to see what he could find out from Dune and Thera and then tell you about it?"

"No," Tristan said immediately, shaking her head. "You know Celes. He's upstanding through and through -- if he thought we were up to anything dishonest, he'd narc on us in a second."

"Loser," Evander muttered, and Olivia elbowed him.

"OK. I was thinking that, but I wanted to confirm. So I'm going to ask Hydran, then. I think he'd agree to help and agree to keep quiet about it."

"You *think* he'd agree? O, he'd walk across hot coals and never even question your motives if you asked him to. I think it's safe to take the *I think* out of your sentence." Evander rolled his eyes.

"Have I told you lately that you're annoying?"

"Only like three times today."

"Well here's a fourth."

"OK," Tristan said, trying to get them back on track. "What are you going to say to Hydran?"

"Watch and learn," Olivia said, pulling out her cell phone.

"You're calling him *now?*" Tristan's eyes widened.

"Oceana, it's Thanksgiving!"

"So?" Olivia held the phone up to her ear, speaking just a few seconds later. "Hydran, hi. It's Oceana Wallace. Oh right, of course you knew that, silly me."

Tristan and Evander exchanged a look at Olivia's sweetened up tone.

"Everything is fine. Yes, I will see you next weekend. Me too. Things have been just fine here, and for you? Good. Listen, I'm so sorry to bother you on Thanksgiving; is this a bad time?" Olivia nodded and shot a wink at her siblings. "Perfect. We just got done eating, too. I'm actually outside going for a walk right now because I ate so much. Anyway, I was wondering if you know anything about Orion, the Elder?"

Olivia was quiet for a moment.

"He's just so mysterious, you know? I know they said he's been ill and away, but they didn't really say anything else, and a lot of people seemed to know he's a big deal, but I don't. I don't get it."

More silence.

"Yes," Olivia said slowly. "He is our grandfather. My Mom won't talk about him. I was hoping you knew something, or could find something out, anything that would sort of help prepare us since I'm sure at some point he's going to come looking for my Mom and want to meet her kids. Yes. That would be amazing, thank you so much Hydran. Can you just do me one favor? Can we keep this between us, just our secret? I don't want word getting out that we're trying to get intel on the all-powerful Orion."

Olivia tinkled a laugh, and Evander raised his eyebrows at Tristan, impressed.

"Great. Thanks again, Hydran. I'll see you next week-end."

Olivia disconnected, looking smugly at Tristan and Evander.

"Done. He's going to see what his parents know, play it off like he's asking for his own interests. He'll get back to me ASAP."

"You are conniving," Tristan said, but she was clearly impressed, and Olivia just grinned.

"Poor Hydran. Sucker doesn't even know he's being used."

"Oh stop," Olivia waved her hand. "We're friends."

"You're not friends. He follows you around like a puppy and you let him because you like the attention."

"Oh my gods, you guys, can you give it a rest?" Tristan said, before Olivia could fire back at Evander. "If Hydran doesn't mind doing this, he doesn't mind doing it, and Olivia isn't wrong for asking him. I was joking."

"Thank you," Olivia said, shooting a look at Evander, who rolled his eyes.

"Do you know when your crash will be?" Tristan asked, a few minutes later, looking between them.

"Mine will be on Tuesday. Had my energy surge this morning," Evander replied.

"Don't know yet, so I guess after Tuesday. I'm hoping for Friday. You?"

Tristan shook her head.

"I don't think it's going to happen again this month.

Celes said my crash was because I was sealing constantly, not because I was unsettled, and sealing drains energy, but not a ton, so it's a gradual drain. After the infusion, he said I probably won't have another crash for a few months."

"Lucky," Olivia muttered darkly.

"Am I?"

The trio walked in silence as darkness began to fall. They strolled around the empty downtown, then headed back home, Olivia and Evander chatting about school while Tristan half-paid attention. She was thinking about Orion, thinking about the dream she'd had about him ordering Beckett's execution. It had been chilling at the time, but now it just seemed absurd. Beckett and Orion would never cross paths; Tristan couldn't think of a way it would ever happen short of Beckett coming to her house while Orion was there visiting, but since Sol would pack up the family and move them to the Bahamas before she'd ever allow Orion to set foot on their property, even that scenario would never happen.

Still, as the cool night air chilled her skin, Tristan couldn't shake the feeling that the vividity of that dream had meant it had been more than just a dream; it had come with a sense of foreboding that she hadn't felt in a very, very long time.

That night, Tristan found herself tossing and turning once again. When she finally fell asleep, she again dreamt of Orion, but this time the dream was much more horrifying, much more realistic. In it, Tristan watched a young Sol get dragged up to the top of the clearing, in front of everyone who had gathered. Orion stood looking at her with eyes completely devoid of emotion, speaking words Tristan could not hear. The dream itself was soundless, which made it that much more terrifying. Young Sol was held in place by two giant hooded guards, and though she struggled with all of her might, they barely flinched. She was screaming, her face red, tears streaming down her face, but no one would help her. She looked over, across the crowd, and her panicked gaze met Tristan's. Tristan startled awake, screaming herself; she was trapped in her comforter, the fabric wrapped around her legs, and she forgot to stop screaming as she tried to wrestle herself out of it.

Footsteps thundered down the hall and Tristan's bedroom door flew open, her entire family pouring in.

"What happened?"

"Trinity!"

"What's going on?"

Tristan looked up, breathing hard, in a full-blown panic attack.

"She's stuck in her blanket!" Olivia cried, and Sol and Umbris rushed to Tristan's bedside, extracting her from the offending comforter.

"What happened?" Umbris knelt before Tristan, and Sol sat beside her, smoothing back her hair as though she was seven and not seventeen.

"I'm fine," Tristan said, deeply embarrassed, as she began to calm down.

Evander made a noise of disgust and shuffled back to bed, but Olivia hovered nearby, biting her nails.

"What happened?" Umbris asked again, and Tristan shook her head. There was no way she was going to talk about her dream, possibly ever, and definitely not at two in the morning.

"It was one of those weird dreams combined with real life things. I don't know how I got so tangled up in my comforter, but the sensation must have crossed into the nightmare I was having and I panicked."

Everyone's shoulders sagged with relief.

"I thought someone had, like, broken in and tried to kill you!" Olivia said, yawning. "Gods. OK. Goodnight again, everyone."

She left, and Tristan looked at her parents.

"I'm OK."

"You're as white as a sheet," Sol said, and Tristan avoided her eyes.

"I'm just going to go back to sleep." Tristan said, running her hands over her face.

Sol kissed the top of her head and Umbris squeezed her arm, and they quietly left the room. Tristan laid back down, kicking her comforter off of her bed. Of course she wasn't going back to sleep, how could she? How could she ever close her eyes again without seeing Sol's terrified face, screaming silently in her mind?

CHAPTER 11

Tristan was dozing on the living room couch the next afternoon after work when a knock sounded on her door. She jumped, then stood and yawned before going to see who was there.

"Beckett," Tristan said, surprised and no longer tired. "What are you doing here?"

"Sorry to just show up, but I don't have your number so I couldn't text first. I think I left something in your trunk yesterday."

"Oh," Tristan said. "Oh sure, OK. Hold on, I have to find my keys."

Leaving the door wide open, she disappeared into the house, realizing too late she should have invited Beckett inside.

"Trinity!" Evander bellowed from the top of the stairs. "Who knocked?"

"It's for me!" Tristan called back up to him, finally locating her keys halfway down the couch cushions.

"What?"

"It's for me! Nothing!"

She stepped back outside, giving Beckett a frazzled smile.

"Sorry. Right this way."

Beckett grinned, following her off the porch.

"Did your brother just call you Trinity?"

"Yes," Tristan replied. "We go by our middle names around here, and to our community friends. School is really the only place me and O and Evander go by our first names. File my parents under, why didn't they just name their kids what they actually planned on calling them?"

Beckett chuckled.

"So you're Tristan Trinity Wallace. And Olivia is...?"

"Olivia Oceana. Evander Ember."

"Huh. Evander Ember is kind of awkward, but the other two are nice. Elemental."

Tristan gave him a tight smile, saying nothing.

"The double initial thing is very Southern, isn't it?"

"I don't know, is it?"

"I think so. Almost everyone I know, including myself, has a double initial name. Well, I guess I have a triple, but still."

"Oh?" Tristan turned to Beckett before she opened her trunk. "What's your middle name?"

Beckett shook his head.

"That's confidential information."

"That bad, huh?" Tristan's eyes sparkled. "You have to tell me now."

"I'll take it to my grave."

"You won't." Tristan opened her trunk, finding a bike lock that did not belong to her.

"There we go." Beckett scooped it up. "It must have fallen off when I was jamming my bike in there yesterday."

Tristan laughed, closing the trunk, and she walked Beckett back over to the house.

"How was your Thanksgiving dinner?"

Beckett laughed humorlessly.

"It was just me and my Mom. We had leftovers from the night before."

"Oh, I'm sorry."

"It was better that way," Beckett said cryptically, a frown creasing his brow. He shook his head, his face clearing. "How was yours?"

"It was nice, thanks. I'm sure if we had known it was just going to be you and your Mom, you two could have eaten with us."

Beckett looked at her for a long moment, and then appeared to decide against whatever he'd been thinking about saying. He shrugged.

"It was fine. I better get going. Sorry again to have bothered you."

"It was no bother. I was just falling asleep on the couch. I worked from five to one-thirty today, and didn't really sleep well last night."

"Well then I will let you get back to napping," Beckett said, giving her a charming smile. He started to go, then turned back. "Did you want to give me your number, though? Just in case something like this happens again, or if we need to talk about the project or something?"

"Sure," Tristan agreed. "Good idea."

She gave Beckett her phone number, and he let her know he'd text her so she could save his. Waving, he jumped on his bike and took off down the driveway, Tristan watching him go. Seeing him had been unexpectedly nice, and she felt a pang that he'd left so soon. Apparently she wasn't the only one who ran away from conversations she didn't want to have.

Umbris arrived home from work shortly after Beckett had left, and he, Evander, and Tristan sat down at the dining room table, brainstorming ideas for how to decorate for winter solstice. Actually, to call it decorating for winter solstice was a misnomer; the family celebrated *Yule,* as did everyone in the community, leaving up their decorations for as long as others left up their Christmas decorations -- usually for just over a month. The Wallaces official Yule festivities began on December 21 this year, solstice, and would last through January 5, the twelfth day of Christmas, but they chose to decorate early so they could enjoy the season for as long as possible.

"I think we should do an all white theme this year," Tristan said, nodding. "Frosted yule log, frost covered branches, white candles, icicles, wreath, everything. Sort of like a Narnia vibe."

"Or like a black and white photograph," Evander added, also nodding. "I like it."

"That sounds easy enough," Umbris replied. "We'll see what Mom and Oceana think when they get home and we'll go from there. Should we get started bringing up the bins?"

The three of them headed down into the basement, forming an assembly line in order to get the boxes upon boxes of decorations up into the living room. Once they were finished, Tristan began opening them up, her favorite part of the day. A pleasant, musty scent emanated from each box, and Tristan briefly closed her eyes. It was the smell of nostalgia, of years past and prior celebrations of Yule. It was baking cookies, making a solstice tree in the yard for any animals passing by in search of food, exchanging small gifts, flipping through the radio stations with her siblings to find the most awful Christmas song they could. It was watching the sun rise and set on the solstice with her family, spending the between-hours in the quiet house, reflecting on all that the year had brought them, and then running wild outside with Olivia and Evander when they could no longer take the silence. It was ending the night by lighting five candles, one for each of them, and blowing them out, and then all of them using a long matchstick to light one fat, central candle of unity, in the glow of which they'd eat dinner.

Yes, this time of year was Tristan's favorite, and she had never felt as though she'd missed out on anything by not celebrating Christmas like her non-secular or secular peers. She was unsure of how she'd get to participate in Yule in the future, as soon as next year!, and the thought took her breath away. She figured the community celebration, usually held the weekend before the solstice, would obviously be out, but would she still be allowed to celebrate the way she always had with her family? If she could wish for nothing else to be spared from the consequences of deflecting, she would wish for it to be Yule. Tristan knew rationally that once her decision was made she'd be free to celebrate on her own, to start her own traditions, but having her family celebration ripped away from her would be a wound that would take years to heal.

Once they'd arrived home, Sol and Olivia readily agreed to the theme their family had cooked up; they all got started on picking through the boxes to find what they already had, what they could paint over, and what they would need. The project took up the bulk of the day, so, when evening fell, Sol and Umbris decided to order dinner in instead of cooking. They ate their spicy Thai favorites as a family in the living room, watching mindless TV and laughing together, and Tristan looked around, drinking it all in and committing this night to memory. If this was to be her last Yule season with her family, she was going to remember every moment.

Olivia's cell phone rang a while later, and she quickly looked at Tristan and Evander before leaving the room to answer it. Tristan and Evander followed her outside, waiting on the porch while she paced in the driveway, listening.

"Thanks Hydran," Olivia finally said, her face grim. "I really appreciate you getting back to me about this so fast."

Olivia hung up and stared at her phone for a few beats, then looked up at Tristan and Evander, who could feel the dread rolling off of her in waves.

"What did he say?" Tristan asked nervously.

"Come with me." Olivia gestured, and Tristan and Evander followed her down the driveway and around the edge of the perimeter to the very back of the yard.

"I don't know how to tell you guys this, or where to start," Olivia said finally, looking at them. She looked worse than she had when she'd gotten off the phone, and Tristan's stomach tied itself into knots.

"Just say it," Evander said, his jaw working.

"Did you know Mom had a sister?" Olivia asked.

There was a brief, stunned silence before Tristan and Evander confirmed they did not.

"Her name was Adara. She..." Olivia trailed off, then took a deep breath. "She tried to deflect from the community, years ago, when it was still a law that you couldn't, and Orion..."

"Holy shit," Tristan whispered, her eyes going wide.

It hadn't been Sol she'd been dreaming about. It had been Adara.

"What?" Olivia asked nervously, and Evander looked at Tristan sharply.

"Orion had her killed."

"How did you know that?" Olivia asked, looking more scared than she had been.

"I dreamt about it. Last night, that's what was happening when I was screaming. I thought it was Mom, but it must have been her sister. I didn't see what happened, I woke up before she died, but in my dream there was a gathering, and everyone was watching while two of these giant guards held her in place and Orion was standing there talking. She was screaming and crying, begging for help, but no one would help her."

Tears spilled out of Olivia's eyes as she nodded. "That's exactly what Hydran said. She was executed, right there in front of everyone. Hydran didn't know the details, he said it was so horrific that no one will talk about it."

The three of them descended into an uncomfortable silence.

"What else aren't you saying?" Evander asked, looking curiously at Olivia. "Why are you blocking me? What could be worse?"

"Mom was there," Olivia whispered, her eyes shimmering in the evening light. "She saw it happen."

Tristan covered her mouth. She couldn't fathom it, didn't want to try.

"What else?" Evander demanded. "That's not what you're not saying."

"Ember," Tristan said admonishingly. "Give her a minute, will you?"

"You never block me," Evander ignored Tristan, speaking to Olivia. He looked hurt, his tone bewildered.

"I can't," Olivia said, covering her face with her hands.

"Let me see," Evander said, his voice gentling. "I'll say it. Just let me see."

Olivia uncovered her face, looking at Evander. He focused on her for a moment and then, paling, looked at Tristan.

"What?" Tristan asked apprehensively.

"There are..." Evander faltered, cleared his throat, started again. "There are rumors that they brought Orion back because the community has gotten too progressive for some of the Elders, so they want to review the newer laws that have been passed and see if they can revert any of them back to original law."

Tristan felt faint.

"But that means..."

Evander and Olivia nodded. Olivia was still crying, and Evander looked nauseated. That meant that the law that had been passed saying it would no longer be a requirement for new adults to join the community would be under review. Under the review of one of the most feared and unforgiving Elders the community had ever seen. Under the review of the man who'd had his own daughter publicly executed for trying to reject the community.

Tristan sank down onto the grass, and her siblings joined

her. That law would probably be at the top of the list, so her choices would be to be forced into a life she did not want, to marry a man she did not want and have children she was not ready for, or to be brutally executed in front of the entire community and everyone who loved her.

"Trinity? Oceana? Ember?" Umbris called from the back door, making them all jump. "What are you doing out there?"

"Just hanging out! We're fine!" Evander called back, his voice remarkably steady.

"Can you come hang out in here please? It's getting pitch black out there."

Evander flicked his wrist and the fire pit sprang to life, illuminating the yard.

"Good enough." Umbris went back inside after a beat, closing the door.

"They're going to be listening now," Evander said.

Silence once again descended upon the trio. Olivia stood, making a sweeping motion over their heads, as though she was drawing a rainbow.

"That should hold them off for a few minutes," Olivia said, sitting back down. She looked at Tristan, speaking urgently. "Look Trinity, I know you haven't come right out and said it, but Ember and I, and I think even Mom, know you're not going to join the community when you graduate. At least we know that's what you're planning. But if Orion is going to overturn the law making it optional, you have to join. You *have* to."

"I can't talk about this right now," Tristan said numbly. "I need to do some research. I need to talk to Celes; I know he knows the laws inside out and backwards. There has to be a loophole, or *something*."

"If he gets wind of what you're thinking, you know he'll dime you out in a heartbeat."

"He won't. I don't owe him any explanations about why I'm asking, and if I'm sealed he won't be able to read me."

"It's risky," Olivia said, shaking her head. "I really don't think it's a good idea to involve him in this."

"It'll be OK," Evander spoke up, nodding assuredly at his sisters. "Trinity is smart, and she knows what she's doing. Even if he gets suspicious, she'll keep her cool."

"Trinity," Olivia looked at her, her gray eyes full of worry. "How serious are you about not joining the community?"

"Serious enough that I don't know what I'll have to do to get away, even if one option means dying," Tristan replied, after a few beats.

Olivia covered her face again, resting her head on her knees, and Evander put his arm around her, looking at Tristan sadly.

"I wish it could be different," Tristan whispered, her own eyes filling with tears. "It's just not."

***

Olivia slept in Tristan's room with her that night, claiming she was too freaked out to sleep alone. Tristan didn't mind, was even secretly glad for her company, since she was feeling the same way.

Tristan laid awake long after Olivia had begun snoring softly beside her. There had to be something in the laws to prevent Orion from undoing the progress the community had made. There had to be someone who would dissent, or who could stop him. Just because *some* of the Elders didn't like the new laws didn't mean *all* of them felt that way, right? And Hydran had even said these were rumors he'd heard, so maybe it was all just speculation.

If that was the case though, Tristan's mind niggled, why had she dreamt of Adara? It had seemed pretty clear that it hadn't been a dream as much as a memory, a warning, and nothing Tristan told herself could change that.

Her stomach hurting, Tristan curled into a ball, rolling onto her side. She was scared, genuinely scared, and dreading next weekend's gathering.

Saturday dawned gray and rainy. Thunder was what woke Tristan, who found that Olivia was no longer in her room with her. She crept down the hall and peeked into Olivia's room, finding her sprawled out in her own bed. Relieved, Tristan went back to her bedroom, opening her window and letting the sounds and the smell of the storm fill the space. She took several deep breaths, but still her nerves rattled. Deciding yoga might help, she rolled out her mat and turned on her TV, finding a program to follow along with.

An hour later, Tristan was sweaty and her muscles were relaxed, but her mind was still buzzing. She jumped in the shower and then went downstairs, pouring herself a bowl of cereal and wondering where her parents were. She wandered into the living room, finding a note on the coffee table -- her parents had gone to spend the day in New Orleans; Umbris had business there, and they'd be meeting Dune and Thera Crenshaw for lunch.

Evander and Olivia were still asleep when Tristan left for work, so she put Sol's note on the kitchen table and wrote one of her own, letting her siblings know she'd be home around four-thirty that afternoon.

***

Beckett woke up on Saturday morning from yet another dream about Tristan. He laid in bed, replaying the bizarre memory. The details were quickly going fuzzy, but they'd been in the woods, he was pretty sure, and Tristan had been looking at him in an absolute panic. Beckett couldn't remember why, or who else had been there, or really anything but Tristan's expression and the fact that they were definitely a couple, in his dream. The whole thing was unnerving, but the couple part had been nice.

With a melancholy he'd never admit aloud to feeling, Beckett thought about how his dream scenarios were probably the only way he and Tristan would ever be together. She had finally agreed to something resembling friendship, but even that had basically been akin to Beckett knocking down one wall just to find five more behind it. The most frustrating part was that he got the feeling that she was into him, too, that she was lonely, too, and that they had a lot more in common than either of them realized. Beckett thought back to Thanksgiving, watching Tristan smile and laugh with the diners at the food kitchen. She'd been a sight to behold, more comfortable there than she ever seemed at school. Beckett could have easily spent the entire day with her, would gladly spend any day with her if she'd let him, which he knew she wouldn't.

He sighed, rolling onto his side and looking out of his bedroom window at the pouring rain. He told himself to stop thinking about Tristan, but she'd made herself a home in his thoughts. His mind wandered, wondering what it would be like to kiss her, to hold her body against his, to bring her up here to his bedroom and shut out the world with her. He wanted to find out so badly it was borderline desperate. He didn't understand the pull he felt towards her, how she held him so captive with so little effort and in spite of how little he knew about her, and part of him worried he was setting himself up for a bad burn at her hands. That same part urged him to move on, to find someone else to crush on or even date -- he'd noticed Eva Revet, the new girl, giving him looks lately -- but how could he when Tristan occupied so much space in his head?

Feeling unsettled, Beckett got up and got a shower, annoyed that the rain was keeping him from getting in some roof time. When he'd finished, he opened the bathroom door to the sounds of his parents fighting, again. It wasn't even ten A.M. Shaking his head in disgust, Beckett got dressed and grabbed his backpack, leaving the house. He had homework to do, but there was no way he'd be able to concentrate while the third world war waged one floor below him. He briefly entertained the thought of going to Rise and Grind, but decided against it when he imagined Tristan, if she was there, asking him why he'd come there to do his homework. His parental situation was one he was unprepared and unwilling to talk about, so the fewer questions he had to field, the better.

Beckett headed to Lavelle's public library instead -- an ancient, tiny building that he was pretty sure was haunted. Still better than his house. He set himself up at a table near a window and pulled out his books, getting started on his physics homework. His friend group was going to the movies tonight to see a re-release of *The Shining,* and while Beckett hadn't yet decided whether or not he was going to join them, he wanted to finish up his schoolwork just in case.

He had just moved onto his open-book sociology quiz when he noticed the librarian struggling to carry a large cardboard box from the front desk to a door against the far wall. Beckett jumped up to help, and the librarian, Margeaux Simeon, gratefully handed the box off to him.

"Thank you. We're doing a bunch of reorganizing right now and we're light on staff as it is, and having to move these boxes myself is killing me."

"I'm happy to help," Beckett replied. "Anything else you need moved?"

"There are two more boxes up front if you don't mind."

"Not at all."

"Hey, any chance you're available for hire?" Margeaux asked, looking him over once he'd carried the other boxes with ease, and Beckett looked back at her, surprised.

"Uh, well, I'm in school during the week but I can be available weeknights and weekends."

"If you don't mind doing the grunt work while we re-structure, you're hired. I'll be paying you under the table, and not much, but it's better than nothing, right?"

"Right, absolutely. I'm Beckett Benson, by the way." Beckett introduced himself, giving Margeaux an amused grin as he shook her hand.

"I know who you are; I've only worked this job for thirty years. You don't come here much, but I think I gave you your first library card."

Beckett smiled, nodding. "You did."

"Alright, so I'll let you get back to your work, but if you could come back tomorrow for a few hours, say around noon, we can get started."

"I'll be here. Thanks, Ms. Simeon."

"No, thank *you*, Beckett."

Beckett went back to his table, pleasantly surprised at what had just gone down. His parents did not require him to work while still in high school, and Beckett had some money thanks to the small, unexpected inheritance he'd received from his Paw-Paw when he'd passed, but Beckett often picked up odd jobs around town for extra money anyway; it made him feel better to be doing something to earn any kind of keep for himself.

Beckett finished his homework within the hour, packing up his bag and promising Margeaux he'd come back the next day. He left the library and drove around aimlessly, not ready to go home, not sure where else to go. He ended up driving out to the main road into Lavelle, traveling down a ways until he spotted a small dirt road to his right. He steered the car down the unpaved surface, bumping along slowly, until he got to an equally small parking lot. The rain had finally stopped, so Beckett got out of the car and began walking through the woods to the river. When he got there, he took off his gray hooded sweatshirt and folded it, placing it on a rock before sitting down.

For a long time, he watched the water rush by, thinking about what direction his life was taking. Graduation was still six months away, but at the same time, it was only six months away. Every day spent in his house felt like it lasted twice as long as every day spent out. Every interaction with his friends made him feel like he belonged somewhere, but made him wonder if it was with them. Beckett recalled what Tristan had said about seeming like a good person in spite of the company he kept, a smile tugging at his lips. He couldn't, wouldn't, blame her for how she saw his friends, as they'd never given her any reason to feel otherwise. His smile faded. He'd also never given her any reason to believe he was any better than them, yet she seemed to have at least a tenuous bit of faith in him.

Beckett finally went home late in the afternoon. His Dad was gone, as usual, and his Mom was holed up in the downstairs den, as usual. He went up to his bedroom and flopped back down on his bed. He wasn't in the mood for a horror movie, but he couldn't keep moping around all day, either. His friends were flawed, everyone was flawed, but they were still his friends, and they were still able to lift his spirits in a way he needed at this juncture in his life, so he'd go to the movies tonight and hopefully forget for a while about his own personal turmoil.

CHAPTER 12

Hours later, Beckett left the house again, driving into town just in case the rain picked back up. He met his group of friends out front, noticing they had invited Eva Revet to join them.

"Beckett, hi!" Emmeline greeted, all pearly white teeth and perfectly curled hair.

"Emmeline," Beckett greeted with a nod, before stepping around her to go and greet Jason, Henry, Wade Leveau, and Charlie Melancon.

Beckett looked over at Tyler, who was chatting with Olivia Wallace, no surprise there. She noticed him looking and smiled a greeting, and he smiled back at her, waving.

"Hi Beckett," Eva said from behind him, and Beckett turned, grinning at her.

"Hi Eva. Didn't expect to see you here tonight."

"Henry invited me," Eva replied, sweeping her long, dark hair behind her shoulders. Then, quickly, "Not as a date."

Beckett nodded, glancing at Henry, who winked at him smoothly before resuming his conversation with Jason.

"It's nice you could make it."

"*The Shining* is one of my favorite movies," Eva told him, her blue eyes sparkling excitedly. "Have you ever seen it?"

Beckett nodded.

"I have. I can't say I'm much of a fan of the bathtub scene, but the rest is OK."

Eva laughed, and Beckett smiled. Olivia, who was still talking to Tyler, shifted so she could keep Beckett and Eva in her line of vision. She didn't know much about Eva Revet -- pronounced Reh-vay, she'd be sure to tell you -- the girl having transferred to Jamestown Academy at the start of the year, and the reading Olivia was getting on her was worryingly murky, but that could have been because she was trying to read Eva while also trying to focus on Tyler.

Olivia knew Tristan wasn't ready to admit that she had a crush on Beckett, at least not out loud anyway, but she didn't need her sister to own up to anything in order to know the real deal. It was for this reason that Olivia was keeping an eye on Beckett and Eva -- Olivia had never known Tristan to be interested in anyone, and, as far as Olivia could tell, Beckett was a good egg. In fact, whenever Beckett was near her sister, Olivia got a vibe she was unfamiliar with, almost a familiarity between him and Tristan that went beyond whatever surface relationship they were very slowly building. It was something she kept meaning to explore, but there was never enough time, as either Beckett or Tristan was always coming or going when she approached them.

"Olivia, no Evander tonight?" Hattie asked her, and Olivia frowned in her direction.

"No Evander until the new year, remember?" Olivia corrected. "Grounded for breaking Theo's nose."

"But wasn't it an accident?" Hattie asked innocently, and Olivia looked at her for a moment, never able to tell when she was being genuine and when she wasn't. It was the very reason she steered as clear of Hattie as she did Emmeline.

"From what I've heard." Olivia coolly flicked her eyes over Hattie, who turned away to talk to Emmeline and Bailey.

"You're gonna sit next to me, right?" Tyler asked, and Olivia pretended to look confused.

"I don't know, I hadn't really thought about it. Why?"

"I'm gonna need someone to hold me when I get scared." Tyler gave her a cheeky smile, his dimples on full display, and Olivia laughed.

"I thought that's what you have Jason and Beckett for."

"We better go in," Emmeline said, and the group made their way inside the theatre.

Olivia casually maneuvered herself until she was behind Beckett, who was behind Eva.

"How's it going, Beckett?" Olivia asked, and Beckett twisted around, looking surprised that she was speaking to him.

"It's going," Beckett replied, nodding his head. "How's it going with you?"

"Well. Can't say the same for my brother."

Beckett laughed.

"I heard he's grounded until the new year."

"At least." Olivia shook her head. "Tristan and I tried to plead his case, but it didn't do much. Saved him from a lecture maybe, but not from a pretty harsh punishment. Being suspended from the games has been the biggest hit he's taken, though."

"I can imagine. It would be for me, too."

"What games?" Eva asked, not bothering to pretend like she hadn't been listening, and Olivia just looked at her.

"Football," Beckett replied, turning away from Olivia.

"You play football?"

"Yes," Beckett said slowly, laughing.

"I've never been to a game," Eva explained. She paused, then gave Beckett a sly look. "Maybe I'll come to the next one."

"You should," Beckett bobbed his head. "They're usually a good time."

"Where did you move here from?" Olivia asked Eva. "Not somewhere local?"

"No, not somewhere local," Eva confirmed with a smile, tilting her head just slightly. "We moved here from Virginia. Deltaville, specifically."

"Ohh, the faux south. That's why you don't really have an accent."

"The faux south?" Eva raised her eyebrows, and Olivia and Beckett laughed.

"You know, because it's so north it's barely south...? No? Anyway, I'm kidding. Mostly."

Eva laughed weakly, looking at Olivia like she wasn't sure what to make of her. She turned her gaze back to Beckett, and her smile went up a few watts.

"Have you ever been to Virginia?"

"Williamsburg with my parents, a long time ago," Beckett nodded. "We had a good time."

"Williamsburg is nice, but there is so much more to Virginia than there and Busch Gardens. Virginia Beach, for example, is gorgeous, or Shenandoah National Park in Front Royal, if you're more of a mountains guy than a beach guy."

"I am a both guy," Beckett grinned affably, and Eva grinned back at him.

"My kind of guy."

The group filed into the theatre, and Olivia sat to the right of Eva, Beckett on her left; she was going to get a read on Eva Revet if it killed her. Tyler sat beside Olivia, of course, and Olivia laughed, rolling her eyes at him. The theatre darkened, the trailers beginning, and Olivia ignored them in order to focus on reading Eva.

A few minutes later, Olivia frowned. She found, generally, that most of her fellow teenagers read OK. Emmeline and Hattie were two immediate exceptions that Olivia could think of -- they read as rotten as they acted, and while Bailey, Tara, Eloise, and Georgiana were better, it wasn't by much. Theo Fitelson was also a bad egg. Eva, however, was different from all of them -- her reading was turbulent, and while it was not bad in the way Emmeline's was or Theo's was, it was bad all the same. It made Olivia extremely uncomfortable, especially since Eva acted very happy and bubbly on the surface; at least the others who read badly didn't really bother trying to pretend they were anything other than what they were.

Eva looked over at Olivia, and Olivia looked back at her, raising her eyebrows just slightly. Eva gave her a bright smile, then leaned over and said something to Beckett, who murmured back to her, an amused expression on his face. This was no good. No good for Tristan, who couldn't possibly have expected Beckett to continue being interested in her when all she did was shut him down, and not good for Beckett, who Olivia couldn't even warn away from Eva, because what would she say? *Hey Beckett, I can read someone to get an idea of what kind of person they are on a soul-deep level, and you might want to run in the opposite direction of Eva Revet?*

The movie finally began, and Olivia pushed her thoughts aside, focusing on the film instead. There was really nothing she could do, even if she wanted to, short of influencing Eva or Beckett's thoughts to keep them away from each other. That wasn't fair, however, and more than being unfair, it was an abuse of power. Beckett was not in danger with Eva, as far as Olivia could tell, and Tristan would never speak to Olivia again if she ever found out Olivia had intervened on her behalf. No, it was tempting, but Olivia had to mind her own business.

Eva talked the whole way out of the movie theatre, and Beckett just watched her and listened, thinking about how cute she was as she chatted away about the brilliance of Stephen King.

"No thanks, Tristan is right there," Beckett heard Olivia say, out on the sidewalk, and his head whipped around. Tristan was parked a little ways up the street from the theatre, leaning against her car, looking at her phone.

Olivia shot a quick look at Beckett, then ran a hand through her hair, hiding a smile to herself. So maybe she hadn't *completely* minded her own business after all. Missing a ride home with Tyler was worth the way Beckett was now staring at an oblivious Tristan, confirming what Olivia had known all along -- regardless of his flirtation with Eva, Beckett was totally into Tristan.

"Coming!" Olivia called down the block, and Tristan looked up, nodding. She glanced at the group, doing a double-take when she saw Beckett standing with Eva Revet, who was smiling up at him, but staring at her. Her eyebrows raised very, very briefly, and then she looked back down at her phone.

A few seconds later, Tristan looked up again, shaking her hair out of her face. She must have remembered the truce she and Beckett had called between them, because she sent a small wave his way, and Beckett waved back at her.

"Who's that?" Eva asked.

"You don't want to know," Emmeline said, and Olivia turned and looked at her.

"No offense," Emmeline said, giving Olivia the fakest of smiles.

"That's Tristan, my sister," Olivia told Eva.

"Oh. *Ohhh*," Eva said, recognition finally dawning. She glanced at Emmeline, who smirked.

"See you guys Monday," Olivia said, rolling her eyes.

"Thanks for keeping me safe in there," Tyler grinned. "Now instead of nightmares of Jack Nicholson, I'll have sweet dreams of you."

Olivia winked at him, blowing him a kiss and wiggling her fingers in goodbye before she sauntered away to meet Tristan at her car.

"Why did you need me to pick you up?" Tristan asked, frowning as Olivia drew closer to her. "I thought Tyler was giving you a ride home."

"Oh, he wasn't going right home," Olivia lied, shrugging.

Tristan rounded the car, looking up the street again as she went, noticing that Eva had moved in front of Beckett, blocking her view of him. She got into the driver's side, telling herself not to ask, and of course immediately disregarded that advice.

"Was that Eva Revet with Beckett back there?"

"Mmhm," Olivia grunted, and Tristan looked over at her. "They didn't show up together, but they'll probably leave together."

"Not a fan?"

"She reads really weird."

"Oceana."

"What? You know me, I read everyone."

Tristan was quiet for a moment. Then, "What do you mean she reads weird?"

"Bad weird. Not bad like Beckett is going to end up in pieces in the Mississippi, I don't think, just, like, *off* weird."

"Super descriptive."

"Ha ha. I don't know how to explain it. Like, Emmeline reads heinously because that's who she is to the core, and she acts it. Same thing with her bitchy friends. But Eva acts super sunshiney and bubbly, meanwhile her reading was *dark*, Trinity. Like unstable, disturbing dark. And I am talking about a reading of who she is, not a reading of her aura."

"But Beckett isn't in danger?"

Olivia shook her head. "No, I really don't think so. But I also can't be one hundred percent sure, so that's why it's weird."

Tristan thought for a moment, then shrugged.

"Then there's nothing than can be done. He'll have to find out for himself whatever her deal is."

"And you don't care that they were getting all flirty with each other?"

Tristan looked at Olivia sharply.

"No, I don't. Why would I?"

Olivia answered her question with a question.

"You do know that as your sister, I'm on your side, right? That you can actually tell me things and whatever you tell me will be safe with me?"

"Debatable."

"What do you mean debatable?" Olivia demanded, scowling.

"Oceana," Tristan looked at her knowingly. "I believe you have good intentions and you'd never blab anything I told you on purpose, but I know you drink when you go to parties with your friends."

"So?"

"So I'd never, ever run the risk of someone getting something out of you while you weren't sober."

"I don't get blasted and I'm not a blabbermouth!" Olivia snapped defensively. "I would never repeat anything you told me in confidence. Hello, I can't even drink that much for my *own* sake so I don't spill any of my *own* secrets!"

"It's nothing personal, O. It's just not a risk I'm taking."

Olivia harrumphed, crossing her arms over her chest and looking out the passenger side window.

"Are you looking forward to the Solstice Celebration in a couple of weeks?" Tristan asked, trying to change the subject.

"No." Olivia glared at her. "It's the same night as Jamestown's Christmas dance, and I would one thousand percent rather be going to that."

"With Tyler Daniels?"

"With none of your business, Trinity!"

Tristan laughed, and Olivia continued to fume.

"Meanwhile, I'm the exact opposite. I'd one thousand percent rather be going to the gathering than to any event at Jamestown on a night I am not supposed to be there."

"Well good for you," Olivia grumbled. Then, "I'm surprised by that, though. Two gatherings in one month would usually be a nightmare for you."

"I didn't say I *want* to go," Tristan pointed out. "I'm just saying I'd choose it over Jamestown if we actually had a choice."

They lapsed into silence then, and Tristan pulled into the driveway. Before they got out of the car, Olivia turned to her.

"You know, the real reason I asked you to pick me up tonight was so Beckett could see you. Don't tell me anything because you don't trust me, but remember that I know things regardless of whether or not you say them out loud. Eva's reading wasn't the only reason I wanted Beckett to remember you exist tonight."

Not waiting for a response, Olivia got out of the car, slamming the door behind her. Tristan stared at where she'd been sitting, her mouth hanging open.

***

The truth was that this newfound *thing* between Beckett and Eva did bother Tristan. What bothered her even more than that, however, was that as Beckett and Eva got friendlier around Jamestown Academy, something strange was happening between Tristan and Beckett. It felt like whatever unspoken tension they had going was ramping up in intensity while simultaneously staying exactly the same, but the only tangible thing Tristan could pinpoint as different was the way Beckett looked at her throughout the week -- he seemed to have stopped rearranging his features to look friendly whenever he saw her, and instead just looked at Tristan like... well... almost like he was *longing* for her. It was the way Tristan would expect him to look at Eva, who could now be found at Beckett's side whenever he took to the halls of Jamestown, and the entire thing made no sense no matter how Tristan tried to examine it. It frustrated her endlessly that a look, or a handful of looks, as the case may be, could be such an all-consuming preoccupation.

On top of the weirdness with Beckett, Tristan's week was crowded by thoughts of the approaching gathering. She was growing increasingly nervous as Saturday approached, and Olivia and Evander were no help, as they were right there in the same boat. Olivia, who had graciously decided to forgive Tristan, had tried a couple of times to relieve Tristan's worry, the way she'd done at the last gathering, but between her lack of energy from her crash and her own nerves, it didn't take. Tristan knew she was going to have to find a way to calm down, even if that meant asking Sol for help, otherwise by the time Saturday came she'd be doubled-over with painful knots of anxiety in her gut.

It was in surprise that Tristan watched Beckett come to meet her alone at their bench on Friday after school. She'd been certain that Eva would be accompanying him, had even prepared herself for it by arming herself with more research than she'd ever brought to their meetings since they'd started.

"Hey, sorry I'm late." Beckett greeted her, sitting down. He flopped his head back, closing his eyes against the harsh December sunlight.

"You're not late," Tristan replied. "I'm early. I have a ton of material this week, so I was just sorting through it so it's in some semblance of order."

Beckett looked at Tristan, not realizing until that moment that he'd missed her. *Missed her?* Yes, missed her. Eva had made herself an extension of his hip all week, even though they'd not seen each other outside of school since Saturday night, so he and Tristan hadn't gotten to chat in the hall between classes, or before class in the morning, or at all, really, outside of English class, where they hadn't been partnered up for their project. They also kept missing each other in the lunch line, which happened occasionally and didn't usually bother Beckett, but this time he resented that they'd fallen out of sync. Eva was nice, cute as hell, but relentlessly cheerful, and yes, Beckett had missed Tristan's quiet, even-keeled demeanor and dry sense of humor.

"Whatcha got?" Beckett asked, leaning over interestedly.

Tristan turned the stack of papers in her lap.

"I found this website that is a resource jackpot for ESL teachers. There's everything from course material to games to how to best interact with the students."

Beckett looked impressed, maybe even excited.

"That's amazing! So we'll build the project around

this?"

"That's what I was thinking." Tristan nodded, looking pleased.

"All right. Let's see what's in here." Beckett moved closer to Tristan on the bench, and, as she watched him look over the papers, the old familiar crush sensation swept through her stomach.

"How's the job going?" Beckett asked, as he flipped through the pages.

"As thrilling as ever," Tristan replied, to Beckett's chuckle. "No, I do actually enjoy it."

"I just picked up a job recently myself."

"Oh? Where?"

"The library."

Tristan squinted at him, giving him the look she used to give him back when they'd first started meeting, the one where she couldn't tell whether or not he was being serious.

"Ohh, there's that face again," Beckett said, pointing and starting to laugh as his eyes went wide. "The *Beckett, are you dumb or do you think I am?* face. I've missed it!"

Tristan laughed at Beckett's exaggerated impression of her, her cheeks turning a lovely shade of pink. She had just opened her mouth to respond when Eva suddenly appeared.

"Hi Beckett."

Beckett jumped, turning, and Tristan looked up, her laughter fading.

"Eva, hey. What's up? What are you still doing here?"

"I had music practice so I thought I'd come see if you

were still here before I left, and here you are." Eva smiled at him, ignoring Tristan.

"Here I am. Have you met Tristan Wallace? She's Olivia's sister." Beckett gestured to Tristan.

"No," Eva said, looking at Tristan. Her expression cooled several degrees and she said nothing else.

Tristan looked back at her, also saying nothing.

"Are you almost done?" Eva asked Beckett.

"We just got started," Beckett replied, shaking his head, his brow creasing. "You don't have to wait. I'm not sure how long this will take."

"Well it *is* Friday and you *do* have a social life, right?" Eva grinned at him. "You can't stay here forever."

Tristan, who could already see how this was going to go, began straightening up her papers.

"It's OK, Beckett. Why don't you take those home, I'll take these, and we'll talk about it next week?" Tristan suggested.

Beckett frowned. "No, I'm not in any rush. We can do this here."

"It's fine," Tristan said again, her tone reassuring.

"But--"

"Great!" Eva said brightly, giving Beckett a dazzling smile. "I'll walk you to your car."

Beckett looked at Tristan, who he knew was intentionally not looking at him.

"You don't mind?"

Tristan finally glanced up and, damn it, there was that look again. The longing. The looking at her mouth, her eyes, her whole entire face like he was two seconds from leaning over and kissing her. She smiled, pretending not to notice, and looked into his eyebrows instead of his eyes.

"We have five months to finish this, Beckett. Have a good weekend, OK?"

"OK," Beckett said reluctantly, standing.

"Finally!" Eva clapped a little, and Tristan watched them walk away, Eva's hand snaking around Beckett's bicep.

Her stomach crunched a little bit, a little pit opening up, and Tristan forcibly pushed it aside. There was no way, in any lifetime, that she and Beckett could ever be together, so it was a waste of time and an abuse of her heart to let herself have feelings for him. Tristan knew it, believed it, but feelings were never rational and didn't care for being censored, so her gut persisted even through the stern talking-to she was giving herself. *You could be together,* it was saying. *His friends would talk, but he would choose you over them.*

"*Stop it,*" Tristan whispered fiercely to herself.

Beckett looked back at Tristan, who was still sitting on their bench, slowly putting her things away. She was frowning, and Beckett knew he'd chosen wrong. He should have stayed to work on their project, should have stayed to spend time with her.

"Beckett?" Eva asked, and Beckett looked at her, clearly having missed a question.

"Sorry, what?"

"I was just asking if you have plans this weekend."

"I have the last football game of the year tomorrow night, and after the game a bunch of us usually go to Mack's diner, across town. Free Sunday. How about you?"

"No plans right now, but I'm thinking I might come to the football game tomorrow. If you don't mind."

Eva smiled at Beckett, and he told himself to give her a chance, reminding himself that his crush on Tristan was fruitless, since she was never going to feel about him the way he felt about her. Beckett smiled back.

"I don't mind at all. You wanna come to Mack's with us afterwards?"

"That would be really nice," Eva replied, nodding, and Beckett smiled at her again.

***

Late Friday night, Tristan found Sol in the kitchen, sitting at the table reading and sipping tea.

"Mom?"

Sol looked up, setting down her book.

"Hi honey."

"Hi. I was wondering if you could help me with something?"

"Anything. What do you need?"

"I'm really anxious lately, and it's starting to make me feel sick. I was wondering if you can help me calm down? I tried everything myself, but it didn't do much." Tristan twisted her fingers together as she talked, a nervous habit she'd had for as long as Sol could remember.

Sol surveyed her daughter's pale face, the anxiety she mentioned evident; Trinity was sealed, as usual, but there was tension in every bit of her frame.

"Come sit," Sol gestured to the chair beside her, and Trinity sat, looking grateful.

"Is it school, getting to you?" Sol asked.

"It's... A lot of things," Trinity replied in a careful voice. "I'll be OK, I think, I just sometimes can't get a handle on my worrying."

"You know if you ever need to talk, I'm here? Without judgment."

Trinity's face momentarily flooded with emotion, and Sol's heart ached for her daughter. She did not miss navigating being a teenager.

"Thanks Mom."

Sol nodded, then took Trinity's hand.

"OK. Close your eyes and try to relax."

Tristan did as she was told, and Sol closed her eyes as well. Within minutes, a sense of peace Tristan had been desperate for settled over her. She relaxed for the first time in what felt like weeks, and the crushing mental load she was under lifted substantially. She opened her eyes and so did Sol, nodding and releasing her hand.

"Thank you," Tristan said gratefully. "I feel so much better now."

"You're welcome, Trinity. Go get some sleep now; the gathering will be here before we know it."

"I will. I love you."

"I love you too." Sol watched Trinity go, sadness filling her heart. Her daughter was in constant emotional upheaval, and if what Sol suspected was true, it would only get worse for her before it got better. She really needed to find the right time to talk to Trinity about rejecting the community, before it was too late.

Tristan slept better that night than she had in ages. She slept so well, in fact, that when she awoke on Saturday, she was shocked to find that it was after ten A.M. Getting out of bed, she went downstairs and made a bowl of cereal, flipping on the TV and watching reruns of *Criminal Minds* while she ate. Everyone else was sleeping, and Tristan would be going back to bed when she was finished breakfast, but for the time being she enjoyed the stillness of the house. It gave her time to think out from under the strain of anxiety, and with new resolve she decided she wasn't going to care that much about Beckett and Eva after all. *Senior year was not the time to get caught up in emotion,* she had to keep that mantra in the forefront of her mind; graduation was in six months, and with luck she'd be leaving Lavelle for good only a few months later. No sense in putting down any roots to this town now.

CHAPTER 13

The December gathering was at the same place it had been last month, the area bringing back unpleasant memories of being held hostage by the guards when Tristan and Celes had wandered too far. Despite Sol's help, Tristan's nerves jangled as she and her siblings once again stepped out of the car by the water, into the pitch black night. What if Entros had revealed her secret and the Elders were going to ambush her after worship?

Dune and Thera came to greet them once again, this time joined by Sanguin who, as usual, said nothing more than hello. Tall and thin, extremely pale and preferring to wear her black hair long and usually partially obscuring her face, Sanguin creeped Tristan out, if Tristan was honest. It wasn't just her appearance, of course, though the faint scowl she always wore didn't help, it was that she was always so *silent* that she was pretty much a human shadow, which was quite unnerving. Tristan could tell Olivia and Evander felt similarly by the way they gave her a wide berth, which made Tristan feel slightly less guilty about her unfavorable thoughts.

The group boarded the same rickety old boat they'd taken last month, and Olivia looked at Tristan apprehensively. Tristan squeezed her hand, and Olivia held onto it. The ride was quiet, which was unusual, but Tristan understood. Sol and Umbris had exchanged anxious looks during the drive, communicating silently and privately, Olivia and Evander blocked from listening in. They didn't need to, however --

Hydran had given them enough information that they could surmise why Sol was on edge.

Several times, Tristan tried and failed to imagine how she'd ever look at her father if he had one of her siblings executed. It was so absurd, so horrific, that she just couldn't quite get her head around what Orion had done.

Celes greeted them at the opposite bank, helping Tristan off of the boat even though she didn't really need help. She pulled her hand away quickly, giving him a tight smile, and Celes, unruffled, walked beside her.

"How have you been, Trinity?"

"Hanging in there," Tristan replied. "And you?"

"I've been fine. Have you been safe?"

"Yes." Tristan looked at him curiously. "You seem to think that I'm in some kind of danger, though, or will be. You want to tell me about that?"

Celes shook his head. "Not right this second. We'll walk later."

"But not too far," Tristan said, and Celes nodded, smiling wryly.

"Not too far."

***

The Jamestown Wolves won the football game, and Beckett grinned up at Eva, jumping up and down and clapping in the bleachers. He chuckled to himself when he saw Emmeline shoot an oblivious Eva a dirty look -- a leopard never did change its spots.

After he'd showered and dressed, he met up with his friends back down at the field.

"What did you think?" Beckett asked Eva, holding open his hands.

"It was exciting! I didn't think I'd have a good time, but I'll admit it, I was wrong!"

"You need a ride to Mack's?"

Eva nodded, her eyes sparkling in the field lighting. She bit her lip and grinned, and Beckett led the way to his car. She was obviously into him, and Beckett wasn't mad about it, but still Tristan lingered in his mind. Would she ever come to a football game? To the diner afterwards? Would she ever look at him the way Eva was looking at him? No. Beckett knew the answer was no, so the sooner he got her out of his head, the better.

"OK, I'm just going to get this out of the way," Eva said, once they reached Beckett's car.

Before Beckett could ask what, Eva grasped the open front of his hoodie and pulled him to her, kissing him. Beckett wasn't sure in what order things happened next, or even how, but thunder suddenly boomed overhead, and the sky absolutely opened up. At the same time, he had what he could only describe as a vision of Tristan. She was in the woods, like she'd been in the dream he'd had about her, but there was a large, shadowy figure standing behind her. The look on her face was not one of fear, also like it had been in his dream, rather she, oddly, looked like someone had just hurt her feelings.

Eva pulled away from Beckett, shrieking about the rain, and as quickly as Beckett had seen Tristan, she was gone. He hurriedly unlocked the car doors and he and Eva scrambled inside, soaked and laughing. He drove them to Mack's, the need to concentrate on seeing the road through the buckets of rain cascading down the windshield driving all thought of Tristan from his mind.

***

"Trinity? Trinity." Celes touched Tristan's shoulder, and she nearly jumped a mile.

"Sorry!" Tristan said, shaking her head, squinting against the suddenly pouring rain. What had just happened?

"We need to go back," Celes said, shaking his hair out of his eyes. "They'll have protected the clearing from the rain."

"But you didn't tell me why you think I'm not safe!" Tristan called, hurrying after Celes.

"It's Orion," Celes said over his shoulder. "He is paying special attention to your family."

"Wait, what?" Tristan grabbed Celes's arm, stopping him. "What do you mean?"

"Trinity," Celes said, exasperated. "Can we not do this here in the rain?"

"It's just water!" Tristan snapped, and Celes sighed. She suppressed the shivers that were threatening -- yes, it was just water, but it also happened to be ice cold.

"Orion is paying special attention to your family. It's probably because Sol is his daughter and he's never met you and the twins, but there are... concerns... that he's angry with Sol, and that's what's behind it. That's all I know."

"Who has concerns? What concerns?" Tristan asked.

"Trinity, all I know is what I told you. Can we please keep going?"

Tristan nodded reluctantly, and they kept moving. Thunder boomed again, and Tristan finally had time to think about what had happened back there. She and Celes had been walking, and Tristan had thought she'd heard something. She'd stopped, looking around, and at the exact moment the storm began, Tristan had seen Beckett and Eva embracing, lips locked, in front of his car. It was as though all three had materialized right in front of her, and she'd felt like she'd been punched square in the gut. As quickly as they'd appeared, however, they'd disappeared, Celes's voice rising over the next clap of thunder, and Tristan had been left breathless and confused. Why had she seen them? Had she really been seeing them? Were Beckett and Eva going to be official now? But most importantly, *why had Tristan seen them?*

Tristan and Celes reached the clearing, and, as they passed through the entrance, four people in black hooded jackets swept their hands over them. Tristan and Celes thanked them as their clothes and skin dried, nice and warm.

"Trinity, there you are!" Olivia called, rushing over to Tristan and Celes.

"We got caught in the rain," Tristan said. "Listen, I need to--"

"No," Celes said sharply, and Tristan and Olivia looked at him. "Not here."

"But--"

"Trinity, I said not here." Celes's voice was authoritative, and Tristan and Olivia raised their eyebrows in unison.

"You don't tell me what to do," Tristan said, stepping up to Celes until they were toe to toe, and, *damn it,* there it went again -- a flash of attraction, lightning fast between them. Celes stared down at her and, though he was clearly irritated, he also looked like he might grab her and kiss her.

"Trinity," Olivia said, sounding alarmed. She grabbed

Tristan's arm. "Come on, Mom and Dad were looking for you."

Olivia pulled Tristan away, muttering things Tristan couldn't hear.

"What?" Tristan said finally, getting her wits about her. What was going *on* tonight? Was it the extra charged atmosphere, a result of the gathering and the thunderstorm combined?

Olivia ignored her, practically thrusting her towards Evander and her parents.

"There you are!" Sol said, her relief palpable. "Trinity, I thought I told you this last month, but no going off alone or with just Celes or anyone, OK? For the time being, I need you to stay close."

"OK, I'm sorry," Tristan said, nodding.

Olivia pulled her arm again, dragging her a few feet from their family, and Tristan shot her an annoyed look as she rubbed her bicep.

"What is wrong with you?" Olivia hissed. "You looked like you were about to jump on Celes back there!"

"I don't know!" Tristan said, her eyes wide. "Maybe I'm ovulating!"

"Ew!" Olivia recoiled, scrunching her face in mild disbelief.

"Sorry!"

"Get it together," Olivia said, giving her a small shake. "You know you can't do this if you're going to you know what, you know when."

"Shut up, Oceana!" Tristan whisper-yelled, looking

around frantically. "Are you crazy?!"

"*You're* making me crazy!" Olivia whisper-yelled back, jabbing Tristan's chest with her finger.

Tristan glared at Olivia, who glared back at her, crossing her arms tightly over her chest.

"Look, I need to talk to you about something. Not what Celes told me not to, but something else. Something happened back there."

Olivia groaned.

"I do *not* want to hear about whatever the something was, especially if you're going to say the word ovulating again."

"Grow up." Tristan gave Olivia a dirty look, then leaned in closer to her. "Listen..."

Tristan told Olivia what had happened, when Beckett and Eva had appeared in front of her just to disappear in a flash, Olivia listening intently. She thought for a few silent moments, and Tristan could practically see the wheels turning in her mind, trying to puzzle together what was going on.

"Has that ever happened before?"

"Them kissing? How would I know?"

"Gods give me strength, I thought you were the smart one." Olivia cast her eyes skyward, before looking at Tristan like she was a toddler. "*No,* Trinity, I *mean* have you ever seen Beckett before, like you did tonight?"

"Not like that, no."

"But somehow?"

Tristan hesitated, and Olivia raised her eyebrows, waiting. On a sigh, Tristan told Olivia about the night of Matteo's party, and the episode during the last gathering when both she and Entros had seen Beckett shirtless in his bedroom.

"OK, that second part is really alarming and we need to talk about that separately, but has Beckett ever mentioned to you that he's seen you? Or that anything weird has happened to him involving you?"

Tristan shook her head.

"No, he hasn't. Why? What are you thinking?"

"I don't know yet. I've been getting this vibe, though, when I'm around you two, and if either of you would stay in the same place long enough in front of me, I might be able to find out more."

"But you look and sound like you have a suspicion as to what's going on."

"I do now, but I'm not ready to tell you about it."

"Why not?" Tristan demanded.

"Because it's... because. Just trust me, OK? And maybe the next time you're with Beckett and you see me, don't run off or let him run off in the opposite direction? You'll get an answer much sooner that way."

"You're infuriating."

"So are you." Olivia stuck her tongue out at Tristan, who rolled her eyes.

"Dad is giving us the hairy eyeball," Tristan said, glancing over at Umbris. "We'd better get back over there."

Tristan and Olivia walked back over to their parents and Evander, and Sol turned to them, her face, as usual anymore, stressed.

"Girls, listen. As soon as they begin the closing tonight, we are leaving, so be prepared, OK? Don't make eye contact with any of the Elders, don't answer any questions anyone may ask as to why we're not staying until the end, just follow your father and Ember and I. Got it?"

Olivia and Tristan nodded nervously. Leaving early was not a violation, but it was uncommon and would garner attention. The community had been restless enough last month over Orion's reappearance that the Wallaces early departure hadn't raised eyebrows, but this month it almost certainly would.

"Mom?" Tristan said, trying to think ahead. "Isn't there a chance that Orion will call you out specifically if he sees us trying to leave early?"

Sol's head snapped around, her gaze sharp.

"Why do you say that?"

Tristan swallowed, twisting her fingers together. Celes would have had a good reason for not wanting Tristan to discuss what he'd told her here, and despite how she felt about him trying to boss her around, she generally deferred to his warnings when it came to the community. He kept his finger on the pulse of the goings on, not in the hope of climbing ranks, but just so he could be prepared for all possibilities. He'd told her that years ago, and Tristan had no reason to believe he'd been lying.

"I... I just... I mean he's your father and he just came back after how many years away? I... I just could see him calling out to you because he might feel like he has the right to do that."

"She's right," Umbris said, and Sol moved her tempestuous gaze to him instead. He shook his head apologetically. "Sol, you know I understand why you want to spend as little time as you can out in the open, but moving as part of a crowd will make you a lot harder to single out than us trying to leave while everyone is still seated."

"Couldn't he just come find us right now, while everyone is standing around waiting for worship to begin?" Evander asked, looking around at the crowd.

Umbris shook his head.

"He's still very weak. He will rest until it's time for him to make an appearance at the end, and he'll need to rest again after that. When he regains his strength is when he'll seek a reunion, I'm sure."

The announcement for everyone to move to the perimeter of the clearing was given, and Tristan ended up standing shoulder to shoulder with Celes.

"I'm sorry," Celes said, leaning over just slightly.

"It's OK," Tristan replied, glancing up at him. Their eyes locked briefly, but then Olivia coughed, bumping Tristan, and she looked away.

Tristan knew what was happening. She'd never admit it out loud, but she'd figured it out when she'd had a moment away from Celes. Her feelings were hurt over Beckett and Eva, and she was reacting. Beckett would have no idea, which made the reaction ineffective, of course, and it unequivocally was not fair to Celes for Tristan to suddenly seem interested in him... but her irrational hurt was like a festering little being of its own, and it drove her to play Beckett's own game, even at Celes's expense. She glanced at Celes again.

"Trinity, I swear to the gods," Olivia said, through clenched teeth, and Tristan shot an irritated look her way.

"Why are you so invested in this?" Tristan leaned over, hissing into Olivia's ear.

"How many reasons do you want?" Olivia shot back. "Grow up."

When the worshipping pillows had settled into the clearing, Tristan followed her family and sat, unsure how she'd get through the hours ahead. If she'd thought she was unsettled before, it was nothing compared to how she was feeling now.

***

Beckett dropped Eva off at her house after the diner, but not before she'd practically jumped into his lap in the car. It took him his entire drive home to get his racing heart under control, which was also when he fully realized he'd agreed to take her to the Winter Dance the following Saturday night. He hadn't planned on going at all, not being much of a dance guy, but that had been hard to remember while Eva's body had been pressing against his, her hands wandering way south, her lips grazing his own as she'd told him how much she was looking forward to it.

Beckett still didn't really know Eva, hadn't gotten much time to talk to her to find out more than the basics about her, but she didn't seem to mind and so he decided to follow her lead. She had told him that she'd had her eye on him since the start of the school year, which had flattered him, but the way she'd said it had kind of reminded him of Emmeline, and he sincerely hoped he wasn't about to start dating the latest iteration of Emmeline Strandquest. He'd really have to question his judgment then.

***

Tristan made it through worship, though it felt about twice as long as it usually did, and the family stayed through the news and closing ceremony. They blended into the rest of the crowd that streamed out of the clearing, as suspected, and Sol gave her a relieved smile as they reached the dinghy with the Crenshaws.

Tristan yawned broadly, and Celes smiled at her.

"Aren't you tired?" Tristan asked, squinting against the rising sun, and Celes shook his head.

"I'll be good until tonight."

"How?"

Celes laughed, and both families got on the boat. They crossed the river without incident and all said their good-byes, the adults agreeing they were looking forward to the Solstice Celebration the following weekend. Tristan fell asleep pretty much as soon as she got in the car, her head propped on her arm, which she rested on the window ledge and folded beneath her head. The Solstice Celebration, the looks she knew she'd be getting from Celes when she was all dressed up and now this newfound urge to maybe let him look at her that way, was the very, very last thing she wanted to think about just then.

CHAPTER 14

Tristan had held out some small hope that, though Beckett and Eva had their tongues down each other's throats on Saturday night, it had not gone any further, but school on Monday morning dashed that hope entirely. As Tristan made her way to her locker, she passed Eva and Beckett, who were at Eva's, their heads close together as they talked.

"Morning Tristan," Beckett greeted, as usual, and Tristan smiled at him. She was not going to punish him for finding someone who made him happy, especially since she herself had done nothing but keep him at arm's length since October.

"Morning Beckett."

Eva did not turn around, so Tristan didn't bother with her. She looked away from Beckett, continuing on to get her books, reassuring herself that she'd done well, and that eventually seeing them together would stop bothering her. She also reminded herself, once again, that *senior year was not the time to get caught up in emotion.*

***

"Taco Tuesday," Beckett said from behind Tristan, the next day at lunch.

Tristan turned, grinning.

"Taco Tuesday."

"I'm glad you came around. You can thank me at any

time for opening your eyes."

Tristan laughed, shaking her head.

"How was your weekend?" Beckett asked.

"It was fine. The same as always, really. You know you don't have to ask me that every week? I don't ever do anything but work or see family."

Beckett shrugged. "I still want to know."

Tristan looked away, biting her lip. Her lines were blurring with him, her rules falling out of place the more she saw him. Nothing could or would come of a friendship with him, but it was getting tiring caring about the bigger picture.

"My weekend was good too, not that you asked."

Tristan turned back around with an apologetic smile.

"Sorry. I'm glad you had a good weekend. Did you do anything fun?"

"Football, Mack's, the usual." Beckett shrugged.

Tristan nodded, waiting to see if he'd say more, but he didn't. Instead, he suddenly looked like he remembered something, and a mix of confusion, fear, and urgency crossed his face while he looked back at her. Tristan raised her eyebrows.

"Are you OK?"

"Where were you this weekend?"

Tristan frowned.

"Excuse me?"

"Were you home all weekend?"

"Uh." Tristan looked around nervously. "No, not all weekend. I went out of town, to see family, on Saturday."

"Were you OK?"

"What's with the questions?" Tristan prickled, still frowning.

"I just..." Beckett shook his head. "I don't know. It would sound crazy if I even told you. Maybe I got struck by lightning or something."

"Do you need to go to the nurse?" Tristan asked, squinting at Beckett. She touched his forehead, which was cool. "Lie down?"

Her touch seemed to snap him out of whatever was going on, and Beckett blinked, watching her hand as she pulled it back.

"Sorry," Tristan said immediately, embarrassed. Her cheeks burned. Had she seriously just felt his head?

"No, I'm sorry." Beckett shook his head. "I guess I should have said my weekend was weird, because that's what it was."

Tristan was dying to know what he meant, getting the distinct impression that perhaps they'd shared the same experience on Saturday night, but she couldn't put herself at risk to ask, so instead she smiled.

"I know how that is."

Tristan paid for her lunch and picked up her tray.

"See you around, Beckett."

"See you."

Beckett watched Tristan go, his thoughts all in a jumble, his skin tingling from where Tristan's hand had been. Was skin supposed to do that? Maybe he *did* need to see the nurse.

***

Tristan closed her locker on Wednesday morning, turning to find Emmeline and her crew standing less than a foot from her. She jumped.

"Jesus."

"Don't you dare speak his name." Emmeline looked personally offended, and Tristan stared at her.

"What do you want?"

"I want to know how many times I have to tell you to stay away from Beckett before you listen."

"I want to know how many times we have to have the same conversation before *you* listen. It's like three times a week at this point, isn't it? Also, isn't Beckett dating Eva Revet? That was a fast breakup between you two."

Emmeline snorted.

"Please. He's trying to make me jealous by sleeping with the easiest girl in the junior class, which won't work, by the way, not that it's any of your business."

Tristan ignored the now-familiar pit in her stomach. She did not want or need to know who Beckett was sleeping with.

"He's getting a lot of weird attention this year," Emmeline said, looking Tristan up and down. "First from you, now from Eva. I have you both on my radar."

"Is that a threat?" Tristan asked, annoyed.

Emmeline smiled.

"It's a courtesy warning. Ciao, Tristan."

Lightning fast, damn her, Emmeline flipped Tristan's books out of her arms, then walked away laughing with her friends.

Tristan closed her eyes, summoning strength she barely had to not chase Emmeline down. Instead, she picked up her books and, clutching them to her chest the way she should have been in the first place, she headed to class, mentally calculating how many days were left until graduation.

There must have been something in the air that day, or Emmeline had gotten to Eva, as well, because every time Tristan and Eva passed each other in the hall, the icy vibe Tristan caught from her nearly chilled her to the bone. The accompanying angry stare did the same. The bizarre thing, however, was that Eva was her usual sunshine and rainbows self whenever Tristan saw her with Beckett. *Actually,* Tristan corrected herself, the *truly* bizarre thing was that Tristan was seeing Eva alone at all with such frequency -- as a junior, they typically would not have as much overlap between classes as they suddenly did, and Tristan knew for a fact that she hadn't seen Eva around Jamestown so much before she'd gotten involved with Beckett. It was all extremely unnerving, and Olivia's warning about Eva bounced around in Tristan's skull.

The whole strange week had put Tristan on edge, so on Friday afternoon, when Beckett unexpectedly approached her at her locker, Tristan nearly jumped out of her skin.

"Sorry," Beckett said, looking slightly surprised by Tristan's reaction. "Didn't mean to startle you."

"It's fine," Tristan replied, putting a hand to her chest. "What's up?"

"I need to go right home after school today."

"Oh OK, no problem. We can meet Monday or something."

"No." Beckett shook his head. "I'm not bailing on you two weeks in a row. Do you want to just meet at my house instead of at the bench today?"

"Your house?"

"Yes, my house," Beckett said, looking exasperated. "To work on our project."

"OK," Tristan agreed, noticing that Beckett was unusually stressed; she didn't want to make things harder on him by enforcing her arbitrary friendship rules that she was barely enforcing these days anyway.

"Great. I'll meet you there." Beckett disappeared without waiting for an answer, and Tristan watched him go, frowning.

"Is it me, or is this week weird?" Olivia asked, appearing beside Tristan. "Is it because the solstice is coming?"

"It is," Tristan replied. "But around here I think it's because winter break is coming. What are you doing here?"

"I was following Eva," Olivia said casually, pointing at Eva, who Tristan had not even noticed go by.

"Olivia!"

"What?" Olivia asked. "I was trying to see if she was stalking you or Beckett."

"Stalking? What are you...? You know what? I have to get to class. I'll see you at home."

Shaking her head, Tristan closed her locker and headed off down the hall, the same way Beckett and Eva had gone. She made it to English class without incident, looking over at Beckett, who was staring absently at the front of the room. His jaw was working, a dark expression on his face, and Tristan hoped he'd tell her at some point what was bothering him.

Tara caught her eye, raising one eyebrow and smirking at her, then slowly shaking her head. Tristan just looked at her before turning her eyes to Ms. West, who entered the room, greeting the class as she pushed a stand with a TV and a DVD player on it ahead of her.

"If I'm interpreting everyone in this school correctly this week, you all have winter break-itis ahead of the start of the break next Wednesday. As an educator, I like to feel like my students are at least a little bit interested in what I'm teaching, and since I am not feeling it from you, I am not feeling teaching you. So there." Ms. West turned the TV on and picked up a DVD case, holding it up. "Since we've been discussing *1984* this year, I thought I'd show you the movie. We'll watch it today and finish it up on Monday or Tuesday. It should really get you in the Christmas spirit."

"That was a joke," Ms. West said wryly, when no one laughed. Shaking her head, she put the DVD into the player and dimmed the lights.

Tristan tried to focus on the movie, but she'd already read the book twice and seen the movie once before, and her head was brimming with thoughts about Beckett, Beckett and Eva, Olivia, school, and, oddly, Celes. Until the most recent gathering, Tristan hadn't felt nervous about the upcoming Solstice Celebration. In fact, she'd never really felt nervous around Celes at all -- mainly, when they weren't interacting as friends, she felt dread about a future with him. She still mostly felt that way, but it had lessened substantially since she'd spoken the truth of her upcoming decision to Olivia and Evander. Tristan was not joining the community, but she also wasn't going to die over it. She'd run if she had to, lay low and cut all ties with her family until it was safe for her to reach out; she'd think of *something* anyway, if that's what it came to, but she was not living the life expected of her and she was not giving up her own life in exchange. This knowledge had empowered her, even though she was terrified of the fallout, but it had also, ironically, made room for the attraction that had suddenly sparked between her and Celes. It was all bad news, and Tristan knew she should entertain none of it, especially not outside of community gatherings, but again, her emotions worked independently of and with no regard for her rational attempts at thought.

The bell rang, rousing her, and Tristan collected her things, deciding to use her free period to clean out her locker. She grabbed a large trash can and dragged it over to her locker, marveling at the junk that had accumulated in the narrow cavity in just three short months. She took her time, fitting tests and quizzes into one folder, loose homework into another. She threw away hall passes and scraps on which she'd written herself notes, random candy wrappers and stray pen caps. When she was satisfied, she put the trash can back where it belonged, deposited her books into her backpack, and headed out to her car. Before she drove to Beckett's house, she looked in the visor mirror, shaking a hand through her lifeless hair and smoothing balm over her dry lips. She looked slightly better, but felt very blah overall about her appearance, which was unlike her.

Tristan was about to pull out of her parking spot when Evander and Olivia approached. She rolled her window down instead.

"I'll be home later. I'm going to Beckett's so we can work on our project."

"Oooh." Evander wiggled his eyebrows, and Tristan made a face at him.

"We know," Olivia said, glancing at Evander. She tried to keep a straight face, failed. "We walked by Beckett explaining to Eva in great detail why she couldn't go home with him today. It legit sounded like he was talking to a pre-schooler."

"Stage five clinger," Evander said, and they both laughed.

"I was still trying to think of how to warn him about her, but she's doing my work for me."

Tristan watched her siblings in mild amusement.

"You guys done?"

"Probably not," Olivia said, still laughing. "We'll see you at home, though."

Smiling and shaking her head, Tristan waved goodbye to them, taking off. She was surprised to see Beckett's car parked out front when she got there -- he hadn't been joking about needing to go right home.

Butterflies in her stomach, Tristan walked up to his door, raising her hand to knock when he pulled it open.

"Come in." Beckett ushered her inside, and Tristan followed him to the kitchen.

She looked around as they walked, the small house sparsely decorated and very dark, all of the curtains drawn. The kitchen, however, was bright and sunny, a pleasing shade of yellow with dated ivory appliances and oak cabinets. Beckett's backpack was tossed onto the long kitchen table, also made of oak, and Tristan set her bag down on one of the matching chairs, sitting beside it. Beckett, who had been looking out the kitchen window, finally turned to face her.

"Should we get started?"

"Sure." Tristan unpacked her bag, pulling out the same materials she'd brought with her to the bench the week before.

Beckett took out his notebooks and opened his laptop, and to his credit he was totally focused, in spite of whatever was going on. Nearly an hour later, they had a rough curriculum outlined, which was more progress than they'd managed to make since they were assigned the project in October.

"This is amazing," Beckett said, scrolling through the document. "You really did hit the resource jackpot with this."

Tristan nodded.

"We might actually finish this by May, at this rate."

Beckett laughed, then sobered as Tristan packed her bag back up.

"Thanks for coming here today. I'm sorry I couldn't meet at school."

"It's OK." Tristan looked at him carefully. "Is everything OK?"

"Everything is--" Beckett turned to look out the window behind him, and then raced to the front of the house, pulling back the curtains on one of the front windows instead. Tristan, more confused than ever, walked over to the kitchen window to see that a car had crept up the street towards the house, but stopped. After a few seconds it peeled away, shooting off down the street with a squeal of its tires.

"I knew it," Beckett muttered, dropping the curtain in disgust. He was still shaking his head when he came back into the kitchen.

Tristan just looked at him, starting to get an idea of what was going on. When he looked up at her, the anguish on his face confirmed.

"I'm sorry," Beckett said.

"Don't be."

"They fight all the time," Beckett told her, shaking his head. His eyes were glassy, and Tristan's heart ached for him. "They have been for almost two years now. I don't know why they won't get a divorce. I know they can't stand each other. But I thought that was as far as it went, until recently. I got this suspicion, you know, that my Dad was doing something he shouldn't be? I got home a couple of times and things in the house looked weird, like they weren't that way when I left in the morning, but who actually pays attention to that kind of thing? Well I do, apparently. He was just about to pull into the driveway with the woman he's cheating on my Mom with."

"I'm so sorry, Beckett." Tristan, not really thinking about anything other than the pain he was in, hugged him.

Beckett's arms came around her immediately, and it was mere seconds later when Tristan became very, very aware that she was in an embrace with Beckett Benson. His body was warm along the length of hers, his shoulders broad, his hug strong. She felt safe, standing there, like they'd weathered storms together before and she knew they'd protect each other if they ever had to do it again. Tristan could feel Beckett's heart beating against her chest, and though she knew she needed to back off immediately, she closed her eyes, committing every feeling she was having to memory. If this was all she would ever get with him, and it probably would be, she was going to remember it until the day she died.

Tristan finally pulled back, putting a foot or so between her and Beckett.

"I'm sorry," Tristan said again, her eyes wide, face flushing.

Beckett shook his head, giving her *the look* again.

"Don't be."

They stared at each other for what felt like an eternity, and Beckett was finally the one to look away. He ran a hand over his hair, and, when he looked at her again, there was regret written all over his face.

"You should probably go. It's not really safe for you to be here."

Tristan looked at him with alarm.

"Not safe? Are you in some kind of danger, Beckett?"

Beckett chuckled to himself.

"No. I mean it's not safe for you and I to be here, alone together."

"Oh." Tristan's eyes widened. *"Oh."*

Beckett looked at her affectionately, and Tristan tried to pretend she wasn't completely out of sorts. She went to move past him, but he moved the same way, and then it happened again when she tried to redirect. Beckett laughed as Tristan squeezed her eyes shut, shaking her head, and he stepped aside, out of her way.

"I'll see you Monday."

"See you Monday."

Tristan practically ran out of his house, and Beckett watched her, wishing he'd done things differently. Wishing he hadn't let her go, or had gone after her, or had done a million things other than telling her she should leave. She'd felt right at home in his arms, and now that she was gone, his body was demanding to know why. Beckett knew that suggesting she go was the right thing to do, but that didn't assuage his regret -- this afternoon had been the first time they'd ever been truly alone together, and he knew that if it had been any of his friends in his position, they would have taken full advantage and dealt with the consequences later. He just couldn't do that to Tristan; he couldn't have her be something he took advantage of and then maybe discarded because he felt guilty about Eva. He also couldn't do that to Eva, who was innocent in whatever storm was brewing between him and Tristan. What Beckett knew he had to do, however, was sort out his head and his heart, and decide between Eva, with whom things were straightforward and uncomplicated, or Tristan, who he felt he was chasing through a maze that had no guaranteed end.

***

Tristan drove home, replaying the scene in Beckett's kitchen. She couldn't believe she had hugged him, had pulled the pin and thrown the grenade right into the middle of every rule she had for herself when it came to socializing with her peers. Worse still, she had liked it. She had more than liked it. She had touched Beckett and it'd felt like she'd come home from a long journey, his arms so familiar that it scared her. Why had he felt so familiar? Tristan was so freaked out that she nearly missed her driveway, jerking the wheel at the last minute. The car bumped over the curb and up the dirt drive, narrowly avoiding one half of the open gates, and she parked beside the house, sitting behind the wheel for a minute to try and get her wits about her.

Apparently she sat there for more than a minute, because there was a tap on her window, and Tristan looked up to find both Olivia and Evander standing silently beside her car like the twins from *The Shining*.

"We took bets on whether or not you made out with Beckett," Evander called to her through the glass. "What's the verdict?"

"You two are so annoying!" Tristan snapped, pushing open the door and them out of her way.

"I'm going with no," Evander said to Olivia, who nodded in agreement.

"Too bad."

"It looks like she agrees."

Tristan let out a growl of frustration and stomped into the house, right up the stairs to her bedroom. Sometimes being given siblings was the worst gift she'd ever received.

CHAPTER 15

Evander dropped Tristan off at Rise and Grind the next morning. He'd decided within the last couple of weeks that he could work around his grounding by dropping Tristan off and picking her up, and Sol and Umbris didn't fight him on it. Tristan didn't mind, either, enjoying the break, though drives to her early shift were not always relaxing, because Evander usually complained about being tired the whole time. Saturday was one of those mornings.

"No one made you drive me," Tristan finally snipped, when Evander had yawned loudly for the third time over the eight minute drive.

"Wake up on the wrong side of the bed this morning?" Evander asked, by way of response, and Tristan ignored him.

"I'm done at one-thirty," Tristan told Evander, when he'd pulled up out front. "Don't be late."

Evander made a face at her, and Tristan got out of the car, entering the shop to find Amos firing up the grill.

"Morning Amos," Tristan called, and Amos greeted her loudly in return. He was deaf in one ear.

Tristan opened up the shop's shutters, propped open the shop door, then turned on machines and restocked supplies before Ellie arrived. Their usual Saturday morning customers trickled in, and Tristan welcomed them, engaging in the small talk that was her least favorite job function. Time flew once Ellie got there, though, the duo falling into the routine that was as smooth as peanut butter for them now, and Tristan was genuinely surprised when it was time for her to go home.

"That shift flew," Tristan said to Ellie, removing her apron, and Ellie nodded.

"Some days do, if we're lucky. Forty-five more minutes for me."

"Good luck. I hope it goes just as quickly."

"Oh, Joe wanted me to ask you if you can pick up some extra shifts these next couple of weeks? Mainly nights and super early mornings. I guess he thinks it's going to get busy because of the holidays. He said to come in if you can and he'll just check your timesheet, you don't need to give him a schedule."

"Sounds good."

Tristan waved to Ellie and exited the shop, getting into the car with Evander.

"Hey."

"Hey. How'd it go?"

"Fine. How's everything at home?"

"Fine."

"Good talk."

Tristan and Evander exchanged a grin and rode home in silence, Evander understanding that Tristan needed to decompress for a little bit after work. When they arrived, Tristan jumped out of the car, hurrying into the house to shower and get ready for the Solstice Celebration that evening. The Celebration was different from the gathering in that it began shortly after sundown and ended shortly after midnight;

Tristan was thankful for this, but it also gave her less time to get ready, seeing as how they had to drive an hour just to get there. To her family's relief, the event was being held at the community's old bayou near New Orleans -- apparently Orion was not up for a party just yet.

When she'd finished in the shower, Tristan went into her room to find a black dress lying flat on her bed. It was short and sleeveless, with a full, lacy skirt, deep v-neck, and, from the waist all the way up the bodice and over the shoulders, it was covered in an intricate fabric feather detailing. The dress was gorgeous, and had to have come from Olivia -- Tristan had laid out a plain black skater dress with three-quarter sleeves and an off-the-shoulder neckline before she'd gotten in the shower.

"I couldn't resist," Olivia said from behind her, and Tristan turned to see Olivia looking like a movie star. She was dressed in a long-sleeved black lace and illusion netted crop top, paired with a high-waisted, floor-length black satin skirt. Her hair was parted on the side and barrel curled, and, as usual, she was rocking a perfectly smoked eye.

"You look amazing. I am going to look ridiculous in this," Tristan said, looking dubiously at the dress. "What's wrong with the dress I had picked out?"

"It was boring. So boring it put me to sleep when I looked at it. I promise you're going to look amazing too. Try it on; if I'm wrong, I'll give you your boring dress back."

Tristan nodded reluctantly.

"I have to blow dry my hair first. I'll let you know when I'm dressed."

Olivia nodded and disappeared, and Tristan closed her bedroom door. She dried her hair and then, deciding it looked blah, swept it over one shoulder and into a loose braid.

She applied mascara and her usual lip balm, hooked a pair of black beaded chandelier earrings into her ears, and once again eyed the black dress with apprehension.

"Here goes nothing."

Tristan shimmied into the dress, the bodice just a tiny bit tighter than she would have preferred. With some effort, she got it zipped, and she stood staring at herself in the mirror before calling in Olivia, who had not been wrong.

"See?" Olivia said, reappearing in Tristan's doorway. "Amazing."

"Where did you even get this?" Tristan asked.

"Some brand sent it to me." Olivia waved her hand. "You know I do those online makeup tutorials? They offered to send me that dress if I'd wear it in one of them. I did, but it's just a little too big on me, so now it's yours."

"It's gorgeous." Tristan could not stop staring at the fabric feathers, and she saw Olivia nod in the mirror. "Thank you."

"You're welcome. Your shoes." Olivia held out a pair of black leather booties with a spiked heel, which Tristan took gratefully.

Evander appeared beside Olivia in a black suit with a black shirt and tie, and the girls complimented him on how dapper he looked. They all went to meet up with their parents downstairs -- Umbris in a tuxedo, Sol in a floor-length, glittering black sheath -- and the five of them got into the car to head to the Celebration.

"Wait!" Olivia cried, as they drove through downtown Lavelle.

"What's the matter?" Umbris asked, hitting the

brakes.

"I forgot my lipstick!"

"Seriously?" Evander asked.

"Oh my gods, Oceana." Tristan rolled her eyes.

"Oceana!" Sol scolded.

"I cannot go to this thing without lipstick. Dad. Please can we stop at the pharmacy real quick? I will be two minutes, tops. I promise."

"Oceana--"

"Dad, please!" Olivia begged, her voice rising.

On a sigh, Umbris steered into the pharmacy parking lot. Makeup was life to Olivia; there was no way out of this one.

"Come on," Olivia said, nudging Tristan's arm, and Tristan made a face at her.

"No thanks."

"Ugh, Trinity, just come with me. I need your opinion! And I gave you that dress, so you owe me!"

Tristan shook her head, blowing out a breath, and got out of the car, Olivia following her. They entered the small pharmacy, sticking out like two black thumbs in their formal wear.

"OK, so this is going to be hard. The selection sucks. Ugh, how could I have forgotten?" Olivia wailed, scanning the racks of makeup, and Tristan shook her head. She couldn't imagine having this kind of meltdown over makeup.

"Oh shut up," Olivia muttered at her, and Tristan smirked.

The bells on the pharmacy door jingled, signaling someone else's arrival, but the girls ignored it. Olivia was in full-on crisis mode, and her stressing was stressing out Tristan.

Beckett headed towards the back of the pharmacy, to where they kept the condoms, when he heard a familiar voice.

"Can't you just pick one? All four of those reds look exactly the same. No, wait, *all* of these reds look exactly the same."

"Oh my gods, Trinity. You're blonde, which means *you* can wear any red. *I* am a redhead, so I can't just pick one!" Beckett heard Olivia snap impatiently, and he smiled to himself.

Mission forgotten, Beckett crept along the back wall, approaching the makeup aisle.

"OK, I think this is the one. Yes. Now give me your face," Olivia said, grabbing at Tristan's face, after she'd put lipstick on herself right there in the store, and Tristan slapped her hands away.

"No!"

"You are really the worst sister. Give me your face!" Olivia grasped Tristan's chin in a grip way too strong for what a petite person she was, and Tristan gave up. "Thank you. You can thank *me* later."

Olivia was applying the red lipstick to Tristan's top lip when Tristan saw Beckett come around the corner into the aisle. She froze, her eyes on him, and he stopped dead in his tracks. Olivia turned, a smile on her face.

"Hi Beckett."

"Hi." Beckett blinked a few times, completely thrown for a loop. "I thought you weren't going to the dance."

"We're not," Olivia replied, though he hadn't been talking to her. "We're going to a family party."

Tristan cleared her throat, making eyes at Olivia, who finished with the lipstick and let go of Tristan's face.

"I'm going to go check out," Olivia chirped, giving Beckett a knowing look as she passed by.

"Hi," Beckett said again, as he approached Tristan, who was rubbing her chin. He couldn't think of anything else to say -- his brain seemed to have frozen over when he saw Tristan in a little black dress that looked like it had been made for her, her legs about twelve miles long in the heels she wore, and he couldn't seem to unfreeze it.

"Hi," Tristan replied, sounding just a little breathless. Her eyes traveled over him, dressed in a navy blue suit with a white shirt and cobalt blue tie. His hair was swept handsomely away from his face and behind his ears, and Tristan wondered if his eyes were more blue than they'd been yesterday.

"You look... wow." Beckett surveyed Tristan from head to toe. "Amazing."

"Thanks," Tristan said, blushing deeply. "So do you."

"I don't." Beckett shook his head, and his eyes crinkled at the corners. "You do."

Though it could not have been more out of character for her, and would certainly end in misery if she did, Tristan found herself desperately wishing she was going to the Jamestown Winter Dance; she understood now how Olivia felt, having to go to the Solstice Celebration instead.

"Done. Ready?" Olivia came back, breaking the spell between Tristan and Beckett.

"Did you get what you needed, Beckett? We can walk up front with you." Olivia asked, and Beckett was sure he saw a mischievous gleam in her eye.

"No, not yet." Beckett gestured vaguely behind him. "You don't have to wait for me."

"If you're sure," Olivia said, grinning. She bumped Tristan with her hip. "Ready?"

"Yes," Tristan replied. She hadn't taken her eyes off of Beckett to that point, but glanced over at Olivia and nodded.

"Have fun at the dance, Beckett. Tell Tyler I said hi."

"I will. He'll be sorry he missed you. Have fun at your party." Beckett inclined his head at both of them.

"Oh, that reminds me, can you take our picture?" Olivia asked.

"O--" Tristan started, but Olivia was already watching as Beckett held out his hand for her phone.

"Ah shoot, I left my phone in the car," Olivia told Beckett, hitting her forehead lightly with the heel of her hand. "Can you use yours and send it to me or us?"

"Of course. Say cheese," Beckett instructed, lifting his phone and smiling, and Olivia and Tristan put their arms around each others waists.

"Done." Beckett took Olivia's number and texted her the photo, lifting his eyes to Tristan when he'd finished.

"You're the best. See you later, Beckett." Olivia smiled at him again, tugging on Tristan's arm.

"See you Monday," Tristan told him, finally finding her voice, and Beckett waved as they left, watching them walk away.

Tristan turned hesitantly at the end of the aisle, looking back at him, and on her face Beckett saw all he needed to see in order to make his decision. He would take Eva to the dance tonight, but he would take her right home afterwards.

***

"Winter is heating up in Lavelle, huh?" Olivia asked, once they were outside, and Tristan glared at her.

"I don't know what you're talking about."

"Sure you don't. You and Beckett were in there smoldering so hard at each other that I'm surprised the whole pharmacy didn't combust."

Tristan groaned.

"You need to let this go."

"You need to stop pretending I don't know, actually literally know, that every time you deny, you lie."

Tristan didn't deign to respond, getting back in the car and turning her head as Umbris pulled out of the parking lot. She wanted to check and see if Beckett had emerged from the pharmacy, but she refused. Olivia was still smirking so much that Tristan was surprised her face didn't get stuck that way, and she would not give her the satisfaction of looking across to her window. Instead, Tristan enjoyed the ride up to their nondescript meeting place near New Orleans, the familiarity a comfort after the tumultuousness of the last few months. The December evening was not nearly as stifling as it usually was, and Tristan unrolled her window, breathing in the sweet, briny air.

The drive went fast, and, as usual, Tristan's nerves sailed into her stomach once they'd arrived at their usual parking spot, which was an extremely narrow dirt road, well off the beaten path, that dead-ended at the water not one hundred yards ahead. The nice thing about this spot was that they were able to walk to the clearing -- once they hit the water, there was a unique, winding wooden bridge they'd follow across the river to the other side of the bayou. Someone had put it there, so someone obviously knew about this isolated spot, but the Elders whose job it was to scope out locations had monitored the site for years on end before giving the green light for everyone to gather in the clearing just a short walk from the bridge's end, and they continued to monitor it to this day.

Tristan could hear music as they approached, and, as they came through the last thicket of trees, Olivia gasped in wonder. The clearing ahead of them had been decorated to the nines -- everything was frosty silver, earthy green, holly berry red, and there was a long train of tables loaded with food. The clearing, of course, had been protected from bugs, wanderers, and the weather alike, and Tristan delighted in the very comfortable temperature they'd chosen.

"Stop."

The family was halted by a photographer dressed in a black turtleneck and black pants, a giant camera hanging around his neck.

"Smile."

They did as told, and the camera flashed blindingly in front of them.

"You can pick up the photo on your way out." The photographer moved out of their way.

Tristan blinked a few times, trying to get the balls of light in her eyes to dissipate. Just ahead of her, Umbris veered away with Sol to greet someone off to their right, and there, in the clearing, stood Celes. He, like Evander and most of the other men at the gathering, wore a black suit, black shirt, and black tie, and he was wearing the hell out of it. It occurred to Tristan that it was not fair to a girl's central nervous system that she should see two such handsome men in two such well-tailored suits in the same evening. His look was edgier than Beckett's had been, of course, but Tristan really appreciated the bad boy vibe he was giving off.

"Trinity." Olivia stepped directly in front of Tristan, who blinked in surprise. "For gods sakes, keep it in your dress tonight. Do you understand me?"

"Oceana!"

"Trinity." Olivia looked at her, her gray eyes completely serious.

"Nothing is going to happen. I am certainly not pulling anything out of my dress," Tristan hissed, noticing that Celes was making his way towards her.

"Don't start anything with him, Trinity. Don't do that to him." Olivia's voice was so quiet she might as well have not even been talking, but her words struck right into the middle of Tristan's heart. Olivia was right.

Nodding to indicate she knew she'd finally gotten through Tristan's thick skull, Olivia stepped out of the way, greeting Celes graciously as he stopped in front of them. Tristan did notice that in spite of her normally aloof nature, even Olivia was appreciating the sight of Celes in his suit.

"Oceana, Trinity. You both look gorgeous."

"Don't we?" Olivia grinned, then picked up her skirt. "I'm going to go find Aurelis Knight. Have you seen her?"

"I think so, back by the fountain." Celes swept his arm across the clearing, and Olivia nodded, taking off with one last knowing look at Tristan. Celes watched her go for a moment before turning back to Tristan.

"The fountain?" Tristan echoed, looking around him to where, sure enough, a massive, intricately carved fountain, made of ice, stood at the opposite end of the clearing. "Huh."

"Do you want to go see it?" Celes asked, and Tristan wondered if his voice had always been so deep.

"Sure."

They began walking, Tristan noticing Celes looking her over as they went.

"It's not like you to not share what you're thinking," Tristan said, glancing up at him.

"I wouldn't share in polite company," Celes replied evenly, and the bottom dropped out of Tristan's stomach. She blushed, a flaw she found herself cursing on a daily basis anymore, and looked away.

"D-Do you have plans for Solstice?" Tristan asked, having a much harder time than usual playing it cool.

"Same as every year," Celes said, nodding. "We go up to Mandeville to be with family. They live right on a bayou and hold the Solstice festivities for us each year. You don't remember?"

"I do," Tristan said. "I just didn't know if you had changed it up this year."

"Have you changed up your plans this year?"

Tristan laughed, shaking her head.

"No, we haven't."

They reached the fountain, and Tristan reached out, touching the smooth surface.

"Incredible."

Celes nodded, but he wasn't looking at the fountain. Tristan was not sure she was going to survive the night this way. She glanced over at Olivia, who was chatting with Aurelis, and Olivia raised both eyebrows at her. Thankfully, Tristan was spared from having to navigate through the next little while when both the Crenshaws and her family approached her and Celes.

"Just think, next year you'll be here as an engaged couple," Thera said, smiling at Tristan and Celes, and Tristan wished she would just fall through a wormhole right then and there. Celes looked at her, and she forced a laugh, hoping the sheer panic she was feeling was not written all over her face.

"Let's get her through graduation first," Sol said, a beatific smile on her face, and Tristan could have wept. "Trinity, Mrs. Odilia was just saying she hasn't seen you in a long time. Celes, you don't mind if I borrow Trinity for a little while, do you?"

"Of course not," Celes said graciously, and Sol put her arm around Tristan's shoulder, guiding her away.

"You do look very beautiful tonight," Sol told her, as they walked. Well, Tristan walked. Sol glided.

"Thanks. So do you."

"It was nice of Oceana to give you that dress, though I heard her using it as leverage over you."

Tristan laughed.

"Is that surprising? It is Oceana we're talking about."

Sol smiled.

"Not surprising, no."

"Mom, about back there--"

"We can talk about it later, Trinity. No need to discuss it now. Just try to enjoy yourself tonight, OK?"

"OK." Tristan remembered Olivia saying that Sol was pretty sure she knew what Tristan was planning for after graduation, and Tristan looked up at her, trying to see for herself if there was any indication of that. Sol, as usual, was the picture of collected grace -- her face revealed nothing.

"Terra." Sol touched Mrs. Odilia's shoulder and Mrs. Odilia turned, her face lighting up when she saw Tristan.

"Trinity!"

Tristan smiled.

"Hi Mrs. Odilia."

"My, you're so grown! I guess you would be, almost eighteen years old! When is your birthday?"

"April twenty-third."

"A Taurus. Yes, of course you are." Mrs. Odilia nodded. "This is a big year coming up for you. How are you feeling?"

"Oh." Tristan stalled for a moment, looking around. "Nervous."

Mrs. Odilia nodded, chuckling.

"We were all nervous once. It'll be OK. The community can be a wonderful, welcoming place."

Tristan laughed weakly, and was grateful when Mrs. Odilia began asking her about school instead. When their conversation ended, Sol and Tristan walked the perimeter back to the fountain, stopping here and there so Sol could chat politely with her acquaintances. They mostly ignored Tristan, which she preferred, and Sol remained unbothered by it as well. Tristan knew her Mom was doing this for her benefit, keeping her occupied but disengaged, and Tristan very slowly felt herself begin to loosen up. She'd turned to look across the clearing when Celes approached her again, holding two drinks.

"Drink?" Celes offered, and Tristan took it gratefully.

She took a sip, then looked at Celes.

"There's no way this is nonalcoholic."

"Did I say it was?" Celes asked mildly, and Tristan laughed.

They finished their drinks and Celes went to get them refills, Tristan promising herself this would be the last one. She was just so tired of feeling so uptight all the time, and the drink, which tasted like the little cinnamon hard candies she'd loved as a kid, was helping loosen her up.

"Do you want to dance?" Celes asked a while later, when the upbeat music had slowed down and the lighting in the clearing turned a moody blue.

"Sure, why not?" Tristan followed Celes into the midst of the other couples on the dance floor.

Celes took Tristan in his arms, bringing her close to him, and, though she tried to ignore facts, it was all very romantic. The song they danced to was one Tristan recognized by George Ezra, incidentally called *Hold My Girl*.

Tristan looked up at Celes, who was looking down at her. She knew he wanted to kiss her, she didn't need any special abilities to figure that one out, and, gods help her, she knew she wouldn't stop him if he tried.

The song ended and the music picked back up, and the spell was broken.

"Do you want to go for a walk?" Celes asked, and Tristan, weak and selfish and a little bit tipsy, nodded.

He led her off the dance floor and through the crowd, passing the ice fountain, against which Evander was leaning, talking to Aeris. He did not see Tristan go by.

Tristan and Celes walked in silence for a bit, until Tristan stopped, nervous.

"We shouldn't go too far."

Celes nodded, standing beside her.

"Can you show me again?" Tristan asked, looking up at him.

Celes smiled down at her briefly, then lifted his chin. Just like he'd done at the gathering a month ago, he flipped the landscape so they were standing among the stars instead of the forest. Tristan looked around, marveling, and looked up at the eerie sight of the forest suspended above their heads.

"I can't even tell it's a mirage," Tristan said, putting her hand out. She trailed her fingers through the air, and Celes caught her hand.

"Celes--"

But he didn't wait to hear what she had to say. He stepped forward, his hands slipping around her waist, and kissed her. Tristan braced herself, not sure what was going to happen, if anything, and... not much happened. It was her first kiss, it couldn't have been in a more romantic setting, but the attraction she'd felt for Celes, that she'd been semi-afraid of because she'd worried it would only grow and consume her, sparked but didn't grow. The spark did not catch. Tristan knew that it most likely would, in time, but also knew she'd never find out. She slid her arms around Celes's neck anyway, figuring she might as well enjoy herself, and Celes pulled her close. There was a spark again, bigger this time, and Tristan pulled away.

The immediately apparent problem with deciding to enjoy herself, in spite of knowing they were going nowhere, was that by ignoring Olivia's warnings and allowing Celes to kiss her, Tristan had misled him, had allowed him to believe there would be more where this one kiss had come from. She saw it on his face when they parted, saw how he looked at her with heat in his eyes, and Tristan knew she'd made a terrible mistake.

"Celes--" But Tristan quieted. She couldn't tell him. Not here; not now.

"We'd better go back," Tristan said finally, and Celes nodded.

He once again raised his chin, then lowered it so the landscape righted itself.

"Thank you for showing me again," Tristan said quietly, and Celes took her hand.

"Any time, Trinity."

They reentered the clearing, and Tristan didn't dare look around for Olivia, not that it mattered. She'd know soon enough.

Tristan and Celes danced a few more times, Tristan resting her cheek on his hard chest, listening to his steady heartbeat and staring absently into the distance. She wondered how the Winter Dance was going at Jamestown, both relieved and sort of disappointed that she'd had no visions of Beckett tonight. She supposed having seen him in person, in his suit, had been vision enough.

Celes kissed her cheek when the Celebration ended, and Tristan smiled at him, saying goodbye. She could feel Olivia fuming beside her, didn't really blame her, but she couldn't bring herself to look at her. Tristan knew what she'd say anyway, and Tristan would deserve every bit of it.

***

"You've got to be kidding me." Eva stared at Beckett in disbelief, her face illuminated by the dashboard lights.

"I'm sorry," Beckett said, and he was.

"I don't understand," Eva said, shaking her head. "Things were fine. What happened?"

Beckett sighed.

"It's not you."

"Oh, the old *it's not you, it's me.* Please, spare me," Eva said disdainfully, crossing her arms over the front of her blue dress. The one she'd matched to the tie she'd bought Beckett.

"It's true. I'm sorry."

"Does this have to do with Tristan Wallace?"

"Nothing happened," Beckett answered honestly, figuring that if he had his way, the cat would be out of the bag very soon anyway. "But yes."

Eva laughed bitterly, shaking her head.

"Oh my God. OK. Good luck with that Beckett. And hey, thanks for completely wasting my time."

"Ev--"

But she was already out of the car, slamming his door and storming up the pathway to her house. Sighing, Beckett pulled away from the curb, driving home. That had gone about as well as he'd expected.

CHAPTER 16

"Good morning." Beckett leaned against the locker beside Tristan's on Monday morning.

She looked over at him, squinting as she stifled a yawn.

"Is it?"

Beckett laughed.

"How was your weekend?"

Tristan shook her head, but she was smiling as she closed her locker.

"It was fine. How was yours?"

"It was interesting."

"Oh? In what way?"

"Well, the DJ's computer went down at the dance, then one of his speakers blew, someone spiked the punch, and Eva and I broke up."

Tristan blinked.

"Wait, what?"

"How was your family party? You were very dressed up, not that I minded."

"Uh, it was fine. It wasn't just family, it was friends of our family too," Tristan replied distractedly. Beckett had broken up with Eva? Why? And was he flirting with her right now, here in the open hallway?

"Did you party hard and that's why you're so tired this morning?" Beckett grinned at her, and Tristan shook her head, trying and failing not to yawn again.

"I worked a double yesterday, and I'm working every night this week. I'm tired just thinking about it."

The bell rang, and Beckett straightened up.

"Walk together to homeroom?"

Tristan eyed him suspiciously, and he laughed.

"I have to go that way too. I can walk a few paces behind you, though, if you'd like."

He and Tristan walked down the hall together, Tristan incredibly self-conscious. They passed Eva, who glared hard at them both, and Tristan glanced at Beckett, who looked untroubled. He waved to Tristan at the door of his classroom, and she waved back, shaking her head as she continued on to her homeroom. Clearly this was going to be another strange week.

***

The next night, Tristan was nearing the end of a late shift she'd picked up at Rise and Grind, working alongside Ellie, when Evander entered the shop.

"Just about ready, sis?" Evander asked, leaning his forearms on the counter.

"Five minutes," Tristan replied, looking at the clock.

"Hi Evander," Ellie said, almost shyly. Tristan looked at her.

"Ellie, right?" Evander asked, and Ellie nodded. "How's it going?"

"It's going OK. Very busy, but OK."

"How's college life treating you?" Evander asked, grinning at her.

Ellie blushed. Wait, *blushed?* Tristan looked between Ellie and Evander, her confusion growing. Were they... *flirting?*

"Well, this semester I'm doing online courses from home; I had to stick around because of a family situation, but I'm hoping to transfer onto LSU's campus next semester."

"I'm going to go..." Tristan gestured to the back, but didn't bother finishing her sentence. Neither Evander nor Ellie were paying attention to her anyway.

Making a face as she headed for the back, Tristan quickly cleaned up the counters and the grill, removed her apron and hat, and clocked out.

"I'll be outside," Tristan said, walking by Evander and Ellie, who once again ignored her.

She left the shop and walked the short distance around the corner to the parking lot.

"Hey," Tristan said, surprised to see Olivia leaning against Evander's car, inspecting her cuticles. "I didn't know you were here."

"Ember made me wait outside." Olivia rolled her eyes. "Don't ask me why."

"He's in there flirting with Ellie." Tristan wrinkled her nose. "It's so bizarre witnessing your sibling flirt."

"Isn't she like eighteen? Why's she bothering with Ember?"

"She's going to be nineteen soon I think," Tristan said.

"Celes will be twenty soon, and he graduated a year before her."

"So weird."

Tristan nodded, leaning on the car next to Olivia.

"Who has two thumbs and a date with Ellie Williams in New Orleans on Sunday?" Evander asked, finally joining Olivia and Tristan beside his car in the empty parking lot, gesturing to himself.

"Yeah right," Tristan snorted, while Olivia said, "What?"

"It's true. I just asked her. I've always liked older women."

"What about Aeris?" Olivia frowned.

"Nothing's happening there," Evander waved his hand. "She's not into me."

"There is no way you're going to New Orleans on Sunday, Ember," Tristan said, looking at him incredulously.

"Why's that?" Evander crossed his arms, looking bored.

"First of all, you're grounded until the new year, remember? And second, even if you weren't, Mom and Dad would never let you go. You're *sixteen*. I know you think you're so much older and wiser than our classmates, but you're not."

"Oh, that's rich coming from you," Evander sneered.

"What is that supposed to mean?" Tristan demanded.

"Judging everyone we go to school with, claiming you can't stand them because they're morons, yet *I'm* the one acting like I think I'm older and wiser than them?"

"No, see, this?" Tristan waved her finger up and down in front of Evander, raising her voice. "*This* is what I can't stand. This parroting what those *morons* say every day, sounding exactly like them. You and Oceana lead totally different lives than I do, Ember, so don't you dare pretend I have no right to judge the people who have made high school hell for me."

"But you take no responsibility for your part in that!" Evander exploded, surprising Tristan and Olivia, and three birds that went flapping and squawking off of a wire above their heads. "They're just kids, Trinity, just like you and me and Oceana! They have power over you because you let them! They're nothing in the grand scheme of what our lives are going to be, or could be, but you let them treat you like they're something!"

"Keep your voice down!" Olivia cried, looking around nervously at the still-empty parking lot.

"You say that, but at the end of the day, those are the people *you've* chosen to be friends with! Don't come at me telling me they mean nothing when you're usually running off to parties with them every weekend! Ugh!" Tristan spun around, starting to walk away, but Evander called after her and she turned back around.

"And again you're judging them, yet you walk around *pining* for Jamestown Academy's very own offensive lineman, who *is* one of them! The hypocrisy never ends with you!"

"Oh, I am so *sick* of this!" Tristan shouted, throwing up her hands. "All year so far you've been needling me and needling me and for the last time, Ember, Beckett is *nothing* to me, he's just my senior project partner! How many times do I have to tell you that? Nothing!"

Evander and Olivia had gone quiet, Tristan realizing too late why Olivia was furiously shaking her head, and from a few feet behind Tristan, a voice spoke.

"Ouch."

Closing her eyes, her stomach dropping into her toes, Tristan slowly turned to see Beckett, who had just come around the corner of Rise and Grind.

"Hi, Wallaces. Pardon the interruption; I didn't realize it was y'all having a shouting match on a public street." Beckett nodded at the trio, clearly trying to look good-natured. He scratched his eyebrow. "Tristan, I came to check if you were still working, but I see your shift is over, so I'll just see you at school tomorrow instead."

"Beckett--"

He left quickly, not stopping when she said his name. Tristan watched him go for a moment before looking at Evander with tears in her eyes. Shaking her head, she took off after Beckett.

"You are *such* an asshole," Olivia said, crossing her arms and glaring at Evander.

"She said it, not me," Evander retorted, but he looked just slightly uncomfortable.

"What is your actual problem, Ember?" Olivia demanded.

"I'm just frustrated! I'm trying to live and enjoy my life, and I'm so tired of being unsettled because *she's* constantly walking around unsettled because she won't just come out and say that--"

"Ember, don't say it. Mom and Dad could be listening," Olivia said sharply, and he rolled his eyes.

"She won't just come out and say what we know she's going to tell us in a few months anyway, and we're *all* suffering for it."

"She's your sister, Ember, and you know what happens when someone makes the decision she's going to make, so maybe you can stop thinking about yourself for one second and act like her brother!"

"Beckett!" Tristan called again, but Beckett, who was walking very swiftly, got into his car, closing the door. He pulled out of the parking spot and drove away, never even looking at her.

Tristan watched him go, burning with embarrassment and regret. *What had she done?* She'd been so annoyed with her siblings and their constant teasing about Beckett that she'd snapped, wanting to convince them once and for all to leave her alone about him. How could she explain that to Beckett without him calling bullshit? She would, in his position.

Tristan, emotion making her stomach churn violently, began walking, leaving Evander and Olivia in the parking lot around the corner. Dusk had fallen and night would too, before she got home, but she didn't care. The evening air was crisp -- Louisiana crisp, anyway -- and Tristan used the long walk to organize her thoughts and plan what she'd say to Beckett at school tomorrow. She was prepared to grovel if she had to; she just needed to fix it.

The long, tree-lined road to her house loomed ahead of her, and Tristan randomly remembered Olivia telling her a while back that she had a bad feeling that something was coming up the pipe. Nothing had ever materialized, thankfully, but Tristan still suddenly felt uneasy, looking over her shoulder and picking up her pace once the sky had turned indigo. A car rolled by slowly, and Tristan recognized it as

Evander's. She hoped he'd keep going, and he did. Good. She wasn't sure when she'd be ready to talk to him again anyway.

Tristan breathed a sigh of relief when she closed the property gate behind her. Trying to shake off her nerves, she walked up to the house, greeting her parents once inside. She chatted with them for a few minutes, half-wondering where Olivia and Evander were, before excusing herself to go shower. Her siblings left her alone for the rest of the night, which was fine with her, though she hoped Olivia knew she wasn't mad at her.

Tristan fell asleep immediately upon getting into bed that night. She slept soundly and could not remember her dreams once she awoke.

CHAPTER 17

On Wednesday morning, Tristan took a deep breath and entered a wing of the Academy she generally tried to stay out of, except to go to class. It was the wing that contained the lockers of Beckett, Emmeline, Tara, Eloise, Jason, and Tyler, and, as she headed to Beckett's locker, where he stood getting his books, people nudged each other and whispered. As usual, Tristan ignored them, noticing with relief that only Eloise was present, not the whole unholy trinity.

"Hi Beckett," Tristan said to his back, and he paused, not turning around.

"I... I wanted to talk to you about last night. I'm sorry, for what you overhead. For what I said." Tristan's voice was quiet, trying to hang onto a shred of privacy. "I--"

"You know how they say drunk people are the most honest?" Beckett asked, interrupting her. He slammed his locker door closed with a bang that had people turning to look at them, and crossed his arms over his chest. "And drunk people say alcohol makes them say things they don't mean, but the reality is they *do* mean them, they just lose the inhibition to keep quiet when they drink?"

Tristan nodded, a puzzled look on her face.

"Well I have this theory that siblings come in a close second to honest drunks. No or low inhibition, so you're more inclined to tell them the truth than you would anyone else."

"That... seems like a reach," Tristan said, frowning. "But--"

"Whoa, whoa, whoa." Jason Dalton chose that moment to approach, interrupting loudly. "Tristan, you're standing a little close to my man Beckett here, looking a little tense. You trying to put a spell on him or something?"

"Go away," Tristan said, giving Jason a nasty look.

"No no," Beckett said, holding up his hand. Jason looked as surprised as Tristan did by that. "He doesn't have to go anywhere. We're walking to class together."

"Look, can you please just meet me at the bench after school, to talk?" Tristan pleaded in a low voice, searching Beckett's face, which was cold and closed off. She was already bright red with embarrassment, but if she could just get him to agree--

"The only business we have worth meeting at the bench for is our project, and since we just met on Friday, it's a little soon," Beckett said flatly. "I know *you* have no social life, so you probably have more material to add after this weekend, but I actually *do* have a life outside of school, and I'm not gonna be ready with more until after break."

Tristan jerked back, stung. Beckett looked like maybe he regretted what he'd said, but at Jason's laughter, his face quickly shifted back into a neutral expression.

"Oh shit son, you just got a one way ticket to voodoo doll town," Jason drawled. "Lookit that face."

Beckett *was* looking at that face, and he hated what he saw. He hated himself for the pain etched into every one of Tristan's features by his words, so much like those his friends hurled at her regularly. But she'd hurt him too, this time, and so while Beckett told himself to back off, that she'd gotten the message loud and clear, he was experiencing the temporary, terrible desire to make her hurt as much as he was.

"This is how it's going to be then?" Tristan asked, gritting her teeth and ignoring Jason again.

"Why would it be any other way? I'm nothing to you and you're nothing to me. We're just project partners. Right?"

"Off you go, freak, before you make us late for class." Jason made a shoo gesture with his hands.

Tristan looked at him and then at Beckett, nodding as she backed up. She felt the backs of her eyes prickling, but she would die before she cried in front of either of them. She turned quickly and, as she did, noticed Tyler watching the scene unfold, his face somber. He looked at Beckett, then back at Tristan like he wanted to say something to her, but Tristan rushed past him, the laughter in the hallway ringing in her ears as she fled.

***

The rest of the day was nearly unbearable. Word had spread quickly about the embarrassment Tristan had made of herself that morning, and it was just juicy enough to chum the waters. A spell of sorts had been broken when she and Beckett had turned their backs on each other, a protection Tristan hadn't realized she'd been under was gone, and even underclassmen were making cutting comments whenever they saw her. Eva Revet, regardless of the fact that she herself had been dumped by Beckett over the weekend, outright laughed in Tristan's face when she'd passed her in the hall. Tristan spent her lunch break in a bathroom stall, crying quietly into a wad of paper towels to muffle the noise.

To their credit, Olivia and Evander had been telling people off left and right, which helped, but not much. Emmeline was gloating like Christmas had come early, and that emboldened the people around her. Beckett steadfastly ignored Tristan for their remaining classes together, though once or twice she could have sworn she saw him glancing over at her during English class, and he'd been conveniently close by when Theo Fitelson had begun leering at her on the way to Chemistry, which he'd stopped immediately upon seeing Beckett.

Tristan could not get out of school fast enough at the end of the day. It was as she rushed to the parking lot, by way of the east side of the building that faced the woods and was not often trafficked, when she was intercepted by Emmeline and her crew. She'd taken that way because it was the quickest route to her car, which Tristan figured Emmeline had guessed she'd do.

"Tristan, you look terrible," Emmeline said in mock surprise, as her friends formed a loose circle around Tristan. "Bad day?"

"What do you want?" Tristan asked through her teeth.

"I heard what happened this morning with Beckett, and I'm going to be honest with you Tristan, I'm scared." Emmeline's green eyes were rounded, her face earnest.

"What?" Tristan frowned.

"I'm scared, for Beckett. I pray for him every night, but I'm scared that my prayers won't be any match for a scorned witch."

"Oh my God with the witch thing again." Tristan laughed humorlessly. "Tell me Emmeline, how is it that I'm a freak and a weirdo and all manner of things because you made up a rumor that I'm a witch, but no one bats an eye about you believing witches exist?"

"Because they do. I see evil in your eyes, Tristan Wallace, it surrounds your whole family like a storm cloud they can't get out from under, and I also know what I saw in the fifth grade." Emmeline stepped closer to her.

"What?" Tristan asked again, her frown returning. "What are you talking about?"

"Class trip to Brentworth Park. You wandered off and I followed you because I wanted to know what you were up to. I saw you parting the flowers as you walked, without touching them, so they jumped right back into place behind you unharmed. *I saw you.*"

"That did not happen," Tristan said, though she was sure it probably had; she hadn't exactly been careful about where she'd practiced her ability back then. "And if the flowers were moving, it was probably on the breeze."

"Liar," Emmeline hissed. "You're an evil force in all of our lives, always have been, and I know Beckett is in danger now that he's gone and rejected you. Well I love him and I also know we're gonna get back together no matter what weird choices he makes this year, so I'm not gonna let anything happen to him, or to anyone in this town, even including your own family."

Emmeline nodded at her friends, who closed in around Tristan.

"What are you doing?" Tristan asked, the hairs on her arms rising.

"Everyone knows every witch has a mark from the devil himself. We're gonna find yours, and we're gonna expose you to everyone for what you really are."

Before Tristan could react, Tara, Hattie, Bailey, Eloise, and Georgiana were on her. They grabbed her arms, yanking off her backpack, and pulled her hair, pinching and slapping her.

"Ow!" Tristan cried, struggling. "Get off of me! Are you crazy?"

"Get her to the ground," Emmeline instructed calmly. "She'll be easier to manage that way."

The group wrestled her down, punching and kicking her, and Tristan thrashed about, yelling. Georgiana and Hattie pinned her arms out to her sides, and Eloise sat on her legs. Tara reached down, ripping open Tristan's blazer and blouse, exposing her bra and her torso.

"Look everywhere," Emmeline commanded, sneering as she watched her friends do her dirty work, her arms crossed neatly over her blazer.

When they began to pull at her skirt, began trying to force her knees apart, Tristan began to scream at the top of her lungs. Georgiana clamped her hand over Tristan's mouth, and Tristan bit her.

"Fucking bitch!" Georgiana yelled, punching Tristan as hard as she could in the face. Pain exploded behind her left eye, and Tristan cried out again.

Tristan looked around desperately as the girls relentlessly kept up their attack, noticing that Eva was slowly passing by. Their eyes met, and Eva *smirked,* deliberately turning her head and continuing on her way. Angrier than she could ever remember being, Tristan thrashed and screamed like a woman possessed, which only made things worse for her.

"HEY!" A nearby voice bellowed ferociously, and the girls looked over to find Beckett tearing towards them. "HEY!"

Beckett plunged right into the middle of them, causing them to scatter away from Tristan, who he immediately pulled to her feet, closing her blazer with one hand. He brought her to him and held her fast against his chest, her face buried in the crook of his neck. She was shaking like a leaf, scratched and muddy and red in the face, and she clung to him like a life raft.

"What the fuck? What the *fuck?*" Beckett's eyes were wild as he yelled the only thing he could manage at Emmeline, who, after a moment, bolted, leaving her friends to fend for themselves. The girls, however, were hot on her trail, disappearing within seconds.

"Tristan!" Olivia was dashing across campus to Beckett and Tristan, and Evander caught up to her easily. "Oh my God, Tristan!"

"I've got you," Beckett murmured, holding Tristan tighter as she began to sob. He pressed his lips to her temple. "I'm so sorry, Tristan. I'm so sorry for all of this. I've got you now."

"Get away from her!" Olivia screeched, her eyes like fire as she pointed at Beckett. Evander looked like he was ready to kill, and Beckett figured he probably could in that moment, they both probably could, but still Beckett couldn't bring himself to let Tristan go.

"I didn't, it wasn't me, I--"

"Bullshit it wasn't you!" Olivia gently pulled Tristan away from him, passing her off to Evander, but she was almost vibrating with anger as she shrieked at Beckett. "You threw her to the wolves this morning, all because your *ego* was bruised! You're just as responsible for this!"

Evander swept Tristan away while Olivia shielded them, and Beckett looked after them, desperately wanting, no, *needing* to see Tristan's face. To know she'd be OK. To know they hadn't broken her. He took a step forward.

"Don't look at her!" Olivia, still yelling, stepped closer to him, blocking his view. For someone so much smaller than him, she sure could be awfully intimidating. "Don't think about her, don't talk to her, don't even *dream* about her! We thought you were good, but you're just as rotten as the rest of them! All of you can go straight to hell!"

"Olivia--" Beckett's voice broke, but Olivia wasn't going to hear it. She spun on her heel and sprinted to catch up with her siblings, putting her arm around Tristan when she had.

Beckett watched them go, his heart racing painfully. He was out of breath and shaking, everything having happened so quickly. One minute he'd been clear on the other side of the building, getting ready to go home, and the next he'd heard Tristan screaming like she was right there in the hallway with him. He'd run then, unsure where she was and how he even knew it was her, but in no time he'd rounded the corner to see her being attacked while Emmeline watched. There hadn't been a thought in his head other than to help her, and his body ached where he'd cradled her now that she was gone.

The most painful part, however, was that Olivia had been right; Beckett was just as culpable as Emmeline and her crew. His bruised ego had clouded over everything, creating a dangerous path for Tristan to walk amongst their class-mates. The popular crowd didn't take kindly to one of their own being hurt, but more than that they lived to go for the jugular -- these two things combined created a perfect storm that Tristan had never seen coming.

Beckett knew what he had to do. Picking up Tristan's dis-carded backpack, he went up to the school and to the Dean's office, where he dropped off the bag and reported what had happened. Dean LeFebvre, looking deeply disturbed, thanked Beckett, letting him know that she would handle the situation. Before he'd even left the office, the Dean was on the phone with the school's video monitoring service, advising she needed the afternoon's footage pulled.

***

Olivia sat in the back of Evander's car with Tristan for the ride home. She kept her arm around her battered sister, who rested her head on Olivia's shoulder, unnervingly silent. Evander kept looking at them in the rearview mirror, visibly shaken, which was new for him.

Olivia couldn't believe she and Evander had been too late. By the time Tristan's distress call had come through, and they had summoned into their minds what'd happened as they ran across campus, Emmeline and her friends were already running every which way through the school's parking lot, Eva was nowhere to be found, and Beckett had Tristan in his arms like he was some kind of hero and not the catalyst for the whole attack. Not hearing her in time to intervene was proof, Olivia realized, that Tristan really was separating from the community. By the time she made the official decision, Olivia and Evander, along with Sol and Umbris, wouldn't be able to hear her at all.

Tears welled up in her eyes, and Olivia quickly brushed them away. Evander pulled up to the house and jumped out of the car, opening Tristan's door and helping her out. Before Olivia had exited, Sol and Umbris were by Tristan's side, guiding her into the house.

Olivia and Evander watched them go, and Olivia already knew what she was going to do. Using their abilities at school was a major no, but Emmeline and her cowardly friends had chosen to attack Tristan right before school closed down for two weeks. Using their abilities in Lavelle was ill-advised, but not forbidden, and so the girls were now fair game.

"We're responsible too, you know?" Evander's voice was tight as he responded aloud to Olivia's thoughts. "We're not best friends with Emmeline and hers, but we run with them. We're all to blame for this."

He walked away, and Olivia watched him go, knowing he was right. It had been easy to pin everything on Beckett because he'd been there, but the uncomfortable truth was that Olivia and Evander themselves had turned a blind eye and ear many, many times so they could climb socially, all at Tristan's expense.

Tristan accepted a bag of ice from Umbris and let Sol walk her upstairs, but Tristan insisted she be left alone once they'd reached her bedroom doorway. She shut her door, walking over to her full-length mirror to look at herself.

She and her uniform were muddy from head to toe, and her hair was a rat's nest. Her left eye was swelling up while a bruise was blossoming across her right cheek, her bottom lip was bloody, and scratches covered her legs and torso. Her blouse and blazer hung open, most of the buttons missing on both. Her entire body ached, but the physical pain was the only thing she felt as she stared at her reflection. Her emotions had fled, and she was numb.

Tristan turned away, undressing and wrapping herself in her thick, fluffy pink robe. She headed down the hall to shower, standing under the too-hot water until her skin had gone as numb as her insides. When finished, she carefully combed the knots out of her hair, then walked meticulously through her skincare routine -- exfoliant, toner, serum, moisturizer. Tristan found that doing things step-by-step helped her focus; she kept getting overwhelmed to the point of breathlessness otherwise.

She went back to her room and took a few painkillers, then dressed in a pair of leggings and her softest, long-sleeved t-shirt. She laid on her bed, staring unseeingly at the mobile above her head. Some time later a soft knock sounded on her door, and Tristan looked over at it, but said nothing. Her voice had apparently gone on vacation with her emotions.

"Trinity?" Sol poked her head in the room. "Can I come in? I won't stay long."

Tristan nodded, and Sol entered, perching beside her on the bed.

"Your father and I have a meeting tomorrow morning with Dean LeFebvre, Mr. and Mrs. Strandquest, Mr. and Mrs. Benson, and the chief of police. It's at eleven A.M. I don't want to pressure you in any way, but if you're up to it, I'd like to hear what happened before we go. I don't want to intrude by fetching the memory myself, but if that would be easier for you, I will."

Tristan closed her eyes, placing her hand over Sol's and un-sealing. It would be easier this way. Sol took a deep breath, and Tristan felt Sol enter her thoughts. Beginning with what Beckett had overheard the night before, Tristan guided Sol through the events as they'd unfolded. When she'd finished, Tristan opened tear-filled eyes, staring up at the ceiling.

"Justice will be served," Sol said, standing. Her face was ashen, but her voice was rock hard. "Rest now. We'll take care of this."

Tristan listened to the soft click of her bedroom door closing, and Sol's footsteps fading down the hall. Vaguely, she could hear Evander's TV, and Tristan rolled off of her bed, going to open her window.

She laid back down, much more interested in letting nature

occupy her ears than the mostly pressing silence of her own bedroom or the tinny sounds of a sitcom.

After a long while, when the sun had started to set, Tristan heard the doorbell ring. Umbris called up for Olivia, and Tristan heard her go by, pausing just slightly at Tristan's door before continuing downstairs.

Several minutes later, Tristan heard voices in the backyard. Olivia's, and someone else's -- a male? She told herself not to snoop, but she wasn't good at listening to herself, especially when her defenses were down.

Tristan crept to her window seat, sitting down gingerly behind one of the opened curtain panels, out of view from the yard below.

"How is she doing?"

"How do you think she's doing?"

"Right. Dumb question."

"What are you doing here, Tyler?" Olivia asked, her voice tired.

"I just wanted to check on you, and Tristan."

Olivia laughed. "Check on Tristan, right, because you've ever spoken to her. Well, we're all just great. Real great. You can go now."

"Why are you mad at me, O?"

"I'm mad at everyone!" Olivia's voice shook. "Myself and Evander included. We all have a hand in what happened to Tristan; can you imagine how that feels as her sister? I'm done, Tyler. With everyone. I'm out. No popularity in the world is worth even a fraction of this, and it's *definitely* not worth my loyalty to my sister."

What happened to Tristan. It had already become *what happened to Tristan,* which Tristan hated. She hated that she'd been targeted, hated that she'd been overpowered, hated that she'd lost control.

"No, I can't imagine how that feels," Tyler said quietly. "I'm sorry. And I know you're right about all of us being responsible for this, and I'm sorry for that too. I saw what went down between her and Beckett this morning, and I was going to say something and... I didn't. I don't know why."

"Do you feel better having confessed that?" Olivia asked icily.

"No, I don't. I don't feel good about any of this. Olivia..."

There were a few moments of silence.

Then, "O, you know I've been backing away from everyone since the beginning of the year, just slowly backing off because I finally realized that I'm part of this groupthink that high school is the be all end all when it's not. I graduate this year, and I don't want to spend it clinging to my Jamestown roots. I want to spend it like I'll be out of there come June and the whole world will be at my feet."

"Why are you telling me this?"

"Because you helped me realize all of this. You've always had this cool, just passing through vibe, and you walk the walk. You say you're done with everyone now, and I believe that. I just... I want to be part of what's next for you, and I want you to be part of what's next for me."

"Tyler--"

"I know we've joked about our crushes on each other through the years, O, but I'm not joking anymore."

"Tyler, please don't do this. Please just go. I can't--"

"Don't be done with me. I take responsibility for the role I've played in Tristan's exclusion, and I'm bound to fuck up again, but if you're done with everyone, I'm done too. And I know Beck is, too. He's all broken up over what happened to Tristan, feels like he's solely responsible."

"You need to go. Do not talk to me about Beckett Benson."

"But Olivia, me and Beck, we're the same. We've both been pulling away from the group because we feel like we can finally see what you see, and what Tristan has always seen. Hell, he broke up with Eva because of Tristan. We made mistakes, we will make mistakes, but we are trying. We just want to be good enough for you and Tristan."

"Well, you're not."

Olivia's words crashed through the quiet evening like an anvil, and Tristan grimaced, closing her eyes. She had long suspected how Olivia felt about Tyler, and Tristan didn't want her giving up on him for her benefit.

"Please go home."

Tyler said nothing, and before long, Tristan heard the back door close. She walked across her bedroom, Tyler's words echoing in her ears, her mind reeling. *Beck and I are the same. He broke up with Eva because of Tristan. We just want to be good enough for you and Tristan.*

Tristan opened her door as Olivia was coming up the hallway, her eyes red-rimmed. She looked up in surprise, trying in vain to put on a happy face.

"Trinity, hey. You OK?"

"Yeah, I just... Did you want to come in?"

"Oh." Olivia glanced down the hall, clearly trying to compose herself. She sniffled. "Oh, no thank you. I uh, I'm really tired, so I was going to go to bed. But if you need me or you need something, just tell me and I'll stay up."

"No," Tristan shook her head quickly, her voice reassuring. "I don't need anything, I'm fine. I'll see you in the morning."

Olivia nodded, continuing down the hall, and Tristan felt a pang of sorrow. Olivia tried so hard to be there for everyone, and almost always succeeded -- was Tristan failing her by not being there for her right now?

"O, are you sure you're OK?" Tristan called after her. "If you need to talk..."

"I'm fine," Olivia said, without turning around. She opened her bedroom door, sniffling again, and her voice wobbled when she spoke. "Goodnight Trinity."

CHAPTER 18

Tristan spent most of the night lying awake. Sometime around one A.M. her emotions had returned, and she'd had a panic attack that had culminated in an ugly cry into her pillow that she thought would never end. She'd fallen asleep for a couple of hours after that, just to jerk awake again.

Tristan felt hollow, and, for better or for worse, she couldn't stop thinking about Beckett. Yes, he'd hurt her feelings yesterday morning, after she'd hurt his the night before, but it had been his friends who had chosen to take his dismissal of her as their cue to run wild. It had been Emmeline and her minions who had chosen to attack her, something Tristan was sure had not just been planned that day, and it had been Eva who had seen what was happening and done nothing. It had been Beckett, while clearly smarting, who'd intercepted Theo in the hall, who'd surreptitiously checked on her in English class, who had come to her rescue for the second time in less than two months, had held her tightly and made her feel safe until Olivia and Evander had arrived.

Tristan must have fallen asleep again, because her alarm, which she'd forgotten to disable for break, startled her awake at six-thirty. She reset it for nine and went back to sleep, and when it went off again, she got out of bed, her mind made up.

After she'd gotten dressed, Tristan swept both sides of her hair back, securing them with bobby pins, and looked at her bruised face in the mirror; it had gotten so much worse overnight, she had a hard time not immediately turning away from her reflection. Instead, Tristan's mouth set in a determined line, and the usual fire flared back to life in her eyes. Her body was stiff and sore, and her emotions felt as fragile as a dandelion, but Tristan gave the mirror a firm nod and went down to the dining room, where Umbris and Sol were having breakfast.

"Trinity," Sol said, putting her coffee cup down and taking in Tristan's skinny jeans and blush colored sweater. "You look great, but where are you going?"

"To the meeting with you." Tristan sat down, and Ruby brought her out a breakfast plate. Tristan thanked her, and Ruby stroked her cheek, looking regretful, before disappearing back into the kitchen.

"I'm not sure that's a good idea," Umbris mused, and Tristan leveled a look at him.

"There is no doubt in my mind that Emmeline will be there with her parents, weeping like she's the victim, so I'm going. I am not letting her rewrite history for her own benefit this time."

Umbris raised his eyebrows and, after a few beats, nodded.

"OK. Fair point."

"Trinity, honey, are you sure you're up to this?" Sol asked, surveying Tristan shrewdly.

"Positive."

Tristan finished her eggs, finished her orange juice, and stood, toast in hand.

"I'm going to go sit on the front porch."

And then she was gone, leaving Umbris and Sol to regard each other in astonishment.

***

"Hey." Evander greeted Tristan tentatively, coming out onto the porch and sitting beside her on the top step.

"Hey."

"Mom and Dad said you're going to their meeting."

Tristan nodded. "I am."

"Good for you."

They sat in silence for a while.

"I'm sorry you're frustrated that my being unsettled is unsettling the whole house. You're right that it isn't fair."

"Did Oceana tell you I said that?" Evander looked surprised, but Tristan shook her head.

"I heard you."

"Was I still yelling?" Evander frowned.

"I don't know," Tristan said, and she didn't. She'd been focused on Beckett, but still able to hear Evander clearly.

"I'm sorry I yelled at you," Evander said, after a pause. "That wasn't fair of me. And really, I'm not that unsettled because of you. It's nothing compared to how you must be feeling, and will be feeling for a while."

"I appreciate it." Tristan gave him a small smile.

Umbris and Sol came outside, and Evander and Tristan stood.

"Give 'em hell," Evander said, and Tristan smiled wider, nodding.

The nerves didn't hit Tristan until Umbris steered the SUV

into the Academy's parking lot. She took a few deep breaths, closing her eyes; she could do this.

"We're right here with you," Umbris said, meeting her eyes in the rearview mirror, and Tristan nodded.

They walked into the silent school, turning left at the end of the hallway to find a small group standing outside of Dean LeFebvre's office. Tristan's stomach swooped -- in addition to the parents and who Tristan assumed was the chief of police, Emmeline had indeed shown up, already crying, but so had Beckett. His gaze hit hers head-on, and Tristan's breath hitched just a little bit. Relief flooded his features as he looked at her, followed immediately by a mix of anger and sorrow, and even Emmeline took a break from making pathetic noises into her tissue to stare at Tristan, who once again cursed her lack of mind reading abilities.

The trio joined the group, and Dean LeFebvre pulled open her office door, stopping short.

"OK, I guess we're doing this in the teacher's lounge. Give me a moment."

Dean LeFebvre disappeared back into her office, reemerging moments later with a stack of files and her laptop.

"Follow me."

They walked the short distance in silence, Umbris and Sol placing themselves between Tristan and the others, their iciness rolling off of them in waves. The other adults, and Emmeline and Beckett, looked uncomfortable, and Tristan knew they were picking up on it too. She was pretty sure one would have to be dead to not be able to pick up on it.

Everyone entered the teacher's lounge, a soaring, lushly decorated room with a squishy patterned carpet in hues of rich blue, marigold, and burgundy, a wall of stained glass windows, and many pieces of comfortable-looking furniture. Dean LeFebvre led them to a long couch, in front of which sat a mahogany trunk-style coffee table, behind which sat a love seat and an armchair. Everyone sat, and, after a brief surveillance of Tristan's face, the Dean began the meeting.

Tristan looked over at Emmeline, seated just a foot away from her, who was blatantly refusing to look back at her. Figured. Her eyes moved next to Beckett, seated diagonally across from her, who was staring at her. Also figured. She stared back at him, and his eyes traveled over her face once again, his expression pained. Tristan wasn't sure where she stood with him at the moment, but she observed that he at least appeared to feel as badly as Tyler had claimed -- in fact, he looked like he hadn't slept a wink the night before, dark shadows haunting his eye area. That made two of them.

"Mr. and Mrs. Wallace, Mr. and Mrs. Benson, Mr. and Mrs. Strandquest, thank you for joining me here this morning," Dean LeFebvre finally spoke, her face grave. "With us is Chief of Police Randall Bordelon, and today we'll be discussing the actions taken against Tristan Wallace by several of her classmates, under the direction of Emmeline Strandquest, and the consequences that will follow. Chief Bordelon is here in the event you would like to press charges, Mr. and Mrs. Wallace and Tristan.

"Yesterday afternoon, it was reported to me by Beckett here that Tristan had been attacked on school grounds. Everyone was gone by then, but Jamestown Academy has cameras in multiple places on campus, including on the side of the building where the attack took place."

Tristan looked at Beckett, surprised to hear he'd been the one to report to the Dean. He looked back at her for a moment before his eyes flickered to Emmeline, who was glowering at him.

"Before we view the video, which I will warn you is hard to watch, I'd like to hear from you, Tristan, or one of your parents if you'd prefer, your version of events."

All eyes turned to Tristan, and she swallowed nervously. Sol put her hand over Tristan's, which Tristan knew was an inquiry, and she shook her head slightly. Tristan cleared her throat and, starting from running into Emmeline and the other girls outside of school, described what had happened. She avoided looking at Beckett, feeling an embarrassment she knew she shouldn't feel, and instead mostly kept her eyes on Devin Strandquest, who was scrolling through his phone.

"Emmeline, anything to add?" Dean LeFebvre asked, and, to Tristan's utter shock, Emmeline shook her head.

"Do you agree with Tristan's version of events?"

"Yes ma'am."

Tristan gaped at Emmeline, who still wouldn't look at her. In fact, she seemed to not really be looking at anything, upon closer inspection, her eyes glassy. Tristan looked at Umbris and Sol, whose faces were perfectly neutral, and then over to Beckett, who looked like he was ready to burn the world down.

"Excuse me, this is ridiculous," Victoria Strandquest spoke up, sitting forward.

Dean LeFebvre looked at her.

"I'm sorry?"

"You heard her." Victoria inclined her head at Tristan, but kept her eyes on the Dean. "Emmeline didn't do anything but stand there. Certainly those other girls should be in here answering to the Chief of Police -- which is excessive, by the way, I'm sorry to be the one to point out -- instead of my daughter."

"I did hear Tristan," Dean LeFebvre said, looking at Victoria with distaste. "I heard her explain how Emmeline directed the attack, and I heard your daughter agree with Tristan."

"OK, so what do we need to do?" Devin asked, finally looking up. His expression was mildly irritated, and he checked his watch. "How much do we need to donate to the Academy to make this go away?"

Tristan's eyebrows shot up along with almost everyone else's.

"To cover all of our bases," Dean LeFebvre ignored Devin's question, "I'm going to play the video of the attack now for you. Any questions can please be reserved for afterwards. Mr. and Mrs. Benson, thank you for coming in, and I apologize for inconveniencing you for such a short amount of time. I just wanted you to be aware of what is happening, and to commend Beckett for coming to me immediately once he saw Tristan was safe in the care of her siblings. You can stay, or you may go now, whichever you prefer."

Raymond stood, but Gabriella Benson stayed seated. She looked up at Raymond incredulously.

"What?" Raymond snapped, and Tristan looked at Beckett, who was looking at the floor.

"You want to leave?"

"You want to stay? You don't trust the Dean's word that we're done here? I don't want to see Tristan being attacked, do you?"

Gabriella's face turned red, and Tristan looked away, up at the stained glass windows. She wished desperately that she hadn't witnessed any of that, realizing that if this was how the Bensons acted towards each other in public, she could only imagine how they acted towards each other in private.

"Thank you, Dean LeFebvre," Raymond said, holding out his hand, which the Dean shook reluctantly. "We're very proud of Beckett, and appreciate you looping us in."

"Thank you again for coming."

"Tristan, hang in there," Raymond said, and Tristan thanked him, caught off-guard. She watched as Beckett stood, following his parents out of the lounge, a miserable expression on his face. Tristan willed him to turn around, and, when he reached the door, he did just that. Tristan held up a finger, then ran it into her hair as though she was scratching an itch in an attempt to be inconspicuous, and Beckett nodded.

Dean LeFebvre turned the laptop at an angle everyone could see, and hit play. Tristan chose not to watch -- she'd lived it, had been reliving it, and didn't need to see it captured on film to remember how everything had gone down.

When the video finished playing, you could hear a pin drop in the room. Dean LeFebvre looked horrified, though she'd already seen the footage, and Chief Bordelon looked disgusted. The icy vibe Sol and Umbris had been throwing had rapidly changed to pure, red hot anger, and while Victoria had opened her mouth to say something that was probably going to be flippant, she glanced at the Wallaces and thought better of it.

Emmeline was back to weeping quietly into her tissue, but everyone ignored her.

"Mr. and Mrs. Wallace, Tristan, if you would like to press charges, Chief Bordelon will be happy to assist."

"Now I don't think that will be necessary," Devin spoke up, holding out his hand. "Emmeline made a mistake. She dared her friends to do something stupid while they had Tristan surrounded, and they did it. It's not her fault they listened to her. And if you ask me, that girl who walked by and smiled should be the one getting charges pressed against her!"

"Dared?" Sol repeated, her voice scarily quiet. *"Dared?"*

All eyes on Emmeline.

"It was planned," Emmeline said in a small voice, not looking at anyone. "We'd been planning it for weeks."

"Emmeline!" Victoria snapped, and Emmeline looked at her helplessly.

"I don't want to press charges," Tristan spoke up, carefully rubbing her dry eyes with two fingers. "I agree that isn't necessary."

Emmeline finally looked at her, fear on her face, and Tristan looked away.

"Mr. and Mrs. Wallace? As Tristan is still a minor, you are able to press charges if you wish."

"We respect Tristan's decision," Umbris said on a nod.

"Very well. Chief, thank you for being here today. I appreciate your time."

The Chief bid everyone goodbye, leaving Dean LeFebvre to it.

"Emmeline, as you know, Jamestown Academy has a zero tolerance policy in place for bullying, and in place for violence, both of which you've violated."

"She only violated one!" Devin protested, and the Dean quieted him with a look.

"I wasn't bullying her!" Emmeline cried. "I was look-ing for proof, to show everyone once and for all that what I've been saying all these years is true. She's a witch, and this town is in danger as long as she lives here! And I wasn't even going to do it yesterday, but that Eva Revet somehow knew about the plan and followed Tristan until she saw she was alone, and then she told me to do it in the name of the Lord!"

"Here we go," Tristan muttered.

"A... witch?" Umbris frowned, looking from Emme-line to her parents.

"Tristan can do things, supernatural things, I've seen it with my own eyes! I saw her do it more than once when we were kids, and I haven't seen her do anything in recent years but that's probably because she got smart about hiding it! I have to go home and pray every single night after school just to get rid of the chill she gives me in my bones."

Victoria gathered Emmeline to her chest, looking at the Wallaces in horror.

"She's insane," Tristan said, and Sol bumped her knee.

"I'm not! Something even happened to me right here in this office! I didn't say those things about planning her at-tack of my own free will, I was forced to say them!"

"Ms. Strandquest, that is quite enough!" Dean LeFeb-vre raised her voice, and everyone quieted down. She pinched the bridge of her nose, then took a deep, calming breath. "As it's your senior year, I believe expulsion would be a punishment that borders on cruel, though make no mis-take that it would be a punishment that fits the crime. In-stead, you will be serving a one-month out of school suspension, effective the day you are to return from winter break. Mr. and Mrs. Strandquest, Emmeline, if you'll stay once I advise the Wallaces they may go, we will work out the details privately."

"Oh this is ridiculous! A suspension will still go on her permanent record!" Mr. Strandquest yelled, throwing up his hands, but Dean LeFebvre continued to ignore his ranting.

"Additionally, before Emmeline may return to school, she must complete four consecutive weeks of outpatient counseling services. This is crucial to her return to Jamestown Academy, and no amount of arguing, or money, will change this. This is not the first report I've gotten of Emmeline's radical religious claims, and I believe she will benefit from a thorough evaluation. It wouldn't be the first time we've had a student crack under the pressures of their senior year."

"Crack under-- now that is not your call to make! You have gone too far now!" Devin spluttered, standing and pointing right in Dean LeFebvre's face. "My daughter does not need therapy. She is a devoted servant of our Lord and Savior Jesus Christ, and if she says she has seen and felt evil, I believe she has seen and felt evil!"

Devin pointed to Tristan, who merely raised her eyebrows as Umbris slowly rose to his feet.

"I'll ask you once, Devin, and there will be no asking a second time. Leave my daughter out of this; she has been through enough at the hands of your family and your beliefs. If for some reason you choose not to, I'll be more than happy to meet you at the Lavelle police station after this so we can get started on pressing those charges."

"We're leaving," Devin said, spinning to face his family. "Let's go, now."

"If you go, you'll have to come back," Dean LeFebvre said, also standing. "If you refuse to come back to meet and go over the details of Emmeline's suspension, I will be forced to push through an expulsion in its place."

Tristan thought Devin might explode. Meanwhile, Emmeline was crying noisily into Victoria's chest, and Victoria had her eyes closed tightly, praying in a low voice. Tristan couldn't believe the gall of any of them. They were outraged over the idea of a suspension going on Emmeline's record, but nothing else? Their blatant refusal to see that Emmeline had brought this on herself, had created her own problem that she was not getting out of so easily this time, was mind-boggling, but also explained a lot about who Emmeline was as a person.

"Mr. and Mrs. Wallace, Tristan," Dean LeFebvre turned to them. "You can go. I will have the other girls and their families in over the next couple of days to discuss their consequences. Thank you so much for coming in today. Tristan, once again, I am so incredibly sorry you've had to go through this."

"Thank you," Tristan said genuinely.

"Oh, before you go, your backpack is in my office. Beckett brought it up to the school yesterday afternoon. Let me grab that for you."

Tristan and Sol stood with their backs to the Strandquests, while Umbris kept his eye on them. Dean LeFebvre returned shortly, handing Tristan her gray and white bag, and Tristan slipped the gray leather straps over her shoulders, thanking her once again.

The three of them left the lounge, Tristan exiting first. At the far end of the hall, she could have sworn she saw a flash of copper disappear around the corner, but it happened so fast she couldn't be sure. Besides, Tristan was distracted by her disappointment of the empty halls -- Beckett had not waited after all.

"Are you OK?" Sol asked, as they walked back to the Academy's entrance.

"Yes. That was strange though, wasn't it?"

"Hmm." Sol seemed to agree, but said nothing more.

They stepped out into the afternoon sun, and there was Beckett, leaning against one of the large concrete blocks flanking the Academy's steps. He looked up as they approached, then straightened up when he noticed Sol and Umbris looking at him.

"Beckett," Umbris said, coming to a stop in front of him, and Tristan looked at her Dad, her heart starting to race. What was he doing?

"Mr. Wallace, Mrs. Wallace," Beckett greeted.

"We owe you for stepping in on behalf of Tristan yesterday," Umbris said, holding out his hand, and all Tristan could think about was how weird it was to hear him call her Tristan. "We will not soon forget your kindness."

Beckett shook Umbris's hand.

"It was the least I could do, sir."

"I'll be right there," Tristan told her parents, inclining her head towards the parking lot. They nodded and walked off, talking quietly to each other.

Tristan looked at Beckett.

"Thanks for waiting. I didn't think it would take that much longer."

"It was fine. I didn't mind." Beckett hesitated, and

when he spoke again, his voice was tender. "How are you?"

"I'll be OK. Thank you, for yesterday," Tristan said, her eyes searching his. Her gaze dropped to his throat as he swallowed, nodding, but roamed back up over his face. She wanted to live in the way he was looking at her. "I owe you, too."

"No," Beckett said fiercely, shaking his head. "No, you don't, Tristan. Don't ever think you owe me anything."

Tristan looked to her right, seeing Umbris and Sol watching her and Beckett from where they stood, beside the school's fountain.

"I guess I should go." Tristan scrunched her mouth to one side. "Do you want to stop by later? Maybe we can talk."

"Yes," Beckett said immediately, his shoulders sagging with relief. "I would like that. What time?"

"Any time. I'll be there."

Beckett nodded, and Tristan gave him a small smile, walking off to join her parents.

"So which one of you got to Emmeline?" Tristan asked, once they were in the car.

"What do you mean?" Sol twisted around in her seat to look at Tristan.

"Oh come on. You know she wasn't lying about being forced to confess."

"It wasn't us, honey," Sol said, shaking her head. "I thought she was acting."

"I did too," Umbris agreed.

Tristan sat back in her seat. She knew Sol and Umbris wouldn't lie to her, so what was going on?

"So Beckett is coming over later?" Sol asked lightly, and Tristan groaned.

"Really guys? Eavesdropping?" Tristan looked out the window, a smile on her face. She was almost always grateful for her parents, almost always annoyed by their overstepping, but this morning was different. This morning, everything had changed.

***

Beckett showed up a few hours later, and Tristan stepped out onto the porch, pulling the door closed behind her.

"Hi."

"Hi." Beckett smiled at her, and Tristan smiled back, wrapping her arms around herself.

"Do you want to walk?"

"Sure. Lead the way."

Tristan nodded, and they set off around the house to cut through the backyard. As they came around, they ran into Olivia, who was lying in the grass. She bolted upright.

"What are *you* doing here?" Olivia asked Beckett, a storm cloud passing over her face.

"I invited him. It's OK, O," Tristan said, her voice even.

Olivia looked at Tristan with a mixed expression and then, eyeing Beckett one more time, flopped back onto the grass, looking up at the sky and ignoring them both.

"She's really angry with me," Beckett commented, once they'd gotten a good distance away.

"She's angry with everyone right now, herself and Evander included."

"I know how she feels."

Tristan said nothing. She and Beckett entered the woods at the back of the property, which provided much-needed shade. Tristan pulled a tiny bottle of bug spray out of her pocket and quickly sprayed the air in front of them, so they passed right through the chemical cloud.

"The bugs can get bad back here," Tristan explained needlessly, and Beckett smiled.

"Thanks for looking out for us."

They walked in silence for a bit, Tristan wanting to take Beckett to her favorite spot, but her body was sore and tired, and she didn't know how far they'd get. She must have been making a face, because Beckett looked at her curiously.

"Are you OK?"

"Yes, I just--" Tristan winced, a sharp pain in her left ribs interrupting her. "I just need to take a rest for a second."

"Tristan, maybe we shouldn't be doing this," Beckett said, watching her clutch her side. "I didn't even think to suggest we just sit and talk, and I should have, I'm sorry."

Tristan leaned her back against a tree for support. "Don't be sorry. I should have realized myself that this wasn't a great idea."

"Do you want me to carry you back?" Beckett asked earnestly, and Tristan laughed.

"No. I'll be fine."

And after a few minutes she was fine, so they went back the way they came, Olivia nowhere to be found when they arrived in the yard. Tristan and Beckett sank down into the grass, and Beckett looked at his hands before speaking.

"I am so sorry for how yesterday went down. I shouldn't have said what I did to you. I was up all night feeling guilty for setting everything off. Seeing you yesterday afternoon, on the ground..." Beckett trailed off, and Tristan pulled her knees up to her chest.

"How did you know to find me?" Tristan asked quietly, and Beckett shook his head, frowning.

"I don't know. I was at my locker and I heard you screaming, so I just ran. I didn't know where I was going, but I guess I just followed the sound to where you were."

It was Tristan's turn to frown. "You heard me screaming from your locker? On the other side of the building?"

"I know it sounds crazy. I haven't figured it out either, but yes. Very clearly."

It didn't sound crazy to Tristan; it sounded like they'd once again connected psychically, but *how?* How did that keep happening?

"Tristan." Beckett looked at her, his eyes so soulful that she could happily stare into them for an eternity. "Things are going to be different now. I'm sorry I've stood by so passively all these years. I can't change that, but I can change going forward. I will change."

"Those are nice words, but I guess we'll see what happens after break, right?" Tristan responded honestly, scrunching her nose a little bit. Her tone was kind, which softened the rejection of his sentiments, and she looked down at her fingers, which she ran back and forth through the soft grass.

"That's fair," Beckett replied, nodding, his expression serious. "I look forward to proving it to you."

The sun disappeared behind the clouds, and Tristan looked up, noticing a storm rolling in.

"We're gonna get soaked in a few minutes if we keep sitting here."

"I should probably get going anyway."

They stood, and Tristan walked Beckett back around to the front of the house.

"Thanks again for waiting after the meeting today."

"You're welcome. It was fine; I had company." Beckett winked, and Tristan tilted her head.

"Who?"

Beckett looked surprised.

"Evander. Olivia was there too, but she avoided me."

"What?" Tristan frowned. "The twins were here, not at school."

"Then I must have been hallucinating." Beckett grinned. "I'll see you tomorrow?"

"Tomorrow?" Tristan echoed, distracted.

"I was thinking maybe I could stop by again, if that's OK."

"Oh. Oh, sure, OK." Tristan nodded, and Beckett gave her a smile that made her stomach tremble.

"Alright. See you tomorrow then, Tristan."

Tristan nodded again, watching him, and Beckett lingered, not wanting to leave her. He finally forced himself to turn away, feeling all wrong for doing so, and the skies opened up just as he got in his car, as though they agreed he'd made the wrong decision.

Tristan stayed on the porch even after Beckett had disappeared from sight, and Olivia came out to join her.

"Hey." Tristan looked her over.

"I don't get you," Olivia said, looking like she was still hurting. "How can you even look at him?"

"It wasn't his fault."

"It *was* his fault, at least partially. He knew what kind of shit everyone was putting you through all day and he just watched it happen. Why wouldn't Emmeline and her crew have thought it was OK to go after you?"

"I don't know what you want me to say," Tristan said, her eyes welling up. "Anything I say won't matter."

Olivia's face softened.

"I'm sorry. Gods, what happened to you really has me fucked up, so I can't imagine how you're feeling."

"I keep seeing him, at random times but usually at the gatherings, probably because there's so much energy there and it opens up a pathway, and I know he's seen me when he shouldn't have. You know none of this is supposed to happen with a commoner, but I even stress signaled to him yesterday -- *that's* how he knew where to find me, and when he did he didn't hesitate. He bowled right into the middle of them to get to me. He has stepped into physical attacks on me twice now in the last couple of months, and he's defended me to his own friends. You really can't understand why I'm not walking away from him?"

Olivia let out a long sigh, shaking her head.

"Of course I understand." Olivia paused. "Plus there's the whole destiny connection thing that makes this inevitable anyway."

Tristan went still. "What?"

Olivia's eyes met hers, and she nodded.

"That vibe I was getting? I had enough time to figure it out on Saturday night. There's a destiny connection between you two, Trin. That's why you keep psychically connecting even though he's common."

Tristan sat down on the top step of the porch, needing to process what Olivia had just told her.

"So even if I..." Tristan trailed off, thinking out loud, and Olivia sat down beside her.

"Yes. *Even if you,* it wouldn't matter. Somehow you and Beckett would get back to each other, as many times as it took until it stuck."

"But destiny connections, they're so rare. And they're temperamental, and can be dangerous. Oceana, are you sure?"

Olivia nodded seriously.

"I'm sure. But you're not in danger; you're thinking of star-crossed, which you guys are not. A destiny connection like yours is not actually all that rare, it's just easy for people to ignore. Of course, they don't realize that ignoring it is the root cause of most of their problems, but I digress."

Tristan scrubbed her face with her hands. Her head hurt, this information just a bit too much for her today.

"I didn't mean to overwhelm you," Olivia said quietly.

"You didn't. It's just a lot. But a lot of things also make sense now, so I'm glad you told me." Tristan surveyed her sister carefully. "I heard you and Tyler talking last night."

Olivia said nothing, just shrugged.

"O, I know you'll probably end up joining the community when it's time. You and Ember are brilliant and talented and will fit in wonderfully. But you need to live now, right now, while nothing much is expected of you. You've had a thing for Tyler for *three years;* please don't shut him out on my behalf, OK? I'm telling you, right from the horse's mouth, I don't want you to do that."

It was Olivia's turn to well up, and Tristan put her arm around her sister's shoulders.

"I don't know how things will be after break," Tristan said. "But I'm going to hope they'll be different. All I want is to be left alone, and I think I might have a few people in my corner now who will help make that happen."

"I just feel so guilty," Olivia whispered, tears rolling down her face. "So many times I've ignored what they've said, or have just given them dirty looks, or have asked them -- *asked* them, and *politely,* too, like how ridiculous is that, to stop talking about you. I didn't want to rock the boat when they all decided to start paying attention to me, and it was at your expense. Tyler is a part of all of that and I don't know how to separate him out. I'm so, so sorry Trinity. I'm a terrible sister."

Olivia wept, and Tristan hugged her. Of course it stung a little bit, Olivia acknowledging aloud what Tristan had already known, but that was the thing -- Tristan *had already known,* and she understood. High school was a savanna and popularity was an ongoing territory war; she *wanted* her siblings to have a different experience than she'd had.

The door opened, and Evander stepped outside, coming to sit on Tristan's other side.

"I'm due to give you an apology, too," Evander said without preamble. "Everything Oceana said also applies to me. I've been a shitty brother, and I'm truly sorry, Trinity."

Tristan hugged Evander next, assuring them both they had nothing to apologize for, though she appreciated it.

"And now that you're both here, can we confirm or deny that Beckett saw you at the school today?"

"Umm," Olivia said, scrunching up her face like she was trying to remember, while Evander tapped his lips in thought.

"I don't know."

"I can't even remember."

Tristan laughed.

"So it was you two who influenced Emmeline to confess. On school grounds. Breaking rule number one."

"I mean, if we *had* been there, which we can't remember, I think it would have been bending more than breaking? Because school is out on break," Evander posited.

"You can't do that again," Tristan told them seriously. "It's too risky."

"Oh we won't," Olivia said. "But that reminds me, we do have to run some errands tonight. Do you need anything while we're out?"

"Run what kind of errands? Aren't you still grounded, Ember?" Tristan asked.

Olivia and Evander exchanged a look.

"Just errands. Mom and Dad are fine with Ember coming along." Olivia smiled, and Tristan shook her head, deciding she didn't want to know after all.

CHAPTER 19

Beckett came over again on Friday afternoon, noticing that Tristan looked a little bit worse than she had the day before. Her bruising had gotten nastier, which he knew was a healing mechanism, but the discoloration on her skin had him angry all over again. Additionally, Tristan was pale, and faint circles had developed under her eyes. Still, she smiled when she saw him, a genuine smile, and it took everything in him to not pull her into his arms.

"Do you mind if we just sit out here on the porch?" Tristan asked, stepping outside, and Beckett shook his head, looking at her closely.

"Whatever you want to do. How are you today?"

"Tired. I haven't been sleeping well since Wednesday, I..." Tristan shrugged, walking to the end of the porch, where she hoisted herself up onto the wide rail, resting her back against one of the wooden support beams. "Every time I close my eyes, I end up reliving what happened."

"Well, if you ever want to come to my house to nap or whatever, let me know," Beckett said, and Tristan creased her brow, a puzzled smile crossing her lips.

"What makes you think I'd sleep any better at your house?"

Beckett shrugged.

"Your day started here. You came back here after the

attack. Maybe it would help to try and rest in a space that doesn't have any direct ties to it."

"I'm not coming to your house to go to sleep, Beckett," Tristan laughed, briefly closing her eyes. "That would be so rude."

"The offer stands. It wouldn't be rude. I'd just do school work or something while you slept."

"I appreciate the offer." Tristan opened her eyes, smiling at him, and Beckett nodded.

Beckett joined her on the porch rail, resting his back against the beam opposite her, and for a while they sat in silence.

"Any plans this weekend?" Beckett finally asked.

"Tomorrow is the first day of winter, the solstice, so the five of us usually have a little celebration here. We're winter people. Sunday I was supposed to work, but Joe told me to not worry about coming back until Monday. You?"

Beckett laughed.

"Winter people living in a place that doesn't actually get winter, huh? I will be helping out at the library both days."

"You never did tell me what you're doing there."

"Grunt work, mostly. They're reorganizing, so there's a lot of heavy lifting that needs to be done."

Tristan sat up, folding her legs in front of her.

"It's nice of you to help them."

"Well, they're paying me, so it's not entirely altruistic," Beckett grinned, and Tristan laughed.

"I help out in the school library a lot," Tristan said,

looking out over the front yard. "If I'm not in the cafeteria at lunch, that's probably where I am. Shelf reorganization is my favorite, though I know people putting books back where they don't belong is the bane of every librarian's existence."

Beckett laughed.

"Well right now most of the books are off the shelves at the Lavelle Free Library, so I'll let Margeaux know she can call you to come shelve them when they're ready."

"Please do." Tristan nodded seriously, and Beckett laughed again.

"So is that what you want to do when you graduate? Become a librarian?"

"I've thought about it," Tristan replied, and then shook her head. "But no. My dream job is to be a researcher, for an author. If someone wants to write a book about something that requires extensive research, I want to be their person. I would do the same thing in the scientific field, for journals and such, but to research material for authors, preferably fiction, is the goal. We'll see how it pans out; it's an incredibly tiny field."

"That sounds interesting, and like it would suit you well," Beckett told her honestly. "Though I feel like you'd probably crush whatever goal you set for yourself anyway."

"What about you? Do you know what you want to do?"

"I think I'd like to get into psychiatry, with a specialization in veterans affairs."

Tristan was surprised. She blinked a couple of times, and Beckett looked at her, an amused expression on his face.

"What?"

"Nothing, that just wasn't what I was expecting you to say. That's... very noble."

"My Paw-Paw was failed by the system when he came home. If I can help one person get the care they need to live a mostly normal life when they come back from deployment, I'll feel like I've actually done something."

Tristan nodded.

"I understand. It really is noble of you; I wasn't trying to be condescending. I think you'd be great at it."

"We'll see. Have to see how the Ward Livingston psych program is, assuming I get in."

Tristan's head snapped up.

"WLU?"

Beckett nodded.

"My dream school."

Tristan gaped at him.

"WLU is *my* dream school."

Beckett smiled, nodding again.

"Yeah I know. I heard you talking to Dolores on Thanksgiving."

"Have you applied?" Tristan asked, and Beckett confirmed.

"So you know the torture of the wait." Tristan sagged back against the beam behind her, blowing out a breath.

Beckett chuckled.

"My hopes aren't real high, I'll be honest with you,

so I'm pretty much preparing for Tulane or LSU while still dreaming, distantly, of WLU."

"Well, I have enough hope for the both of us, and Ward Livingston has enough room for the both of us," Tristan said, her chin setting in the same stubborn way Beckett had often seen Olivia's, and he felt unexpectedly touched as he surveyed her face.

"Did you want anything to drink, or eat, or anything?" Tristan asked, suddenly remembering her manners.

She swung her legs over the railing and hopped down, losing her balance in the process, and Beckett jumped up to catch her. She grasped his forearm, his hand on her waist, and looked up at him, laughing nervously.

"Sorry."

Beckett shook his head.

"You really need to stop saying that."

Her hair had fallen over one eye, and, as the breath froze in her lungs, Beckett moved it away from her face, his thumb grazing the bruise on her cheek so slowly and gently that a shiver ran down her spine. He was looking at her the same wanting way he'd looked at her after the meeting yesterday, the same way he'd looked at her the whole time he'd been quasi-dating Eva, maybe the same way he'd always looked at her, in this and other lifetimes, and Tristan gazed back at him, knowing her expression probably mirrored his, wondering if he could hear the galloping of her heart that sounded like thunder in her own ears.

"Tristan."

He said her name like a prayer, and Tristan moved closer to him, knowing what was coming, wanting it so badly she ached from head to toe. Beckett's eyes dropped to her lips, and at that very moment, because it was so fitting for her life these days, Tristan heard a car coming up the driveway, and she and Beckett turned to see a silver SUV slowly approaching the house. Tristan did not recognize the vehicle, but she immediately hated whoever was inside for interrupting her moment with Beckett.

"Expecting company?" Beckett asked, his voice rough, and Tristan shook her head.

"No, I was only expecting you today."

Tristan walked around him, going to stand at the top of the steps, and as the car pulled up to the house, she nearly fainted. It was Celes, and his eyes were bouncing between Tristan and Beckett, though she knew he most likely couldn't have seen what had been about to happen on the porch.

Celes got out of the car, looking larger than life outside of a gathering setting, and Tristan twisted her fingers together as Beckett came to stand beside her. Why was Celes here? Why now? Why, right at this moment, when Beckett had been standing not a foot from her, ready to finally, finally kiss her?

"Ce-- Canton, hi," Tristan greeted, catching herself. She glanced at Beckett, who was looking at Celes with a faint frown on his face.

Celes made a face at her use of his common name, but nodded all the same as he approached the steps.

"Tristan."

"W-What are you doing here?"

Celes came up the steps, finally turning his gaze on Beckett. They sized each other up, and Tristan wished for a swift and sudden death.

"Are you a friend of Tristan's?" Celes asked Beckett, not unkindly, and Beckett nodded.

"Beckett Benson."

"Nice to meet you." Celes held out his hand. "I'm Canton Crenshaw, a family friend."

Beckett shook it, looking wary, and his eyes moved to Tristan, who looked even paler than she already had. He had the strangest feeling of déjà vu meeting this guy, whoever he was, and it was clear Canton was trying to establish his dominance, all of which made Beckett uneasy. The way Tristan was looking at Canton -- like he made her nervous, confirmed by the twisting thing she did with her fingers when she was anxious -- was not helping that feeling.

"Your Dad called to let my parents know what happened to you. I'm so sorry." Celes did look genuinely sorry as he took in her bruised face, and Tristan nodded.

"Thank you."

"I told him I'd probably come down to see you today, before we leave for Mandeville, but I can see he didn't relay the message."

"No, he didn't," Tristan said, wondering whether or not that had been intentional.

Celes looked at Beckett again.

"Your name sounds familiar. You're the one who found Tristan?"

Beckett nodded.

"Thank you," Celes said, and Tristan wondered what they would do if she just went inside and closed the door and never came back out.

Beckett's face settled somewhere between defensive and amused.

"You're welcome."

"Tristan means a lot to me and my family," Celes half-explained, looking between Beckett and Tristan.

"Right." Beckett eyed Celes, and then looked over at Tristan. "I'm gonna get going, I think. Are you OK?"

"I'm fine, but you don't have to go," Tristan said, looking at him regretfully.

Beckett gave her a reassuring smile.

"It's OK. Let me know if you want me to come back over later, or on Sunday, or whenever works for you. And don't forget the offer stands for you to come sleep at my house whenever you need to."

Celes crossed his arms, and Tristan ignored him, smiling at Beckett, who'd winked at her.

"I'm not napping at your house. But I'll let you know about the rest."

"Nice meeting you, Canton." Beckett held out his hand to Celes, who shook it, and then he reached out, squeezing Tristan's hand. "And I'll talk to you later."

"Talk to you later." Tristan watched him go, her hand tingling where he'd grabbed it, and she finally turned to Celes once Beckett had disappeared on his bike.

"Sorry about that. Like I said, my Dad didn't tell me you were coming today."

Celes looked at her for a few beats before speaking.

"I should be the one apologizing. I didn't mean to

interrupt you and your friend."

Tristan shook her head.

"It's no big deal. He was here yesterday, too, and will probably be back again. He only lives about ten minutes from us."

Celes was still watching her, not saying much, which was making Tristan nervous. She was sealed, as usual, but she was positive the very basic female element of her was signaling all over the place that Beckett was the one she had feelings for.

"Do you want to come in?" Tristan asked, gesturing at the house. "Hungry? Thirsty?"

Celes shook his head.

"I ate before I came here. We can go in, though. I didn't think it got much more humid than New Orleans, but it's brutal down here."

Tristan laughed, letting Celes go into the house before her.

"We're due for another storm. We've been having a ton lately, but the humidity will let up when the next one blows through."

"Celes," Olivia said in surprise, when they walked into the living room. Her eyes darted to Tristan, and then the empty space behind them, presumably looking for Beckett. "What are you doing here?"

"I came to see how Trinity is doing," Celes replied, sinking down onto the couch. "Your Dad forgot to tell all of you, I see."

Olivia nodded.

"He sure did. How was the drive?"

"It was fine."

"I thought you were going to Mandeville, for the Solstice?"

Celes looked surprised that Olivia had remembered.

"We are. I'll be leaving from here and driving up there myself, so I'm not staying long."

"Too bad. Barbecued ribs for dinner tonight." Olivia shot him a friendly grin, and Celes smiled back at her.

Tristan looked between them, getting the strangest, vaguest feeling. She told herself to remember this interaction -- it seemed inconsequential now, but also seemed like it might be relevant later.

Celes stayed a while longer, and Tristan relaxed once her hormones had a chance to settle down. She'd forgotten that for the most part she could enjoy Celes's company, and for not the first time she felt an enormous sense of guilt over what he had no idea was coming. He left without attempting to touch her in any way, and Tristan was relieved, closing the door behind him and leaning on it.

"Worlds collide," Olivia commented, walking by and shaking her head, on her way to the kitchen.

"Hey," Tristan said, and Olivia turned. "Have you talked to Tyler?"

Olivia bit her lip, looking down at her phone, which she clutched in her hand.

"Not yet. I've been typing and deleting all day without sending."

Tristan nodded.

"It'll be OK, O. He's not going to give up on you that

easily."

Olivia nodded, looking apprehensive.

"Maybe I'll just text him and ask him to come over so we can talk in person."

"That's probably the best idea."

Taking a deep breath, Olivia switched on her phone, her fingers tapping the touchscreen in quick succession.

"There. Will you wait with me until he responds?"

Tristan nodded and followed Olivia into the kitchen. Olivia set her phone on the island and began pulling food out of the fridge, assembling a sandwich. She was in the middle of telling Tristan about her latest makeup tutorial Instagram post, trying to convince her to make her own account so Olivia would gain another follower, when her phone vibrated. Olivia and Tristan exchanged a look.

"Can you read it? I can't." Olivia looked panicky, and Tristan nodded, reaching for the phone.

She smiled. *"I was hoping you'd ask me this. Tell me when to come over."*

"You're lying," Olivia said, her hands creeping up towards her mouth as she got teary once again.

"I wouldn't do that to you," Tristan said, handing over Olivia's phone.

Olivia beamed, typing a quick response, and then rushed out of the kitchen. She stopped at the doorway.

"I have to go get pretty. You can have that sandwich!"

And then she was gone, and Tristan smiled after her, glad Olivia had taken her advice for once in her life.

***

Beckett spent his bike ride home trying to figure out why Canton Crenshaw had seemed so familiar to him, but, more importantly, what Canton's relationship was with Tristan. He'd seemed comfortable around her, and at the house, like he belonged there, and it struck Beckett that he had no idea about the life Tristan kept outside of Jamestown Academy. Sure, she claimed she never did anything besides work and get together with her family, but Canton was clearly not a relative, so who was he? How did he know him? Did he have to show up just as Beckett was about to kiss Tristan? He made a mental note to ask Tristan the next time they were alone together.

Beckett had only been home a couple of hours when Tristan texted him, asking if he wanted to come back over. She explained that Tyler had come to see Olivia and was sticking around for dinner, being grilled by Umbris, so Tristan figured she'd see if Beckett wanted to come back. He did, of course, this time taking his car over.

Beckett parked in the driveway next to Tyler's car and walked around the house, the smell of barbecued food intoxicating. He entered the yard to see Tyler sitting in the middle of the younger Wallaces, in a circle of chairs that had been placed around their massive fire pit. Umbris was at the grill, a black apron covering his suit, which Beckett had to stop himself from laughing at, and Sol was walking over to the fire. She spotted him first, smiling as he approached.

"Beckett, Trinity told us you'd be joining us for dinner."

Beckett greeted her and Umbris, then went to join Tristan, Olivia, Evander, and Tyler by the fire. They all said hi to him, and Beckett shot a sly thumbs up at Tyler, who was holding

Olivia's hand. Tristan saw but pretended she hadn't, looking away across the yard and smiling over her shoulder. Beckett sat beside her and grinned.

"Hi again."

"Hi. I'm glad you came back over."

"I wouldn't have missed barbecued ribs for the world," Beckett replied, looking longingly in the direction of the grill.

Tristan laughed.

"Well, hold on to your hat, because there's also going to be corn on the cob, crawfish, and coleslaw."

"I can't take it," Beckett put his hand to his chest, laughing at Tristan's laughter.

"There's no stopping them now," Sol said to Umbris, looking over at Tristan and Beckett. "You know how a traumatic event can bring two people together."

Umbris nodded, a deep frown knitting his brow.

"I warned her to stay away, mostly for her own good, but I suppose she's going to have to find out for herself. Getting involved with him is going to make it that much harder on her when she leaves him to join the community."

"If," Sol gently corrected. Umbris looked at her, and she gave him a knowing look in return, a gentle reminder that Tristan had a choice.

"*If*," Umbris said begrudgingly.

When the sun had set, the food had been eaten, and the fire had burned down to smoldering ash, Sol and Umbris went inside, Evander following not long after. Olivia walked Tyler to his car after he said goodbye to Tristan and Beckett, which left the latter two alone beside the fire pit.

"I guess I should get going too," Beckett said a bit later, looking over at Tristan. His eyes sparkled in what glow was left of the fire. "Do you think you can roll me home?"

Tristan laughed, standing up. She held out her hand.

"I can't, but I can at least help you up."

Beckett took it, and she pulled him to his feet, both of them laughing. He ended up very close to Tristan, and held onto her hand when she went to let go. Tristan looked up at him in the dying light, and he smoothed her hair away from her face, his fingers weaving into the strands as he looked at her. Then, as though he was afraid they'd be interrupted again, his arm went around her waist and he brought her to him.

Cupping the back of her head, Beckett finally kissed her, and it was everything Tristan had hoped it would be. Her heart blossomed, opening up to his, every cell in her body rejoicing that she'd come home at last. The spark -- no, the *inferno* -- that she'd been missing with Celes ignited between her and Beckett, and they pressed together, tongues meeting, holding each other like they'd never let go again.

Beckett broke the kiss but didn't move away from Tristan, rather he rested his forehead against hers, trying to catch his breath. He framed her face with his hands, gently tilting her head back so he could look at her, wanting to know if the wonder on his face matched the wonder on hers. It did. They had both felt whatever it was that had just happened between them.

Beckett kissed her again, softly, and Tristan clung to him, her arms around his waist.

"I wish you could come home with me," Beckett murmured. "I don't want to leave you. I don't want us to be apart anymore."

"I don't either," Tristan whispered.

"Walk me to my car?" Beckett asked, and Tristan nodded, knowing she'd walk him to the ends of the earth if he asked.

The walk was too short, and, when they got to the driver's side of his car, Beckett pulled Tristan to him once again, wrapping his arms around her. Tristan breathed him in, her face in the crook of his neck just the way they'd been on Wednesday, but it was much sweeter this time, and for a much better reason.

"When can I see you again?" Beckett asked, his intense eyes searching her face, wanting to memorize every detail.

"Sunday," Tristan said breathlessly. "I'm free all day."

"I have to work a few hours in the morning, but I'll come here when I'm done," Beckett promised, and Tristan nodded.

Beckett kissed her one last time for the night, a kiss that nearly made her toes curl, and Tristan waved as he backed down the driveway, her whole body on fire, her brain hardly able to process all that had just happened, save for one thought: she was in *so* much trouble now.

CHAPTER 20

Solstice dawned clear and cool. A thunderstorm had rolled in overnight, breaking the humidity just as Tristan had predicted. The whole family got up before sunrise, getting into their SUV and traveling a short distance to a small clearing on the river. They followed Sol in a special yoga routine as the sun rose, giving thanks for all they had received since the summer solstice, letting go of anything that would bring negativity into the new year with them, and celebrating the rebirth of the sun. This was something the family had done for years now, this day as sacred to them as Christmas or Easter was to the non-secular crowd, and Tristan closed her eyes, inhaling and exhaling, feeling a weight lift from her soul.

The months leading up to the winter solstice had been turbulent, to say the least, but in a matter of days things had started to turn around. It wasn't just her budding relationship with Beckett -- he was a bonus, maybe the nicest bonus she'd ever been the recipient of -- it was that her attack at the direction of Emmeline Strandquest had changed her. Tristan was sure the intention had been to break her, and through those first numb hours after Beckett had scared the girls away, Tristan had thought maybe Emmeline had succeeded. As she'd emerged from the shock, however, she'd found that what the attack had done instead was liberate her. It had knocked down the last secret wall of insecurity she'd had, the one concerned with how her classmates saw her and privately had her taking their jabs and insults personally. In being humiliated, Tristan had lost it all, but she'd unexpectedly risen from the ashes.

Evander's words about her letting the popular crowd have power over her, giving her a hand in how her high school experience had panned out, had finally stopped hurting and started sinking in, as had Tyler's to Olivia about how the real beginning came once high school was over. Tristan knew she wouldn't have believed it any sooner than the moment she'd started -- it was nearly impossible to be in such a uniquely isolating environment day after day and not be affected by the idea that everything that happened within the school's walls, and everything that happened on the branches that shot out from those walls, was the be all, end all -- but as the new year approached, her graduation year, she'd finally seen the light.

As Tristan moved into the Warrior I yoga pose, she vowed to herself that the path forward would be the only path she walked now. No more turning back in fear, stepping on and off the path, distracted by what ifs -- she'd known since she was a child that the community life was not going to be the life for her, and she was going to start allowing herself to feel secure in that knowledge. She'd focus on maintaining her grade point average, focus on volunteerism, wait for the acceptance or rejection letters from the colleges she'd applied to and come clean to Sol and Umbris when all of those letters had come in. She'd focus on Beckett, on whatever time she had with him now that would be dictated by where in the country their lives took them in the Fall, comforted by Olivia's revelation that even if things fell apart for them this go round, they'd eventually come back together. Finally, when she had built her confidence up as high as she could, she would let Umbris and Sol know what her decision was going to be upon graduation.

Tristan knew all of these changes and decisions wouldn't

happen right away. She knew there might come a time or two where she'd waver, where the old retreating method would feel as enticing as a favorite pair of well-worn jeans, but she had to be as strong as her certainty that a common life was the life she was always going to choose.

When they'd finished their sunrise yoga, the Wallaces headed back to their house, chatting happily about the day ahead. Umbris got to cooking breakfast when they'd arrived, and they all took turns showering and getting dressed, each family member wearing some item of blood red -- the color of the root chakra, the grounding chakra that connected them to the Earth itself. Their clothes stood out especially against the stark white decorations that festooned the house, and Tristan looked around, smiling. There was really nothing quite like the solstice.

After breakfast, they headed outside to a grand old oak tree that stood in the very back of the yard. Working together, they scattered grains and seeds at the base, hung strings of nuts and berries from the lower hanging branches, and left a wide, shallow basket of fresh vegetables for the deer who frequented their woods. When they were finished, they linked hands, smiling at each other.

"Happy Solstice," Umbris said, looking around at them, and they returned his sentiment.

Sol and Umbris went back inside then, and Tristan, Olivia, and Evander sat at the patio table, a bare wreath made of grapevine resting in the middle. On either end of the table sat bins of materials they'd use to decorate the wreath, which would then hang on their front door until summer solstice, when they'd burn it in a bonfire. They chatted as they worked, about how strange it always was to welcome winter when their temperatures were summer temps to people up North, how they looked forward to the twelve days of Christmas, and, briefly, how special this particular year and its celebrations were. Olivia and Evander both looked sad about this, and Tristan understood their sorrow, wishing there was a way to spare them the inevitable pain of her separation from their community. When all was said and done, the siblings had opted to decorate their wreath with evergreens, for their strength, sprigs of holly, as a nod to the Holly King, bits of oak, as a nod to the Oak King, clusters of faux bayberries, for luck, and leaves of laurel, for prosperity. Olivia tied a pair of perfect, small brass bells to the upper left side of the wreath, a folklore symbol that was used to chase away the unknown waiting in the darkness brought by the winter solstice, and, as a finishing touch, Tristan tied a piece of raw ruby to the lower right hand side with twine, to help manifest their intentions for the coming year.

Evander went to fetch Umbris and Sol, who came outside and stood beside the table with their children.

"Another Yule is upon us," Umbris said, looking around at his family. "Another cycle of rebirth, another chance to refocus on our higher priorities, goals, and missions. With thankful hearts for what the summer solstice brought us, let us look forward to this new cycle with fresh eyes."

Sol gingerly lifted the wreath, smiling, and set off around the house, the family following her. She hung the wreath on the front door, then stood back, nodding.

"Beautiful work, as always."

They went inside, each person retreating to their own space in the house. For the next several hours they'd meditate in the silence -- well, Sol and Umbris would. Tristan, Olivia, and Evander would meditate for a while and then try not to fall asleep, at which they usually failed, and then they'd drive to the nearest trail entrance and go for a walk through the woods.

Tristan was tempted to pull out her phone, to see what Beckett was up to, but she refrained, reminding herself that when the sun finally set and they did their unity candle tradition, their observation of the solstice would end, and then she could reach out to him.

Instead, Tristan sat cross-legged on her bed, closing her eyes and turning her palms upward. She had never been good at meditation and did not expect this year to be any different, but she'd give it her best shot.

***

The day passed quickly, the siblings arriving home from the woods refreshed and relaxed. Before they'd started off, Olivia had touched Tristan's back, granting welcomed relief to her still-aching body. Sol had also offered to heal Tristan after the attack, but Tristan had resisted, the pain and the bruising fueling her fire of rebirth; Tristan had only accepted Olivia's offer today so she wouldn't be the reason they'd have to modify their yearly nature walk.

It had been a long time, too long, since the trio had just hung out with each other and talked about everything other than school; they delighted in each other's company as they walked, stopping along the way to feed small animals like rabbits and chipmunks, identify interesting plants, and turn their faces up at the sun, shining with all its might in the cloudless sky. The trappings of who they'd become as self-conscious teenagers fell away until they were just siblings, just themselves, their bond as strong as it had ever been.

By the time they got home, the sun was preparing its early descent into the horizon, and the family set up in the yard to follow Sol through one more specialized yoga routine. The winter sky was a peaceful navy blue by the time they'd finished, and Umbris disappeared into the house, coming back out with a small tin box and this year's Yule log. The log had been spray painted white and wrapped with red ribbons and dried holly leaves, per tradition.

Umbris reached into the tin box, handing Sol and the children a few loose, dried holly sprigs and a single acorn, and then dumped the remaining contents into the fire pit -- charred wood and ash from last year's log -- and added dried kindling. He looked around at his family, smiling as he held the Yule log in his hands.

"I know this is your favorite part," Umbris said to his children, who smiled back at him, exchanging looks.

"For as long as time has existed, so have the Holly King and the Oak King -- one king with dual souls, locked in an eternal battle between dark and light. At winter solstice, the Oak King rings triumphant, promising and slowly bestowing the Earth with bounty, growth, new life, marching forth through the waning cold and the melting frost, only to reverse this bounty in equally slow measure. Alas, when midsummer comes, the summer solstice, the Holly King, having had six months to regain his strength, takes back the battle, overseeing the Oak King's destruction and ultimately allowing for the letting go of the old to make way for the new. There cannot be one without the other; all dark has light, all light has dark. Without death there cannot be rebirth, and the price of rebirth is death. This solstice, we give thanks to the twin kings, and we welcome back the strengthening sun, by which we are energized and guarded."

Umbris, whose voice had resonated around the dusky yard, fell silent. The family stood still as dusk rapidly gave way to dark, contemplating the old legend and their own triumphs and losses of the year gone by, as well as their plans for their own private rebirths in the coming year.

He placed the Yule log into the fire pit, and, with a sweep of his hand, the kindling ignited.

"We bid farewell to the old calendar year, and in doing this we banish newly developed bad habits, lingering negativity, and the personal pains we've experienced over these last twelve months."

One by one, led by Umbris, they tossed their leaves into the fire, and Tristan hoped she'd never again experience the kind of personal pain she'd gone through just days ago. When the Yule log itself lit, Umbris held out his acorn in the palm of his hand, dropping it into the fire as he spoke once again.

"My hope for this year is peace for my family and myself, as we all embark on our new chapters and new endeavors."

"My hope for this year is strength for my family and myself, as we all embark on our new chapters and new endeavors," Sol said next, exchanging a nod with Umbris and releasing her acorn.

"This year, I resolve to work on my sense of responsibility, to my family, our community, and myself," Evander said next, tossing his acorn into the flames.

"My resolution this year is to stand firm in what I know is right, no matter the personal cost, for the betterment of my family, our community, our society, and myself." Olivia, her chin set, threw in her acorn.

"My resolution this year is to work on my fearlessness, following in the footsteps of the examples I've had in my family and the community." Tristan was the last one to sacrifice her acorn, and, once she had, Olivia grinned at everyone.

"Let's do this."

The five of them launched into a terrible rendition of *Deck the Halls,* not one of them able to carry a tune in a bucket, and finished the song through peals of laughter. When Tristan and her siblings were young, Sol and Umbris had tried to lead them through a reverent version of the carol, but the children had been unable to marry the solemnity of the Yule log ritual and the absurdity of their singing of what had become a commercial carol, so it had quickly devolved into an ice breaker of sorts, or a signal that the reverent observation of solstice was ending, and the rest of the evening would be enjoyed in relaxation, ordering in Chinese food -- another absurdly out of place yet favorite ritual -- and eating by the light of their unity candle.

When Umbris had extinguished the fire and scooped the new remnants into the tin box, the five of them headed inside the house to get their dinner order going. While they waited for the delivery, Tristan cleared the dining room table and helped Sol set out five red candles, the fat white unity candle, and five long matchsticks.

The food arrived and Umbris plated all of it, Olivia and Evander helping him bring it into the dining room, where they set it at the other end of the long table. Evander hit the lights, plunging them into darkness, and they joined Tristan and Sol, taking their seats in front of the circle of red candles. In the middle of the circle was the unity candle, brand new each year.

"We light these candles as individuals to acknowledge the path of rebirth each of us must ultimately walk alone. We understand that the light symbolizes our internal light that guides our way, protecting us against outside influences and temptations, as well as the sun, the most important source to life on Earth. We also light them in the presence of each other, to symbolize that we are never far from each other be it in spirit or in body, and as a symbol of the support we offer each other unconditionally and unwaveringly as we walk our individual paths."

Umbris nodded, and one by one they lit their candles. He nodded again, and they blew them out, sitting for a moment in the silent darkness.

"And now we light this unity candle to acknowledge the strength and bond of our family unit. We ask that blessings abound for us this coming year, in exchange for thankful and complete devotion to the universe and its abundant gifts. With this lighting, we resolve to keep our bond the priority above all other bonds, and we affirm our obligations of loyalty and honesty to each other."

Umbris nodded again, and the matchsticks lit in unison. The five of them joined their sticks at the wick of the unity candle, which blazed proudly to life. They smiled at each other.

"The light of renewal remains in our hearts. Happy Solstice, everyone."

"Happy Solstice."

Umbris stood, waving his hand, and several ivory candles around the room lit themselves, affording them enough light by which to eat. Everyone grabbed their plates and sat back down, talking happily in the glow of the candlelight.

It had been a long day, introspection more tiring than Tristan remembered, and she went up to her bedroom shortly after dinner. She laid on her bed and grabbed her phone from her nightstand, finding a handful of texts from Beckett waiting for her.

Thinking about you.

Still thinking about you.

Guess what I'm doing? ....Thinking about you.

Now I'm thinking about your phone. Is this your number, Tristan Wallace? I'm gonna be so embarrassed if it's not.

Just kidding, I know it's your number.

I miss you.

Tristan smiled, composing a message back to Beckett.

Were you thinking about me today, by any chance?

Nope. The response came immediately, and Tristan laughed.

I'm sorry I'm just getting back to you. We have a "no electronics on the first day of winter" rule. Family day.

How was your family day?

Really, really nice. Really, really tiring. How was your day?

Really really boring. Except for the parts I was thinking about you. Still not sleeping?

You're sweet. I'll be happy to see you tomorrow. And no, not really.

You could come sleep here.

Don't tempt me, Beckett Benson. I'm getting desperate. Hey, you never did tell me your middle name.

And I never will. Go to sleep. I'll see you tomorrow at 7 AM.

...Just kidding. Let me know when you want me to come over tomorrow. I'll be done at the library before 12.

I will. Goodnight Beckett.

Goodnight Tristan.

Tristan smiled again, switching off her phone and holding it to her chest. She stared up at her mobile, her heart full to the brim. So much had happened in the last few days after seventeen and a half years of not a whole lot happening, and her head was spinning in the best way.

Tristan must have drifted off to sleep, because the next thing she knew, she was in the woods. It was dark, and she was alone, heading through thick underbrush and dense trees to a destination she couldn't see quite yet.

Eventually, the trees thinned and she stepped onto a dirt pathway. She looked down, jolting in surprise when she saw she was wearing a wedding dress. It was jet black, a ball gown with a long, tiered skirt and a heavily beaded bodice. Her hair was twisted back into an intricate updo, soft tendrils framing her face, on which Tristan could feel makeup had been layered. A black lace veil brushed her bare shoulders like ghostly hands, and she lifted the skirt of her dress, revealing black satin ballet slippers. On her left hand sat a ring of diamonds, a square stone sitting high and proud in the middle. Her fingernails were glossy, jet black in the moonlight.

A fog rolled in, overtaking the pathway and the forest around her, everything cast in misty gray. Still, Tristan walked, intuitively knowing where to step. As she rounded a corner, she came upon a gathering. This gathering was different, however, in that the community members were already seated on the worshipping pillows, which had been separated to form a long, narrow aisle. Everyone, dressed in black hooded robes, had their heads bent downward, and no one moved when Tristan came to a stop at the end of the aisle. Tearing her eyes from the eerie sight, Tristan looked up, noticing that at the head of the clearing, in front of a grand ivory altar, Celes stood waiting for her. Pele stood with him, her hands clasped in front of her over a small black leather book, black hood pulled so that only her grim, angular face showed. Tristan's family was nowhere to be found, nor was

Celes's, but Tristan figured they were probably in the front, heads bent like the other worshippers.

Tristan walked forward, locking eyes with Celes, which triggered a cavalcade of memories to play in her mind, sped up like someone had hit the fast forward button on her. The two of them in the car, windows open, hair blowing around as they laughed about something together. On a beach at sunrise, Celes spinning her around in his arms. On a green couch she somehow knew was theirs, snuggled together in front of a roaring fireplace. And then more intimate memories -- Celes lifting her onto a kitchen counter so she'd be as tall as him, kissing her once she was seated. Tristan poking her head out of a blue and white polka dotted shower curtain and Celes kissing her before leaving the bathroom. Tristan, in black lingerie, sitting in a shirtless Celes's lap as he--

Her face flamed, and Tristan could swear Celes smirked at her from where he stood, just ten feet away now, waiting for her. He wore a black tuxedo with a black shirt and tie, and his hair was styled back away from his handsome face. Tristan reached him, coming to a stop before him, and Celes looked at her, his expression guarded now, which was strange.

"Trinity Wallace," Pele spoke, and Tristan looked over at her. "What say you to the accusations that have been brought forth before us today, that you have betrayed the community, sullied your family's name, and destroyed the sacred bond of trust between you and your intended spouse, Celes Crenshaw?"

"What?" Tristan asked, swallowing hard as panic rose like bile in her throat. The fog had begun to roll into the clearing, and Pele's voice was as hard as her eyes. "This is my wedding, why are you doing this?"

"This is not your wedding. This is your trial."

"But..." Tristan looked at Celes, who had disappeared. In his place was Orion, and fear like she'd never known gripped Tristan's heart as she gasped, stumbling back a few steps. She looked at Pele in a panic, only to find the altar behind her had also disappeared, in its place two large, hooded guards, faces obscured. Tristan looked down to find her beautiful ensemble had been replaced by a long, plain black T-shirt, sleeveless and shapeless and reaching her knees, and her hair hung loose and limp around her shoulders. She wore no shoes, and her feet were filthy, her legs scratched and muddy, thin bands of blood mixing with the dirt. Instinctively, she knew she'd been running from just this, but had been lured in and trapped by Celes's manipulation of reality.

Tristan looked at the worshippers, who were now standing, staring at her, waiting to see what happened next. Her family was crying, and Celes stood near them with his arms folded, looking conflicted.

"What did you do?" Tristan whispered to Celes in horror. He looked away.

"This is about what you did," Orion said, his voice as chilling as ever. "This is about the double life you've been leading, as though you'd never be caught."

"Double life? What are you talking about?" Tristan cried, bewildered.

Orion lifted his arm, and in the air above the heads of everyone at the gathering, Tristan's sins played out for all to see. Tristan, accepting her role in the community at the acceptance ceremony after she'd graduated high school. Accepting Celes's formal proposal. Moving into a small, charming house with Celes. Waiting until he left for work and making a phone call. Opening the front door to find Beckett waiting to come in.

Tristan covered her mouth as it went on.

Pulling Beckett inside and embracing him. Kissing him. Leading him up the stairs. Tristan pressing a kiss to a jagged, dark red scar on the front of Beckett's bare right shoulder, her own shoulders bare. Greeting Celes with a kiss at the end of his work day. Going out to dinner with Celes, only to find Beckett's eyes across the room as he dined at the same restaurant.

Tristan's heart was all ache as she watched herself with the two men -- the one she'd been chosen for, and the one she'd been meant for. She'd never wanted to hurt Celes this way; why had she joined the community? When had she started sneaking around with Beckett? She couldn't remember anything, yet the memories playing in the air rang true all the same.

"I told you I loved you then and nothing has changed," Beckett's voice filled the clearing, and Tristan jumped, looking up as this last memory played with sound. She knew she didn't have to look, however, as *this* one, this memory, was pressed indelibly into her very soul.

This had just happened, maybe mere days ago. She and Beckett had gotten caught in the rain in Tristan's private spot by the river, and Beckett had pulled her close, not caring that they were getting soaked.

"How many times can I beg you to leave him, Tristan? Please. Please come with me. We'll leave town, get the hell out of this state, we'll start over together. Say you will." Beckett had rested his forehead against hers, his thumbs stroking either side of her face, his voice a whisper under the weight of his emotion. "Tristan, say you will."

"I will," Tristan had whispered back, and it was those words now that echoed in the clearing as the memory dissipated, the gathered community murmuring amongst themselves.

"This isn't fair," Tristan said, beyond humiliated, her teeth clenched. "Why do I have to publicly atone for my sins? I've broken no laws. Why don't we play yours next? Or Celes's? Or anyone here's? Everyone is guilty of something!"

"Silence." Orion waved his hand, and Tristan could no longer speak. She stared at him, hatred burning in her eyes, which were already sore from crying. A strange sensation washed over her, but as quickly as it had come, it had gone.

Orion turned to the community.

"Do you hear her? She speaks in threats and nonsense! She shows no remorse and claims she's broken no laws. She's a liar and a traitor down to the very fibers of this community, and there's no doubt in my mind that if I hadn't stripped her of her powers just now, she'd try to use them against us all! She stood before all of us one year ago and pledged her allegiance to this community, to you, and ran off almost immediately to maintain her sex life with a *commoner,* with whom she was planning to abandon this life, as you just heard."

Stripped her of her powers? That was what she'd felt just now? Tristan looked around desperately, but Pele had vanished and now it was just her against Orion. Powerless. An impossible imbalance. Where *were* the other Elders? Why was Orion alone running this show? Would it even matter if the rest of the committee was anywhere to be found?

Orion turned to Celes.

"Celes. You did good work, harvesting this evidence and keeping Trinity's suspicions low over the last six months. On behalf of the Elders and all of us in this community, please accept our apology that your plotted life has gone wayward. We will find you a new arrangement as soon as we can."

Celes nodded, and Olivia looked over at him, loathing all over her face.

"How could you do this to her? To us? To me? All because she hurt your little feelings?"

"Silence!" Orion snapped, lifting his hand, but Sol lifted hers, too, and Olivia shot Orion a smug look as Sol blocked him.

Tristan looked at her parents, who would not look at her, which cut as deep as any knife. Why wouldn't they look at her? Did they agree with all of this? Did they know there was no way out for her, and it was too painful to watch? Had they known, warned her away from Beckett, and she'd ignored them?

Celes was looking at Olivia, anguish on his face, and Tristan thought her brain might explode. He was in love with her sister, it was as plain as day, yet Tristan was on trial for betraying him.

"There is a difference between thought and action," Orion said, slowly approaching Tristan. "And that difference is law. You would have been protected if you'd just rejected the community the way you'd planned, if you hadn't done what you thought was right though it wasn't what you wanted, but you didn't. You accepted your role here and with it you accepted the consequences of any law you'd go on to break, and the law against deflecting after accepting stands."

Tristan was either going to throw up or pass out, maybe both.

"She was forced into accepting and you know it!"

Olivia yelled, bless her feisty soul. "And then our Dad went back on his word to our Mom and he changed Tristan's path to make joining the community seem like the best option and-- no! She deserves to know this, everyone does! Ember!"

Tristan looked around Orion to see Olivia struggling against Umbris, who was trying to lead her away, hand over her mouth.

Evander, hesitating only a moment, grabbed Umbris's arm, stopping him. He pulled Olivia easily out of Umbris's grasp and Olivia fought her way back to the front of the clearing while Evander blocked Umbris's way.

"Is it true?" Sol asked, turning to Umbris, whose face was gray. "*You* changed her course? You said she agreed that your decision was for the best. You... You lied? You broke your vow?"

"Save your family turmoil for the privacy of your home," Orion commanded. "It doesn't matter here. Regardless of the specifics, Trinity accepted into the community and broke the law. That's clear if nothing else is."

"I'll never forgive you for this," Olivia told Celes, taking a step toward him. "This has undone everything you've ever said to me, every tie that has ever bound us."

"What say you?" Orion asked Tristan, who knew she was going to die as sure as she knew anything.

"I'm only sorry that my family has to see this," Tristan said clearly, and the community gasped. She looked at Sol, who was finally looking at her, the pain on her face nearly unbearable. "You should go. You don't have to watch history repeat itself. Take Oceana and Ember and go."

Tristan's eyes moved to Umbris.

"The least you can do is remind me how you changed

my course. How you set off the chain of events I would continue that brought me here."

Umbris closed his eyes and Tristan closed hers. A flashback played in her mind on borrowed powers, Umbris bargaining for Beckett's life after Beckett had been caught by Entros and his guards.

"I'll wipe his memory. Just let him go."

The flashback jumped to when Umbris had come home after the wiping.

"Only tonight, right?" Tristan had asked tearfully, and Umbris had nodded, avoiding her eyes and going silently upstairs.

But he'd lied. Tristan remembered now. He'd wiped Beckett's memory back to September, erasing everything that had happened between him and Tristan, which Tristan didn't find out until his number, all of his messages, all of their photos, all traces of him had been gone from her phone and her life the next day. And on Monday at school Beckett had looked at her in the hallway and then kept going, oblivious.

Tristan had collapsed. Had been taken home, where, lying in her bed for the next two days, her anger had built until it exploded. Her power had come back in a rush that had nearly electrified her, and she'd hurled her bed through her window and the surrounding wall, screaming until she was sure she'd permanently lose her voice.

She'd graduated numbly. Accepted her role into the community numbly. And then, in his final betrayal and driven by the guilt of seeing his daughter broken, Umbris had restored Beckett's memories, and Beckett had reached out to Tristan just days after the acceptance ceremony.

All of it was cruel. All of it had led here, to her trial, to her sentencing, to what she knew would be her execution.

"Can I see him, one last time?" Tristan asked quietly, and Orion laughed coldly.

"You've seen enough of him; we all have, after tonight. I'd almost admire your nerve in asking if I wasn't part of the family onto whom you've brought such shame and disappointment. Trinity Wallace, by order of the community and its laws, established thousands of years ago and proudly upheld despite generations of change and progression, I hereby order your execution, on this night of July third."

"No!" Olivia screamed, running back through the crowd, past Orion, to Tristan. Olivia stood in front of her, shielding her, and reached back, grabbing Tristan's wrists.

In stunning clarity, Beckett appeared in Tristan's mind, and her heart shattered into a million pieces as she closed her eyes. He was in his bedroom, lounging on his bed with schoolwork spread out around him. He had no idea what was happening, and Tristan preferred it that way. She wanted his last memory of her to be a good one.

"I'll find you," Tristan whispered, though she knew he couldn't hear her. "I'll find you again."

Olivia released her, and Tristan opened her eyes to discover that the Elders had finally managed to wrestle her away from Tristan.

"Thank you, Oceana," Tristan croaked, her throat thick with tears, and in her mind Olivia told her she loved her. "I love you too."

Tristan opened her eyes, gray morning light filling her bedroom. She couldn't move, could barely breathe. With every cell in her body she wanted to believe that had just been a dream, but she knew it had been a premonition. Tristan had no idea how the events that brought her to what she'd just seen would transpire, still couldn't fathom how Beckett would ever end up at a gathering in the first place in order to be captured by Entros, but that didn't matter much. She'd seen her future, and it ended just as Adara's had.

"Oceana," Tristan whispered, closing her eyes, and not two minutes later Olivia hurried into her room, climbing into bed beside her.

"What's wrong?" Tristan had clearly woken Olivia, but to her credit, her eyes were sharp and she was ready to hear what had happened.

Tears rolled down Tristan's face, and she tried to decide if she should tell Olivia what she'd seen or show her. Deciding to spare her how she could, Tristan told her.

"OK," Olivia said when she'd finished, looking freaked out but also thoughtful. "OK, OK. I don't know if I'm ready to call this a premonition. It's really choppy and there are lots of missing pieces and consequences being doled out based on assumptions. How on earth would Beckett end up at a gathering? He wouldn't. That's the first thing. Second thing, Dad would not double cross Mom to get you to join the community. He made a *vow* to her, Trinity, not some casual promise. Also, you said yourself that even the penalty of death wouldn't immediately make you join the community, but even if you could be tricked or forced into it, Dad would never do that to you. His actions were heinous; that wasn't our Dad."

Tristan took a deep breath, Olivia making valid points.

"Now if you decided to join the community on your own, everything but Beckett showing up at a gathering and Dad wiping his memory and all that becomes a lot more plausible. Have you been thinking of changing your mind?"

"No," Tristan said immediately, and Olivia nodded.

"I didn't think so. I think you're just under a lot of stress, Trin, and you haven't been sleeping well since the attack, so I think your brain is just sort of spazzing on you right now. But look, it's only December. You have just over five months until you really need to worry about any of this, and you just started dating Beckett. You should be focusing on that and enjoying that right now. Live now, right?"

Tristan laughed, wiping her face.

"Right."

"Right. OK, I'm going back to bed. Maybe put on some music and your earbuds and try to fall asleep without thinking about all of this crap."

Tristan nodded, and Olivia left the room. She'd probably been right, but the feeling in Tristan's gut lingered -- the warning that sometimes the impossible or implausible did happen, that fate was a tricky mistress and would find a way in spite of all doubt, and, most importantly, that not all premonitions were created equal.

Tristan did not go back to sleep that morning.

***

Beckett texted Tristan shortly after noon that day, asking if she wanted to come to his house or if she'd like him to come to hers. Tristan, still unsettled from her dream that morning, let Beckett know she'd come to him.

As he'd done before, Beckett answered his door before she'd gotten a chance to knock, his hair wet from the shower. He smiled at her, opening the glass storm door, and Tristan stepped inside.

"Hey, come on in. My Mom is in Barataria visiting her sister this weekend, and my Dad..." Beckett trailed off, his face darkening, then shrugged. "Who knows where he is?"

"Thanks for inviting me over," Tristan replied, nodding.

There were actually lights lit in his house that day, and Tristan looked around. The door opened up right into the living room, which contained a couch, a loveseat, a small fireplace, a decorated Christmas tree, and a long, low entertainment center, on top of which sat a TV and various accessories and was flanked by two bookcases housing both DVDs and books. To her right was an archway that led through a short hallway and into a small dining room with a six-person table and not much else. Down that same hallway was the kitchen, Tristan knew from her last visit, as well as the staircases to both the upstairs and the basement.

"I'd give you the grand tour," Beckett said, following her gaze, "But you can see everything from where you're standing."

Tristan laughed.

"It's homey. I like it."

"It's too small and getting smaller by the day," Beckett replied, then shrugged. "How was your morning?"

Tristan did not want to talk about her morning.

"It was OK. I've been up since five-thirty, though."

"I can tell. Still not sleeping?" Beckett looked at her with concern, and Tristan had the most ridiculous urge to cry. She'd never functioned well on prolonged broken sleep.

"Not really."

"Why don't you sit down? Take off your shoes, get comfortable." Beckett pointed to the couch. "I'll get us snacks and we can just hang here, watch a movie or something."

"That sounds perfect," Tristan said, meaning it.

She sank down onto the navy couch, the cushions embracing her, and she decided she'd be content to never move again. Beckett came back shortly with two bottles of water and a giant bowl of popcorn, and he flopped down beside her, grabbing the remote and switching on the TV. He flipped through the menu for a while, suggesting movies here and there, until they finally settled on the newest Thor movie.

"This reminds me of Halloween," Tristan said, grinning. "I thought about you in that Loki costume for weeks afterwards."

Beckett laughed, then lifted his eyebrows suggestively.

"I still have it upstairs. You want me to go get it?"

Tristan nodded, and Beckett started to get up. She grabbed his arm, laughing and pulling him back down onto the couch.

"I'm kidding! Maybe on our third date."

"You are feisty and I like it." Beckett, still laughing, settled back in beside her, putting his arm around her shoulders. Tristan tucked her legs up beside her and snuggled into him, still not quite daring to believe this was happening.

"So where in Alabama did you move here from?" Tristan asked Beckett, grabbing a handful of popcorn from the bowl. "And why on Earth did you move to Lavelle? Not that I'm complaining."

"Prichard, Alabama. My Dad worked in Mobile. He

was promoted and his new job was a telecommuting position, and around the same time my Mom's sister, my Aunt Olive, the one who lives in Barataria, fell ill. My Mom wanted to be closer to her, so this was where we landed."

"How is your Aunt now?"

"Still sick. She was diagnosed with breast cancer, so she's been undergoing treatment, but the treatment is making her sick. It's working, though, so she says it's worth it."

"I'm sorry," Tristan replied.

"Thank you. Have you always lived in Lavelle?"

Tristan nodded.

"My Mom and Dad both grew up in New Orleans. They moved to Lavelle when they were first married, for privacy," Tristan snorted. "The house we live in belonged to my great-grandmother but sat empty when she died until my parents bought it. No one else in the family wanted it."

"Why? It's a nice house."

"It is," Tristan nodded. She hesitated, unsure how much to say. "My great-grandmother was not a nice woman, and you know how families can be superstitious? Mine is one of them. No one wanted to take on the potential bad energy."

Beckett nodded.

"I getcha. But your parents did. So what's the verdict?"

"No bad energy I've ever experienced," Tristan replied, shrugging.

They settled back into comfortable silence, and before long Tristan felt herself drifting off. She tried to shake herself awake, but Beckett began stroking her hair, slowly and steadily, and, though she knew what he was up to, she was too tired to fight him on it.

Beckett waited until Tristan was out like a light, which didn't take long, and then he shifted, settling her head into his lap. She sighed in her sleep, her arms pulled up against her chest, and he looked down at her perfect profile, still having trouble believing this was happening. He continued running his fingers through her hair, fanning the strands out behind her, over his leg and stomach and down onto the couch. The movie ended and he searched through the channels again, looking for something else to watch. It was a perfect afternoon, and Beckett felt more content than he would have imagined feeling in this scenario with anyone else.

Nearly three hours had passed before Tristan stirred. She sat up suddenly, looking embarrassed, and Beckett smiled at her.

"I'm glad you took me up on my offer."

Her face turned red and she smoothed her hands over her hair.

"Oh my God, I'm so sorry. I'm so embarrassed. What time is it?"

"Don't be," Beckett frowned. "Tristan, you needed to sleep. Did you have any bad dreams?"

Tristan shook her head, reaching for her water bottle. She hadn't, which was truly the first time since the attack on Wednesday.

"Good."

Tristan still looked embarrassed, so Beckett leaned forward, looking at her until she met his eyes.

"Hey."

"What?"

"You don't ever have to be embarrassed with me, about anything. I'm never gonna mock you or make you feel awkward on purpose, and if I do it by accident, I want you to tell me so I can apologize and kiss the ground at your feet until you forgive me."

That got a laugh out of Tristan, and Beckett took her hand. He pulled her gently to him and wrapped his arm around her waist. Tristan looked at him, her eyes just as dark up close as they were from far away, her lips parting as he stared at her. Briefly shaking his head, Beckett kissed her, and Tristan would have given anything to know what he'd just been thinking. She kissed him back, her hands on either side of his face, and he brought her up against him, his free hand disappearing into her hair.

"I can't believe I missed out on you these last two years," Beckett said, when they'd come up for air. He studied her face, tracing the curve of her cheek with his finger. "You were right in front of me the whole time."

Tristan grasped his hand, flattening his palm against her cheek.

"I know what you mean."

"I dreamt about you," Beckett said, and Tristan looked at him in surprise.

"About those eyes of yours. Every time you looked at me in the hallway, even before our assignment, I'd dream about you for days. And then we were paired up and it happened more and more. I thought the only way I'd ever be with you would be in my dreams."

"That's what I thought," Tristan whispered.

They kissed again, and Beckett rested his forehead against hers.

"I don't want you to go home tonight. Stay."

"Beckett--" Tristan said, looking uncertain.

"We don't have to rush into anything. We can just sleep. You can have my bed and I'll sleep down here, or we can both sleep in my bed, or we can both sleep down here. I can hold you or give you space, whatever you want. I'm never gonna force you into anything, Tristan."

Tears threatened again. What Beckett was offering was so tempting it hurt; spending the night in his arms was so far beyond her wildest dreams.

"I don't know how I'd explain it to my Mom and Dad. They're not really thrilled about this, us, to begin with."

"Why's that?" Beckett looked mildly put-off.

"They don't want me to lose focus at school, especially now in senior year. I told them school is the most important thing to me so I won't, but you know parents." Tristan half-shrugged.

"Fair enough. Want me to sneak into your bedroom and sleep with you instead?"

Tristan laughed.

"We'd be caught in a red-hot second. My family misses nothing." Tristan thought for a moment. "Maybe in a few weeks we can tell them we're going camping. And then we can either go or stay here."

"I like the way you think, Tristan Wallace. But you're gonna collapse before a few weeks gets here if you keep not sleeping."

"I'll be OK," Tristan assured him.

"Well the good news is we still have a long break from school ahead of us, so at the very least you can come over here and nap if you need to."

"Beckett, I lost three hours with you this afternoon because I fell asleep. Three hours! I'm not doing that again."

"But you're still here, and I'm definitely not letting you go home any time soon, so does it really matter?" Beckett grinned, and Tristan shook her head on an eye roll, fighting off a smile.

The rest of the day passed criminally quickly, Beckett ordering pizza for them for dinner, and they were in the middle of a lively debate about whether or not pop music of the old days sounded as bad and cheesy to those teenagers as pop music of the now days does to them, when Raymond Benson arrived home.

"Hey Beckett," Raymond greeted, looking surprised to see Tristan. "And Tristan, hi, how are you feeling?"

"Hi Mr. Benson," Tristan returned politely. "Better by the day, thanks."

"You can call me Ray. I'm glad you're feeling better. You look better. It's just awful what those girls did to you."

Tristan nodded in agreement.

"Where were you?" Beckett asked casually, but Tristan could feel the tension rolling off of him in waves.

"I was up in New Orleans. You remember Jensen Sanders, who I worked with in Mobile? He and his family are visiting, so I went up to have lunch with him."

Beckett looked surprised by this, and Tristan quickly read

Ray, which confirmed he was telling the truth.

"I'm gonna be upstairs if you guys need anything. Nice to see you again, Tristan."

Ray disappeared, and Tristan looked at Beckett, who shook his head.

"It's always hard to know when he's telling the truth or when he's lying."

"He was telling the truth," Tristan said without thinking, and Beckett looked at her funny.

"How do you know?"

"Oh, I'm just good at reading body language," Tristan said, embarrassed. "It's usually pretty obvious when someone is lying, even if they're a good liar. Nervous eyes, scratching their nose, repeating the lie, looking almost indignant while they're lying when the situation doesn't call for being indignant, that sort of thing."

"Can you read my body language?" Beckett asked, and Tristan smirked, nodding.

"What's it saying?"

Tristan's eyes moved over him slowly and deliberately, from head to toe and back again. She was being cheeky on purpose, but her focus gave her an unintentional reading, and what she read was a mix of things, but in that mix was love. By the time she met his gaze again, her fool heart was pounding erratically, and Beckett was looking at her expectantly.

"Um," Tristan said, her brain going blank.

"Is it that I'm going to pounce on you? Because I am."

Before Tristan could react, Beckett launched himself on top of her, wrestling her down onto the cushions while he tickled her sides. Tristan shrieked with laughter, quickly crying Uncle, and Beckett, also laughing, stopped immediately, resting his elbows on either side of her head and smiling down at her.

His weight on top of hers was the best thing Tristan had ever felt, and she stared up at him, trying to catch her breath.

"You gotta stop looking at me that way," Beckett murmured, shaking his head. "You're killin' me."

Tristan shifted beneath him, feeling his hardness through both of their jeans, and he briefly closed his eyes. He was killing her, too, and she gave some serious thought to throwing caution to the wind and letting things keep going from here.

"Beckett," Tristan whispered, and he gazed down at her, the love she'd read on him shining like a beacon directly into her heart. She knew she had to stop this now, before Ray wandered downstairs into something he'd never unsee, and, more importantly, before she'd had a chance to get herself on birth control.

"Tell me your middle name," Tristan continued, still whispering, and the tension broke as they both dissolved into fits of laughter.

Beckett took his cue to sit back up, pulling Tristan up with him, and he impatiently waited for the blood to start recirculating through his whole body.

"OK, OK," Beckett agreed, to Tristan's surprise. "But you can't make fun of me."

"I wouldn't make fun of you," Tristan said seriously, and Beckett smiled.

"I know. And I'm just joking; you can laugh if you need to. It won't hurt my feelings."

"It can't be that bad," Tristan replied, waiting.

"It's Bartleby."

Tristan sucked her lips in, trying in vain to keep a straight face.

"Oh," she squeaked, and Beckett looked at her in mock outrage.

"That's..." Tristan began, frowning hard in an attempt to keep her face under control. "That's not bad."

"It's terrible," Beckett said, laughing. "And I'm kidding. It's actually Beauregard, which is not *much* better, but definitely *better*."

"Oh thank goodness," Tristan let go of the breath she'd been holding, laughing and shaking her head.

"I appreciate your efforts in keeping a straight face there though," Beckett told her, his eyes crinkling at the corners. "It was almost Herculean."

***

As it approached eleven o'clock, Beckett walked Tristan to his door.

"Thanks for letting me spend the day here," Tristan said, her hand on the doorknob.

"Thanks for spending the day here," Beckett replied with a smile.

Tristan tucked her hair behind one ear, suddenly looking nervous, and Beckett put his hands around her waist, walking in close to her. He kissed her, and Tristan grasped his biceps, kissing him back.

"When can I see you again?" Beckett asked, pulling

away just slightly.

"Um," Tristan blinked, forcing her brain to start working again. "Tomorrow morning I have a doctor's appointment, and then I'm working from twelve to eight. You can come see me at the shop, if you want, or I can see you on Tuesday when I'm done work. I'll be home by two, probably."

"I might come by the shop, but I'd like to take you out on Christmas Eve, if you're free."

"I'm free." Tristan smiled.

Beckett released her, looking sorry about it.

"Great. Then I will see you either tomorrow or Tuesday."

"Goodnight Beckett."

"Goodnight Tristan."

CHAPTER 21

Early the next morning, Tristan drove across town to the Lavelle Free Clinic, signing in and having a seat, pulling out her phone to pass the time while she waited. Nearly one hour and a brief, perfunctory exam later, she left the clinic with a birth control prescription in one hand, and four sample pill packs in the other. She drove from the clinic to the pharmacy, avoiding the eyes of Gerald Franklin, who'd been the pharmacist since Tristan was born, as she slid the paper across the counter. Ever the professional, Gerald said nothing as he keyed the script into his computer, his face rivaling that of the best poker player. Tristan knew, rationally, he probably didn't care, but it didn't make the whole exchange any less awkward.

"If you wanna wait, it'll take about fifteen minutes."

Tristan nodded, sitting down in one of the four plastic chairs lined up in the tiny waiting area. The time passed quickly, and she thanked Gerald as she took the white paper bag, shoving it into her crossbody and beating a hasty retreat.

To her relief, no one was in the immediate area when Tristan got home, so she went straight up to her room and shoved her sample packs into one of her desk drawers, the newly opened blister pack following once she'd dry swallowed the first pill. Her parents, or Sol, at least, would most likely not care that she was starting birth control, but it was a conversation Tristan was in no rush to have right away.

She dressed for work and went downstairs, joining her family for breakfast before it was time for Evander to drive her to Rise and Grind.

The day was slow, likely because it was two days before Christmas, but the bright spot was Beckett stopping by shortly before her shift ended, offering Tristan a ride home. Tristan agreed, texting Evander to let him know he didn't have to come get her.

"So I don't know if you heard," Beckett said, as they pulled into Tristan's driveway. "But Dean LeFebvre called in everyone who attacked you and their families. They're all suspended with Emmeline."

Tristan shook her head.

"I hadn't heard, but good."

"Apparently they all corroborated what Emmeline said at the meeting. That she'd been planning it for awhile, and that Eva had been following you that day and had told them where you were."

Beckett put the car in park and looked at her regretfully.

"I'm so sorry, Tristan."

Tristan shook her head.

"Don't be sorry. It's not your fault."

"I knew Emmeline was a bitch, but I didn't realize how terrible she was until this past year. And I swear to you I had no idea about Eva at all."

"Beckett," Tristan said, looking into his eyes. "I'm not blaming you for what happened. Please stop blaming yourself."

Beckett nodded, running a hand through his hair, but he still looked troubled.

"So tomorrow," Tristan said, trying to distract him from his guilt. "I was thinking of going to volunteer over at the food kitchen for the dinner rush. Do you want to come?"

"Sure," Beckett nodded, smiling. "Good idea. You're working until two you said?"

"Yes. I'll probably come home and shower and head over there around four."

"Do you want me to pick you up? I was thinking afterwards we can go for a drive, try to find the worst Christmas decoration setup we can."

Tristan laughed.

"That sounds perfect," she said honestly.

"Perfect," Beckett echoed, his eyes meeting hers in the glow of the dashboard lights.

"I'll see you tomorrow," Tristan said, staring at his mouth. Talk about perfect. "Thank you for the ride home."

She kissed Beckett, and he slipped his hand around the back of her neck to kiss her back, which was quickly becoming her favorite thing he did.

She floated into the house, out into the kitchen to make a late dinner, which she ate in the living room with Oceana and Ember, ignoring their playful jabs about Beckett. She zoned out in front of the TV, thinking of Beckett, of how comfortable she felt around him already, a thrill of anticipation growing outward from her belly when she thought about their days to come.

Tristan's glow was dimmed only by the thought of returning to school -- she didn't know how Beckett would marry the social life he currently enjoyed with a relationship with her, but she had to believe they would figure it out together.

CHAPTER 22

Tristan arrived at work, bleary-eyed, at five A.M. the next day. She had suspected the shop would be dead due to it being Christmas Eve, and she was right. Aside from maybe three of her regular customers coming in for their usual, downtown Lavelle in its entirety was a ghost town.

Tristan decided to sit at a table by the window, because she wasn't sure that she wouldn't fall asleep standing up if she stayed behind the counter. She scrolled through her phone, sipping a cinnamon latte and enjoying the music that played softly over the loudspeakers. The shop door bells jingled, and Tristan looked up, surprised to see Joe, who she'd thought was in New York.

"Good morning," Tristan said, standing. "I thought you were going back up to New York for the holidays?"

"I am," Joe said, disappearing into the back and reappearing behind the counter. "I forgot to do the deposit last night, so I just need to grab that before I go. You got any plans for Christmas?"

"We don't really celebrate Christmas, per se," Tristan replied. "But we like to do the twelve days of Christmas, so tomorrow we'll start exchanging small gifts until January sixth."

"You guys pagans or something?" Joe asked, and Tristan suppressed a smile.

"Something like that, I guess."

"Well I don't care what you are, your Dad is a genius and I am forever grateful for that, so I hope you and yours have a nice holiday."

Tristan frowned.

"Sorry, my Dad?"

Joe looked at her like she should know what he was talking about.

"Yeah, your Dad. Urien? He saved Rise and Grind."

"What?" Tristan asked, surprised. "What do you mean?"

"I was struggling bigtime my first year here in Lavelle. I didn't have a pot to piss in, but I took a chance and I contacted the first consulting firm I found in New Orleans to see if there was any saving this rinky dink little shop that had always been my dream. Your Dad is who they sent me. We met three times, and on our third meeting he said to me, 'Joe, if this doesn't save your business, I promise you I'll pay your consulting fees in full. You won't be out another penny.'" Joe shook his head. "You don't find people like your Dad anymore, you know? Anyway, he didn't just save my business. He made it boom. If things keep going this way, I'm gonna open a second shop in New York."

Tristan was flabbergasted.

"I had no idea."

"Why would you?" Joe shrugged. "Anyway, I'm outta here. Give your family my best. And if this place is still this dead at noon go home if you wanna, OK? Also, in case you're gonna ask, no, your Dad isn't the reason I hired you."

Tristan laughed.

"OK. Merry Christmas, Joe."

"Merry... whatever you celebrate, T." Joe waved his hand at her and left the shop, and Tristan shook her head, sitting back down with a smile. She knew very little about the kind of work Umbris did, but it was cool all the same to hear he'd facilitated Rise and Grind flourishing.

The shop traffic did not pick up, but Tristan stayed until one-thirty anyway, needing to make as much money as she could. She had one more customer before her shift ended, and then she cleaned everything until it was sparkling, restocked, straightened up, and went home.

Beckett picked her up just before four o'clock, and they headed to the food kitchen for the dinner shift. The evening passed quickly, the place swarming with people; the atmosphere was warm and welcoming, the Christmas music cheerful, and the giant pine tree at the front of the room pleasantly scented the air around it. Tristan and Beckett stayed to help clean up, and finally left close to nine o'clock.

They drove through Lavelle in Beckett's old green Jeep, out through the main road into the adjoining communities, talking and laughing as they took in the best and worst displays of Christmas cheer they could find. When Beckett pulled into Tristan's driveway after midnight, she was sorry their night had come to an end so quickly once again.

"Tomorrow we're gonna go see my Aunt Olive, so I won't be around," Beckett said, looking regretful. "But I'll see you on Thursday?"

"I'm working in the morning and my whole family is going to the food kitchen to volunteer for a while in the afternoon, but I bet I can squeeze you in somewhere." Tristan grinned.

"I bet I can squeeze you in somewhere, too," Beckett said, reaching over and hoisting Tristan across the console and into his lap.

Tristan squealed in surprise and, laughing, settled into his arms. Beckett kissed her, his lips soft yet firm against hers, and Tristan clung to him, the rush of passion between them sweeping her away. Beckett's hand crept beneath her shirt, his hand warm, and he held her waist, his thumb stroking over her skin.

Tristan broke their kiss first, looking at him while she tried to catch her breath.

"I was thinking maybe we really can go camping in a few weeks, if you want. There's this little place by the river that I go to a lot, to be alone. I think I'm the only person in Lavelle who knows about it. There's just enough room for a tent and a little fire."

Beckett nodded.

"Let's do it."

Tristan kissed him again.

"I should go in."

Beckett nodded.

"You should."

Tristan looked surprised, and Beckett gave her a rueful smile.

"You being in my lap is getting painful."

He shifted beneath her for good measure, and Tristan struggled to keep a straight face.

"Sorry."

"You should be." Beckett grinned, kissing her one last time, and Tristan slid back into the passenger seat.

"I'll see you on Thursday. Have a nice visit with your Aunt."

"See you Thursday, Tristan. I will." Beckett smiled at her, and Tristan waved at him before hopping out of his Jeep.

She crept into her dark, quiet house, going up the stairs just as soundlessly. In the privacy of her bedroom, she lay back on her bed, biting her lip and grinning like a goof over the power she wielded over Beckett's libido.

CHAPTER 23

Christmas morning dawned gray and glaring, and Tristan got out of bed in a huff much earlier than she wanted. She yanked her curtains closed, plunging her room into darkness, and crawled back under her covers for the next several hours.

When she'd awakened again, in a much better mood, Tristan joined her family downstairs. Though they did not celebrate Christmas day, Umbris had made a full breakfast spread that had Tristan's stomach growling. She loaded up her plate with French toast, bacon, and eggs, poured herself a glass of orange juice, and joined her siblings in the living room.

Beckett had messaged her to say Merry Christmas, so Tristan chatted back and forth with him for a while before he let her know they'd arrived in Barataria and he'd talk to her later.

The Wallaces spent the remainder of the day at the house, Sol painting the shed in the backyard with the occasional assistance of Evander, and Umbris holed up in the den, working.

In the late afternoon, Evander came back inside, pointing at Tristan.

"You're it."

"I'm not dressed to paint," Tristan complained, looking down at her leggings and gray t-shirt.

"You couldn't be *more* dressed to paint," Evander corrected, heading up the stairs to shower.

On a groan, Tristan rolled off the couch, Olivia looking at her sympathetically.

"Why can't you go?"

"I have cramps," Olivia said immediately, and Tristan rolled her eyes.

She slipped her feet into her sneakers and went outside, crossing the yard to where Sol stood looking at the mostly finished shed, which she'd painted a deep, rich turquoise with bright white trim. She wore denim overalls over a white tank top, her hair pulled back in a low ponytail, and she looked all of about twenty years old.

"Oh, Trinity, there you are," Sol greeted, smiling over at her as Tristan came to stand beside her. There was a smudge of white paint on her cheek.

"Evander tagged me in," Tristan replied, taking the paintbrush Sol held out to her.

"All that's really left is the trim, but I appreciate your help."

They got to work in comfortable silence, Tristan focused on the task at hand. When she noticed that Sol had glanced at her a few times without saying anything, she looked over at her.

"What?"

"What?" Sol asked, sounding mildly bewildered.

"Why do you keep looking at me?"

"Because you're so pretty." Sol smiled, and Tristan rolled her eyes, her own smile tugging at the corners of her mouth. Still, she waited.

"You and Beckett," Sol began casually, swiping her paintbrush back and forth over the wood. "Are now a you and Beckett?"

"We are." Tristan tensed, but Sol's face barely changed as she nodded.

"I figured that would happen."

Tristan didn't know what to say to that, so she didn't say anything.

"He seems nice."

"He is nice."

"So far."

"So far?" Tristan raised her eyebrows.

"It's easy to be nice when no one's watching." Sol glanced over at Tristan, who was opening her mouth to retort. "Though Beckett is good, so he'll probably do the right thing when school starts up again."

"I guess we'll see."

While her immediate reaction had been defensive, Tristan would not pretend she didn't share Sol's reservations.

"Do you know where he's looking to go to college, if he's planning on going that path?"

"Ward Livingston University is his top choice, but he doesn't think he'll get in, so he's expecting Tulane or LSU."

"Does he know what he wants to major in?"

"Psychiatry," Tristan replied, still inexplicably surprised. "With a specialization in veterans affairs. It's a cause close to him; his Paw-Paw was a veteran."

Sol raised her eyebrows briefly, nodding.

"I'm impressed. I didn't think most seventeen and eighteen year olds had any idea what kind of career path they'd like to walk."

"Well we *are* talking about very prestigious Jamestown Academy students, you know," Tristan replied, grinning.

"And how about you, Trinity? What career path do you want to take?"

Tristan froze, her eyes on the trim in front of her. The question felt like a trap, though she knew Sol had no malicious intent. She didn't respond right away, instead watching her paintbrush move back and forth over the same spot.

"If that were to be the path I chose," Tristan finally said, her tone careful, "I think being a researcher sounds interesting. You know, like the people who are paid to research subjects for authors?"

Sol nodded, smiling fondly.

"That doesn't surprise me to hear."

Tristan again said nothing, knowing the less she said, the less she'd incriminate herself.

"And what is your dream school?"

"Oh," Tristan waved her hand. "I haven't really looked much into it… but I did also actually check out Ward Livingston in passing, and I can see why it's Beckett's first choice."

"Hmm."

Tristan moved around the back of the shed, still not looking at Sol. She was a terrible liar, always had been, and she was sure Sol already knew she was lying, but she didn't want to look up and have her face confirm it.

"Have we talked about the acceptance ceremony coming up in June?" Sol asked, and Tristan's stomach clenched as she shook her head.

"Well, you probably already know about it, but just in case you don't, it will take place a week or two after you graduate. All new recruits have to wear white, of course, and you will all line up before the adults in the community, since no children are invited, in front of this gorgeous altar all lit up with fiery torches. Two of the Elders, usually the oldest and the youngest, will greet you and the crowd, and ask for volunteers to come up to lead you through your vow. They'll say it first, and all of you will repeat after them. When that's finished, the Elders will come around and seal you into the community by placing their hands over yours. Your hands will feel very pleasantly warm, there will be a flash of gold as they seal you, and it will be over. Not much pomp and circumstance for a ritual that has such importance placed upon it."

Tristan felt sick, and she dared not open her mouth in the event she vomited; she knew about the acceptance ceremony, not because she'd heard about it, but because she'd seen it in her premonition.

"Maybe too much importance," Sol mused, and Tristan's senses began to tingle.

"I don't think anyone really talks about the alternative, do they?" Not waiting for an answer, Sol continued. "Probably because the last person to deflect from the community did it at least ten years ago, after the laws had changed."

Sol lapsed into silence, and Tristan peeked over at her to find her staring off into the distance. Sol shook her head, shrugging as she resumed painting, and Tristan did the same.

"Anyway. Deflection is rare, but it does happen. I don't know a ton about that path, but I know for certain it's not an easy one to take, if for no other reason than having the community turn its back on you after being there from the first breath you ever took. And of course you lose your abilities, and any psychic connection you have with anyone in the community, including your own family, and you lose the life that had been mapped out for you and the person it was mapped out with. It's incredibly lonely and isolating, from what little I've seen, though due to the law changes it's probably easier now, in a way, than it ever was. Used to be that the family of the deflector was forbidden from reaching out to them once they made that choice, until and even after they were caught and brought back. That I do know, and all too well."

Tristan was openly staring at Sol now, but Sol was miles away, heartbreak written all over her face as she remembered Adara.

"I think it's also hard because once you break, that's it. The wagons circle around the community members who are inevitably injured by the deflection, leaving the deflector to grapple alone, with the exception of their family, and maybe not even always. You just immediately live life as a commoner. No more connections to help you with your future path, or inclusivity into neighborhood schools and events, not that everyone cares about that." Sol resumed talking like she hadn't stopped, and Tristan continued to stare at her, paintbrush suspended in the air. "I think we don't realize, being uncommon, what a privilege we have as community members. But common people do it every day, and some have a much harder time than others. It all works out eventually, or so it seems. It's just not a path I'd ever choose for myself, or for my children."

Sol finally looked over at Tristan, who blinked several times, at a loss for words.

"It's not up to me to choose, though, and you and the twins know your Father and I will support you in whichever direction your compass spins you. I didn't mean to dump all of this on you at once and at random, but we haven't gotten to talk much lately, and I feel like your Father and I have hardly talked to you at all about what's on the horizon for you."

"It's OK," Tristan said, her voice sticking in her throat. "Everyone has been busy."

"Yes." Sol surveyed Tristan over the shed roof. "I'm glad we had this opportunity."

"Me too," Tristan replied, meaning it. Her voice was soupy with emotion, and she knew Sol would have to be blind to miss the tears in her eyes, but Sol just gave her a placid smile and kept on painting.

When they'd finished, they headed back inside, Tristan feeling both heavier and lighter than she had been as she made her way upstairs to shower. Before joining her family in the dining room for dinner and their small gift exchange, Tristan shook her head hard, trying to clear it. Like Oceana had said, it was only December, and to fret over June now seemed both silly and like an exercise in futility. It would do Tristan and her anxiety a world of good to take each day as it came until she could no longer put off what loomed ahead.

CHAPTER 24

Tristan left for work the next morning when everyone was still sleeping, per the usual for her offensively early shifts. Business had clearly resumed as though Christmas had not been the day before, judging by the frazzled greeting Ellie gave her as Tristan hurriedly joined her behind the counter.

"How was opening?" Tristan asked when they got a moment to breathe, looking at Ellie's short hair, which was standing on end.

"Horrific," Ellie replied, smoothing down the chestnut strands. "There was a line out the door before six, and we had three allergy orders in a row."

Tristan pulled a face.

"I'm so sorry."

"You've done it yourself more than once," Ellie said dismissively. "It's fine now that you're here, but man there are a lot of angry people the day after a holiday. Also, where did they all come from? Lavelle is not that big, and I didn't recognize at least half of the faces."

Tristan laughed.

"Friends and families in town for the holidays?"

"Probably. I need to get me some friends and family who would go on six A.M. coffee runs for me. Hey, how's Evander? He canceled Sunday but didn't really say why."

"Oh," Tristan replied, feeling awkward, "He forgot he's grounded until the new year."

"For what?" Ellie's eyes widened, not a trace of shame in them for prying.

"He got into a fight at school. Broke his football teammate's nose."

"Damn," Ellie replied, looking both impressed and startled.

"The guy deserved it," Tristan assured her, giving her the Cliff's notes on what had happened on Halloween.

"Theo Fitelson *is* a jerk," Ellie nodded, scowling. "I remember him too well, which is saying something considering he was a sophomore when I graduated."

Tristan's shift was short that day, two o'clock arriving before she felt like she'd had a chance to even blink, and she waved goodbye to Ellie before rushing home to change before the whole Wallace clan headed to the food kitchen.

Dolores was delighted to see Tristan back so soon, and beside herself when she saw the entire family had come, too. Sol took Tristan's usual place beside Dolores to assist with the cooking, and Tristan, Umbris, and her siblings manned the food station.

The Wallaces arrived home after the dinner rush and subsequent cleanup, and Beckett showed up shortly after that. He and Tristan sat out on the front porch, watching the thunderstorm that had rolled into Lavelle on Beckett's drive over.

"It's a shame we never get snow," Tristan commented.

Beckett shook his head.

"It's not."

Tristan laughed.

"Not a fan?"

"I have never actually seen snow and I'm in no rush. I am a warm weather guy through and through."

"Boston has all four seasons, you know."

"Well if I'm lucky, we'll both get into WLU and I'll have you to keep me warm when my cold intolerant self is shiverin' in my layers of fleece and wool."

Tristan laughed.

"I don't think it gets *that* cold, but I'll be happy to if it works out that way."

Tristan rested her head on Beckett's shoulder, looking up at him as he gazed back down at her.

"It has to work out that way," Beckett murmured, and Tristan hoped it would more than anything.

CHAPTER 25

The rest of winter break passed more quickly than Tristan was ready for, for a few reasons. First, she and Beckett had seen each other every day of their break, had rung in the new year together alongside Olivia, Tyler, Evander, and Ellie, and though they would see each other at school every day also, Tristan did not want to relinquish the freedom of doing whatever they wanted with their time together. A very close second, however, was Tristan's unpreparedness for how things would be once she and Beckett returned to Jamestown Academy as a couple. Third was her unpreparedness to return to Jamestown Academy at all -- the high school's social network was connected in a way that assured gossip got around before it had even fully left the lips of the informers, so by now everyone knew what had happened the day school had let out, and what punishments had been doled out for Emmeline and her squad.

Tristan believed that Beckett would do the right thing and defend her against anyone who had anything to say, and she knew that having Olivia in her corner, too, was priceless, considering Olivia was probably the mouthiest thing to walk the halls of Jamestown Academy, but Tristan dreaded her return all the same, and was not very comforted by the knowledge that Emmeline and her friends would not also be returning at the same time. On the contrary, Tristan felt as though their later return was only delaying the inevitable.

For his part, Beckett was steadfast in his reassurance that everything would be fine. Though he didn't say it, Tristan got the impression that he'd spoken to his immediate circle of friends and they now knew better than to try and antagonize her. He hadn't mentioned this, either, but Tristan also suspected his friends hadn't taken the news of their coupling as well as Beckett had been assuming they would -- more than once, she'd seen Beckett scowling at his phone after he received a message, but her anxiety had kept her from asking for details.

"Hey," Tristan called out to Olivia on the Monday morning they returned to school, as Olivia passed by Tristan's bedroom door.

"Hey," Olivia replied, stopping and leaning against the door jamb.

"Do you have any lingering bad feelings?" Tristan asked, twisting her fingers together. "Or did they disappear after the attack?"

Olivia studied her for a moment, her gray eyes somber.

"There is something residual, yes. It's weaker than before, but it's there."

Tristan nodded.

"I was hoping it was just my usual anxiety, but something told me to ask you anyway."

"It will be OK, whatever it is. Beckett has you, me and Ember and Tyler have you. If anyone corners you for whatever reason, just stress signal or, if you can, just walk away and come find one of us. It sucks so bad that you have to do this, Trin, but please do it."

Tristan nodded.

"I will."

Olivia smiled.

"Do you want to ride to school together?"

"I would love that."

It turned out that Tristan had worried for no reason, at least that day. Plenty of people stared, at her and at her and Beckett together, and there were more whispers than usual ricocheting off the walls of the old building, but no one approached Tristan and no one said anything to her outright.

Just as he'd promised, Beckett's friends, who clearly had their reservations and allegiances to Emmeline and her besties, also acted very neutrally towards Tristan. She didn't imagine she'd ever reach the point of friendliness with them, but Tristan wasn't interested in that, anyway -- she could live very contentedly with neutrality.

The first week back, as a whole, was only brutal in the way of their schoolwork. There was no such thing as easing back into the curriculum at Jamestown, and with mid-year finals approaching at the end of the month, the heat was on. Tristan also had the January gathering the first weekend after she'd returned, which she told Beckett about on Friday as they sat on their bench during their free period.

"Another family reunion?" Beckett asked, raising his eyebrows. "You guys really like each other, huh?"

Tristan laughed.

"Yes, there are get-togethers every month. Once I graduate I won't have to keep going, but for now..." Tristan shrugged.

Beckett frowned good-naturedly.

"Your family reunions are mandatory? And are they still reunions if you have them every thirty days?"

Tristan laughed again.

"I know it sounds ridiculous. Families are strange, aren't they?"

Beckett nodded, dropping the subject, and Tristan was relieved.

"Do you want to go to the movies tonight?" Beckett asked. "Our local theatre has been playing old movies, and this weekend is *The Haunting,* from 1963."

"Sure," Tristan smiled. "What time?"

"Good question." Beckett pulled out his phone, looking up from the screen a few minutes later. "There's a nine o'clock showing. Does that work?"

Tristan nodded.

"I'm working until eight. Do you want to pick me up from Rise and Grind or shall I meet you at the movies or what?"

"I can pick you up from the shop."

"It's a date," Tristan said through a grin.

She and Beckett gathered their things and he walked her to her car. At the driver's side door he kissed her, a quick one, and Tristan watched him go, grinning when he looked back at her over his shoulder with a smile. She hurried home, running late for her shift now, and threw a change of clothes into her bag before going right back out the door to Rise and Grind.

"T," Joe said, as soon as Tristan came through the door.

"Joe?"

"Can you work tomorrow night?"

Tristan pulled a face.

"I'm sorry, I can't. I have a family thing."

"Ellie has a family thing, too. I really need to hire a weekender."

"I'm sorry. You know I'd do it otherwise."

"I know, I know. Alright, let me get a sign posted in the window for a weekend position, and I'll cover tomorrow night myself."

Tristan clocked in and tied her apron around her waist, listening to Joe tell Ellie about his New York holiday as he did inventory. Joe didn't usually take on shifts at Rise and Grind -- he preferred to work at home whenever possible, trusting the shop in Ellie and Tristan's hands. Tristan was glad he was going to hire someone else for the weekends, however; even though their town was small, and coverage wasn't normally a problem, it would be nice if Tristan didn't have to pick up Ellie's slack *quite* so often.

The shop door opened, and Emmeline, Hattie, Tara, and Eloise entered. Tristan's stomach dropped into her toes as they approached the counter, and she had never been more thankful that Joe had decided to come in that evening. Joe, who knew what had happened to Tristan and who had been responsible, stepped forward. Ellie made a face, and Tristan smiled her way -- she knew Ellie would have been just as happy to go to bat for her.

"Hi," Emmeline greeted Joe sweetly. "Do you have any drinks called The Snitch? I'm a big Harry Potter fan, see, and I notice quite a few drinks on the menu up there are named after movies."

"Do you see one up there called The Snitch?" Joe asked, and Ellie snorted.

Emmeline's cheeks turned very faintly pink, but she merely raised an eyebrow. Her friends, who had been laughing, instead looked offended on her behalf.

"No secret menu in this rinky dink place, then." Emmeline's eyes moved to Tristan, and for a few seconds the two of them had a staredown.

"Secret menus are for chains. Do you want to order something or do you want to let one of your friends order instead?" Not waiting for an answer, Joe turned to Tristan. "T, do me a favor and grab a new bag of the Cape Cod dark roast from the back, would ya?"

Tristan nodded, grateful beyond words for Joe, and disappeared into the back. Rise and Grind didn't carry a dark roast Cape Cod blend, which Tristan laughed quietly about once the door had swung closed behind her. She busied herself with organizing the stock shelves until the door behind her opened and Ellie poked her head in.

"They're gone. You'll never believe this, but they didn't actually want to order anything."

Tristan laughed.

"You don't say."

Ellie shook her head.

"Are they still bothering you, at school?"

"They're all suspended until February, but judging by how tonight went, I am assuming they will get right back to it when they return."

Tristan went back out into the shop, thanking Joe for handling Emmeline and the other girls.

"Wicked," Joe muttered, shaking his head. "Wicked,

wicked girls."

"Are you safe?" Ellie asked, and Tristan looked at her in surprise, thinking she sounded just like Celes.

"Sorry?"

"Like, they're not going to try anything else right? You don't think they'll go after you again?"

"They will be expelled if they do, so no, I don't think so. I am sure the comments will probably be nastier than ever, but that's OK. They don't bother me anymore."

"Pathetic." Ellie shook her head in unison with Joe, who hadn't stopped.

The rest of Tristan's shift was uneventful, and, once she'd clocked out, she changed in the bathroom for her date with Beckett. She hadn't really been paying attention to the clothes she grabbed, so Tristan was relieved to see she'd picked jeans and a long-sleeved, v-neck green shirt instead of, say, jeans and a pair of leggings.

Tristan said goodbye to Ellie and Joe, and went out to meet Beckett, who was waiting for her in the parking lot. He smiled at her when she got in the Jeep.

"Did I ever tell you that you look great in green? And red. And black. And white. And blue."

Tristan laughed.

"I think you've mentioned it. Thanks. How was your night?"

Beckett shrugged.

"My parents were just warming up their vocal chords when I left, so probably by now the neighbors are listening to the dulcet tones of them screaming at each other."

"I'm sorry." Tristan took his hand, and Beckett squeezed it.

"*I'm* sorry that I'm always complaining about them."

"Don't be."

Beckett drove them to the theatre, and he took her hand again as they approached the old building. Tristan smiled at him, and then looked ahead, her eyes widening in surprise.

"Hi!" Olivia greeted, grinning from where she stood beside Tyler, who greeted them as well.

"Fancy meeting you here," Tristan replied, smiling back at them.

"I figured you wouldn't mind if they joined us," Beckett said, and Tristan shook her head, confirming.

The classic movie was campy in the best way, and good for several unexpected jumps. Tristan, who did not normally enjoy horror movies, enjoyed the experience with Beckett and Olivia and Tyler. When the movie ended, the four of them went to Mack's Diner, and Tristan was relieved to not see anyone who would ruin the extremely good night she was having.

As it always seemed to go, however, Tristan had relaxed too soon. As they were wrapping up their meal, Eva Revet approached their table.

"Hi Beckett," Eva said, her voice ice cold and her eyes even colder.

Beckett just looked at her, and Tristan felt him tense up beside her.

"Go away, Eva," Olivia said, a warning in her voice.

"No." Eva looked at Olivia, raising her eyebrows.

"It's fine, we're leaving anyway." Beckett nodded at Olivia and Tyler, and Olivia slid out of the booth, drawing herself up in front of Eva and making it as far as her eyebrows, not that she cared.

"So this is what you do, I guess, you take your dates to the movies and then to Mack's? How original of you," Eva said, turning away from Olivia to Beckett, who was still ignoring her.

Beckett had positioned himself in front of Tristan, and he twisted around to look at her, taking her hand.

"Ready?"

Tristan nodded.

"You can ignore me all you want, Beckett, but sooner or later you won't be able to."

"Um, creepy," Olivia said, making a face at Eva.

Beckett strode out of the diner, pulling Tristan firmly along behind him, and she looked at him once they got outside, her eyebrows raised.

"Are you OK?"

Beckett nodded, but his jaw was working and he said nothing.

"What a weirdo," Olivia muttered, shaking her head as she and Tyler appeared behind Beckett and Tristan.

Tristan nodded, still wondering about Beckett's reaction.

"I'll see you at home, I guess?" Olivia said to Tristan, looking from her to Tyler.

"See you at home," Tristan confirmed.

The couples went their separate ways, Beckett still silent

beside Tristan as he drove. She had just opened her mouth to ask him what was going on in his head, when Beckett's phone rang.

He frowned at it, not recognizing the number but noticing the area code was local. He pulled over, putting the phone to his ear.

"Hello?"

"Beckett Benson?"

"Yes?"

"This is Officer Grieg, from the Lavelle police station."

"Yes?" Beckett asked, tensing up, and he saw Tristan frown over at him, worry creeping over her face.

"Your Dad asked me to call you. He and your Mom were brought in earlier for a domestic dispute, and they'll be here awhile. He didn't want you to worry when you got home to an empty house."

"Thanks for letting me know," Beckett said woodenly, disconnecting.

"What's going on?" Tristan asked, studying his profile anxiously.

"My parents are at the police station. Domestic dispute."

"Beckett, I'm so sorry."

"Will you come home with me?" Beckett asked, looking vulnerable in the glow of the dashboard lights, and Tristan nodded.

"Of course."

Tristan texted Olivia, who agreed to cover for her, and she and Beckett rode the rest of the way to his house in silence.

"Do you mind if we go upstairs?" Beckett asked, once they got inside. "Sometimes when I need to clear my head, I like to climb out onto my roof and sit there for a while."

"Whatever you want."

Tristan followed him up the stairs and through his bedroom, which she couldn't get a good look at in the dark, but which was bigger than she'd expected compared to the rest of the house. She glanced at his bed, confirming it looked exactly as it had the night she'd seen him from the gathering, and she was thankful the darkness hid her flushed face.

Beckett climbed out his window and then helped Tristan out, and they sat together, leaning against the house.

"I need to get out of this house," Beckett said, shaking his head. "I keep telling myself that graduation will be here in no time, but it's not getting here soon enough. And it's not like I'm leaving right after graduation anyway, though I've thought about a short-term lease somewhere in town between graduation and starting college."

"How long has this been going on?" Tristan asked quietly.

"At least two years now. The screaming matches started about a year ago, but the fighting started within a year of us moving here. I don't know why. My Dad claimed up and down he was fine with the move from Alabama, but I think it became pretty clear pretty quick that he actually really resented it."

Tristan, sensing Beckett wasn't finished, kept quiet.

"I have asked my Mom point blank why she doesn't

leave him. She knows he's having an affair, and it's clear she hates him. She hasn't been able to answer me, but I have the worst feeling it's because of me."

"Beckett--"

Beckett shook his head.

"I think she feels like she needs to stay because she knows *he* won't leave, and if *she* does it's going to throw my life into upheaval in my senior year, and she doesn't want that. At this point I'm just hoping she'll leave or kick him out once I go away to school."

Tristan nodded.

"No matter the reason, though, it's not your fault. OK?"

Beckett gave her a sad smile, and Tristan linked her arm with his, resting her head on his shoulder. They sat in silence for a long while before Tristan spoke.

"So can I ask what was up with your reaction to Eva back there?"

"I'm just really angry at her and the other girls. I don't want to talk to or even look at any of them, and she's the worst because not only did she tell them where you were, she decided to stroll on by and watch what was happening to you. What kind of sociopath do you have to be to do something like that?"

"Beckett, I'm OK. I--"

"And I'm not OK, Tristan," Beckett interrupted, turning to look at her with a distressed expression on his handsome face. "You're so strong, and I know that the attack awoke something in you that has helped you come to terms with it, but I'm not as strong as you. I still have dreams about finding you the way I did that day."

"I'm not that strong," Tristan confessed, shaking her head. "Emmeline and a few of the others showed up at Rise and Grind tonight and my stomach about fell through the floor."

"They what?" Beckett's jaw clenched, and Tristan frowned.

"I'm going to have to get used to it. They're going to be hellbent on antagonizing me now that they didn't get away with something for once. Maybe not at school, but definitely if they see me outside of it."

Beckett pulled out his phone, shaking his head.

"What are you doing?" Tristan asked, alarmed.

"I'm sending Emmeline a message."

"No." Tristan gripped Beckett's arm, and he looked over into her pleading face. "Please don't. Please, Beckett. I ignored them tonight, just the way you ignored Eva, and that's what I'll keep doing. I just want to move on."

Reluctantly, Beckett switched off his phone screen. Guilt lanced through him as he took in Tristan's upset expression, and he wrapped his arm around her, pulling her closer to him.

"I'm sorry. You're right. Ignoring is the best thing to do."

"Thank you for wanting to fight for me," Tristan whispered, her lips just inches from his.

Beckett kissed her then, urgently, and Tristan kissed him back, shivering as his cold hand snaked around to the back of her neck.

"We should go in." Beckett pulled away, but kept his face close. "You're cold."

"So are you."

Beckett stood and pulled Tristan to her feet, climbing back inside his bedroom and then reaching down to help her in, as well. They stared at each other in the dim lighting for just a moment, before reaching for each other.

Beckett cradled Tristan's head in his hands, kissing her, and she kissed him in return. He slowly walked forward, until Tristan's back pressed against his bedroom wall, and she tilted her head as he kissed her neck. Her heart was pounding erratically, her nerve endings in overdrive, and she was nervous in the best way for what was about to happen. Beckett pulled back and looked at her, his thumbs tracing her bottom lip.

"We can stop if you want to," Beckett told her, eyes on her mouth, but Tristan quickly shook her head.

"No."

Beckett grabbed the hem of Tristan's shirt and pulled it over her head, discarding it, and then removed his own. He pressed against Tristan, torso to torso, his skin hot against hers, and Tristan's fingers trailed down his bare back.

Beckett moved them again, this time towards his bed, and when Tristan's knees hit the back of it, she undid her jeans with shaking hands, shimmying out of them. Beckett went next, and the feel of him, hard against her, made Tristan tremble all over.

Beckett guided her down onto the bed.

"Beckett," Tristan palmed his chest, and he looked up from where he'd been planting kisses along her collarbone.

"I... I'm... I haven't..."

"We'll go nice and slow," Beckett told her, his lips brushing hers as he spoke, his eyes earnest. "If you want to stop, you just tell me and we'll stop, OK?"

Tristan nodded, biting her lip.

"OK."

True to his word, they went slow. Beckett eased her into each step, waiting until she was comfortable before he continued, leaving her only to grab a condom from his dresser across the room. By the time they got to the actual act, Tristan thought she was going to die from wanting him.

The expression squicked Tristan out, but nevertheless, Beckett made love to her, giving her time to adjust around him and acclimate to the initial pain before he settled into a slow, rolling rhythm.

The whole time, he kept his hands by her face, brushing his fingers lightly over her skin or gently through her hair. He watched her for any sign that she needed to stop or wasn't enjoying herself, but she just stared up at him in awe, occasionally closing her eyes and biting her bottom lip.

Beckett had known it already, before this moment, but as he watched Tristan watching him, he wondered how obvious it was now that he'd fallen in love with her.

***

Later, Beckett held Tristan close to him. He hadn't told her he loved her, not wanting to scare her away, so instead he hoped she could tell by his actions.

"Do you have to go?"

Tristan nodded regretfully.

"I do. I wish I didn't."

"Me too." Beckett pressed a kiss to Tristan's forehead. "I'm not going to see you until Sunday, right?"

"Right."

"What if I just didn't let you go?" Beckett grinned, tightening his arms around Tristan.

"That would be fine with me." Tristan smiled back, her hand sliding up his chest and coming to rest on his shoulder as she kissed him.

Beckett turned onto his side so his body fit against the length of hers, and Tristan wrapped her arm around his neck.

"There's still so much I want to do with you in this bed," Beckett told her in a low voice, and Tristan smiled at him almost shyly.

"Thank you for being so gentle," Tristan whispered, her black eyes catching and absorbing the watery moonlight that filtered in through his bedroom window.

"I'll never hurt you, Tristan," Beckett said seriously, as he smoothed a strand of Tristan's hair away from her face. "Not on purpose, not unintentionally, not in any way. I promise you that."

"I promise, too."

Tangling their limbs together, Tristan and Beckett stayed that way for a while longer until, on a sigh, Tristan sat up.

"Will you be OK if I go?"

Beckett nodded, one hand splayed over his bare chest, the other behind his head, his eyelids heavy with fatigue. Tristan took a moment to appreciate the sight of him before she slipped out of his bed, pulling her jeans back on.

"You don't have to walk me out," Tristan said, holding out her hand as Beckett started to get up. "You look so comfortable."

Beckett smiled, shaking his head.

"I'll get comfortable again."

They walked downstairs, and at the front door Beckett gently pulled Tristan to him.

"Have a safe drive home. Thanks for staying with me awhile."

"I will." Tristan studied his face in the glow of the porch light, and Beckett smiled at her again.

"Beautiful girl."

Tristan kissed him softly, slipping her arms around his waist and hugging him, and Beckett squeezed her back, not wanting her to go, knowing she couldn't stay.

"Keep me posted about your parents?" Tristan asked, and Beckett nodded. "I'll see you Sunday, then."

"See you Sunday, Tristan."

Tristan left reluctantly, getting in her car to discover it was nearly three A.M., which was nearly three hours past her curfew. Pulling a face, Tristan hoped Olivia had done a good job covering for her. She drove home, her stomach rippling with the memory of what she and Beckett had just done. Tristan couldn't have hoped for a better first time -- she wasn't so sure that many other guys her age would have taken the time to make sure it had been as comfortable and enjoyable as possible. She was sore now, but she knew it would pass, and she looked forward to the next time. Tristan grinned to herself the rest of the way home, switching off her headlights when she rolled into the driveway.

As it turned out, turning off her headlights was not necessary; as Tristan approached the house, she noticed a light glowing in the living room, and her nerves began to jangle. She should have known better than to think she'd get away with anything under Sol and Umbris's roof, should have known better than to ask Olivia to cover for her. On a sigh, Tristan got out of the car. She would be honest with her parents when they asked what had kept her out, at least to an extent. There was no point in lying -- aside from being terrible at it, Tristan knew they'd see right through it anyway.

Tristan looked in the living room as she approached, and both Sol and Umbris looked up.

"Hi." Tristan grimaced and, to her amazement, Sol and Umbris looked more amused than angry.

"Let me guess. You forgot you had a curfew?" Umbris asked dryly.

"Is that the best Oceana could come up with?" Tristan muttered. She sighed again. "I didn't forget. Ray and Gabriella Benson are at the police station, they were taken in over a domestic dispute. Beckett didn't want to be alone, so I waited with him as long as I could, and my phone was in my bag so I lost track of time. I should have called instead of asking Oceana to cover for me. I'm sorry."

Sol and Umbris exchanged a glance, Sol's eyebrows lifting in surprise.

"Don't let it happen again," Umbris said, and Tristan nodded.

"You better get to bed." Sol looked up at Tristan tiredly. "You're going to be suffering at the gathering tomorrow night, missing out on all of this sleep."

"And you guys will too, because of me. I'm sorry,"

Tristan apologized again, twisting her fingers together. She hadn't even thought about it, which was unlike her.

"We'll be fine," Sol said, looking at Umbris again.

"Goodnight. Love you." Tristan waved and trudged up the stairs, guilt gnawing away at her gut.

She had just reached her bed when her bedroom door opened and Olivia slipped in.

"Forgot I had a curfew, really Oceana?" Tristan asked, turning and crossing her arms.

"I'm sorry! I didn't know what else to say, and "she probably fell asleep" sounded lame!"

Tristan smiled in spite of her frustration.

"It's OK."

"Are they super mad?" Olivia asked, looking nervous.

Tristan shook her head.

"Surprisingly no. They just said not to let it happen again."

"Oh, it must be nice to be the golden child," Olivia quipped good-naturedly.

"Why are you still awake?" Tristan asked her.

"I was texting with Tyler until like an hour ago and when I realized you still weren't home, I couldn't sleep." Olivia shrugged. "How was the rest of your night?"

"Uhh, good. Fine. You know," Tristan replied, turning towards her mirror and braiding her hair. As she watched, Olivia's mouth dropped open behind her, a mischievous glint creeping into her eyes. "Don't even try it. You know I seal the second I step foot onto this property."

Olivia grinned.

"I don't need you to be unsealed to know what you were up to tonight."

Tristan blushed from the roots of her hair all the way down to her chest, and Olivia cackled behind her.

"Go to bed, Oceana!"

"Your aura is totally orange," Olivia said, still laughing. "Oh gods, and you just had a conversation with Mom and Dad!"

"Get out!" Tristan cried, mortified, and Olivia laughed herself all the way back to her room.

Tristan pressed her hands to her red cheeks, her eyes wide and panicky. Was her aura really orange? She hoped not, or she would never be able to look Sol and Umbris in the eye again.

CHAPTER 26

The next evening, Tristan stared at herself in the mirror, thinking about how tired she was of being nervous to attend these gatherings and how now, on top of her regular nerves, this month she also had to worry about her orange aura. Tristan had never been able to read auras -- if she concentrated very hard, she could maybe see some very watered down colors, but it gave her a headache and she didn't care, so it wasn't something she'd ever worked to cultivate. Tristan turned from side to side, looking at her black jeggings, black turtleneck sweater, and black booties, feeling unsettled, trapped in her own skin, in a way she hadn't in a long time. She swept her hair into a high bun and sat on her bed, staring unseeingly out her window.

Celes was going to know something, probably exactly what, had happened with Beckett. Despite Tristan sealing, despite the fact that she was not going to be his ever, but at least until June as far as he knew, he was going to know and she was not prepared for what his reaction might be.

"Hey," Olivia spoke from her doorway, and Tristan twisted around to look at her.

Olivia was dressed stylishly, as usual, in black leggings, a lace-front black shirt, and black leather moto jacket. On her feet were Tristan's black and white Adidas sneakers, which, as usual, she hadn't asked to borrow.

"We're leaving soon."

Tristan nodded.

"OK."

Olivia sat next to her, looking at her carefully.

"You know I was joking about your aura, right?"

"What?" Tristan's head snapped around, and Olivia had the good grace to look sheepish.

"I was just giving you a hard time."

"Oceana! I've been avoiding Mom and Dad all day!"

"Sorry!" Olivia held her hands up, and Tristan shook her head, blowing out a relieved breath.

"So how was it?" Olivia asked, after a few beats.

"Oceana," Tristan groaned.

"You're right, weird question, sorry."

Tristan laughed, then sobered.

"Celes is totally going to know."

Olivia nodded.

"Probably. It's not really any of his business, though."

"No," Tristan agreed. "But there was that whole kiss thing at the Solstice Celebration..."

"Oh, the exact thing I told you not to do, you mean?"

Tristan gave Olivia a look, who gave her one right back.

"You should tell him *something*, though, Trinity. I'm not suggesting you tell him you know what, but you probably should tell him you're dating Beckett."

"You just said it's none of his business," Tristan

pointed out.

"What goes on between you and Beckett isn't," Olivia clarified. "But Celes is a good person, and you ignored my good advice to not lead him on, so the least you can do is be honest with him that you're dating someone."

Tristan sighed.

"I know you're right, I just..."

"I know." Olivia gave her a sympathetic face, then stood, holding out her hand. "Ready?"

Tristan took it, letting Olivia pull her up, and followed her downstairs. Her phone vibrated in her hand, and she smiled when she saw a message from Beckett.

I miss you.

I miss you too. How is everything going?

Quiet. I can't tell which is better, them fighting or them not speaking at all.

Beckett had messaged her earlier to let her know that his parents had arrived home around four that morning, escorted by Officer Grieg. Beckett had fallen asleep on the couch waiting for them, and neither of them spoke when they came into the house -- Ray had gone upstairs, and Gabriella had gone down. Tristan ached, wishing she could or would have stayed with Beckett, hoping her presence would have been a comfort if nothing else.

For not the first time, and for what she was sure would not be the last, Tristan did not want to go to the gathering that night. She wanted to see Beckett, to invite him over to her empty house and have him spend the night with her. It was this fantasy that she lost herself in on the drive to the gathering, leaving her surprised when they pulled into the familiar

New Orleans-adjacent bayou.

"Something is wrong," Umbris said immediately, and everyone in the car tensed.

"What's going on?" Olivia asked, but Umbris and Sol did not reply.

"We have to turn around." Sol looked at Umbris, a frown creasing between her brows.

Brake lights lit in front of their SUV and then went out, the car, which had suddenly appeared through the darkness, stopping just short of hitting them. A man approached the driver's side window, and Umbris rolled it down.

"Ventis," Umbris greeted Ventis Dearing, a fellow community member.

"The gathering has been moved to next weekend, to the alternative meeting place on the southern point. This one was discovered. The guards are still managing the situation."

Tristan felt ill. She didn't want to know what Ventis meant by "managing the situation". She exchanged an uneasy look with Olivia and Evander as Umbris nodded and Ventis headed back to his car.

"If this was discovered, does that mean we can't come here at all anymore?" Evander asked.

"I'm not sure," Sol replied. "I guess it depends on what actually happened and how the guards are handling it."

"I think we know how they're handling it," Olivia snapped, contempt in her voice. "They live for this kind of thing going down."

"That's not fair, Oceana." Sol frowned as she looked back at her.

"Fair or not, it's the truth. You'd think by now they could choose something less barbaric than slaughter; what about memory wiping? Why does death have to be the go-to?"

"Death isn't always the go-to, it depends on the circumstances. But it's not our job to know why they make the decisions they make, Oceana," Umbris said, looking at her in the rearview mirror.

"Well maybe it should be." Olivia crossed her arms and stubbornly lifted her chin, and Umbris and Sol let the subject drop.

"So that's it?" Evander asked. "We just go home and try again next weekend?"

"Yes."

Tristan smiled, pulling out her phone to text Beckett.

So the reunion was canceled tonight, last minute. It was moved to next weekend instead, so we're on our way back home now. Are you busy tonight?

Busy seeing you when you get home. Are you hungry? My Mom just left for my Aunt's house for the night and once again I don't know where my Dad is, so I was going to order dinner from Perry's Pizza.

Tristan confirmed she could eat, letting Beckett know she'd see him in a little over an hour for a movie and pizza. The drive home seemed to take much longer than the drive to the gathering, but at long last Umbris pulled into the driveway, and everyone got out, stretching their legs.

"I'm going to go over to Beckett's, if that's OK," Tristan said to Sol, who looked over at Umbris.

"Will you remember your curfew tonight?" Umbris

asked, and Tristan nodded, trying not to roll her eyes.

"Midnight sharp." Umbris gave her a stern look before turning and heading towards the house.

Tristan followed her family inside, grabbing her purse and her car keys before driving over to Beckett's house. A thrill ran through her when he opened the door, looking at her like he hadn't just seen her less than twenty-four hours ago.

"Hi beautiful," Beckett drawled, inviting her in, and Tristan smiled.

"Hi."

Beckett closed the door behind them and wrapped his arms around Tristan, kissing her hello.

"I'm glad you're here," Beckett said, his lips brushing hers, and Tristan smiled up at him again.

"I'm glad to be here."

Tristan was more thankful than Beckett knew to be at his house that night; though wanting to spend all of her free time with him was her biggest motivation, she was also relieved to the point of near tears that she didn't have to think about facing Celes for another week.

CHAPTER 27

Tristan twisted her fingers nervously as she watched Celes, who had said nothing for the last several minutes. Tristan had used the week between gatherings to figure out what she was going to say to him, and had settled on, as usual, a modified version of the truth delivered in as few words as possible.

She knew Celes had known as soon as he'd seen her that something had changed, could tell by the way his smile had dimmed and a frown had come to settle on his brow. Tristan had to ask him to go for a walk that night, which was further proof that he knew.

Tristan hadn't been sure how to broach the subject, but Celes took care of that part for her.

"You want to talk to me."

It had been a statement, not a question, and Tristan had nodded.

"I wanted to let you know I'm seeing someone. A commoner."

"*The* commoner. The one who rescued you."

Again, a statement. Tristan bristled at the idea she'd been *rescued,* but she let it slide, nodding again. Celes had gone silent then, and Tristan watched him, his expression displeased but not revealing much else.

"We should go back," Celes finally said, turning and

heading back to the clearing without waiting for Tristan.

"Celes, wait." Tristan caught his arm, and he turned to look at her in the dark, still frowning. "I'm sorry. I--"

"It doesn't matter. What you do and who you do it with until June is not my business."

Until June. Tristan swallowed around the sudden hard knot in her throat. Oh gods, she was dreading hurting Celes more than she'd dreaded anything else in her life so far. How was she going to do it? Where would she get the strength?

Celes walked off again, and Tristan trailed behind him, cursing herself for not listening to Olivia the night of the Solstice Celebration. Still, there was a small sense of relief in having come clean to Celes; if nothing else, he would probably give her a wide berth until June. *Until June.* Ugh.

Tristan sought out Olivia when she reentered the clearing, and Olivia took both of her hands, squeezing them.

"I should have listened to you," Tristan said miserably, and Olivia nodded.

"Yes, you should have."

That made Tristan laugh, and Olivia laughed too, hugging her.

"It's going to be OK."

"Maybe." Tristan eyed the Elders, who were gathered at the head of the clearing in a tight circle, their faces tense as they talked amongst themselves. "Something is going on."

Olivia agreed, following Tristan's gaze. A breeze blew through the clearing and Tristan shivered -- the occurrence reminded her too much of her premonition for comfort.

"Did you get to talk to Celes about the laws?" Olivia

asked, thinking along the same lines as Tristan.

"I didn't, and I'm sure he won't be thrilled to talk to me now." Tristan shook her head, frustrated.

"That's OK. I'll talk to him." Olivia set her chin and started to walk away, but Tristan grabbed her elbow.

"Oceana, no."

"It'll be fine, Trin. Celes and I are friends, kind of, and I can be discreet when I need to be."

Tristan hesitated, but ultimately let Olivia go, watching her cross the clearing to where Celes stood with his family. He looked surprised to see her, but curious, and much friendlier than he would have looked at Tristan, probably. Tristan recalled the part in her premonition when she'd realized Celes was in love with Olivia, and she wondered if that was at all based in reality. She chewed her thumbnail, watching them with interest as they stepped away from Dune and Thera, but she saw nothing out of the ordinary.

The thought of Celes and Olivia was a strange one for Tristan -- she envisioned years of awkward family dinners, at minimum -- but, oddly, she could also see how it could work between them; they were both smart and ambitious, both generally rule-followers by nature, and both honest nearly to a fault.

Snapping out of it, Tristan blinked a few times, looking away from Olivia and Celes. What was she thinking? Olivia was dating Tyler, happily, and after June, Tristan was sure none of the Crenshaws would want to have anything to do with *any* of the Wallaces. Plus, gods knew Olivia didn't need Tristan playing the weirdest game of matchmaking ever for her, and Tristan didn't even know if Olivia would end up joining the community herself. Tristan shook her head, refocusing on the task at hand.

A few minutes later, Olivia came back over to Tristan, looking serious, but not anxious, which gave Tristan hope.

"Well?" Tristan asked her, and Olivia looked over her shoulder before she answered.

"The committee of the Elders can review any law at any time, be it current or terminated, and the rumor right now is that one of the main reasons Orion has been brought back is to do just that." Olivia spoke quickly and quietly, so quietly that Tristan had to lean all the way in to hear her. "But, and this is a big but, every single Elder has to agree to abolish or reinstate a community law. There is no majority over minority ruling -- if they all can't agree, it doesn't happen. Supposedly Orion is not thrilled with this, but there's nothing he can do about it."

Tristan looked at the group of Elders once again, thinking about how most of them looked around, or at least close to, Orion's age, which didn't make her feel great. There were two on whom Tristan could potentially pin her hopes, though -- Bayle Vencroft and Abrus Macimier, both closer to Umbris and Sol's age than not, and both fairly newly appointed to the Elder committee.

"Did Celes say when they're going to be reviewing the laws?"

Olivia shook her head.

"He said it's just a rumor at the moment, but that could mean that it's in the future plans or it's actually going on right now. Hard to tell without having inside information."

"Did he suspect anything about your questions?"

Olivia shook her head again.

"No. He likes to talk about the community and the rules, so I don't think he really thought anything of it, and my questions were pretty innocuous, if I do say so myself."

"Thanks for doing this, Oceana," Tristan said genuinely, and Olivia smiled at her.

"We're not out of the woods, but at least things don't seem as dire as they did when I talked to Hydran."

Orion did not end up making an appearance at that gathering, much to Tristan's relief. Still, a time or two the odd breeze would pass through the clearing, and she couldn't help but remember the same thing happening at the gathering where Orion had made his comeback a couple of months ago.

"Ember." Tristan sidled up beside Ember, speaking to him as quietly as Oceana had spoken to her.

Evander looked around, his eyebrows rising in surprise when he saw Tristan standing beside him.

"Did you say my name?"

"Yes."

"Why are you talking so quietly?"

"Because," Tristan hissed. "Listen, are you getting any weird feelings?"

"Only from you," Evander said, already looking bored.

"Hilarious. I'm serious. Have you noticed that random breeze that keeps passing through here?"

"No. But it's January, even down here in the bayou. There probably would be a breeze."

Tristan shook her head.

"Do you remember the gathering a couple of months ago when Orion came back? Do you remember how, when they introduced him, a breeze went through the clearing? That's what I keep feeling."

"I don't remember that."

Tristan glared at Evander, who made a face at her.

"I'm sorry, Trin. I'm not trying to be a dick -- I didn't notice it then, and I haven't noticed it tonight."

Tristan turned away from Evander, looking for Olivia instead. She spotted her across the way, talking to Aurelis Knight, and went over to interrupt.

"Hi Aurelis." Tristan smiled briefly. "Do you mind if I borrow Oceana for a sec?"

"Not at all." Aurelis wandered away, and Olivia looked expectantly at Tristan.

"Have you noticed a breeze moving through here tonight?"

Olivia frowned.

"What?"

"A breeze, through the clearing? Have you noticed it? It's happened like twice now."

Olivia shook her head.

"No, but I can't say I was really paying attention. Why would a breeze pass through, though? Aren't we sort of sealed off from the elements?"

"Exactly. Do you remember the night Orion was introduced a couple of months ago? It happened then, too."

Olivia shook her head again, concern in her eyes.

"No, Trinity, I don't remember that happening then either."

Tristan fell silent for a few beats, frowning.

"OK. I'm going to go ask Mom and Dad."

Tristan disappeared before Olivia could respond, locating Umbris and Sol talking with Ventis Dearing.

"Mom?" Tristan asked, from behind Sol, and Sol turned with a smile.

"Hi honey."

"Mom, have you noticed a breeze moving through here tonight?"

Sol shook her head.

"No, I don't think so. Why?"

"It's happened twice now, which I thought was strange since there wouldn't really be any reason for a breeze in here."

"That would be strange."

"It..." Tristan faltered, tried again. "It also happened the night the Elders introduced--"

Sol's eyes had gone wide before Tristan had finished her sentence, her face turning so white that Tristan grabbed her arm in alarm.

"Mom? Are you OK?"

"Trinity," Sol whispered urgently. "Seal. I want you to seal, and I don't want you to unseal no matter what anyone says to you, OK?"

Tristan hurriedly sealed, her heart starting to pound. Olivia, having watched the exchange from across the way, rushed over.

"What's going on?"

"We need to have a family meeting tomorrow," Sol said, turning and touching Umbris's shoulder. He bid Ventis goodbye and joined them, Evander closing the small circle they formed.

"What's wrong?" Umbris asked, looking at Sol's distressed face with worry.

"Family meeting tomorrow." Sol looked at Umbris, who, after a few beats, nodded, understanding crossing his face. He looked at Tristan, Olivia, and Evander, his face grave.

"Have either of you felt this breeze Trinity mentioned?" Sol asked the twins, who shook their heads.

"I need you to tell me immediately if you do, do you understand?"

Olivia and Evander nodded seriously. Evander opened his mouth, but Sol shook her head.

"We'll talk tomorrow."

"Are we in danger?" Olivia asked calmly, but Sol and Umbris didn't respond right away.

"You could be."

The Wallaces turned to find Celes looking just as grave as Umbris. He swept his hand in an arc over the five of them, which Tristan knew would temporarily shield them from intrusion from everyone, even the Elders.

"All of us?" Olivia asked him, and Celes nodded.

"We talked about this the last time you came to New Orleans," Celes said, addressing Sol and Umbris. "The suspicion we had about Orion watching you. It's no longer a suspicion."

"Is he closing in?" Tristan asked, her stomach dropping.

"It seems that way, but it's hard to tell. The Elders are the most powerful in the community; their abilities are almost limitless, though it's their duty to keep themselves in check. We know what we do about Orion because he's permitting that much, but there's no telling what he's really up to at any given time." Celes addressed Tristan's parents again, "The best thing you can do is go on as normal; the less you know, or appear to know, the better."

"Is he targeting Trinity specifically?" Olivia asked, and Celes visibly hedged, saying nothing.

"Celes," Olivia said, a pleading note in her voice.

"He could be," Celes said finally, looking at Olivia and then Tristan with an expression that said he was sorry to be the messenger. "Again, it's almost impossible to tell, but I overheard your conversation just now about the breeze and... I can't say I've felt it either, which makes me think only Trinity has, intentionally. She's the eldest and she's up next to join the community, so it's not a stretch to think he'd be paying special attention to her, even teasing her."

All eyes on Tristan. She looked back at everyone, lifting her chin and mentally shelving her nerves.

"I'm not going to live in fear over this. I assume if he's particularly interested in me, he'll eventually come for me no matter what I do, and I'll deal with it then."

"I won't let that happen," Sol said fiercely. "He won't

be coming for any of you. Mark my words."

CHAPTER 28

February saw Jamestown Academy's Valentine's Day dance, and Tristan very, very, very, very reluctantly agreed to go with Beckett. Emmeline and her friends had returned to school just in time for the dance, and Tristan was anticipating a verbal Valentine's dance massacre, which didn't exactly thrill her.

Even more reluctantly, Tristan agreed to let Olivia dress her for the dance. It was this decision that led to Tristan shaking her head, unable to stop, as she looked in the mirror a mere half hour before Beckett was set to arrive to pick her up.

"No. No, no, this is not going to work. I look completely ridiculous, Oceana."

Her dress was red, and comprised of two pieces -- a sleeveless, intricately embellished cropped top, and a short, flouncy tulle skirt with an embellished high waistband. On her feet were the same black leather booties she'd worn to the Solstice Celebration, and Olivia had styled her hair into an updo, with a French braided fishtail that swept back into a loose bun at the crown of her head. She'd also done Tristan's makeup -- completely neutral except for a fire engine red lip that Olivia swore would survive the apocalypse, not that Tristan wanted to test that theory.

"You look completely *amazing,* you mean," Olivia corrected, coming to stand beside her. "You're gonna knock Beckett's socks off."

For herself, she'd gone with a short, backless champagne colored dress, with a deep v-neckline, spaghetti straps, and all-over beading in a creeping ivy pattern. For her own hair, she'd pulled it back into a wide, loose braid and woven a thin vine of tiny, faux ivory flowers through it. Her makeup was also neutral, including her lips for a change, and she looked ethereal, like a sprite or an alien from planet gorgeous.

"Oceana, I never wear this kind of thing. I don't know what I was thinking, I--"

"You were thinking that you looked beautiful in it, and you were right," Oceana interrupted. "You *are* beautiful, Tristan, and your body is banging. You should show it off more often. Now let's go downstairs; our dates will be here soon."

Beckett's face when he came through the front door of her house made the dress worth it, Tristan decided, watching Beckett take her in. He looked stunned, and, as he raised his eyes to hers, Tristan had to suppress a shiver.

"Hi," Tristan greeted, as he approached, dressed in a black suit with a white shirt and red tie.

"Hi, beautiful," Beckett referred to her by the now-familiar pet name, which always made Tristan smile.

Beckett slipped a rose corsage onto her wrist and then took her hands, looking her over.

"You look incredible, Tristan."

"Thank you. You do, too." Tristan meant it.

After Sol and Umbris had taken photos of Tristan and Beckett, Olivia and Tyler, and the four of them together, they finally left the house, getting into Beckett's Jeep.

"No Evander tonight, huh?" Beckett asked.

"He's on a date with Ellie. She said she'd die before she stepped foot back in Jamestown, so they went to dinner and a movie in Winslow," Olivia replied, and Beckett laughed.

"Fair enough."

They arrived at the school before Tristan had time to prepare herself, and Beckett waved Olivia and Tyler ahead of them, stopping Tristan and sliding his hands up and down her arms as she twisted her fingers together.

"I'm not going to let anyone ruin your night. You're here with me, you are more beautiful than any other girl here could even hope to be, inside *and* out, and we're gonna have a good time. And if we don't, we'll leave and start our camping trip early. OK?"

"OK." Tristan smiled at Beckett, who smiled back at her before kissing her and taking her hand firmly in his.

Tristan wasn't sure what she'd been expecting the dance to be like, but the reality was much more boring than whatever she'd been imagining. After his pep talk, Beckett and Tristan had caught up with Olivia and Tyler, entering the academy together and taking a seat on the bleachers among most of the other attendants. There were some round tables with chairs set up near the bleachers, covered in long, shimmering white tablecloths with centerpieces of rich crimson roses, but they were all already occupied. To the far left of where the foursome sat, there was a long table laden with a punch bowl, small cups, and various finger foods. Straight across from them, on the opposite side of the gym, was the DJ, and to their far right was the backdrop and set for the official Valentine's dance photos. The entire gymnasium had been transformed into a veritable explosion of frothy, red, white, and pink decorations, and Tristan looked around in half-wonder, half-revulsion.

"Wow," was all Tristan could think of to say, and Beckett, Olivia, and Tyler nodded in agreement.

They sat there for a while, chatting, and eventually the boys wandered off to get drinks and food. Tristan looked around nervously, feeling strangely exposed without Beckett beside her, and Olivia squeezed her hand.

"Try to chill out," Olivia said, not unkindly. "I don't think Emmeline and her friends are going to try anything, not so soon after coming back and definitely not with teachers crawling all over this place."

She had a point, and Tristan nodded, her shoulders relaxing.

"Plus, I'll clock anyone who tries anything." Olivia's voice was casual, and Tristan laughed, though she knew Olivia meant it.

Once Beckett and Tyler had returned and they'd eaten and drained their cups, Beckett stood, holding out his hand.

"Shall we?"

As though Beckett had timed it himself, the DJ began to play a slow song that Tristan didn't recognize, but that moved pleasantly through her ears. She smiled, standing and taking Beckett's hand. They walked to the dance floor, Tristan ignoring the looks they were getting in favor of looking at Beckett.

Beckett took Tristan in his arms, pulling her close. He was warm and solid, familiar, and Tristan smiled over his shoulder at the feel of his fingers against her bare skin. As they danced, she thought again about how strange it was to still be partially in disbelief that she was dating Beckett Benson, but also to partially feel like their getting together had been a reunion after a long, long time apart. She shivered, realizing that side of things was more than likely their destiny connection, and Beckett pulled back to look at her.

"Are you OK?"

"I'm fine." Tristan gazed at him, and she watched his eyes take in hers, their aquamarine depths seemingly fathomless, saying more than he'd ever said aloud.

The song ended and Tristan blinked, breaking their stare. Beckett looked dazed for a moment longer before smiling and running a hand through his hair. There was a look on his face that Tristan was having trouble reading, and she briefly frowned.

"Are *you* OK?"

"I'm... fine." Beckett shook his head, his face clearing, and Tristan made a mental note to ask him about it later.

"I'm going to run to the bathroom," Tristan told him, looking around for Olivia.

"Do you want me to walk you?" Beckett asked earnestly, and Tristan laughed.

"No, it's OK. I'm going to grab Olivia."

Beckett nodded, and Tristan made her way to Olivia, gently touching her arm. Olivia turned sharply, her face relaxing when she saw it was Tristan.

"On edge much?" Tristan asked, and Olivia made a face.

"Ha ha. What's up?"

"Can you come to the bathroom with me?" Tristan asked lamely. She felt embarrassed, but was grateful that Olivia nodded readily.

"Sure. Let's go."

The sisters exited the gym and walked the short distance to the bathroom, passing various couples who were making out in the shadowy hallway. The bathroom was empty save for one occupied stall, and Olivia leaned against the sinks, waiting for Tristan, who quickly did her business.

Tristan was washing her hands, Olivia using her pinky to fix her eye makeup, when the stall door behind them opened and Eva Revet exited, bringing with her such a malevolent air that even Tristan felt it sweep over them. Olivia turned immediately to face Eva, while Tristan eyed her in the mirror. Holding Tristan's gaze, Eva wordlessly walked up to the sink beside her, washing her own hands and then just standing there, continuing to stare, dripping water all over the floor and her tall black heels.

Tristan would not be the one to speak first. She stared back at Eva, her body tense, anger slowly creeping into her bones and muscles. In vivid clarity she flashed back to the afternoon of her attack, to Eva's smirk as she strolled by, knowing full well what she'd done and what she'd done nothing to rectify.

As though Eva could read Tristan's thoughts, an identical smirk crossed her strangely wan face. Tristan gripped the sink's edge, and Olivia stepped around her, planting herself firmly in the narrow space between the two of them.

"Can we help you with something?"

Eva, maddeningly, still said nothing. She merely stared down at Olivia, her eyes as hard as the tile beneath their feet, shadows etched into the skin beneath. The smirk left her face, and again Tristan felt the absolutely wretched vibes rolling off of her in waves.

"If you think you're intimidating us, you don't know us at all," Olivia spoke in a low, hard voice, leaning towards

Eva until their noses were practically touching. "If I were you, I'd stay far away from my family."

"Is that a threat, Olivia?" Eva finally spoke, her voice brittle, almost hoarse, which Tristan also found extremely odd. She frowned.

"It's a word of advice," Olivia responded icily. "Advice I wouldn't advise going against."

"You have no idea who you're messing with," Eva said, sneering, looking almost amused.

"I am not messing with anyone," Olivia shot back. "But you apparently haven't learned your lesson. Was a month-long suspension not enough for you? Will you risk expulsion in your senior year?"

Eva started to answer, but Olivia cut her off.

"I don't care. Stop trying to intimidate my sister. This is the last time I'm telling you."

"You'll be sorry. All of you." Eva bent her head so her eyes were level with Olivia's, and Tristan felt Olivia move back just a fraction of an inch. Eva stared at her for a few long seconds more, then walked out of the bathroom, not giving them a backward glance.

Tristan blew out a noisy breath.

"Gods, she's creepy. Should we go back to the gym?"

But Olivia didn't move. Tristan frowned again.

"O?"

Tristan walked around the front of Olivia, looking at her. Olivia looked terrified, which threw Tristan's stomach for a loop. She grabbed Olivia's shoulders, giving her a gentle but firm shake.

"Oceana."

Olivia looked up at Tristan, and gradually the fear faded from her face.

"What's going on?"

"I don't know," Olivia whispered, trembling. "I don't know."

The bathroom door opened and one of Olivia's fellow underclassmen, Samantha Braje, entered, giving Tristan and Olivia a funny look.

"Are you OK, Olivia?" Samantha asked, looking at Tristan with a mixture of nervousness and suspicion.

Tristan glared at her while Olivia smiled at Samantha, nodding.

"I'm good, thanks. Tristan, shall we?"

Olivia took a deep breath and turned her smile on Tristan, who nodded and reluctantly followed her out of the bathroom.

"What happened?" Tristan asked in a low voice, when she saw there was no one within earshot at their end of the hallway.

"I thought I saw..." Olivia trailed off, shaking her head. "Nothing, it couldn't have been. Eva is just super creepy, like you said. She really freaked me out back there."

"You thought you saw what, Oceana?" Tristan asked quietly, not letting it go that easily.

"Nothing. Really." Olivia gave her a smile that didn't quite reach her eyes. "I've been so stressed lately, and not sleeping well, and I think I'm just a little more paranoid than usual. Plus you know, I am pretty tough, but I'm also pretty small, and sometimes my brain forgets that and then re-members it at the most inconvenient time, usually when I'm toe to toe with someone who has a half a foot on me."

She was lying, but Tristan would not keep pushing her here at their school. She made another mental note to follow up with Olivia about it tomorrow, nodding mildly in the mean-time.

The rest of the dance was uneventful, Eva nowhere to be found. Tristan relaxed enough to enjoy herself, and didn't stiffen up too much when Beckett and Emmeline's mutual friends came over to chat and dance beside them. A few times, Tristan did catch Emmeline throwing bitter looks her way as she danced with Beckett, but nothing more came of it.

Still, the end of the dance in sight was a relief, and Tris-tan rolled her eyes, giving in with a laugh, as Beckett pulled them over to the photography station, not missing the chance for them to have their souvenir photo taken. He stood behind her, solid as a brick wall, his body pressed against hers from chest to knees. He wrapped one arm around her waist, the other holding her arm in the typical "prom pose", and Tristan hoped her smile didn't give away her accelerating heart rate.

He held her just as close for the last dance of the night, singing along with an again unfamiliar song in not a terrible voice, right in Tristan's ear. She smiled, resting her temple against his cheek, listening.

***

Once the dance had ended, Tristan and Beckett parted ways with Olivia and Tyler, who were spending the night at Tyler's house, and headed off to Tristan's house to change and make their way through the woods to where they'd be camping. Umbris and Sol had gone out for the evening, and Ember was still out with Ellie, so the house stood empty and dark as Beckett pulled into the driveway.

"I'm not sure when my parents will be home, so let's be quick," Tristan told Beckett, who nodded as she unlocked the door. She pointed down the dark hall towards the kitchen. "There's a bathroom right in that hallway to your right. I'm going to run up to my room."

Beckett hesitated.

"Uh, is there a light we can switch on?"

Tristan smiled, hitting a switch on the panel beside the door.

"Sorry."

"No need. I'm just not real crazy about big dark houses."

Tristan gave him another apologetic smile and kissed him quickly, scurrying upstairs. She was back down in record time, having changed into her favorite dark wash jeggings, warm black boots, and a thick black sweater over a white tank. She'd left her hair and makeup the way it was, and Beckett eyed her in appreciation when she came into view.

"Ready?" Tristan asked, and Beckett nodded.

They got their backpacks, the tent, and a small bag of equipment out of the back of Beckett's Jeep, and Tristan led the way through her backyard and into the woods. Their only light was the moon, which totally disappeared in some places particularly dense with foliage.

"Hang on." Beckett stopped, and Tristan stopped as well. Moments later, his phone flashlight lit up the immediate woods in front of them, and they resumed walking.

Tristan supposed the woods, especially on a windy, blustery night such as that one, would be considered creepy to most people, Beckett being one of them. To her, however, the semi-turbulent weather matched her semi-turbulent state of being most days, and Tristan found the big, bright moon nearly as soothing as the daytime's big, bright sun. Plus, she'd grown up with these woods; she'd explored them inside out and upside down, every trail, every overgrown path, every twist and turn they had to offer in their modest patch of Lavelle. She knew the wildlife, knew the greenery, knew there was nothing threatening lurking in the shadows or behind some of the trees which were as wide as two of her. Tristan could probably walk to the river with her eyes closed by now, not that she'd attempt it. She smiled into the dark as she led the way through the last bit of forest to "her" clearing.

"Here we are." Tristan held out her arms, and Beckett looked around, his impressed face illuminated in the moonlight. The river, less than ten feet from where they stood, rushed quietly, and the overgrown grass whispered soothingly in the wind as Beckett let his eyes adjust.

"Wow. How did you find this place?"

"I grew up here. Well, you know, with my back to the woods. I used to love, still love, going off by myself to explore, and a few years ago I found this place. I've been coming back ever since. There is literally no one here, ever, so when I need to be alone and think, this is where I come."

Beckett nodded, and they got to work setting up their tent and the small, portable campfire pit. Beckett had it going within minutes, and they sat down beside it with their s'mores ingredients, grinning at each other.

As far as Tristan was concerned, that night was one of the

best she'd ever had. Between the dance and being alone with Beckett -- totally alone with next to no chance of being interrupted -- under the stars in her favorite place, she couldn't remember the last time she had felt so happy. Hours later, she drifted off to sleep with Beckett's bare chest pressed against her back, his warmth radiating through her thin t-shirt, and his arms enveloping her against the February chill that permeated the tent in spite of the small space heater running on high.

Tristan slept blissfully until the night had begun to give way to the dawn. She wasn't sure what stirred her out of her slumber, but her pounding heart let her know that whatever it had been, it was terribly out of place in their secluded clearing. Her eyes opened wide and took stock of the tent, which looked just as it had when they'd fallen asleep. Tristan stayed perfectly still, just listening. Beckett was still wrapped around her, sleeping peacefully, and she tuned out the sound of his even breathing. For endless minutes she listened, her ears straining against the deafening silence... Wait, *why* was it so silent? Why couldn't she hear the river?

"Trinity."

Her name, a whisper on the morning wind. Tristan's stomach clenched painfully, her heart still pounding, and her breathing grew panicky.

"Trinity. Trinity. Trinity."

All around the tent now, in different volumes, her name. She couldn't identify the voice, couldn't tell if it was male or female, but she felt it rebound in her skull, over and over, a sense of dread unlike she'd ever known settling over her.

Tristan twisted around and shook Beckett's shoulder, but he slept on, oblivious. She didn't know how, but she knew he would not wake up for this no matter how hard she tried to rouse him.

"Trinity."

The voice boomed right outside the tent flap, and Tristan jumped, sitting up. She quickly pulled on her jeans, sweater, and boots, and she scooted to the opening, unzipping it and squinting against the freezing cold and the stark whiteness that awaited her.

Snow. Everything was covered in a thick blanket of pure white snow, so bright it was nearly blinding. She shielded her eyes, stepping out of the tent, and looked around. There was no one there. She shivered as the wind blew, snowflakes catching in her hair and eyelashes, the tiny particles also seeming to glow against the ombre lavender sky. Where had this weather come from? The forecast had not mentioned a word about snow, which was impossible -- snow was something they never got in Lavelle; it would have been the top story all over the local news stations.

"Trinity."

The voice again, ringing across the clearing from every direction; its reverberation intensified until her very bones felt like they were rattling, and Tristan had to stop herself from covering her ears. It wouldn't make a difference anyway. To her left, a thick tree branch cracked beneath the foreign weight of the heavy snow, and fell to the ground with a muted thud.

"What do you want?" Tristan cried out, her voice reedy with terror.

"You. This is a warning. Relent. Relent in your selfish pursuit. Follow the path your ancestors have laid for you. Follow your bloodline. Relent. Relent, or disobey at your own peril."

Tristan's hands flew to her mouth. She knew the voice now. It was Orion. He had found her, away from her family, powerless. How? Wasn't he still too weak to travel away from the swamp in which he'd been hiding? More importantly, though, *what the hell was she going to do?* Tristan looked back at the tent in which Beckett innocently slept, knowing she would protect him no matter what came next, and an incredible anger coursed through her. Who was Orion to follow her here and threaten her? What kind of coward was he, waiting until she was isolated from her family and then swooping in? What right did he have?

"I won't." Tristan spoke loudly and clearly, with bravado she didn't even remotely feel. "Joining the community is no longer a law. I am free to choose, and you cannot force me onto the path I have always known I will not take."

For a few moments, there was silence. Then the woods to her right rustled, and Tristan's head whipped around as Eva Revet emerged, still in the dress and heels she'd been wearing at the dance. Tristan's heart dropped through the ground. Eva was smirking, always smirking, and her long, raven hair rippled in the wind as she approached Tristan. She walked right up to her, stopping mere inches from Tristan's face. Tristan lifted her chin, trying to channel Olivia and her courage, refusing to step back though she wanted nothing more than to somehow wake Beckett so they could run as far away as their feet would carry them.

"Relent."

Orion's voice boomed out of Eva's mouth, and she lifted her hand, placing it dead center on Tristan's chest. Pain detonated in every part of Tristan's body, and she screamed until she was sure her throat was bleeding.

"Tristan! Tristan!"

She was shaking, a voice was yelling beside her ear, and Tristan opened her eyes. She looked around, panicked, and saw Beckett with his hand on her shoulder, his expression mirroring her own. Tristan scrambled past him, fumbling with the tent flap with violently shaking hands until she got it unzipped. She stared outside in horror -- while it was dawn, the sky the same lavender it had been, there was no snow. No Orion. No Eva. Tristan looked down. She was still in her t-shirt and underwear, her clothes still piled where she'd discarded them last night. Her chest was pale and undisturbed, her body felt fine. It had been a nightmare. Just a nightmare. Right?

"Tristan?" Beckett's voice was heavy with sleep, full of apprehension. "What the hell?"

Tristan flopped back into the tent, staring at the ceiling as she struggled to catch her breath.

"I'm sorry," she said finally, turning her head to look at Beckett. "I had a nightmare."

Beckett laid down beside her, his hand on his chest. He blew out a long breath.

"I hoped I would never have to hear you scream like that again."

"What?" Tristan asked sharply, and Beckett's troubled eyes met hers.

"You were screaming like... like you were being attacked again... and I couldn't wake you right away. I was shaking you and calling your name for at least two minutes until you came around."

Tristan rolled towards him.

"I'm sorry."

Beckett shook his head.

"Don't apologize. It was just, uh, quite a way to wake up."

Tristan smiled in spite of her still-jangling nerves, and Beckett wrapped his arm around her, pulling her close. He kissed her forehead.

"Do you want to tell me about it?"

Tristan shook her head, knowing she couldn't even if she wanted to.

"No. It was... dumb. I'd rather just try to forget about it as quickly as possible."

She felt Beckett nod as he began running his fingers through her hair, and Tristan drifted off into her own thoughts. Had that really only been a nightmare? She couldn't remember ever having had one so realistic. She'd been able to feel the brush of the snowflakes on her skin, the cold wind that blew off of the river. Everything had been as vivid as though it'd really happened, but it couldn't have. How could it have if she was still in the tent, still undressed, and Beckett had confirmed she'd been sleeping?

Tristan knew it ultimately didn't matter; while her nightmare about her execution had technically only been a nightmare, she was sure that this most recent incident had been a premonition, too. Another warning from Orion. Another confirmation that he was circling above her head, closing in. What did he want with her? Was Eva working for him? Why was it so important to Orion that she, what had he said, follow her bloodline? Was it really just a matter of pride? Was it really just that he didn't want her to embarrass him by turning her back on the community? He seemed to be making an awful lot of fuss, if that was the case.

Something told her that was not the case.

CHAPTER 29

Celes had been right that Tristan's next crash would come in March. Her energy surge came while she was at school on a Friday, in the form of the light above her head in Chemistry class suddenly growing brighter and brighter until the long tube had shattered completely, causing a dull tinkling sound as the glass shards were caught by the plexiglass that housed the lightbulbs, extinguishing the offensive glow. Emmeline had looked at Tristan with trepidation, but Tristan kept her face as interested as her other classmates as she glanced upward, shrugging before she returned to her test.

Sure enough, her crash followed on Wednesday. She'd told Sol the day before, so Sol didn't even bother to check on Tristan that morning before she called her out of school for the day. Tristan stayed in bed happily, having forgotten how absolutely exhausting a crash was, snuggling back under the covers and closing her eyes, hoping she'd sleep until Saturday's gathering.

An indeterminable amount of time later, Tristan felt her arm being squeezed, vaguely heard her name. She cracked one eye open, her brain immediately protesting the disturbance, and saw Olivia standing beside her bed.

"Beckett is here," Olivia said in a low voice. "Downstairs. He was worried when you didn't come to school or answer his messages all day."

"Did you tell him I'm sick?" Tristan asked, her words so heavy with fatigue that she was nearly slurring.

Olivia nodded.

"He's persistent."

"Well what am I supposed to do, Oceana?" Tristan asked, with effort, her eyes closing again.

Olivia sighed. She placed her hand on Tristan's arm, and Tristan opened her eyes as she felt energy flowing into her. Her brain's immediate reaction was to shake Olivia off, but the energy flow was like finding water in the desert, so she hesitated for a good thirty seconds or so, basking in the feeling.

"Stop." Tristan sat up, finally pulling her arm away. "You don't have it to spare."

Indeed, Olivia looked tired and wan, her crash having been on Monday, but she merely shook her head.

"I'll be fine, Trinity. Feel better enough to go downstairs and see Beckett?"

Tristan swung her heavy legs out of bed and stretched, her shoulders slumping when she finished, resting.

"Gods, this sucks."

"Well this is probably the last time you'll have to deal with it, if that helps." Olivia gave her a dejected smile, and Tristan stood, squeezing her hand.

"I'm just going to use the bathroom and then I'll come downstairs."

Olivia nodded and left the room, and Tristan pulled her hair into a ponytail, grimacing at her deathly pallor. She freshened up in the bathroom as quickly as she could, then made her way downstairs.

Beckett stood as Tristan crept into the living room, his eyes immediately scanning her face in concern.

"Hey, beautiful. How are you feeling?"

Tristan sat on the couch, leaning her head back against the cushions and briefly closing her eyes.

"I'll be OK."

Beckett sat beside her, giving her a once-over. She was as pale and sickly looking as she'd been back on Halloween, and it suddenly occurred to him that he'd never gotten around to asking her what had really been going on at the time. To be fair, however, things were different between them then -- the odds that she'd actually tell him were not even remotely in his favor. Maybe she'd tell him now.

"Is this the same thing you were dealing with back on Halloween?" Beckett's voice was low; though Olivia had disappeared into the depths of the house and Beckett hadn't seen Evander or their parents at all, he couldn't be too careful.

Tristan hesitated, then nodded, her eyes still closed.

"And is it... Is there something I should know, Tristan?"

Beckett's tone had Tristan turning to look at him. His voice had been filled with dread, matching his expression, and his eyes were hooded with worry.

"It's nothing chronic or terminal, if that's what you're asking," Tristan said finally, trying to sound as reassuring as possible.

Beckett blew out a long, relieved breath.

"That answers that. But also doesn't really answer a bunch of other things."

Tristan nodded. It wasn't the first time Beckett had attempted to ask her about something he found strange or puzzling, community-related things, and Tristan had side-stepped his question. She couldn't find a way to explain to him why she and her family really were kind of odd when you spent time with them up close, how they all seemed to know so much with so little conversation passing between them, how Evander was so strong for someone so slight and why Olivia was forever looking at people like she knew what their exact intentions were. She couldn't answer at all for the obvious calm vibe Sol carried with her from room to room, or the obvious powerful vibe Umbris carried with him. Tristan knew it frustrated Beckett, though he'd always accepted her hedging, and she was always quick to apologize to him and then send up a silent prayer to the universe that he wouldn't grow tired of her secrecy before June, when she could finally let him in on some things.

"I know. I'm sorry. The best I can give you right now is that it won't always be this way."

Tristan looked genuinely torn. That cryptic answer also didn't offer him anything, but Beckett didn't want to be a jerk and push her to talk about things she clearly wasn't ready to talk about. He was as curious as anything, but he would have to content himself, for now, with the knowledge that Tristan was not dying. He forced aside a flash of frustration -- these conversations never seemed to be productive or satisfying -- reminding himself that just because they were dating it did not mean he was entitled to her secrets, or really anything about her at all. His biggest fear was pushing her too hard, right out of his life; though they'd only been dating a short time, entertaining the idea of a future without Tristan was no longer an option, whatever it took. The thought, sudden and intense, alarmed him.

"Are you OK?" Tristan frowned, watching his expression rapidly shift, and Beckett confirmed he was.

"I'm fine. I'm just glad you're OK."

Tristan continued to look at him, knowing he was lying, but accepted his answer. What else could she do? It would be laughably hypocritical of her to demand he tell her what was on his mind when there was so much she herself was withholding from him. She sighed, her eyes drifting closed once again.

"I'm sorry I'm rotten company today."

"Don't apologize. I should actually probably get going and let you get back to bed. I just wanted to make sure you were alright." Beckett took her hand, his thumb stroking over the back, and Tristan gave his a faint squeeze.

"Thank you for coming to check on me."

Tristan stood and Beckett protested, but she waved him off. She walked him slowly to the door, and rested her head against the frame as he stepped out onto the porch.

"Can I kiss you?" Beckett asked, and Tristan smiled, nodding.

Beckett kissed her softly, and Tristan cupped his face.

"I'll see you tomorrow."

As usual, Beckett looked like he didn't want to go, but he reluctantly stepped back, giving her a short wave as he descended the porch steps. He drove home, continuing to muse over Tristan's mysterious, non-contagious, non-terminal illness, as well as the many other mysteries she presented. Though he reminded himself again that they were still a new couple, the more Beckett thought about it, the more he realized Tristan was almost a total stranger to him. He wouldn't push her to divulge anything she didn't want to, but he was going to do some light digging the next time he saw her.

***

Sol administered mini-infusions to both Olivia and Tristan that night, enough so that Olivia's color returned and Tristan felt wiped out, but not completely useless. She was still as pale as alabaster, but she could deal with that until the gathering.

The gathering. Tristan could not believe another month had passed so quickly, could not believe that she was now just three months away from making the biggest decision of her life. She had the ceaseless feeling that she was facing more than just rejecting the choice expected of her -- she felt as though the clock was running down, that the very hands of time and space were wrapping slowly around her throat and starting to squeeze. She was in danger, she knew it and she'd known it since her nightmare in the woods, and waiting for Orion to make his actual move had her nerves constantly on edge.

Tristan knew, rationally, she should lay it all out for Umbris and Sol. She knew she should come clean, confess what she was planning and prepare them for it. She knew she should tell them about the visions she'd had through her dreams, that Orion seemed to have a purpose in mind for her that went far behind her joining the community and starting a life with Celes. But it was fear that kept her frozen and, maybe more than that, it was her desire to avoid the whole mess and pretend everything was normal until she could no longer keep up the charade. It was the coward's way out, Tristan knew that, too, but denial was more powerful than she was, and so she kept it all to herself and as often as she could tried to completely ignore that the community existed at all.

That method didn't work too well when a gathering was mere days away, however. Tristan was distracted for the rest of the week, not able to lose herself in the time she spent with Beckett the way she usually did. The way he usually did, Beckett could tell something was up -- Tristan could see it every time he looked at her, but she pretended not to notice. She was starting to hate the person secrecy was turning her into, but, again, fear had her in a chokehold.

On Friday afternoon, at their bench after school, Beckett closed his laptop after trying and failing, twice, to get Tristan's attention. She stared out over the lake, a million miles away, absently chewing on her bottom lip. They'd made really good progress on their project and were set to start the community service aspect in a couple of weeks, so Beckett didn't mind that Tristan was contributing nothing that afternoon. He did mind that she answered him vaguely when he checked to be sure she was OK, that she changed the subject if he started questioning her health, that she twisted her fingers together constantly anymore, any time something wasn't occupying her hands.

"Tristan." Beckett placed his hand on her knee, and Tristan jumped, looking at him guiltily.

"Sorry." Tristan looked at Beckett's closed laptop, then back up at him. "Sorry."

Beckett shook his head.

"I don't want you to apologize. I want you to talk to me. You're a ball of nerves and you have been all week. What is going on?"

Tristan sighed. For a few minutes she said nothing, and Beckett started to wonder if she was just not going to answer his question at all. Still, something told him to let her gather her thoughts, so he kept quiet.

"I have this... grandfather," Tristan began, and Beckett raised his eyebrows. "Estranged from our family, and with good reason. Or he was estranged, for a long time. But recently he's come back into the picture, sort of, and..."

Tristan cast her eyes around the lake, as though she was trying to think of how much or what to say next.

"You know how the very presence of someone can stress you out? They don't even need to be near you, necessarily, or talking to you, just knowing they exist and that you're on their radar is enough? That's sort of how my whole family feels right now, and has been feeling for the last couple of months. To say things have been tense since his return would be a huge understatement."

"Is he dangerous?" Beckett asked.

Tristan looked at him, surprised, hesitating again before she answered.

"Possibly."

Beckett nodded, thinking.

"Why don't I come with you?"

"What?"

"To your family reunion. Bring me with you; I can keep you safe."

Tristan vehemently shook her head, had started shaking it before he even finished talking.

"No. No way."

Beckett's eyebrows lifted, and hurt flashed across his features.

"OK."

"*Not* because I'm ashamed of you, or anything like that," Tristan said forcefully, putting her hand on Beckett's arm. "I know this is frustrating. I know… I know not being able to share certain things with you makes you feel excluded or like I'm hiding something, and I'm sorry, Beckett. It's just… Family stuff is so complicated, and I…"

Tristan sighed again, trailing off. There was nothing she could say beyond what she'd already said, and giving Beckett even a little bit of information was too risky at this point, for both of them. She felt tears prickling at the corners of her eyes, and she blinked quickly, trying to pull herself together.

"Hey." Beckett put his arm around her shoulders, pulling her close. "Hey, come on. It's OK. I don't understand what's going on, but I trust you when you say you'll tell me when you can."

Tristan rested her head in the crook of his neck, taking some deep, steadying breaths.

"Let's talk about something else," Beckett said. "Do you have any hobbies I don't know about?"

Tristan laughed, grateful for the change of subject. Grateful for Beckett.

CHAPTER 30

Unbeknownst to Tristan, her family and the Crenshaws had hatched a plan after January's gathering, when Celes had confirmed that Orion had his sights set on Tristan. She hadn't caught on last month at the February gathering, but she did this time. It could have been that they all seemed more on edge than they had before, or that she'd caught Celes talking quietly with her parents while eyeballing her to see if she was listening, or maybe even something that had been there last month, too, but Tristan had been too preoccupied to notice. Either way, after she'd watched Celes look over at her for the fifth or sixth time, she marched up to him and her parents.

"OK, what gives?" Tristan put her hands on her hips, raising her eyebrows at all of them.

Celes, as usual, remained quiet, his expression passive.

"What do you mean, honey?" Sol asked, but her eyes were scanning the crowd, the faintest of frowns creasing her brow.

"What do you keep whispering about over here? I know you don't want me to know, considering you've been watching to make sure I don't come over here," Tristan said, looking accusingly at Celes.

"We're not whispering," Umbris told Tristan, his expression unreadable. "Celes was keeping his eye on you because we asked him to."

"Why?" Tristan frowned.

"I think you know the answer to that," Celes finally spoke, his voice grave.

Tristan nodded reluctantly, looking around with a breeziness she didn't feel.

"Is there something I should know about right now?"

Celes shook his head.

"He's not even here, not yet. It's possible he won't be. I am having trouble confirming, but word is that he attended an Elder meeting in the city last weekend and it really set him back. His health is not great, needless to say, despite the Elders doing everything they can."

"And again, the question is, how is he a threat to me if he's so weak?"

Celes exchanged a look with Sol and Umbris.

"We're still working on that."

"But?" Tristan sensed a but.

"But we know how powerful he is, and we know that when or if he decides to move in, he'll find a way."

Tristan bit her lip, debating on whether or not to mention Eva. Since the dance, she had not seen Eva in the hallways at school, to her surprise, and Tristan had also not had any more nightmares with Eva as the star. She still had a bad feeling about her, exacerbated by Olivia's continued claim that nothing had happened beyond Eva creeping her out in the bathroom, but Tristan figured the lingering feelings probably had to do with the attack and the nightmare more than anything else. On top of that, mentioning Eva was risky -- Tristan knew it would require the Crenshaws coming to town and somehow tracking her to see what she was up to, and that walked a line the community members tried to avoid, especially in this day and age of practically constant surveillance and social media.

"He's not coming." Dune approached the five of them, whose faces simultaneously flooded with relief, and spoke quietly. "The info we have is accurate; the Elder meeting took him down for the count, at least for this month's gathering."

"Thank the gods." Sol put her hand to her chest, but Tristan was still watching Dune, who didn't look as relieved as the rest of them. Celes, who'd been looking at Tristan, turned his gaze on his dad.

"What is it?"

"There's another Elder meeting, being held not far from here to accommodate Orion, in the coming weeks. We have been told to expect news at the April gathering."

"What kind of news?" Tristan attempted to sound normal, but her voice barely broke a whisper. She felt a hand slip into hers, and she turned to find Olivia standing beside her.

"We don't know. We all do know news is rarely good, but that doesn't necessarily mean anything. I believe the Elder committee's main interest lately has been to review the community laws -- there has been some noise about the goings-on behind closed doors, things being brought back into consideration and other things being put on the chopping block. Whatever they come up with will be interesting, for lack of a better term."

"Why do you look worried, then?" Tristan hadn't meant to ask, but nevertheless the question came out of her mouth, directed at Dune.

"I've never done well with change." Dune gave Tristan a rare smile, probably the last one she'd ever see from him. "And there has been lots of it this year. I can't imagine the Elders changing any laws or establishing any laws that would affect me and mine personally, but that doesn't mean I don't worry, don't dislike the secrecy before the big reveal."

Tristan swallowed a guilty lump in her throat, carefully avoiding looking at anyone but Dune as she nodded.

"I understand."

It was time for Tristan and her family to get their infusions, so Tristan and Olivia lined up, once again, behind Evander. Tristan listened mutely to the conversations taking place around her. She couldn't find her voice even if she wanted to, which she didn't; she feared, with the steadily rising panic inside of her, that if she opened her mouth, she might just start screaming and not stop. She took several deep breaths before Evander could admonish her for "getting her mud all over him", but Evander seemed lost in thought, as well.

"Trinity," Glacis said, looking and sounding surprised as Tristan entered the tent for her infusion. "I didn't expect to see you again."

Tristan smiled half-heartedly.

"Surprise."

"Sit, please. How have you been?"

Tristan almost laughed, but bit it back at the last second.

"I've been well, and you?"

Glacis eyed her for the briefest of moments, almost like she knew Tristan was lying -- hell, she probably did know -- but gave her a genuine smile anyway.

"Well also, thank you."

Tristan leaned her head back against the firm cushion, watching as Glacis prepared the infusion.

"OK, and relax. Here we go."

Glacis didn't speak again until Tristan had stood and was about to exit the tent.

"Trinity?"

Tristan turned, startled, and Glacis looked her over for a moment, her light brown eyes contrasting nicely with her short, bright aqua hair.

"Take care, OK?"

Tristan went cold.

"Sorry?"

"Until I see you again," Glacis clarified, frowning so briefly Tristan could have imagined it.

"Oh. Yes. Yeah, uh, you too. Thanks Glacis." Tristan gave her a quick smile and high-tailed it out of the tent.

At this rate, she was going to have a nervous breakdown before June.

***

Beckett's birthday was the weekend after the gathering, and his only request for celebration was to have Tristan spend the weekend at his house. It had been a tough sell to Umbris and Sol, Umbris especially, but in the end they'd relented. Mrs. Benson had gone to spend the weekend with her sister, and Mr. Benson happily -- too happily, Beckett felt -- agreed to find somewhere else to stay both nights as well. Tristan had warned Beckett that she had work on Friday night and

Saturday morning, but he didn't care; he gladly picked her up after work on Friday night, driving her back to his house.

Spending the night with Beckett was bliss. They cocooned themselves up in his bed, entwined like snakes in a jar, and Tristan wished desperately that she'd had the foresight to ask for Saturday off from work. Alas, the new hire -- a Jamestown Academy junior, no surprise there, named Violetta Folliard -- was scheduled for her very first shift, and it was Tristan's turn to do the training.

Tristan's alarm went off at five A.M., and she kissed Beckett awake, softly as not to startle him. His long-lashed eyes fluttered open and he gave her a sleepy grin that had her heart tripping all over itself.

"Happy Birthday," Tristan whispered, and Beckett pulled her to him, kissing her, sorely tempting her to call in sick to work.

A half hour later he kissed her again, this time in his Jeep as he dropped her off in front of Rise and Grind, and Tristan envied that he'd be going right back home to bed. She opened up the shop on a smile, and got everything up and running while dealing with the morning rush. Amos arrived a half hour after she did, and Tristan was grateful that she wouldn't have to be responsible for the grill, as well -- those mornings were by far the most stressful.

Violetta arrived at ten A.M., looking nervous, and Tristan wondered if she'd looked the same way on her first day. Probably.

"You can go through there," Tristan told her, once Violetta had greeted her. She pointed towards the door that led to the back. "Go right, put your things down, stamp your timecard, and come on out."

Violetta nodded, skirting quickly through the door and behind the counter in record time.

"I'm Tristan, by the way," Tristan told her, and Violetta looked amused.

"I know. Olivia and Evander's sister. Dating Beckett Benson. Lucky."

Tristan laughed.

"I have Algebra with Olivia. We've never really talked, but she seems cool."

Tristan nodded politely.

"And I have English with Evander. He's quiet."

Tristan looked at her bemusedly. Violetta's brown eyes were earnest, and she seemed to be getting less nervous by the minute.

"And I know Emmeline Strandquest and her friends attacked you back in December."

Tristan's stomach clenched a bit.

"Yes."

"Bitches."

Tristan hid a smile, turning briefly away from Violetta before turning back and gesturing to the shiny equipment that sat, waiting for her to learn, on the counter in front of them.

"We should probably get to this. I know it looks overwhelming, but you'll get the hang of it in no time."

Violetta nodded, looking nervous again, and pulled her blonde hair into a short ponytail at the base of her skull.

"OK. Let's do this."

Tristan had a better time than she'd anticipated with

Violetta. The girl was funny, rough around the edges and honest bordering on blunt, and Tristan found her refreshing. Violetta had many things to say about many of the people they went to Jamestown with, and Tristan secretly delighted in her assessment of Emmeline and her friends ("vapid, evil, brainless hosebeasts who will never make it out of Lavelle"), as well as Beckett ("dreamy, too good to be true, will probably never come back to Lavelle once he leaves"), Tyler ("have you ever heard him sing? Oh my God, my panties melt -- oh he's dating your sister, sorry"), Henry Aspern ("an Asian dreamboat"), and Theo Fitelson ("definite serial killer"). Her shift ended at two P.M., same as Tristan's, and Tristan introduced her to Ellie, who was just coming in, before they left.

"Oh I know Ellie," Violetta grinned, and Ellie gave her a flinty look, which had Tristan raising her eyebrows. Violetta looked at Tristan, still grinning. "She broke my brother's heart."

"Ah," Tristan said awkwardly, scratching her eyebrow.

"See you gals later." Violetta wiggled her fingers and exited the coffee shop, and Tristan and Ellie looked at each other.

"Really, Joe *had* to hire *her?*" Ellie grumped. "For the record, me and her brother broke each other's hearts."

"Ah," Tristan said again, backing away. "Well, I have to go. I'll see you on Monday?"

Ellie nodded distractedly, and Tristan hurried out of the coffee shop, hoping fervently that she wouldn't be stuck in some awkward third wheel situation with Ellie and Violetta any time soon.

"Hi birthday boy," Tristan greeted Beckett, hopping

into his Jeep. She kissed him.

"Hello beautiful," Beckett returned, but he seemed nervous, and Tristan eyeballed him.

"How was your day?"

"It was fine. Boring. I slept until ten though, so that was nice."

Tristan harrumphed, and Beckett laughed. The short ride was mostly quiet, and Tristan couldn't help but notice that his nervousness seemed to increase the closer they got to his house.

"Are you OK?" Tristan asked, as they pulled up to the curb and Beckett looked downright nauseated.

He turned to Tristan, his face taking on a greenish tinge, and her heart flew into her throat.

"What's wrong?"

"There's a letter inside, for me. It's from Ward Livingston."

Tristan's eyes nearly fell out of her head.

"And?!"

"And I haven't been able to bring myself to open it. It's my birthday, Tristan. What if it's a rejection? What if it isn't? I didn't want to be alone either way."

Tristan nodded, but her own heart was galloping like she'd just run a mile. What if it *was* a rejection? What if it *wasn't?*

"OK. Well. Let's go in and take it from there."

They got out of the Jeep and Tristan followed Beckett, walking slowly, to the house. She was now so jittery herself that she wanted to shove him ahead, make him hurry up. She felt like she'd received her own letter and was dying to know what contents the envelope held.

Once inside, they sat down at the kitchen table, the puffy envelope between them.

"Puffy is good, right? I don't think they send big acceptance packets with the initial letter anymore, but I also think a rejection is just a single sheet and a much thinner envelope." Tristan twisted her fingers, hoping, now that she'd spoken her thoughts, she wasn't wrong.

"One way to find out." Beckett inched the envelope towards him with one finger just barely on the corner, as though it was made of acid.

"Hey," Tristan said, and Beckett lifted his anxious eyes to hers. "No matter what it says in there, it's going to be OK."

Beckett nodded.

"It has to be."

Tristan nodded in return, and Beckett looked back down at the rectangle that was going to change his life one way or another. Steeling himself, he took a deep breath and opened the envelope, holding the folded papers in his hand for a moment.

"Will you come over here and sit with me?"

Tristan jumped up, rounding the table, and Beckett pulled her onto his lap. She looked at him and he looked at her, unfolding the paper.

Tristan's eyes flew to the first line. *Congratulations on your acceptance to Ward Livingston University!*, it read. *Your admission to our highly selective college reflects your outstanding academic accomplishments...*

"You got in." Tristan turned her big eyes on Beckett, who looked utterly gobsmacked. She gently shook his shoulders, so excited for him that she almost hit the ceiling. "Beckett, you got in!"

Tristan hugged Beckett then, who was still in a state of shock. After a few seconds, however, his arms came around her, crushing her to him, and she could feel his whole body smiling, trembling.

"Congratulations," Tristan spoke next to his ear. "I am so, so happy for you. You deserve this so much."

Beckett pulled back, kissing her, his hands framing her face. He held onto her even as he broke the kiss, and she gently grasped his wrists.

"Thank you for being here with me when I did this. If I got mine, that means yours should be coming any day now."

Tristan shook her head.

"Probably not, being at the end of the alphabet. But that reminds me that I need to ask Olivia and Evander to start intercepting the mail for me."

Beckett frowned, puzzled, and Tristan cringed inwardly at her thoughtless mistake.

"Why?"

"I, uh... My parents would probably open the letter or letters before I could, and I want to be the first to know." Tristan knew petty felony probably sounded very out of character for Umbris and Sol, but Beckett seemed to accept her answer anyway.

"So what do you want to do? Can I take you to dinner tonight? Combination birthday and celebration dinner?" Tristan smiled excitedly, still thrilled for Beckett. Her anxious mind tried to start *what if*-ing her about her own impending acceptance or rejection, but she shoved those thoughts aside. It was Beckett's day.

"I would love for you to take me to dinner." Beckett grinned, squeezing Tristan's sides, and she squirmed, shrieking with laughter.

When she managed to jump out of his lap, she shook her head at him, a good-natured smile on her face.

"No tickling. Ever."

"Ever?" Beckett raised both eyebrows.

Tristan shook her head.

"Never, ever."

Beckett eyeballed her for a few beats, and then very suddenly launched himself out of his chair at her. Tristan turned immediately, taking off running through the house, and they both cracked up as he chased her, hot on her trail. Tristan ran upstairs and into his bedroom, and Beckett squeezed through his door at the last second as she tried to close it, grabbing her around the waist and pinning her against the door. He tickled her her until she was writhing against him, until his smile grazed the side of her neck. Beckett's fingers stilled, and he slid his hands around her waist, kissing her neck instead. Tristan's eyes drifted closed as her laughter faded into breathlessness.

***

That evening, both of them having showered and dressed for dinner out, Beckett drove them up to New Orleans. Tristan smiled as they entered the city -- though she'd grown up an hour away, it was still a novelty to her, and she often felt like a tourist whenever she visited. The vibe in the city was unlike anything else Tristan had ever experienced in her relatively short life; she knew people often commented on how the city felt like a living, breathing thing, and she had to agree. There was an energy in the air that could be felt on a visceral level -- a welcoming, easy vitality that was both charming and intoxicating.

Beckett's favorite restaurant, as it turned out, was a small café on Canal Street. Tristan felt a brief flicker of unease as they approached -- Dune and Thera Crenshaw's antique shop was little more than a half a block from the café -- but she ignored it; New Orleans was a city in constant motion, and the odds that Tristan would see Celes or his parents were slim. Besides, Celes knew now about Beckett, which meant Dune and Thera knew as well, so it's not like Tristan was in danger of having her cover blown. The thought relaxed her, and she looked around the café, grinning, as she and Beckett waited for their food.

"So how did this place come to be your favorite?"

"We used to vacation for ten days every year on the Gulf Coast when I lived in Alabama, and the family who owns this place owned one there, too. You wouldn't believe how excited I was when I came here for the first time and found that out."

Tristan smiled at him.

"You're pretty cute, you know that?"

Beckett winked at her just as the waitress arrived with their food. Over shared platters of chicken and andouille gumbo and shrimp and crawfish étouffée, they discussed Beckett's acceptance to Ward Livingston University.

"I know you'll be accepted, too." Beckett leaned across the table, his gaze intense on Tristan's. "If I got in? I'm not even half as smart as you are."

"That's not true at all."

"It is true. You're the smartest in the senior class; it's almost scary how easy everything seems to come to you. Why do you think Emmeline and her friends are so threatened by you?"

Tristan laughed.

"Please. Next you'll tell me they're just jealous."

"They are," Beckett confirmed seriously, and Tristan shook her head.

"I think that's an easy out. Some people are just heinous, no ulterior motive necessary. Anyway, by the way, it might look like everything comes easy to me academically, but I work really hard to get and maintain my grades."

Beckett looked appropriately chastened.

"I know you do. I'm sorry."

"Thank you." Tristan would be lying if she said she wasn't smarting a little, but she appreciated Beckett's quick apology.

"Really." Beckett took Tristan's hand and squeezed it gently until she looked at him, her black eyes guarded. "I know you work hard, and that you take school more seriously than anything else. I am sorry that I sounded like I was dismissing that."

"I appreciate your apology," Tristan replied.

They finished their meal in silence, guilt eating away at Beckett. He hadn't meant to hurt Tristan's feelings; now that the reality of his WLU acceptance was setting in, he was getting nervous about what would happen if, for whatever reason, Tristan wasn't accepted as well, and it was coming out of his mouth all wrong.

Tristan paid for their dinner and they stepped out onto Canal Street, hand in hand.

"Want to walk around?" Beckett asked, and Tristan nodded, but she planted her feet when he started to walk away from the café.

"Let's go the other way," Tristan suggested, and Beckett complied with a nod.

"Why this way?"

"There's a shop in the other direction that I'd like to avoid. Family friends own it, and it would be awkward to run into them."

"Why's that?" Beckett frowned.

"I don't know," Tristan scrunched her nose. "It's always weird to run into my parents' friends when I'm out and about."

"Would these be the friends whose son so rudely interrupted me trying to kiss you on your porch back in December?"

Tristan laughed. "Yes."

"Ah. So is it seeing the parents that would be weird, or seeing, what was his name? Cameron?"

"Canton. And both."

"Uh huh. Because he has a crush on you."

Tristan looked surprised, but nodded.

"Something like that."

"Well I can't say I blame him," Beckett grinned, and Tristan laughed, holding his hand a little bit tighter.

They meandered down the strip, dazzling in the dusky evening light, eventually turning back to where they'd parked when they'd run out of shops to peer into and sights to point out.

Tristan was thankful when they made it to the car without running into anyone familiar, and she and Beckett held hands during the ride back to Lavelle, letting the music fill the comfortable silence between them.

When The Rolling Stones' *Wild Horses* came on, Beckett turned up the volume.

"This is my all-time favorite song."

Tristan gave him her old familiar squint, and Beckett laughed.

"What?"

Tristan looked at him for a few more silent beats before the ghost of a smile crossed her face and she shook her head.

"You just keep surprising me, that's all."

CHAPTER 31

When Tristan arrived home the next day, she asked Olivia and Evander to walk and talk with her. When they were at a safe distance from the house, Olivia swept her hand over them to protect them from Sol and Umbris's potentially prying ears, and the twins looked at Tristan expectantly.

Tristan took a deep breath.

"I'm not joining the community in June."

Olivia and Evander exchanged puzzled glances.

"We know."

"Well, I know you know, but this is the first time I'm saying it out loud, definitively, instead of heavily hinting at it."

Olivia and Evander nodded, and Olivia's eyebrows lifted, impressed.

"You're right. How does it feel?"

"Scary, but good." Tristan took another deep breath. "I need your help. I'll probably actually need your help a lot in the coming months, and I'm sorry for that, but right now all I need you guys to do is watch the mail for me. I applied to a bunch of colleges over the summer, and now is the time where the letters will be coming in, letting me know if I've been accepted or rejected. Since I haven't talked to Mom and Dad yet, I just need you to intercept the mail for me until I do."

"And when are you going to talk to them, Trinity?" Evander asked, crossing his arms and looking wary.

"I don't know. Soon, I hope." Tristan had a hard time looking him in the eye; her cowardice knew no bounds.

Olivia and Evander exchanged another look, seeming to discuss something between them that Tristan could not hear.

"Please," Tristan said softly. "I know it's not fair. I know I'm asking a lot, and I know it's not fair of me to ask you to help me deceive them, but please."

Olivia sighed and Evander looked unhappy, but they both reluctantly nodded.

"OK. To make it easier on all of us, I'm just going to sort of phase remembering to get the mail out of their heads for the time being, that way one of us can grab it when we can instead of stressing every day that we need to make some mad scramble to the box before they do. I'll do the same with Ivan and Ruby."

"Thank you, Oceana, Ember." Tristan gripped their hands. "Thank you."

"You need to talk to Mom and Dad sooner rather than later, though, Trin," Evander said, frowning. "You know it's going to be worse, especially with Dad, the longer you wait."

"I know."

As she watched them walk away, however, Tristan knew that all three of them knew the same thing -- she had no intention of talking to Sol and Umbris any time soon.

***

As though the universe had been listening to the siblings' conversation and took it as the green light for Tristan to start receiving her letters, the Wallace's mailbox over the next few weeks saw a near constant stream of acceptances and rejections from colleges and universities across the country. With an electrifying mix of guilt and elation, Tristan squirreled the letters away in the bottom drawer of her desk, sorted into two large envelopes marked simply with "A" and "R". At night, she pulled out the "A" envelope, thumbing through the growing stack of congratulatory acceptances. Tulane University, Louisiana State University, UCLA, University of Pennsylvania, Flagler College, James Madison University -- all prestigious, all of their acceptances incredibly, gobsmackingly flattering. Tristan's head spun with each response, good or bad, and she was in disbelief to the point of dizziness at times.

Tristan's school counselor, Virginia Wicker, had taken an exhausting amount of convincing to keep Tristan's news on the downlow -- Tristan could not afford for a fuss to be made over any of this part of her high school career, and had eventually told Ms. Wicker flat out that her parents were not aware she'd been applying anywhere and it was a conversation Tristan and Tristan alone had to have with them first before she'd grant the school permission to acknowledge her acceptances and her final decision. Ms. Wicker had involved Dean LeFebvre then and, while neither of the women could quite fit Tristan's story with the impression they'd gotten of Sol and Umbris over the years, they had ultimately, thankfully, respected Tristan's wishes. Beckett, for his part, was beside himself with pride, yet they both still waited with bated breath for the response from Ward Livingston.

CHAPTER 32

By the time April's gathering arrived, Tristan felt like she was living a nightmare. The repetitiveness of the gatherings, almost every thirty days exactly, where she not only had to pretend she was joining the community in June but had to start pretending like she was *excited* to be doing so, was taking a huge toll on her mental health. Her nerves were stretched so thin she was sure they were transparent, and she didn't know how much longer she would last before they snapped and curled in on themselves, causing her to unravel completely.

Not helping matters was how intense her course load was at school now that graduation was rapidly approaching -- between final projects in multiple classes, her big project with Beckett that saw them going into the next town multiple times every week to help tutor ESL elementary students, and beginning prep for final exams, Tristan was barely keeping her head above water. Beckett was dealing with all of the same things plus football, and the only silver lining to the absolutely crushing schedule that Tristan could find was that it kept Emmeline and her friends equally as frantically busy, which meant they left Tristan alone entirely.

On top of all of that, Beckett had started casually mentioning prom, which was being held the first weekend in May, same as the gathering. Tristan had told him she was not interested, had told him that she had her usual family get together that night, but Beckett would not be deterred. Already trying to pour from an empty bucket, Tristan let the subject drop for the time being; she didn't have the energy to do anything but hope that Beckett would start listening to her sooner rather than later.

It was sometime during the infusions that Sol approached Tristan, idling at the edge of the clearing by herself, with panic on her face.

"What's wrong?" Tristan asked immediately, as fear gripped her heart.

"I can't find Oceana. Have you seen her?"

"No," Tristan said, frowning. "I'm sure she's here somewhere."

"I've looked everywhere, Trinity!" Sol snapped, and Tristan's eyebrows climbed all the way up her forehead.

"OK. OK, I'll help you look. Where are Dad and Ember?"

"Looking themselves. Come on."

Tristan took off with Sol, knowing that if she was this worried, it was with good reason -- as they hurried along, Tristan realized that Sol must not be able to psychically locate Oceana; it was the only thing that would explain her panic.

"You can't reach her, can you?" Tristan looked up at Sol, her expression confirming Tristan's suspicions. "Can Ember?"

Sol shook her head slightly, and Tristan stumbled, feeling like she was going to vomit. A twin connection was even more powerful than a parent-child connection -- the only way a twin connection could be broken, as far as Tristan knew, was if one of them...

Tristan shook her head hard, blinking back tears. *No.* There was no way. Maybe she didn't use her abilities anymore, but there was *no way* Tristan wouldn't know if something horrible had happened to Oceana. There was no way none of them would not have somehow known what was happening before it had happened to her.

"We'll find her." Tristan's voice was hard, and she and Sol met up with Celes at the entrance of the clearing.

"Nothing." Celes was pale, and again Tristan fought off a wave of nausea.

Just then, a commotion caught their ears. Tristan, Sol, and Celes turned their heads at once to see a crowd forming at the top of the clearing. They took off, pushing their way through the other community members, some who protested loudly but stopped when Celes whipped his head around to look at them. Sol, slight though she was, charged a path through the horde, Tristan right on her heels. When they reached the head of the clearing, Sol stopped short and Tristan bumped into her.

"Sorry."

Tristan moved around Sol, and a system-shocking mix of dread and relief flooded through her. Olivia was OK, alive and well as far as they could tell, but she stood a few feet from Orion, her eyes locked on him, his on her. Tristan stared at Olivia, trying to determine if she was under some sort of trance, but she couldn't immediately tell.

Orion turned, looking right at Sol, and Tristan gripped her arm.

"Ah, Sol. I see you've found us."

Tristan could feel Sol's anger, and she was sure Sol's eyes would be shooting lasers if they could. When she spoke, it was through a clenched jaw, her voice like steel.

"Get away from my daughter."

Orion had the nerve to look surprised, and Tristan again looked at Olivia. Olivia looked back at her, pissed as hell, which Tristan knew was a good sign, but she also looked unnerved. Tristan heard Celes exhale behind her, and she turned to see his eyes on Olivia as well, relief weighing down his shoulders.

"Oceana? We were just having a chat. She graciously agreed to show me how her abilities are coming along." Orion swept his hand towards Olivia, and she shot him a look, stalking over to where Tristan and Sol stood.

"I was going to collect Ember next, but I see he has come to me." Orion looked over Sol's shoulder, his eyes never once alighting on Tristan, and then looked at the group that had gathered. "There's nothing for you all to see here; just a family reunion."

The crowd took the hint and dispersed, and Tristan eyeballed Orion. He looked startlingly healthy, which Tristan was having trouble understanding; wasn't it just last month that the Elder meeting he'd attended had caused him a major health setback? Sure, he was currently leaning heavily on a jet black, marbled cane, and his shoulders were slightly stooped and his complexion slightly pallid, but all of that just made him look... old. Tristan could still tell that he'd been formidable once -- his shoulders and chest were broad, and his blue eyes were sharp and virulent beneath his snowy white hair. He was also, in spite of the cane, standing with his feet planted in a power stance that belied his very casual demeanor, which was one of the biggest giveaways for Tristan that they were dealing with a snake, and apparently one who had recently feasted. Pieces of the puzzle wanted to come together in her mind, but Tristan could not quite get them to slide into place.

"Oceana!" Evander shot across the clearing and embraced Olivia in a bear hug, not letting her go for several long moments. Umbris was next, and Olivia nodded at them both, wordlessly confirming she was OK.

Tristan had felt sick enough over the idea of something having happened to Olivia -- she could not imagine how Evander especially must have felt, not being able to reach her. Once Evander had released Olivia, he turned his thunderous gaze on Orion.

"Ember. Nice to finally meet you." Orion gazed at Evander, completely unruffled, and Evander glared at him in return.

"If you will." Orion gestured, and Evander began to move forward. Tristan frowned.

Sol put out her hand, and Evander stopped, a vein in his neck throbbing as he cracked his knuckles. Olivia put her hand on his arm and he looked at her, giving her a brief nod as he took several deep breaths in an attempt to calm himself.

"How *dare* you try to manipulate my children, and right in front of me! How dare you cut Oceana off from us, take her away from the gathering and bring her back like you have any right to do these things!"

Sol was yelling, and her children were staring at her, mouths hanging open. Even Umbris looked surprised, but Tristan noticed that he also looked proud, which made her feel slightly less nervous about whatever was currently happening.

"Oh Sol, always such a hothead for such a soft-spoken thing, just like your sister... and your son, apparently." Orion's face was still a neutral mask, but there was a hint of amusement in his eyes that Tristan suddenly and intensely hated him for.

"Do not talk about Adara."

Orion waved his hand dismissively.

"No harm was done to Oceana, anyway. She was more than willing to show me what she's capable of, you may be surprised to hear."

"I was not!" Olivia fired back immediately. "I was cornered, and you vaguely implied there would be consequences if I didn't cooperate with you! And I didn't know you had cut me off from everyone until I saw my Mom and Trinity burst through the crowd looking scared to death!"

Orion took a step forward. Sol held out her other hand, and Orion stopped.

"We don't turn eighteen for another year, so we're still under our parents' protection," Olivia told Orion smugly.

Tristan watched Orion, who was still ignoring her, wondering how he'd play this. Would he continue to escalate? Sol was angry enough to flatten the clearing if she had to, leaving nothing but scorched earth where they stood, Tristan was sure of that, and while Orion was extremely powerful, he was also ill, which left him at a slight disadvantage. There really was nothing like a mother protecting her children, and Tristan could practically see the same wheels turning in Orion's mind that were turning in hers. The idea they had anything in common made her blood run cold.

"I apologize, then, that I misunderstood our conversation." Orion looked across the way at his fellow Elders, who were cloaking up for worship. "If you'll excuse me, I believe I'm needed over there. Ember, I do hope we get an opportunity in the future to chat."

Orion moved slowly off to the other Elders, never having acknowledged Tristan. She watched him go, too smart to fall for what had clearly been a calculated move to ignore her. The desire to follow him, to confront him about what he was planning, what he was doing, was so strong that Tristan had taken a step after him before she realized it. It was Celes's hand on her wrist that stopped her.

"What are you doing?" Celes's face was a storm cloud, and Tristan yanked her arm away from him.

"Nothing."

Celes eyed her, but said nothing, instead turning at his father's call. With one last turbulent glance at Tristan, he stalked off, and Tristan followed her own family to settle in for worship. Tristan tried to focus, she really did, but her mind wandered against her will. She hadn't forgotten that an announcement was coming at this gathering, hadn't been so thrown by her family's interaction with Orion that she wasn't deeply puzzled, and unsettled, over his apparent mostly restored health. How could it be? What had he done? Who had suffered so he could regain a fraction of the power his good health had afforded him? Who had he used and most certainly discarded, or was planning to discard when they were no longer useful?

At that, Tristan's head snapped up. Eva. Tristan had barely seen her since the Valentine's dance, and, as she wracked her brain, she could not remember whether or not she'd seen her at all recently, but Tristan was almost positive she hadn't. The odds of Orion knowing Eva Revet seemed slim, even impossible, but Tristan knew not to underestimate him. Maybe Eva and her family were part of the community, maybe they weren't, but *somehow* Orion had gotten ahold of Eva, Tristan was sure of it. Desperately, Tristan wished she could reach out to Beckett to find out if he'd seen Eva lately, but it was the middle of the night and there was no cell reception on the island anyway. Asking Olivia or Evander would require an explanation Tristan could obviously not get into at the gathering, and one she wasn't sure she wanted to get into with them anyway, lest they started to think she was losing it.

Unsure if it would work, but needing to try, Tristan closed her eyes, forcing out all thought except for that of Beckett. She focused her energy, drawing up her old friend the black funnel, and a shirtless, sleeping Beckett shortly came into view. Lamenting that there was no time to admire him, Tristan focused harder, trying to connect with Beckett's thoughts. The funnel swirled and swirled, and Tristan began to sweat with the exertion of trying to break into Beckett's mind. He jumped in his sleep, rolling onto his back before settling down again. *Come on, Beckett,* Tristan thought, frustrated, and Beckett suddenly opened his eyes. This caught Tristan off guard, but she kept her focus as Beckett slowly pushed himself up onto one elbow. He looked around his room, Tristan knew, for her. He'd heard her voice, probably as clearly as though she was beside him. Awake, it was easier for Tristan to get into his head, and finally the black funnel picked up speed and, as it did, picked up images unfamiliar to Tristan. *Show me Eva,* she thought, and up came the memory -- and the incredible anger attached to it -- of Eva confronting Beckett at Mack's. Impatiently, Tristan waited for the next memory, but it was only a flash of Eva in the gym at the Valentine's dance, by herself, looking in Beckett's direction as he looked at her. There was nothing after that at all. Tristan got out of Beckett's head, hating how scared he looked as he clutched it in his hands, asking himself aloud what was happening. As Tristan watched, he picked up his phone, opening their text message thread. *I know it's late and I'm sorry, but I just need to know if you're OK.* Tristan felt helpless, knowing she would not be able to answer him until the morning.

An elbow jammed into her ribs and Tristan lost her concentration, snapping back into the present. Olivia was looking at her with an incredulous expression -- psychically checking out of worship was a rule you didn't break -- but a furtive glance around confirmed for Tristan that she hadn't been caught by anyone else. Relieved, she nodded at Olivia, who briefly shook her head before turning her face away and closing her eyes.

At long last, worship ended. Just as he'd done months ago, Vitalis stepped up to announce that Pele had news she wanted to share with the community, and Pele soon took his place.

"Good morning, everyone, and thank you as always for joining us for this month's gathering. Like you all, I'm sure, I am thrilled to welcome spring back into the bayou and say goodbye to the winter nights that are far too cold for my liking."

Laughter rippled through the community, and Tristan exchanged looks of disbelief with her siblings. Pele almost seemed jovial, which was so wildly out of character that Tristan wondered if she'd been body-snatched.

"This is not good," Olivia said in a low voice, and Tristan and Evander nodded in agreement.

"Anyway, I won't hold you. There are just a couple of announcements I wanted to make, since it's been some time since you've heard from your Elders about what's happening in your community. As you know, we are coming up on a new class of inductees in just two months from now. We, and they, we're sure, are thrilled. While we have been preparing for that, we've also been working to make some changes behind the scenes for the betterment of our community and your quality of life here."

Murmurs began, and Olivia gripped Tristan's hand so tightly, it had gone numb.

"As you know, throughout the years we like to periodically review the laws, rules, and regulations that keep our community functioning like a well-oiled machine, and we like to make adjustments and additions when and where we find it necessary. This means that occasionally we Elders will get together over a series of meetings to take a look at what is working, what isn't working, and how something could maybe work better if there's an area that's lagging. Since the return of our beloved Orion--"

Tristan, Olivia, and Evander all made the same disgusted face.

"--We have been holding these meetings in New Orleans. While they are fixed at this point in time, meaning, really, we're only just getting started, this morning I am pleased to share with you that the Elders have two important decisions we'd like to make you aware of, effective immediately."

Tristan closed her eyes. This was it. This would be the confirmation that she was either going to pay for her deflection with her life, or she was going to have to disappear and cut ties with her family for an indeterminable amount of time, until it would be safe to contact them again.

"First, as most of you know, years ago the laurel leaf was appointed the flower of our community, though there was no follow-up after that was announced. Recently we've developed a community crest, which Vitalis will share with you when I'm finished, that has incorporated both our beloved laurel leaf and a sprig of holly, to pay respect to our mighty King. As a result of this development, mandatory work will begin on all community houses this coming Monday, to have the seal branded onto the foundation of your home. This is a gesture of solidarity that we hope you will appreciate as much as we do."

Olivia let out a noisy breath beside Tristan.

"Really?"

"The next thing I'd like to share with you is quite a bit more serious in nature."

Pele waited to speak until everyone had quieted down.

"Again, as most of you know, years ago there was a law introduced which stated that there would no longer be consequences for deflection from our community -- it was declared that joining was no longer mandatory, and that the decision for each child of age would be left to the individual families. This law was introduced in a time of great turmoil, and alongside it came a few corresponding rulings that have allowed the community reins to go a bit lax. Nothing to worry yourselves with, of course, but it's one of our responsibilities as Elders to pay attention. All of these laws are currently still being evaluated in relation to the functioning of the community, but since they are our backbone, we plan to keep you updated as we go. There has been one change, therefore, that, as I said, will go into effect immediately, and that is that the law against consequences for deflecting after a sealing has been rescinded."

Gasps. More murmurs. A general air of uneasiness settled over the community, and Tristan took a moment to remind herself to breathe. Of course. She'd heard this in her premonition, hadn't she? It was how Orion still got to call for her execution even though she'd joined the community. She hadn't realized it at the time, hadn't been well-versed enough in community law to know that this wasn't something that was already in place, and her stomach gave a slow turn. Things, little things, were starting to happen that were setting the stage for Tristan's premonition to come true, and panic rose in her throat. Olivia was muttering angrily beside her, and Tristan tilted her head so she could hear what she was saying.

"Freaking unbelievable. A time of great turmoil, *ya think?* Who's *freaking* fault was it that things were so tumultuous, should we talk--"

Evander elbowed Olivia, a heavy frown between his eyes, and she glared at him but shut up.

Pele lifted her hands, and again everyone went quiet.

"I know this is startling, but please be assured, on our honor as a committee, that the changes that are being made are for the benefit of the community as a whole, and are being made with the best interest of everyone in the forefront of our minds. We do not anticipate the reversal of this law being put to use, of course, but in this day and age we unfortunately cannot afford to not be as vigilant as possible, within reason. I ask you now to please save any questions you may have, and forward them to your local Elder leader if you'd like to follow up in private. Thank you all again for coming, and we will see you next month."

Tristan stood numbly, not hearing her family's talk around her. She knew she should be relieved that the news hadn't been worse, that the Elders hadn't unanimously decided joining the community would be mandatory again -- that meant at least *someone* on the committee would not agree to it -- but her premonition weighed heavily on her mind and soul. The wheels were in motion now; was there anything she could do to stop her fate she'd seen unfold? Of course it seemed absurd that Beckett would show up at a gathering -- try as she might, Tristan still couldn't imagine a scenario in which he'd manage that, as she was pretty sure the island was safeguarded against wanderers -- plus, she was still autonomous even if the totally implausible did happen and she did accept into the community, meaning she could choose not to have an affair and plan to run off with Beckett... but Tristan had learned long ago to never doubt that *anything* could happen, no matter how far-fetched it seemed.

"Deep breaths," Olivia spoke in Tristan's ear, and Tristan jumped.

Olivia looked at her worriedly. "Please just try to maintain your cool until we're out of here, OK? You never know who's watching, and your face is too expressive to not reveal every thought you're having."

Tristan nodded, forcing her face into a bored expression. As she fell into step beside Olivia, Tristan looked to the head of the clearing, where the Elders were still gathered.

Orion was staring straight at her, and he was smiling.

CHAPTER 33

Olivia and Evander fell asleep practically as soon as they'd gotten in the car, but Tristan did not have that luxury. She was too wired to sleep, her brain in full on panic mode, and she sat stiffly in her seat, staring unseeingly out the window. She'd texted Beckett as soon as she could, but she knew he'd long been back to sleep. She hoped, for his sake, that the remainder of his slumber erased the memory of why he'd reached out to her at two in the morning in the first place.

Tears threatened, but Tristan fiercely battled them back. She couldn't lose it now, or Umbris would pull over and Tristan would spill everything to him and Sol right there on the side of the road. She desperately wanted Beckett -- she couldn't tell him the truth, but she could maybe tell him enough, and he could hold her and assure her that life outside of the stupid community and stupid Orion and his stupid, bloodthirsty laws was still going and she was still a part of it.

By the time they got home, Tristan could not bear the idea of going into the house. She instead told Sol and Umbris she'd be back later, and she drove to Beckett's. It was barely seven A.M., but by some divine intervention, Gabriella Benson was sitting on the front steps with a mug of coffee and a book.

"Tristan," Gabriella's eyes widened as Tristan approached, taking in her red rimmed eyes and her disheveled appearance. "Are you OK, honey?"

"I know he's asleep, but I just need to see Beckett," Tristan croaked, her voice rough with the restraint of holding back a defcon one level meltdown.

"Sure, of course. Go ahead in." Gabriella stood, moving out of the way, looking at Tristan sympathetically.

Tristan hurried into the house and up to Beckett's room, which was cool and dark thanks to the thick navy curtains pulled closed across his windows. She took off her boots, the thud of them hitting the floor rousing Beckett. He looked up groggily as her black pea coat joined her boots.

"Tristan? What are you doing here?"

Tristan crawled into his bed, sniffling, and settled in beside him, beneath his comforter. Beckett immediately pulled her close, wrapping his arms around her.

"I just need you to hold me," Tristan whispered.

And so he did.

***

Tristan was on a boat. It was large and white, and the deck under her back was made of thick glass, offering her an unobstructed view of the sea. The water was a blue she'd never seen anywhere but Beckett's eyes, impossibly calm, and, though the ocean's bottom was over fifty feet below, she could see straight down to the pale sand and the vibrant coral. The sky was a brilliant azure, puffy white clouds rolled lazily by, and the sun was the best sensation she'd felt on her skin in what felt like a lifetime. Birds called out to each other, and besides them and the gentle lapping of the waves against the anchored vessel, there was no other sound at all.

Suddenly, the boat started to shake. Not violently, but

firmly.

"Tristan."

Someone was saying her name, but who? Tristan opened her eyes, closing them again immediately against the dazzling sunlight, but in that brief glance she'd seen no one.

"Tristan."

It was Beckett, and Tristan's eyes fluttered open. She was not on a boat, after all -- rather, she was flat on her back in Beckett's bed, having slid down off of the pillows, and his deep turquoise sheets and thick, white and navy striped comforter surrounded her. It took her a moment to get her bearings, and she blinked up at Beckett, who was leaning over her, dressed in jeans and a dark green t-shirt. His room was considerably lighter than it had been, and Tristan turned her face out of the shaft of sunlight that broke through the slit in his curtains.

"There you are. Good morning, beautiful, or should I say afternoon?"

"What?" Tristan felt more exhausted than she had when she'd fallen asleep, and she pushed her hair off of her forehead. "What time is it?"

"Almost one in the afternoon."

"What?" Tristan said again, bolting upright.

"Tristan, it's OK." Beckett looked at her with concern, studying her face for a moment before he spoke again. "Not that I mind, in fact if you want to sneak into my room every morning I'll start leaving the front door unlocked, but... what are you doing here? My mom said you showed up before seven and you looked like you'd been crying?"

Tristan ran a hand over her face.

"I'm so sorry I slept so long."

"Don't be; you clearly needed it. What's going on?"

"It's my grandfather," Tristan said, pushing herself into a sitting position. "He got ahold of Olivia at the reunion and really gave us a fright."

"Is she OK?" Beckett frowned.

She's OK, but I'm not, Tristan thought, but she nodded.

"She's fine."

"And you? Are you fine?" Beckett's eyes were concerned, soft at the corners and telling her he knew she was not fine, and Tristan felt the desperate, crushing panic rise in her once again.

"I didn't think so." Beckett gathered Tristan into his arms and she clung to him, more scared than she'd ever been.

"It's OK," Beckett murmured. "I'm here, Tristan. No matter what happens, I'm here."

"Do you promise?"

Her voice was a whisper, but when she pulled back to look at him, her eyes bore into his own with a need and intensity that nearly took his breath away. He promised. He'd promise her whatever she wanted, he knew that beyond the shadow of a doubt. Beckett didn't know what this love was, had not thought anything like it existed outside of the sappy romances his Mom loved to watch, but even those rang hollow now compared to how he felt about Tristan. It shook him to his core -- how he was sure he'd do anything for her, to protect her, to lay down his life for hers if it ever came to that, and this after only a handful of months together. He loved her in a way he hadn't known he was capable of loving; it was easy and familiar, as though he'd loved her before, in other lifetimes, if such a thing was even possible, and as a result he was steadfast and secure in his feelings. It wasn't some silly, hormonally driven infatuation between them, though Beckett knew no adult would believe him if he said that aloud -- not that he needed to be believed by anyone but Tristan. Tristan.

Beckett began a slow tour of her face, taking in the small scar just above her outer left eyebrow that she'd gotten when she'd fallen off of her bike in the second grade; her infinite, unnaturally black eyes; her perfect nose, perfect lips, and the other small, thin scar beneath her chin that had been the result of her face meeting a curb when she'd taken a spill roller-blading at ten years old.

"Beckett."

A whisper, again, and Beckett met Tristan's gaze, which he swore he could feel all the way inside of him.

"I promise you that I am here no matter what happens."

"I'm going to hold onto that."

Tristan was very clearly in a bad place, and helplessness began to weave its way around Beckett's heart as he watched her trying so valiantly to keep it together.

"Just tell me what's going on, please?" Beckett kept his voice low as well, as not to scare her off.

Tristan's eyes filled with tears.

"I can't. I... I can't. I'm sorry."

"You can." Beckett cupped Tristan's face, using his thumbs to wipe the fat tears that spilled down her cheeks. "Tristan, I promise you there's nothing in this world you can't tell me."

The worst part was that Tristan knew he meant it. She knew that he would hear anything she wanted to share with him, and she even believed he would handle the truth thoughtfully and openly, which caused a physical ache in her chest. If telling him wouldn't put him at risk, she would spill everything right where they sat. But putting Beckett's life in danger was not an option, never had been, and Tristan only had to hang on until June. Once she was free from the community, removed from the psychic map and no longer vulnerable to surveillance by the Elders, or her family, or any other community members, then she could tell Beckett everything.

"I believe you. I just can't yet. I know it doesn't make any sense, I know you don't understand, but I just need until graduation, OK? After graduation, I can tell you everything."

Beckett looked at Tristan contemplatively, his brow furrowed just slightly. She looked back at him with a mixture of trepidation and despair, and finally Beckett nodded.

"OK. After graduation."

Tristan exhaled a shaky breath and hugged Beckett tightly, hoping with all of her might that they'd make it to graduation unscathed.

***

Three days before Tristan's birthday, the envelope from Ward Livingston University arrived. Beckett had taken to driving Tristan to and from school every day, so he could be there when she collected the mail in the hopes her letter would come, and, after Tristan had frozen upon opening the mailbox, he gave her hand a gentle squeeze of encouragement.

Taking a deep breath, Tristan picked up the envelope, knowing immediately what the contents inside would say. She had been accepted.

"Dear Miss Wallace, congratulations on your acceptance to Ward Livingston..." Tristan read faintly.

Before her brain could catch up with her eyes and the news could really sink in, Beckett had lifted her off of her feet, spinning her around as he hooted and hollered and kissed her. Tristan laughed, holding on for dear life, closing her eyes and sending a genuine prayer of thanks to the universe for this outcome. The commotion drew Olivia and Evander outside, and the four of them had a mini-celebration right there on the porch over Tristan's acceptance letter.

"Congratulations! Both of you! Oh my gods, what are the odds?" Olivia clapped excitedly, hopping from foot to foot. "It's almost like it was meant to be!"

Tristan gave her the hairy eyeball as Beckett grinned, but Olivia just smiled radiantly at them.

"So now you *have* to talk to Mom and Dad," Evander pointed out, and Tristan's face fell.

"You couldn't have given her like ten whole minutes to just be happy about this?" Olivia snapped, twisting around to look at him accusingly.

Evander, at least, had the good grace to look ashamed.

"Why would that make you unhappy?" Beckett asked, frowning at Tristan, and that was when she and her siblings realized Evander's error.

For a moment, the three Wallaces froze, looking at each other and then at Beckett, who lifted his eyebrows at them in return.

"They don't know WLU is my top choice," Tristan

said eventually, which was at least some form of the truth. "Boston is pretty far from here."

"Will it make a difference if you tell them I got in, too?"

Tristan smiled at him affectionately.

"It might. I guess I'll find out. But I'm going to keep this to myself at least until my birthday -- I just want to enjoy it privately, well, with you four, for a few days."

Everyone nodded, and Olivia and Evander went back inside. Tristan looked at Beckett, who was still smiling at her, and she smiled back at him, hardly daring to believe that after so many stressful months, something truly good had finally happened.

"Now we need to celebrate you." Beckett took her hands in his. "Anything in mind?"

Tristan shook her head.

"I'm still reeling. I'm having a hard time believing this is real; what if tomorrow another letter comes that says they made a mistake and I'm actually not accepted, or waitlisted? That does happen."

As she was talking, Beckett had bent down to pick up a page that had fallen to the porch. He scanned it, and then raised his eyebrows, a smile tugging at the corners of his mouth as he handed the paper to Tristan.

"I don't think they're going to do that."

Tristan looked at the second page of the letter, which explained that not only had she been accepted, she'd been granted an inconceivably generous scholarship. Her eyes widened and she covered her mouth with her free hand.

"My smart girl." Beckett's eyes shone with admiration, and Tristan jumped into his arms once again.

Not wanting to be discovered with her letter by Umbris and Sol, Tristan folded everything back up neatly and placed it in the envelope, which she then tucked carefully into her schoolbag. She and Beckett sat down on the porch swing, Tristan draping her legs over his lap, and Beckett drummed lightly on her knees as they swayed.

"So I've been thinking about this," Beckett started slowly, looking apprehensive, and Tristan cocked her head interestedly.

"About my acceptance?"

Beckett nodded.

"Yes. If we both ended up getting accepted. Do we stay here in Lavelle for one last summer, or do we start looking for a month-to-month rental up in Boston for July and August, before we move into the university?"

Tristan blinked a few times, surprised.

"You're asking if we should move in together in Boston before we start school?"

Beckett nodded.

"Every day in Lavelle, in my house, feels like someone has layered another blanket on top of me. You know I can't wait to get out of here and never look back. If we start looking now, we might be able to secure a place starting July first, and rent for July and August before we move into the dorms. You don't have to answer me right now."

Tristan watched Beckett while he talked, so confident and sure. He really had thought about this. Did she want to move in with him? That would be a huge step for two eighteen year olds who'd only been dating for less than a year and hadn't even exchanged I love yous. Tristan didn't consider herself a prude, but she'd always assumed that moving in with a boyfriend came after, or even during, college -- after the relationship had been established for a couple of years.

On the other hand, did it really matter when they moved in together? It would end up happening eventually, their destiny connection would ensure that. And it would only be for two months before school started, at which point they'd live in separate dorms for a while, so it would sort of be like a trial run before they moved in together for good.

Tristan didn't have an answer, so she was thankful Beckett wasn't expecting one.

"I will definitely think about it."

Beckett nodded, satisfied, and Tristan observed his profile as he looked out across her property. Her mind lingered on the fact that they hadn't yet exchanged "I love you"s -- sometimes she could swear Beckett was going to say it, just based on the way he'd gaze at her, and the love she'd detected in his feelings for her the first time she'd read him had intensified nearly tenfold since that day at his house, but then he'd look like his thoughts had caught up with him and he'd lose his nerve. Tristan knew he didn't have to be the one to say it first, knew that she could tell him before he told her, but she was scared, too; mostly, she was afraid to make herself so vulnerable. There was no taking something like that back once it was out there, and Tristan had never been good at taking chances.

Oh, but she loved him. She loved his intelligent, kind brain, and the surprising way it worked. She loved his steady, mellow personality, and the way he never put on airs to impress other people. She loved his quiet strength, his physical strength, his beautiful eyes, and the way it felt every time he touched her. She loved that when he'd told her she had him, that he would be by her side and not let anyone or anything harm her, he'd stuck to it, even at the expense of some of his friendships. She loved his sense of humor, his vulnerability that he wasn't afraid to show her, the way he cheered her on and picked her up when she couldn't keep going. He was flawed, everyone was, but he was home, and all of the flaws in the world would never change that about him.

"Penny for your thoughts." Beckett sent her a lazy grin, his eyes having met hers a few seconds before, watching her watch him.

"I love you."

Tristan had blurted out the words before she could stop herself, and her eyes widened as she twisted her fingers together painfully. She turned her face away as she went scarlet from hairline to chest, wishing she would fall through the swing, through the porch, and right into the center of the Earth, never to be seen again.

"You… love me?" Beckett's voice was full of wonder.

Tristan chanced a look at him, her mouth forming silent words that wouldn't squeak past her lips, and Beckett suddenly stood, pulling her off of the swing and to him in one fluid motion. Tristan let out a yelp of surprise before Beckett's mouth was on hers, intense and ravenous. His hands plunged into her hair and her stomach bottomed out, desire rushing through her body as she kissed him back with equal fervor.

"Beckett," Tristan gasped, breaking for air, and Beckett pressed kisses along her neck, down to her shirt collar, until she shivered, laughing.

"I love you too." Beckett rested his forehead against hers, and Tristan beamed, framing his face with her hands as she brought his mouth back to hers.

***

Tristan's birthday was on Thursday, so on Saturday she and Beckett went camping again. This time, Tristan had requested they go tubing on the little stretch of the Mississippi next to which they'd be setting up, and Beckett, in his usual fashion, had embraced the idea wholeheartedly. Also different from last time, Olivia, Tyler, and Evander -- sans Ellie, as they'd stopped seeing each other in March -- joined Tristan and Beckett for a day of tubing, but declined to camp overnight.

"I am not being the fifth or the third wheel overnight in the wilderness," Evander had replied when Tristan asked, firmly shaking his head.

"This place creeps me out at night," Olivia had said, also shaking her head.

"How do you know?" Tristan frowned.

"You brought me here years ago, remember? It was getting pitch dark and I said I wanted to turn around and go home, but you swore the best view we could get of the blood moon was from this spot. It's so isolated, it's like it's just waiting for a masked murderer to find it and the unsuspecting dingbats who decide to set up camp here."

"Ha ha. Also, I was right about the moon."

The day was as perfect as Tristan had hoped for -- the sky was a rich, cloudless blue, and a gentle wind rustled the treetops far above them. April in Lavelle already saw temperatures close to eighty degrees, especially so close to May, and Tristan absolutely reveled in the warmth and light.

"Hey beautiful." Beckett's tube bumped gently into Tristan's, and she looked over at him, shading her eyes with one hand. "Did I tell you I love you in that swimsuit?"

Tristan grinned, looking down at what was actually one of Olivia's suits -- a neon pink bikini that was very much out of the realm of her usual style.

"Thank you. Did I tell you I love you shirtless?"

Beckett flexed exaggeratedly, putting his hands behind his head, and Tristan laughed. His abs rippled, and she sighed with pleasure as she turned her face back to the sun. She didn't think she would ever get tired of looking at him without clothes.

At long last, when the sun began to set, everyone got out of the water, toweling off and pulling on clothes before sitting down around a fire Beckett quickly built. They toasted s'mores and gossiped about their classmates, and Tristan drank in every bit of the laughter, the good-natured ribbing, the sweet saltiness of the snacks, and the drying breeze that carried the scent of magnolias. The feeling that her clock was running down had abated for a while in the excitement of her WLU acceptance, but it had returned the morning of her birthday and persisted, though she tried not to pay it much attention. Her emotions lodged in her throat as she looked around at Beckett laughing with Tyler and her siblings, her heart swelling to capacity with how much she loved these people. She hoped with every fiber of her being that her feeling was wrong, that things would turn out OK despite those very same fibers yelling that things would not, and that her time would be better spent preparing for the battle of her life. She carefully committed the happy faces to memory, knowing on some deep level that she'd need to turn to them for strength in the coming weeks.

Tristan shook her head quickly, trying to clear the melancholy that had settled in before someone noticed how quiet she'd fallen. She leaned into Beckett and he gently held her close, rubbing her arm while still in conversation with

Tyler. Tristan's eyes moved to Olivia, who looked back at her knowingly, her own eyes shimmering with sadness for just a moment before they cleared. Tristan knew Olivia was having a hard time with the idea of Tristan deflecting -- for all of the obvious reasons, of course, but also because they would lose the connection that linked them in a way common sisters never had the fortune of experiencing. It made Tristan's heart hurt to know Olivia was grieving, but she also knew that Olivia would be OK, and so would their relationship; they had much, much more that bound them than their abilities.

When darkness began to fall, Olivia, Tyler, and Evander departed, Olivia wishing Tristan and Beckett luck with the night ahead. Finally alone, Beckett turned to Tristan, slipping his hands around her waist.

"I've been waiting for today since Monday."

"Me too."

"Did you have a good birthday celebration?"

Tristan nodded, her eyes lingering on Beckett's lips.

"The best one I can ever remember having."

"Good." Beckett grinned, noticing her distraction. "What do you want to do now?"

Tristan thought it over for a moment, looking behind her at the remaining s'mores ingredients. "Why don't we sit by the fire for just a little longer?"

Beckett smiled and followed Tristan back to the stone circle, sitting behind her and scooting up until she rested against him. He wrapped his arms around her and she leaned her head back, looking up at him for a few wordless beats.

"What's on your mind, gorgeous?"

Tristan smiled.

"For once, nothing. I'm just enjoying being here with you."

"We could stay here. Who needs to graduate, really?"

"Right, and who needs Boston, or a future at all?" Tristan laughed.

"Speaking of Boston, have you thought more about the apartment idea?"

"I have," Tristan nodded thoughtfully. "I think the first step is breaking the news of my WLU acceptance to my parents, and then going from there. But that aside, I don't think it sounds like a bad idea."

"It's a great idea. You and me, alone together, every day, every night..."

Tristan laughed.

"You don't have to convince me to want to spend as much time as possible with you, trust me."

"But?"

"It's just a lot to think about."

Beckett kissed her temple.

"We've got time."

Eventually the s'mores disappeared and the fire burned down to cinder, and Tristan and Beckett climbed into their tent for the night. Beckett pulled Tristan close to him before she had a chance to start changing into her pajamas, and she smiled against his mouth, deciding he had a much better plan in mind.

CHAPTER 34

The following Friday, as Tristan and Beckett sat by the lake putting the finishing touches on their senior project, which had come together earlier and more seamlessly than they had anticipated, Beckett grinned at her, a glimmer in his eye that both amused her and made her feel uneasy.

"Why are you looking at me like that?"

"I have a surprise for you."

"What's that?" Tristan hated surprises.

"OK, hear me out. I know you said no. I know you have your family meeting--"

"Beckett--"

"--But you see them every month and we only get one senior prom, and I want nothing more than to take you. I promise we'll have an amazing night, and we can go into New Orleans afterwards, and we can spend the next day there."

"Beckett--"

Beckett hopped up off of the bench, oblivious to or ignoring Tristan's frustration that had her on the verge of tears, and he pulled two tickets out of his back pocket.

"Tristan Wallace, will you please go to prom with me tomorrow night?"

"I can't." Tristan looked at him incredulously, and his

face fell. "I told you that. Beckett, I'm sorry, but I don't know how I could have made it any clearer. I cannot get out of my family's reunion. I'm sorry."

"You can't, or you don't want to? Because I seem to recall you saying you can't get out of it but also that you don't want to go to prom." Beckett crossed his arms, and Tristan stood.

"I can't. I know you want to go and want me to go with you, so I would if I could... but I *can't*."

"Well then you need to tell me where you really go and what you really do every month, Tristan, because there is no such thing as a family reunion that happens every thirty days and is mandatory."

"There is in my family."

"No, there isn't. Why are you lying to me? Why have you been lying to me? I thought... I..."

Beckett shoved his hands through his hair, looking caught somewhere between angry and exasperated. This was the first time since they'd started dating that they were arguing, the first time Beckett was holding his ground over Tristan's secrecy and weird family rituals, and while Tristan knew to expect it sooner or later, she had been hoping for much, much later. She had been hoping he'd stick to his word that he'd be patient until graduation.

"I'm not lying. Beckett, please." Tristan took a step towards him, but Beckett stiffened up and she stopped, pain piercing her heart. "Please."

"I love you," Beckett said fiercely, his own hurt written all over his face. "But I also know you, and I *know* you're lying to me. I just want to know why. It's killing me, Tristan; every day it kills me a little bit more that there are all these things about you and your life and your family that you won't tell me, but I keep waiting because that's what you've asked me to do. And now I'm asking you to do something that's important to me, like not pressing you for your secrets has been to you, and you won't?"

Tears streaked down Tristan's face and she quickly wiped them away.

"I'm sorry. I don't know what else to say."

"You can say you'll go to prom with me, or you can tell me why you really can't."

"No."

Beckett looked floored.

"No?"

"No. I'm sorry. You should go, though; I think Tyler is going solo since Olivia can't. You should go with your friends and have a great time, but I..." Tristan felt like her insides were being torn apart, evidenced by her wavering voice, but she held her chin high and firm.

She reached out to Beckett again, but he put his hand out, stopping her, and stepped away.

"Please, Beckett. You said you'd stick by me no matter what happened. You said you'd give me until graduation." Tristan's voice was barely above a whisper now, and she knew it wasn't fair to use his words against him, but she needed him to understand just one more time. One more time and if he ever asked again, she'd tell him everything.

"I know what I said."

"Then do it!" Tristan cried. An unexpected wave of bitterness surged through her. "Or were *you* lying?"

"Don't turn this around on me, Tristan. I love you no matter what happens, and I'm *not* walking away from you now or giving up on loving you, I'm just asking you for the truth! That's all I want from you! Stop lying and finally tell me the truth!" Beckett tried to keep his voice down, but the end came out in a shout that destroyed what little restraint Tristan had left.

"I can't tell you the truth!" Tristan yelled back, on a sob. "OK? There! Fine, I'm lying if that's what you want to hear! But I can't tell you the truth yet, Beckett, so you'll either have to deal with that until graduation like you promised, or we'll have to break up!"

Tristan knew in that instant that she would curse her eidetic memory for the rest of her days. Beckett's stunned expression, the absolute heartbreak in his eyes and on every plane of his face, branded itself into each layer of her brain. As Beckett grabbed his backpack and left without another word, all Tristan could do was bury her face in her hands and weep.

***

At home, Tristan sat numbly on the edge of her bed, staring unseeingly out her window. Every part of her ached; her insides were inflamed and raw. She had made the right decision, somewhere deep down she knew that -- Orion was watching her, and telling Beckett what was going on would immediately expose him, make him a target, and that was a risk Tristan would never take, no matter the cost. That knowledge didn't make anything better, however. Protecting Beckett by hurting him, even for the greater good, had been brutal for them both. Sure, so it was only their senior prom he'd asked her to attend, and it wouldn't be the end of the world if neither of them went, but Tristan knew the prom had just been a facade for the months of frustration and bewilderment Beckett was feeling. She knew it had merely been the catalyst for his blow-up, and that while prom probably was important to him, what was most important was knowing why Tristan was lying to him.

Tristan didn't need to put herself in his shoes to know how he was feeling. She knew perfectly well how it looked, and how it must feel to just want answers and to have someone flat out refuse them, or to offer an adequate apology for the refusal.

Tristan heard the front door open and close, and then footsteps come up the stairs.

"Hey, Trin, do y--" Olivia was saying, but she stopped short. "Trinity?"

Tristan cleared the thickness out of her throat, but still didn't turn around. She blinked a few times, trying to get herself together.

"Hey, O," Tristan said flatly.

Olivia eyeballed Tristan from the doorway. Her sister was still in her Jamestown uniform, her braid hanging in a perfect line halfway down her back. Her shoulders were squared, but her vibe was so sorrowful that it had stopped Olivia in her tracks. She bit her lip, popping into Tristan's thoughts with very little effort, which also meant Tristan was unsealed. None of this pointed to anything good.

As Olivia watched, Tristan's fight by the lake with Beckett unfolded. Beckett stormed off, and Olivia was filled with all of Tristan's emotions as he went, which had tears gathering in Olivia's eyes.

"Oh Trinity, I'm so sorry," Olivia said quietly.

Tristan said nothing.

"Do you want company?"

"No thank you."

Olivia nodded.

"Do you think you should--"

"No."

"But maybe you should just tell him--"

"*No.*"

Olivia nodded again. She understood Tristan's motives for keeping Beckett in the dark; it was the only way she knew she could keep him safe. Olivia wanted to point out that Orion was ruthless and it probably wouldn't matter in the end whether or not Beckett knew anything, if Orion decided to go after him to hurt Tristan, but Olivia didn't want to add to her sister's misery.

"If you change your mind about wanting company, I'll be in my room for a while before I go out tonight."

Tristan had lapsed back into silence, and Olivia left, softly closing the door behind her. Tristan sat there for a while longer, then stood and changed out of her uniform, into a pair of soft black shorts and a white t-shirt. She laid on her bed, pulling her knees up to her chest, and resumed her blank stare out the window. The sky gradually changed, bright blue to dusky indigo to the same deep navy as the stripes on Beckett's comforter. Inexplicably, this was what stomped the rest of Tristan's heart flat, and she pulled her legs in closer to her body, wishing she could keep pulling herself into a ball until she just disappeared with a pop. Could this really be it? Could this really be the end of her and Beckett until their destiny connection brought them back together, if it even did in this lifetime? A lie too big to keep fitting between them, a plea for honesty, a refusal. A departure. Their argument had felt like it had stopped time itself, but it had only lasted a few minutes. Amazing how quickly something could unravel if given just a few minutes.

Tristan closed her eyes, but Beckett's face was waiting. Betrayed. Heartbroken. Confused. Not a trace of anger, somehow, which made it all the worse. It would be easier if he'd left angry. It would be easier if his love for her had soured into hatred. Tristan squeezed her eyes shut harder, but the memories were coming now and cared not for her pain. Beckett holding her hand at school, watching only her while the rest of the students watched them, still curious as to how their relationship worked. Beckett pushing her hair behind her ears, his fingers warm and sure on the back of her neck as he kissed her. Beckett holding her in his bed the morning after the gathering, putting her back together without knowing how broken she'd been. Beckett pulling her up off of the porch swing and into his arms when she'd told him she loved him. Smiling at her as they'd tubed on the river. Asking her to stay with him when his parents had been arrested, his face so open and vulnerable. Tearing through Emmeline and her friends to rescue her, his entire body shaking with panic and lividity. Beckett kissing her for the first time, quickly as though if he hadn't, he would have missed his chance. As if he ever would have missed his chance. Beckett, Beckett, Beckett. Tristan had no other memories.

***

Olivia must have filled in the rest of the family about what had happened, for everyone left Tristan alone that night, and even into the next morning. She ate breakfast at the table with them, but she wasn't there, not really, and Sol and Umbris exchanged more than one worried look while Olivia and Evander filled the gaps in conversation that would have normally been filled by Tristan. Still, they let her be.

Tristan excused herself and no one argued, and she headed upstairs to shower before her shift at Rise and Grind. She left the house earlier than she needed to, weaving her wet hair into a braid, and she sat at a table in the back of the café, nose buried in a book, until it was time to clock in. Even Joe, who was generally oblivious and no master of subtlety by any stretch, could tell something was wrong and left her alone.

Alone. Tristan appreciated that no one was prying or saying things like "you're so young, there's plenty of fish in the sea!" or "it's never love at this age anyway, you'll be OK" or "at least this happened now, a month before the acceptance ceremony, instead of at the same time" (that last one was an actual thought she'd heard Umbris have), but alone was a hard thing to be when it wasn't what she wanted, and worse still when the only person who could really make it right didn't owe it to her to try, and wouldn't.

Tristan's face went red at her secret shame. She'd texted Beckett late last night, several times, to say she was sorry and that she wished she could explain but that she couldn't yet. Desperation had compelled her to add that she loved him and always would, had compelled her to beg him to please understand just one last time and trust her that she would tell him everything as soon as she could.

He'd said nothing, which shocked Tristan and didn't. She was saying nothing different than what she'd said when they'd argued, so why would he respond? She was begging him for a mile, but wouldn't give him an inch.

Violetta was the only person who would not handle Tristan with kid gloves.

"I heard you and Beckett broke up," Violetta said unceremoniously, leaning her hip on the counter next to Tristan, who was staring absentmindedly at the wall.

Tristan's head whipped around.

"What?"

Violetta nodded, her face not unkind.

"Of course I heard. Everyone has. You know how it goes."

"Great. I'm so glad he's telling people," Tristan muttered.

"Beckett didn't tell anyone."

Tristan snorted.

"Well that leaves me and I only told my sister, and I know she'd never throw a scrap to the Jamestown hounds. So sorry, but I don't buy it."

"It wasn't Beckett. It was Dean Ward, from my grade. Apparently you and Beckett were yelling at each other by the lake and he overheard."

Tristan's face burned with embarrassment.

"I didn't think there was anyone around."

"You know Jamestown -- there are eyes and ears everywhere."

"So I guess I can expect the bitch brigade, led by Sergeant Emmeline, to roll in any minute now?"

Violetta shrugged.

"Probably. Hosebeasts gonna hosebeast."

"Fantastic."

Violetta observed Tristan for a moment.

"I really am sorry."

Violetta's tone was surprisingly soft, and Tristan looked at her, startled. Her eyes began to well up, and Tristan looked away before she started awkwardly crying all over Violetta's shoulder.

"Thanks."

"Not that you asked, but I think you guys will get back together."

"Doubtful."

"Well, you never know. Anything can happen, right?"

Tristan nodded wryly.

"So they say."

CHAPTER 35

It began to rain as Tristan drove home from work. The drab, oyster-colored sky reflected Tristan's inner turmoil, which was soothing, in a way -- she hated nothing more than a pleasant, sunny day when she was in a state of despair.

In her bedroom, Tristan stared listlessly into her closet. Did it matter what she wore tonight? It seemed like such a waste of time to put any effort at all into her outfit for the gathering -- who was it for? What did it matter? On a sigh, Tristan decided on distressed black jeggings, flat black rain boots that cut off at her ankles, and a sleeveless black shirt. Plain. Boring. Uninspired. She left her hair the way it was, down and wavy from her earlier braid, and skipped her usual light makeup. Turning away from the mirror, she pulled on a thin black raincoat and went downstairs to wait, her phone as silent and heavy as a rock in her back pocket.

Tristan watched mindless TV in the living room until everyone was ready to go, and then got in the car, staring out the window as Umbris began the drive south through the lashing, angry downpour. They passed the entrance of Beckett's street on the way, and though she told herself not to look, Tristan did anyway, noticing that Beckett's car was missing from out front of his house. So he'd gone to prom after all. Good for him. Olivia squeezed her hand, looking at her sympathetically, and Tristan gave her a half-hearted squeeze back. She envied how little drama had occurred between Olivia and Tyler around prom, but then, their relationship was much more casual than hers and Beckett's;

Olivia and Tyler clearly cared for each other, but neither of them seemed to give much thought to a future together. Such a nonchalant approach seemed incredibly appealing to Tristan in her current position, though she wouldn't trade her relationship with Beckett for the world. *Wouldn't have traded,* Tristan corrected herself, her heart aching once again. She supposed she had traded it, come to think of it, but she never could have imagined doing so for the community she wasn't even going to join in the end.

They arrived at the gathering place and Tristan shed her jacket, already sweating, instead opting for an umbrella that Umbris held out to her. The five of them walked to and boarded the small boat to the island, thankfully alone. Tristan didn't know where any of the Crenshaws were, and didn't care. Evander nudged her as they made the short jaunt across the river, his voice low, though it was raining so hard and so loudly that Tristan had to strain to hear him over the heavy drops pelting her hood.

"You OK?"

"Fine," Tristan replied, her voice tight.

"Liar."

Tristan gave him a withering look.

"For what it's worth, he's suffering, too."

"I don't care."

"Liar."

"Do you have an actual point or do you just want to make me feel worse?" Tristan's voice was full of venom.

Evander looked taken aback, his mouth opening and closing a couple of times before he spoke again.

"I was trying to make you feel better. I didn't want

you to think this is easy for him, either."

"I don't really need to think about how this is for him," Tristan replied. Her voice softened as she added, "But thanks anyway."

Evander nodded, and Tristan looked at Olivia, who had been watching them with a rueful expression. Olivia said nothing, just gave Tristan a small, sad smile, and Tristan looked away. She couldn't decide if she wanted to continue being left alone, or discuss what was going on in her head with her family -- the former left a pit in her stomach that was edged by an anxiety she couldn't quite understand, and the latter filled her with a peculiar anger that she also couldn't quite understand.

The Wallaces stepped off of the boat, and it made its way back across the river as they trudged through the mud toward the gathering. Several minutes into their walk, Tristan, who was the caboose of the group, suddenly got the strangest feeling. She looked around the pitch black island, seeing nothing out of the ordinary -- nothing at all, actually, since it was so dark and the rain obscured the landscape almost entirely -- but her scalp prickled all the same.

"Oceana." Tristan tapped Olivia on the shoulder, and Olivia turned. "Are you picking up on any weird vibes right now?"

Olivia stilled, listening, waiting, but after a few beats she shook her head.

"No. Why, are you?"

Tristan made a quick decision, knowing Olivia was currently worried enough about her. She shook her head.

"No. I thought I heard something, but I haven't heard it since."

Olivia nodded and resumed walking, and Tristan followed her, though she looked back over her shoulder a couple of times, bothered. This feeling she had was different than anything she'd felt before -- she didn't think it was related to Orion this time, since it didn't seem malevolent in any way, but she couldn't hone in on it to figure out where it was coming from and why. As they neared the entrance to the clearing, Tristan was quickly distracted by the sight of Celes waiting for her and her family. Seeing him made her stomach flip unpleasantly, and Tristan realized that they were now only a month from her decision. One month until she'd find out if, somehow, her premonition would come to fruition, or if she'd go through with her anticipated plan of deflection. That she didn't have a stomach ulcer the size of Louisiana by now was a true miracle.

"Trinity." Celes nodded in her direction, but otherwise didn't engage with her, and Tristan nodded back at him, relieved.

Tristan followed her family into the clearing, passing by the members who dutifully swept their hands over the Wallaces to dry their clothes and skin. She looked around as they mingled, not really paying attention to the goings-on around her; despite her best efforts, Tristan found herself wondering what Beckett was up to. The temptation to drop in on him psychically was so great that Tristan had to clench her jaw to stop herself -- it would do her no good to keep up this kind of torture, and the sooner she could convince herself of that, the better. Beckett's continued silence told her everything she needed to know anyway.

The C names had just been called for their infusions when there was a sudden, loud commotion at the entrance of the clearing. Someone -- someones, actually, were yelling, and Tristan frowned, wondering what was going on now. Had

Orion, despite Sol's clear warnings, accosted Ember anyway so he could show him what he could do?

Tristan started towards the noise, and had just reached the growing throng of onlookers when Olivia, from several people ahead of Tristan, turned around. The look of terror on her face was so complete that it took Tristan's breath away. At the very same moment, a different voice yelled, a voice Tristan would know anywhere, and her blood ran cold.

Tristan grabbed onto the person beside her, swaying on her feet. This could not be happening. She had to be dreaming. The person looked at her, irritated, and she let go, pinching herself hard and grimacing at the sensation. Getting her bearings, Tristan forced her way to Olivia, who pushed her ahead, through the people at the front of the line. Tristan stumbled out of the crowd and onto a scene so horrific that her brain kept jamming up trying to process it. Panic swelled like an ocean within her, and so did an overwhelming nausea. *How?* Her brain demanded. *How? How was this possible?*

Entros and three of his minions had a struggling Beckett in a stronghold. He was soaked, muddy, bruised and bloodied, and his right shoulder in particular was spilling blood at an alarming rate from a deep, wide wound. He looked up, noticing Tristan with his one non-swollen eye, but all she could do was stare and try not to collapse into a dead faint.

"Tristan! Let me go, you stupid assholes!" Beckett jerked his body, blanching at the pain that must have rocketed through his shoulder.

"Beckett!"

His voice roused her, and Tristan ran towards him, but she was swiftly intercepted by another guard.

"Let me go!" Tristan screamed, thrashing wildly against the guard who might as well have been hewn from the side of a mountain for all he moved.

"Tristan!" Beckett yelled, and Tristan shook her head furiously, wanting him to stop fighting the guards, to stop aggravating his shoulder wound.

"What is going on?" Orion suddenly stepped into the clearing beside Tristan, looking at the guard who held her. "Lutu, I demand you unhand Trinity at once."

Lutu dropped Tristan like a hot potato, scowling at her as he rubbed his forearm where Tristan had dug in her fingernails as hard as possible, puncturing his skin through his cloak. Tristan ran over to Beckett, her hands shaking as she pushed his wet hair out of his face.

"Beckett," Tristan whispered, tears rolling down her cheeks. "Beckett, what are you doing here?"

"I followed you. Not my best idea," Beckett replied, sounding tired, and Tristan noticed how pale he was beneath the dirt and bruising.

"No," Tristan said softly. "Oh, no. Oh, Beckett..."

"Entros, explain." Orion's voice was calm, commanding, and Tristan looked at Entros with hate in her eyes as he stepped forward.

"We caught this commoner not far from here. It appears as though he came in via the west bank, which was unfortunately left unguarded for a few minutes earlier this evening." Entros's jaw briefly clenched as he looked over at one of his guards. "We wouldn't normally have brought him here, we would have dealt with him the way we usually deal with commoners, but he insisted he knew someone named Tristan Wallace and that she was here, in danger. We were concerned another commoner had entered the gathering undetected."

Tristan frowned. What was Entros talking about? It had just been a few months ago that he'd caught her and Celes and had to answer to Umbris -- surely Entros would have connected the last name Wallace, if he didn't remember hearing Beckett say her common name when he'd grabbed her by the shoulders? Had he brought Beckett here on purpose? If so, why? Almost imperceptibly, Entros's eyes flickered to Tristan, and then right back to Orion, who was carefully surveying Beckett.

Tristan moved her body in front of Beckett's, shielding him, and from the corner of her eye she saw her family and the Crenshaws push to the front of the congregation, coming to a standstill as the guards halted them. In silence they took in the scene before them, which was yet another eerie reflection of Tristan's premonition. The rest of the community was whispering and murmuring amongst themselves, but Tristan could not process any specific words. Beckett let out a low moan, and Tristan looked back at him in a panic that was choking her as he swayed on his feet, his eyelids drooping. His shoulder was still bleeding steadily, the right half of what was his white Henley stained almost black, almost down to his wrist, and up close Tristan could tell his injury was more serious than it had originally looked.

"Entros, when you were given your position, were you also given complete power to make such a crucial call as this?" Orion asked, his tone mild, and dread dropped into Tristan's stomach.

Entros looked surprised by the question.

"Forgive me, Elder Orion, but I do not believe anyone is given complete power besides the Elders."

"Correct. And so do you feel you made the right call here? Or do you think, perhaps, you should have called for a consult with the Elders down by the west bank before you marched this commoner into the very clearing to which he should never have been granted access?"

Silence fell.

"I believed I was making the right call," Entros said finally, and Tristan shook her head.

"I see. Well, I'm sorry to say you believed wrong." Orion lifted his hand, and Entros let out one strangled cry before he slumped to the ground, dead.

"No!" Tristan shrieked, whirling around to face Orion. "No! What have you done?"

"Oh my God," Beckett said from behind her. "Oh my God. Is he dead? Did he just--"

There was the sound of vomit hitting the ground, and Tristan turned to Beckett, putting a shaking hand on his back as he expelled the contents of his stomach, groaning in agony as he tried to straighten back up. He stumbled sideways, and the guards roughly righted him, their faces masks of disgust. Tristan glared at them.

"OK. It's OK. You're going to be OK." Tristan was trying not to lose it, but she couldn't stop looking at Entros, at Beckett, at the havoc wreaked already, all because she had refused to tell Beckett the truth.

"Take the commoner up front to be executed." Orion ignored Tristan, ordering the shellshocked guards instead.

"No! No, stop, please! Don't do this!" Tristan threw herself in front of Beckett, whose forehead touched her back as she shielded him from Orion. The guards, probably still too shocked to move, stayed put, and Tristan had the sickening realization that her first premonition had come true, which meant the second one...

"Orion, this is not necessary." Umbris stepped up, distracting Tristan from her distress, and Orion turned his disdainful gaze on him.

Celes, Celes heard Oceana in his mind, and he turned his head slightly to look at her out of the corner of his eye. *I can't go into detail right now, there isn't time, but I need you to manipulate Orion's reality so we can get Beckett and Trinity out of here.*

Oceana, no. You can't ask me to get involved in this. I can't--

Celes, Trinity is about to make a deal with the devil that will end one way, and that is in her execution. Please, there isn't time to explain now how I know this, but I promise I will when I can. Please, Celes.

Even if I could, which I don't think I can, Orion is too powerful. He'd know immediately.

Please try. If you could just make it seem like they're taking Beckett away, that's all we need. Evander is ready to run him back to where the car is parked, and I'll do anything that's needed to get them out of here safely too.

Celes looked at Oceana with uncertainty for a few long moments, and Oceana felt like she was going to explode. If Celes refused, it was over for Tristan. If he refused, Oceana would never forgive him as long as she lived. Finally, he nodded.

I'll try.

"Is that your call to make, Umbris?" Orion asked, unbothered. His fellow Elders finally appeared behind him, taking in the scene with mixed expressions. Bayle Vencroft, Tristan noticed immediately, looked deeply troubled, and exchanged an unreadable look with Axis Daddona.

"I'm asking you to please reconsider. This commoner is harmless; he knows nothing about us, and I assure you even still he has no idea what he's come across tonight. He saved Trinity's life in December, and we are indebted to him for that."

"You know the rules," Orion replied in a clipped voice. "Exceptions are rare and, as far as I'm concerned, should be done away with altogether."

"Of course you'd feel that way," Tristan spat, her eyes burning as she looked at Orion. Her gaze moved to the Elders behind him. "And what of your silence? What of the rule that no decisions are made by one, only by all? You've stood by while he carelessly and needlessly took one life tonight, will you do it again?"

"How dare you address your Elders in such a manner." Orion stepped towards Tristan, but instead of looking angry, he looked utterly delighted. What a lunatic.

"Orion." Bayle stepped forward next. "Trinity is correct. This is not how we are supposed to operate."

"We were having a meeting up at the other end of the clearing," Bayle continued, looking at Tristan and then at the rest of the community. "We didn't hear everything going on right away, but we came as soon as we were notified."

"And you will step in now, that's what you think?" Orion turned on Bayle, and Tristan turned back to Beckett.

"We're going to get you out of here. I'm not going to let anything else happen to you," Tristan said in a low voice, but Beckett seemed dazed and sluggish. She took his face in her hands and forced his eyes to hers, speaking firmly but still quietly. "Beckett. I know you're hurt. I know you've lost a lot of blood, but I need you to stay with me, OK? Just try to stay with me."

"I'm always with you, beautiful. Wild horses couldn't drag me away."

Tristan let out a half-laugh, half-sob, and she pressed a quick kiss to his mouth.

"I'm so sorry for everything."

"I'm sorry too. What the hell is going on? Who are these people?"

"Let him go," Umbris addressed the guards, who looked uncertain. "He's harmless. He's injured. You know he won't go anywhere and if he tries he won't get far."

Maybe it was their loyalty to Entros, or maybe it was something Tristan would never be privy to that made them do it, but the guards released Beckett, and he staggered towards Tristan, who caught him, holding him, careful not to touch his shoulder.

"I love you. I love you, and I'm going to do whatever it takes to get you out of here," Tristan whispered, as Beckett held her with his one good arm.

"Yes, I'm going to step in now that you've killed our head guard," Bayle was saying to Orion, his fury evident on his face. "We all are."

Orion smiled coldly. "Wrong."

Bayle lifted his hand, but before he could do anything, Orion, with a twitch of his head, encased the Elder committee in a dome of watery blue light. They could do nothing, not even protest, as whatever the orb was made of had seemed to stop time for all of them, suspending them, frozen, like spectres of themselves.

"What the fuck? Tristan, what the fuck is going on?"

Beckett looked terrified, and Tristan could only shake her head, more scared than she'd ever been. Orion had gone rogue and he was mad with power; there was no stopping him now.

"Orion." Umbris got Orion's attention once again, though his voice sounded less than sure, which made Tristan's knees shake. "I'm asking you again, just let this boy go and I'll wipe his memory myself. I'll make sure he remembers nothing about any of this, and I'll plant a false memory to explain his injuries."

"You're making a lot of effort for the boy who is the reason your daughter will reject the community next month, Umbris."

Gasps ricocheted through the crowd, and Tristan once again felt like she was going to faint as all eyes were suddenly on her -- the ones that remained, anyway, since a large portion of the community, in the melee, had made the wise decision to flee. She helplessly took in the shock and hurt on Umbris's face, the regret on Olivia and Evander's, and, worst of all, the betrayal on Celes, Dune, and Thera's. It was then Tristan realized Sol had disappeared.

"He's not the reason." Tristan steadied Beckett before she let him go and stepped forward, lifting her chin. She had to get through this, get Beckett through this alive, and then she'd make amends. "My decision was made long before he came into the picture. Let him go. He means nothing to you. I know it's me you've been after."

"Indeed." Orion eyed Tristan. "But he means everything to you, and that makes him valuable to me."

Celes, Oceana urged, but Celes was still staring at Tristan. *Celes! I know you're blindsided, OK, but please focus. We're running out of time!*

Celes slowly turned his head to look at Oceana, an incredulous expression on his face. *You think I'm going to help them now?*

Yes, Oceana said fiercely. *I do. Because you're a good person, and you care about Trinity, and you wouldn't let your ego cost someone his life.*

Celes's jaw worked, but he nodded once again. *Fine. But this is the last time I'll ever have anything to do with your family.*

Oceana nodded back, knowing she couldn't ask for more than that.

CHAPTER 36

Beckett was barely hanging onto consciousness. His whole body throbbed with pain, his shoulder was on fire, and he was having trouble understanding what he'd stumbled into. He was ashamed that he'd followed Tristan and her family, but he hadn't realized what an egregious mistake he'd made until he'd been accosted by a bunch of men in cloaks, like something out of *American Horror Story,* in the pitch black bayou. They'd asked him all sorts of weird questions that he couldn't answer, and when he'd tried to fight them off, one of them had stabbed him in the shoulder with a spear or something. Stabbed him! They'd beaten him too, after that, but he hadn't stopped pleading with them to let him find Tristan, who he knew was in danger with her grandfather.

It had been when Beckett had mentioned Umbris that the guard called Entros, who was now lying dead at his feet, had halted the attack by his minions. They'd hauled Beckett off to the place where he stood now, stared down by a bunch of scared, panicky faces in a sea of black, and confronted with a glowing blue ball in which actual people were somehow trapped.

Nothing made sense. What was an Elder? What was a commoner? Was this a hardcore group of fantasy role players he'd discovered? Was Tristan embarrassed by how seriously they took themselves, and that's why she'd lied about them? What community was everyone talking about? Had Mr. Wallace just said he would *wipe Beckett's memory?* Was Tristan a prisoner of some weird, delusional cult, and she'd lied to protect Beckett from them?

"You."

Beckett looked up to find the hulking guy who'd interrupted his first attempt at kissing Tristan back in December addressing him.

"Do you love her?"

"What?"

"Trinity. Do you love her?"

Beckett looked at the guy -- what was his name? Cameron? -- wondering what his motives were, wondering if he would kill him before the deranged, power drunk senior citizen that everyone kept referring to as Elder Orion got to it. What did it matter, though? Beckett was sure he wasn't getting out of this bizarre wormhole he'd fallen into, anyway; if he wasn't killed, surely he was going to bleed to death. He was already weak, and growing weaker by the minute.

"Yes, I do."

"And does she love you?"

Beckett looked at Cameron, and then deliberately at everyone else, who seemed oblivious to their conversation.

"Is this really what we're gonna focus on right now?"

"They can't see or hear us. Answer me. Does Trinity love you?"

Beckett still couldn't determine his motives, but there was a familiar expression of pain on Cameron's face that Beckett himself had known all too well since the day before, which compelled him to answer.

"Yes. She does."

Cameron nodded, looking at Tristan, who was still in a standoff with Orion, for a long moment.

"Unbelievable. A commoner. It never would have worked anyway, though, I guess. The curse of the destiny connection."

"What?" Beckett wondered if he'd reached the point of no return with his blood loss; Cameron had said words in order, but they were nonsensical.

"Listen to me carefully," Cameron got right up in Beckett's face, leaving him no choice. "If Trinity tells you to run, do not hesitate. Do not wait for her. Run. I know you're weak. I know there's a good chance you'll die from your injuries anyway, making this whole goddamned thing a suicide mission, but do it anyway. Do you understand? If Trinity or *anyone* tells you to run, run like your life depends on it, because it does."

"I'll try."

"No," Cameron said ferociously, leaning even closer. *"You will."*

"Alright, alright, I will."

"He's of no use to you," Tristan's voice broke into Beckett's ears at full volume, startling him. He hadn't realized that all sounds had dimmed while Cameron had been bossing him around. "And there is no need to use him against me. Tell me what you want. Tell me why you've been after me, and if you promise to let him go, I promise to do whatever you want."

"Trinity, no!" Olivia cried, but Tristan ignored her.

This was how it had to be, Tristan knew it now. Orion would not let Beckett live if Tristan chose him, if she chose not to join the community. If she could end this tonight, if she could be the one to tell Umbris to wipe Beckett's memory back to September herself instead of him doing it behind her back, she could change the course of her premonition in that way. She could remove the guilt that would compel Umbris to restore Beckett's memories, leading to their affair that would lead to her execution. It was the only way out of Beckett's and her certain deaths.

Orion approached, stopping uncomfortably close to her. He looked deeply into her eyes, and, in an experience she'd never had before and hoped she'd never have again, Tristan's brain actually began to burn. She gritted her teeth, holding his stare, while the white-hot pain in her head increased until she was seeing spots. Still, she made no noise other than her labored breathing, and she did not look away -- she would give him what he wanted, but he would not break her in the process.

Just when Tristan had started to doubt her resolve, Orion smiled, taking a step back, and the pain immediately stopped. He looked over to the crowd, his smile growing bigger, and Tristan breathlessly followed his gaze to Sol, who had returned from wherever she'd gone.

"You never told her."

Tristan looked between Orion and Sol, who she'd never seen angrier in her entire life.

"Told me what?"

"Told you that you are the one in the bloodline who can restore the old way of governing the community."

This was no big revelation for Tristan, who had no idea what Orion was talking about. The older members of the community, however, and Sol and Umbris, certainly seemed to know, as the murmuring escalated to a dull roar.

"Shameful you've told her nothing." Orion shook his head at Sol and Umbris. He turned to Tristan. "This community was founded by my many greats-ago grandfather and his wife, Orion and Estelle Beltremieux. They governed solely and efficiently until there was a growing discord amongst their people. Cornered and facing the risk of an overthrowing, they agreed to establish a committee of Elders to more fairly oversee the community, which resulted in the first iteration of what you are familiar with today. There was a catch, however, that once the committee had been established, they decided to banish Orion and Estelle from the community, for its safety.

Not to be fully stripped of their dignity, Orion and Estelle warned the Elders and the community that there would come a day where a child would be born into the Beltremieux bloodline who would be more powerful than any of them or their successors, and who would restore the community and its governances to its former glory. You, Trinity, are that child. The deliverance of what ended up being their last act of revenge, as in the eleventh hour they were sentenced to execution instead of banishment."

Tristan stared at Orion, agape, and then looked at her parents, who looked grim.

"That's not possible. I don't use my abilities, I haven't since the age of ten, and I've known just as long that the community life is not the life for me. Surely if I were as powerful as you say, none of that would be true."

Orion sneered.

"Laziness, suppression, and silly notions that can be broken out of you. It is so. Your parents know it as well as I, so don't just take my word for it. Sol, darling, why don't you tell her how you discovered she was the one?"

Sol clenched her jaw, her hands balling into fists.

"No. Trinity will be free to make her own choices, not swayed by false burdens."

"So you'd rather her make her choice without knowing all the pertinent facts to her unique situation? Are *you* trying to sway her in a certain direction by withholding this from her, Sol?"

Sol glared at him with fire in her eyes.

"Of course not."

"No matter." Orion waved his hand, a gesture Tristan was coming to hate. "I'll tell her. You were not yet two, Trinity, and your siblings were infants. Your Mom had been trying to get them to nap for the better part of an hour, and it had been quiet for a few minutes when one of them began to fuss. Not wanting one to wake the other, your Mom left you alone in your bedroom for just a few minutes. Your bedroom, of course, was right up the hall from the twins' room, and the stairs were gated off, so your Mom figured you'd be OK. Imagine her terror, then, when there was a loud crash from your bedroom. She put down the fussing twin and ran to you, just to find you had opened all of the drawers of your dresser and it had fallen on top of you, crushing your tiny body.

Imagine her relief, and her subsequent shock, when you looked up at her with a smile and pushed the dresser into an upright position, and then stood up, unscathed. Such a heavy piece of furniture should have been no match for a powerless toddler, and as we know, community children do not start displaying their abilities until the age of five. She knew then, what you are. I knew, too, though I was terribly sick and didn't know how the next hour would go, let alone the next day. The scene came to me while I slept, and it turned into the lifeline that pulled me through my illness. Just in time for you to accept into the community and fulfill your bloodline."

A chill ran through Tristan. Fulfill her bloodline. The same thing Eva had said in the clearing the morning Tristan and Beckett had been camping.

"Yes, you've heard me say that before. I must admit, posing as a classmate of yours was one of my better ideas, though you and your sister are of stronger will than I had anticipated, and that plan fell flat in the end." Orion's lip curled in disgust, and Tristan felt a fury creeping into her bones and muscles that she could only remember having felt a couple of times before.

"What did you do to Eva?"

"Eva? There was no Eva, not really. There was a Bella Revet, married to a John Revet, but they lost their daughter, Eva, in infancy. It was a terrible shame when she showed up eighteen years later and they went insane. They're now the newest residents of The Winston Friends Psychiatric Institute."

"You were posing as Eva?" Beckett spoke from behind Tristan and she jumped, having temporarily forgotten he was there. His voice was filled with revulsion, and Tristan's eyes widened, remembering Eva and Beckett's brief interlude.

Orion *blew him a kiss.*

"Enough," Tristan said sternly, moving in front of Beckett. The rage was still coursing through her body, but Tristan kept outwardly cool. She knew her brain and her body were preparing for battle with no effort by her, but also knew she couldn't show her hand or it would be over before it began. "I've heard enough. Say you'll let Beckett go, and I will join you. I will fulfill my bloodline."

"Tristan--" Beckett's voice behind her was faint, and her courage briefly faltered.

Tristan heard Beckett drop to the ground like a bag of potatoes, and every cell within her told her to turn around, to say fuck it all and pick him up so they could make a gamble for their lives together, against Orion, but Tristan knew that would be the end. Even if Beckett wasn't injured, wasn't dying, neither of them would stand a chance. Orion would delight in executing them both, maybe even her whole family after that, and who knew what would become of the community then? At least if she agreed to what Orion was asking, agreed to fulfill her bloodline in whatever manner he had in mind, she would have some control over the safety of the community. Over the safety of her family.

Orion is not going to let him go. Oceana's voice entered Celes's head again, and he looked at her, irritated at the intrusion. *He's going to give Trinity his word, but he's going to lie. She will join him, and he'll tell his guards to execute Beckett anyway. Right over there, behind you, his personal guards have just arrived. Celes, this is it. When he orders Beckett's execution, you need to do the manipulation and not hesitate. There is no way in hell I am letting Trinity sell her soul to Orion.*

Celes scowled at Oceana. *I think I know better than you what to do and how to do it.*

Good. So don't let your feelings fuck it up, Oceana shot back, her eyes sending daggers at him from where they stood, less than eight feet from each other.

What makes you think he isn't listening to this conversation right now? What makes you think this will work at all?

I was paying attention once when you talked about how to close off a connection so it's impenetrable to even the Elders. It's one of

the luxuries we'll lose, I'm sure, if Orion gets his way and govern-
ance is taken from the committee and placed in his and Trinity's
hands. For now, I'm using it to my advantage.

Celes actually looked surprised at that, and Oceana raised
her eyebrows, stiffly inclining her head to the Tristan and
Orion standoff unfolding before them in the clearing.

"Trinity, I'm not letting you do this." Sol stepped forward, but a guard advanced on her and she stopped. "The
Beltremieux's Revenge is a myth, a fable. There are no docu-
ments indicating Orion and Estelle had ever placed any
such curse before they were executed; community members
kept meticulous records back then and were just as vigilant
about preserving those records. Yes, you displayed abilities
at a very, very young age, but your path since then has been
clear. You have always known which direction you would
take, and my only regret is not helping you cultivate that
path sooner."

"Such lies," Orion hissed, but Sol merely looked at
him.

Tristan walked around the guard and took Sol's hands in
hers. They were warm, where Tristan's felt like blocks of ice.

"This is the only way. It's the only way I can guarantee
your safety, and Beckett's safety."

"No it isn't." Sol looked at Orion again, her jaw setting. "There's always another way."

"I would listen to Trinity, dear Sol. She's the one who's
been having the premonitions, after all. You see, your darling daughter is as smart as I'd always heard she was -- she
has examined every possible way around and through this,
and she has come to the realization that this ends one of two
ways. One, in her, the commoner's, and your family's execution. Or two, in her taking her rightful place beside me in

exchange for your safety. Trinity has learned what has taken you your whole life to learn, if you have at all -- I am far too powerful to be challenged, even when I'm weakened. You can try whatever you're plotting, and I won't waste my time trying to figure out what it is or stop you before you do. Just know that you will fail."

"You have to get Beckett out of here," Tristan told Sol urgently. "Please. I don't know how much time he has left. You have to get him to the hospital before it's too late. I'll be OK. No matter what happens... I'll be OK."

"Trinity, you don't--"

"Mom, there isn't time!" Tristan exclaimed, her tone bordering on hysterical. She spun around to look at Orion. "Say it. Say you'll let Beckett go unharmed."

"I'll let Beckett go unharmed." Orion looked bored, but he waved off the guards, who had been lingering around Beckett.

Tristan turned to Sol again.

"I love you. Go, please."

"Tristan." Beckett, from his place on the ground, curled up on his left side, called to her.

Tristan dropped to her knees and pulled Beckett's head into her lap. She smoothed back his hair, her hands trembling.

"I love you. Listen to me. We'll find each other again. But now you have to go, you have to let my family take you out of here and to the hospital. You've lost so much blood--"

"No. I'm not leaving you." Beckett struggled to sit up, but collapsed again, his eyes closing briefly. "I'm not leaving you. I'll die here, I don't care. I walked away from you once and it was clearly the worst mistake I've ever made. I'm not doing it again."

"Beckett please," Tristan's voice shook, but she couldn't cry. She had to wrap her insides in steel, had to shove down her emotions or she'd never get through this. "Please go. This is the only way I can keep you safe."

"Trinity." Orion spoke her name, and Tristan kissed Beckett, gently placing his head back on the ground.

"Tristan, no!" Beckett said more forcefully, but Tristan walked away without turning around.

"When he's out of the clearing, I'll follow you wherever you want me to go."

"You'll follow me now." Orion gripped Tristan's wrist, the burning in her head immediately returning, and she cried out. Orion smiled cruelly, looking over at his personal guards. "Execute the boy."

"No! NO!" Tristan screamed trying desperately to pull away from Orion, but the agony in her head, now accompanied by a loud, awful hum, was taking over. It obscured her vision, all of her senses, until she couldn't see, couldn't hear, couldn't even think straight.

CHAPTER 37

Tristan felt a hard pull, and suddenly she was standing beside Sol, who was helping a sobbing Beckett to his feet, her voice soothing as she encouraged him on. Umbris had his other arm, and Olivia stood nearby, her arms wrapped around herself. Tristan turned, seeing herself still held captive by Orion, still desperately fighting him, screaming her head off. Feet away, another Beckett was being dragged off by Orion's guards. The community members who remained were cowering at the far end of the clearing, afraid to move, afraid to stay. Another Sol, Umbris, Olivia, and Evander were standing in front of the group, hands linked, shielding them from whatever may come next.

"What--"

"Trinity, go!" Olivia cried. "Celes is buying you as much time as he can, but you need to go now!"

Tristan's head swiveled to Celes, who was standing in the crowd with his eyes laser focused on Orion and other Tristan. Real Tristan? Who was that? Who was she?

"Trinity!" Olivia screamed.

Tristan sprang into action, helping Sol and Umbris help Beckett stand, and Beckett fell into her, holding her as tightly as he could.

"I thought I lost you. I thought I lost you." Beckett was mumbling into her hair, Tristan was weeping, and Olivia was panicking.

Evander -- another Evander? -- suddenly appeared beside them, gesturing to Beckett.

"Get on my back."

"I'm too heavy."

He was very heavy. Tristan could attest to this, as Beckett was currently leaning all of his weight on her.

"You're not. Help him on," Evander directed Umbris, who awkwardly maneuvered Beckett onto Evander's back.

"Oceana and I will stay here. We're going to help Celes hold Orion off if he needs it. Dad will go with you and Evander and Beckett, get you out of here and get Beckett home." Sol spoke so quickly that Tristan, whose mind was still reeling from seeing two of her doing two very different things at once, was having trouble following. "Dad will wipe his memory once he gets him home and patched up, and he'll plant a false memory of what happened tonight."

Fear seized Tristan's heart, and she shook her head.

"Let me stay. Let me stay and help Oceana and Celes. I need you to go with Dad."

"Trinity, if Orion finds out what's happening--"

"I'll handle it." Tristan cast a nervous look at Umbris, who was not paying attention to her, and she turned so her back was to him. In a low voice, she spoke as quickly as Sol had just been speaking to her. "Mom, I know I keep saying this, but I don't have time to explain everything just now. I know, *I know,* you believe Dad would never betray you and break his vow about not forcing us to choose the community, but if you send him alone or just with Evander with Beckett, Dad is going to wipe Beckett's memory back to September. He's going to decide on the way that all of this was too risky and then he will tell you I agreed that his way was the best way, and that will start an irreversible snowball effect that will end in my... my..."

Tristan was having trouble saying it. Gods, it was so horrible, to have to tell Sol that her husband would be responsible for Tristan meeting her end the same way Adara had if Sol refused to go, but Evander had started towards the entrance of the clearing and Tristan knew it was now or never.

"My execution. I promise to explain everything to you when this is over. Please just go with Dad. And be the one to wipe Beckett's memory if you can."

"Trinity--"

"Mom."

For a moment, Sol and Tristan stared at each other, Tristan willing her to take her at her word. She knew she was asking the near impossible, knew Sol did not believe that Umbris would do something so underhanded, but Tristan also knew that Sol trusted her and her judgment, and in the end she relented. Together, Sol and Tristan jogged over to Evander, Umbris, and Beckett. Beckett slid off of Evander's shoulders, and Tristan pulled him close.

"I'll find you when this is all over, I promise," Tristan whispered. "Tomorrow you'll wake up and I'll be there."

"I don't want to leave you. I can't leave you. I feel like if I go, if you stay behind, I'll never see you again."

"No," Tristan said fiercely, shaking her head and letting out a small sob. "This isn't the end. It isn't goodbye for us, Beckett, not yet, but if you stay it could be, this time. Your shoulder... you're running out of time. You have to go."

"I love you." Beckett, summoning strength Tristan didn't know how he could possibly have left, took her chin in his hand, forcing her eyes to meet his. "I love you more than anything or anyone. If something happens to you, there will be no more me. It won't matter about my shoulder. Tristan--"

"You need to go. I love you, too, but please, please go. Please trust me that no matter what happens or when, we'll find each other again."

Beckett kissed her, a kiss that reached in and wrapped gently around her very soul, and Tristan kissed him back through her tears. Letting him go, letting Umbris hoist him up onto Evander's back and watching them all run out of the clearing, was more painful than anything else she'd endured so far.

***

"I think you owe me some answers," Beckett said, his cheek flat against Evander's back as they ran through the woods. Rain assailed his face, splashing into his eyes, but he barely felt it. "What the fuck is going on? Sorry, Mr. and Mrs. Wallace."

Umbris merely grunted, and Sol ignored him entirely.

"The short version is that my family... Well, we all have certain abilities, of the supernatural variety. Oceana, she is a healer, an influencer, a mind-reader. I read auras and am freakishly strong. Trinity can't do anything. OK, she can borrow energy and get a basic reading on someone, and she can seal, which means none of us can read her thoughts, but that's it. She used to be able to move things with her mind, but she gave it up when she was ten. My Mom and Dad can do everything we can and more."

"What... the fuck?" Beckett said again. "So you guys *are* witches?"

Evander scoffed.

"Witches don't exist. No. We just happen to have tapped into the energy of the universe, whereas most people, common people, can't. We're enlightened, and it's a birthright, it's not something you can just pick up or become. Anyway, there's a ritual that used to be a law, but that law was abolished after Orion had his own daughter, my Mom's sister, executed. The law had said that upon graduating high school the children in the community had to be sealed in, had to join, and the eldest children were entered into arranged marriages to breed the next generation of uncommon kids. Adara, my Mom's sister, deflected and Orion had her killed. The Elders did away with the law immediately and it's been optional ever since, but it's still an expectation in the families. Orion disappeared for a while, but now he's back to fuck things up again -- sorry Mom."

Neither Sol nor Umbris were paying attention, too busy swiveling their heads from side to side to make sure they were still in the clear.

"So then Tristan was supposed to be sealed into your secret society and marry Cameron."

"Canton. Celes. Yes. He was chosen for her when she was ten."

"That's gross."

"I agree. Anyway, we're pretty sure Orion has been trying to have the original law restored before next month, because he's been stalking Trinity and he knew she was planning on not joining once she graduates. He failed, and since he froze the rest of the Elders tonight, I am guessing he won't succeed at all, let alone before next month. There's more to the story, but that's the gist."

"And Tristan telling me that no matter what happens this time, or when, we'll find each other again... did that mean something?"

Evander wasn't even winded, and Beckett would have hated him if he wasn't currently trying to save his life.

"Oh, yeah. There's that too. You and Trin have a destiny connection."

"A destiny connection? Cameron said something about that."

"*Canton,*" Evander corrected, sounding exasperated. "Who goes by Celes anyway."

"Sorry. Celes. He said those words."

Evander nodded.

"So... what is it?" Beckett closed his eyes, so tired, the rhythm of Evander's running lulling him to sleep.

Evander gave him a violent shake, and Beckett jumped, scowling.

"What the hell!"

"No sleeping!" Evander snapped. He ran a bit faster, his boots squelching heavily in the mud. "A destiny connection is basically a fated relationship. Not ill-fated, not star-crossed, just fated. Basically, because you and Trin have one, you can break up and date and even marry other people, but the universe has one job and one job only and that is to put you back together as many times as it needs to until it sticks. No regard for anyone else who may be involved or their feelings."

"That sounds like a load of crap."

"I would suggest you test it to see for yourself, but

Trinity will kill me and I don't think you want to put her or anyone else through that."

"It's kind of nice though. And no man, I don't want to test it. I want to be with Tristan until I die, which I hope isn't tonight. I love her."

"Talk about gross," Evander muttered.

Very suddenly, Evander came to a halt.

"What?" Beckett slurred, not having the energy to lift his head.

"My parents are gone."

"What?"

"They had our sides and now they're gone."

"Maybe we should ke--"

The woods in front of them rustled, branches cracking beneath someone's feet, and Evander stood stockstill as Thera Crenshaw stepped out of the shadows.

"Mrs. Crenshaw?" Evander frowned.

"He's not going to make it," Thera said, approaching Evander, her eyes on Beckett from beneath the hood she had pulled up to shield her face from the rain.

"That's why I'm trying--"

"No. Your running is accelerating his blood loss since no one bothered to wrap his shoulder. He's not going to make it to your destination."

"Where are my parents?" Evander asked suspiciously.

"They're not far behind. They stopped to check in on what's happening in the clearing since it was getting loud; they are going to meet you at the car."

Evander squinted past her, the river just up ahead. He assumed Thera Crenshaw was harmless, but then tonight had proven that nothing and no one could be trusted, not really, and it was suspect as hell that she had appeared now, so close to freedom.

"I'm not here to hurt either of you," Thera snapped, annoyed. She placed her hand on Beckett's shoulder. Beckett, who was not moving.

"Hey!" Evander shook Beckett, yelling loudly, but Beckett didn't stir.

"Stay still," Thera snapped again, then muttered something to herself that Evander did not catch.

After a few minutes, Thera nodded, stepping away from the boys.

"That should last him about two hours, tops. Two hours if he's lucky, Ember. I know your parents want to take him to his house and get him cleaned up and modify his memory, but he has lost too much blood, so tell them to improvise."

Thera looked behind him, her mouth setting in a hard line.

"Go."

Evander didn't wait to find out what she was looking at -- he took off running once again, jumping into the boat that he cursed for being so slow to cross the small river. He could feel Beckett breathing, even and deep, on his back, which he took as a good sign that Thera had not double-crossed them and stealthily killed Beckett while she distracted Evander.

Evander had just stepped onto the opposing bank when he heard Olivia scream in a way that made his knees go weak. His instinct was to go to her -- to leave Beckett on the riverbank and get back to his twin -- but he couldn't. He couldn't have brought Beckett this far just to leave him alone, exposed and dying. *Godsdamnit it all, Trinity,* Evander thought.

"Hurry up!" Evander bellowed into the darkness, wondering where Sol and Umbris were, what was taking them so long.

The good news was that he did not have to wait long; Sol and Umbris appeared practically seconds later, jumping into the boat just as he had minutes ago. The bad news was that their faces were devoid of color, panicked in a way he'd never seen and hoped he'd never see again.

"What's happening?" Evander asked, as they joined him on the bank.

"Orion knows," Umbris said shortly.

"I have to go back. Take him." Evander gently hoisted Beckett into Umbris's arms.

"No, Ember. You stay with us."

"I am not leaving Oceana and Trinity to fight Orion alone. Hell no. Take him and go now. Thera Crenshaw did something to keep him alive for the next two-ish hours, and told me to tell you to take him to the hospital. She said to improvise on the memory thing, but not to take him home because he won't make it."

Evander didn't wait for them to respond. He started to take off once again, but Sol's voice stopped him.

"Ember!"

Evander paused, turning to look at his Mom.

"Tell Trinity he died."

"What?" Evander's mouth fell open.

"You have to tell Trinity that Beckett died. It's your only hope of defeating Orion."

"Mom--"

"Ember." Sol suddenly looked nervous, but she lifted her chin. "What Orion said tonight is correct. Trinity is the product of the Beltremieux's revenge. She doesn't know it, because her path diverted in spite of that mark, but she has an incredible power reserve that she will only be able to access tonight if she thinks she has nothing left to lose. Lie now, apologize later. You *must*."

Evander nodded, knowing this was it, knowing by Olivia's screaming that the end was coming and so far it wasn't coming in his siblings' favor. Sol nodded as well, knowing he understood, and Evander cleared the river in one leap, flying back to the gathering.

CHAPTER 38

Evander arrived to a horror show. Bodies littered the clearing, and Olivia was on the ground, convulsing as she screamed. Celes was nowhere to be found, and Tristan was several feet from Olivia, at the edge of the clearing, motionless. Her left thigh was bleeding steadily, a small crimson pool already forming on the ground beneath her. The Elders were still frozen in their blue snow globe. Some of the older community members had begun fighting Orion and his guards, and Evander used this to his advantage, skirting around the outer edge in a low run until he reached Tristan. He dragged her almost completely out of sight and then conjured ice cold water that poured on her until she came to, gasping and sputtering.

"Wha-- Ember?" Tristan looked momentarily dazed, but then panic set in, clearing the clouds from her eyes. "Ember! He has Oceana! Where's Mom and Dad? Did they get Beckett to the hospital?"

Ember briefly closed his eyes, hoping fervently Tristan would forgive him for this someday. Tristan shook his arm, her voice rising with her anxiety.

"Ember!"

"Mom--" Evander had to clear his throat to get his voice to stop sticking to the sides. "Mom and Dad got back to the car but..."

"But what?"

Tristan was already shaking her head, already starting to hyperventilate. Evander looked sick and was avoiding her eyes. She began to quake from head to toe, her complexion waxy.

"But what?" Tristan whispered, squeezing his arm tight enough to cut off the circulation.

"He didn't make it." Evander's voice broke, and so did Tristan. From far away, she heard him continue. "Beckett. He lost too much blood. By the time..."

Everything went black.

***

When Tristan opened her eyes again, everything was so vivid, it hurt. She squinted. It was the middle of the night, she was certain, but she could see the clearing like it was the middle of the day. The rain had stopped, the colors of the island were vibrant, more vibrant than she'd ever known they were, and the heady smell of wet earth filled her nostrils. Evander was gone, and Tristan stood, her body feeling limber, like she'd spent some time warming up her muscles and was now totally pliable. She flexed her arms, her fingers, finding them painless, just like her head. Hadn't they been hurting just a bit ago, along with the rest of her body? Hadn't there been a gnarly wound on her left leg that had been bleeding fairly steadily? Tristan looked down. Her legs were fine. Great, even, ensconced in her muddy black jeggings. Her body was familiar and foreign all at once, a mildly disconcerting but overall unsurprising feeling.

She tilted her head, listening to the sounds of fighting in the clearing straight ahead. She thought of Beckett, of the great chasm the news of his death had opened inside of her, but even that felt like someone else's memory now. She stepped through the trees and into the clearing, spotting Olivia first.

She was still and silent, but Tristan could see her chest moving. She was alive. Tristan wanted to know where Evander was, and in an instant she saw him in the woods with Celes. Specifically, Evander was running Celes through the woods on his back, away from the gathering. Celes's manipulation, which had allowed Beckett to get away, though all for naught, had made him enemy number one. He was smart to be fleeing.

Tristan wove her hand through the air, transporting Evander and Celes to the Crenshaw's residence in New Orleans. No sense in them sticking around if they didn't have to. Next, she waved her hand over Olivia, sending her home to Umbris and Sol. Tristan didn't know how she knew how to do these things -- this type of ability was unheard of -- but her brain seemed to be working independently of the rest of her, moving intuitively with one goal in mind: clear the obstacles in order to kill Orion.

Tristan also swept her hands over the wounded she passed, including Monse Telarie de Maragon, who was reaching weakly for the hand of her sister, Mortua, who was dead. Her other sister, Mora, and their parents, Terminus and Noxis, were nowhere to be found. Ventis Dearing was another one who had died, the sight leaving her reeling just slightly, but Tristan kept on, moving her hand continuously as she walked, over both casualties and survivors. They would be protected now. Briefly, she thought about releasing the Elders, but her brain gave her a hard no on that one. They were safest where they were, suspended in their ball in the clearing, oblivious to Orion's rampage.

Tristan had never known a day without fear, but as she approached Orion, whose back was to her, she realized she was experiencing it now. In losing Beckett for the remainder of this lifetime, despite making every effort to protect him, Tristan had lost the only thing that had kept her standing, that had kept the ground firm beneath her feet. With her family secure now, there was nothing more Orion could take from her. Nothing more he could do to her.

Tristan had taken down his guards before they ever saw her coming, which left her and Orion alone, facing each other in their final showdown.

They raised their arms at the same time, and Orion's eyes glowed as white as Tristan was sure hers glowed black. A bitterly cold wind, colder than anything Tristan had ever felt, colder than she was sure any human could withstand, swept towards her, and she stumbled back a bit before planting her feet and bending her knees just slightly. She ground her teeth and pushed the gust back at Orion, the air biting at her hands and face, freezing them immediately. The glacial wind was excruciating, and she began to shake violently. Her head pounded with the effort of her concentration, and she felt one of her teeth crack as she kept her jaw clenched, but she persisted, Beckett's face in the forefront of her mind, and gradually she felt Orion start to retreat.

Tristan had virtually no time to recover before Orion launched his next attack -- a lightning storm replete with torrential downpouring and high winds. A bolt struck just to Tristan's left, her body buzzing with the proximity, and she spun on her heel, running through the clearing, thankful she'd opted that night for boots with tread that easily took on the muddy ground. The wind, however, was a different story -- she had nothing to protect against that, and debris hit and scraped her as she was nearly flattened to the earth multiple times.

She kept her eyes squinted, nearly closed, in an effort to protect them, and, working again on intuition alone, Tristan leapt over bodies and dodged the lightning that Orion aimed at her, running into the trees on the opposite side of the clearing. Heading into the trees was not a great option when lightning was the hunter, but it was the best option she had. Her face and hands were prickling uncomfortably with pins and needles, but she ignored them, hoping full feeling would at least return by the next time she'd need her hands.

Tristan tried desperately to think of how to fight off this attack -- she paused in an attempt to push the storm back onto Orion, but that method was not working this time, the wind from his storm was far too strong, and a strike of lightning missed her by a hair. She resumed running as Orion laughed maniacally, willing herself to block him out so she could pull together a plan. She zigged and zagged, working with the direction of the gale force gusts, running as fast as her legs would allow, as the trees around her were hit and caught fire in great flashes of blinding white light. Thick, charcoal colored smoke plumed in spite of the chaos, temporarily obscuring her surroundings, but Tristan kept on. She ran an intricate figure eight as lightning split a tree, and then the ground, to her far left, and for a moment it seemed as though Orion's barrage had caused him to lose sight of her.

That brief reprieve allowed Tristan to think more clearly, and the wheels in her mind whirred at a frenetic pace. It seemed too comedically simple to be a real solution, but if Tristan was dealing with a real weather event, she had to think of what caused real weather events and, specifically, what caused them to clear up and move out. She almost laughed at the preposterousness of elementary school science class coming in handy now, in a supernatural battle for her life, but she had no other ideas and was in too harrowing of a situation to scoff at the absurd.

While tree branches clawed at her drenched clothes and skin, and the ground began to shake for reasons she refused to turn and acknowledge, Tristan reached upward, praying Orion would not catch her off-guard. With great effort she began pulling dry, atmospheric air downward, concentrating on the warmth she could feel in her hands. Sweat beaded on her forehead and her arms quivered, her muscles pushed beyond their limits, but, to her amazement, the lightning stopped, the wind died down, and the rain gradually slowed to a drizzle as the dry air suffocated the moisture. Exhausted, but knowing the fight was far from over, Tristan pushed the now weakened hurricane back towards Orion. She shoved her wet hair out of her face and, after giving herself a full-body shake, ran back towards the clearing.

She'd just made it through the treeline when one of Orion's guards, who had somehow rallied, charged her. His expression one of unhinged ecstasy, Orion appeared in front of Tristan at the same time, conjuring a towering wall of fire which erupted from his hands and sped towards her without warning. Once again planting her feet, Tristan held off the fire with one hand as she turned her head to shield her face, feeling her skin bubble sickeningly into blisters. With her other hand, Tristan crushed the approaching guard's windpipe, sending him immediately to the ground. Orion had taught her that trick when he'd killed Entros.

Orion, spotting a flaw in Tristan's defense against his fire wall, shot his hand out towards her, and, though she dodged to the side at the last second, a blistering pain exploded at her waist as the magic clipped her on the right side, her clothing and flesh immediately burning away in that area. Tristan gritted her teeth, but she was off-kilter now, and Orion had the upper hand. He flicked his wrist this time and Tristan's left leg shattered like glass. She dropped to her right knee with a bloodcurdling scream, but still she pushed back, praying she'd have any skin on her hands and arms left at all by the time this was over.

"Relent. Relent now and join me. We will set aside the hurt we have caused and are causing each other, and together we will govern this community as destined by our blood-line. Relent." Orion's voice boomed in from every direction, and Tristan's arms began to shake, her fingers curling under the unyielding heat from the fire.

She was losing. Somehow, despite being so sure she would defeat Orion, Tristan was losing.

Orion began to laugh again, and this time it echoed deafeningly in her head.

"You are your mother's daughter. Too stubborn to admit I am too powerful to be defeated. I've taken your worthless commoner, and after you I'll take your traitorous family. They will scream like your commoner screamed when I killed him."

Tristan's head shot up, and her eyes locked on Orion's alabaster orbs.

"That's right. I killed him. You thought you could get him off of this island by having Celes Crenshaw manipulate my reality, you silly, stupid girl, but all you did was put a target on your commoner's back, and on Celes's too. One is dead, the other will be shortly. He will scream for his mother too, I'm sure."

Something snapped inside of Tristan then. On an inhuman wail she stood, throwing her head back as her mind burst open with a bone-rattling rip and an unbearable tearing sensation. A black funnel rose in the clearing between her and Orion, and she screeched endlessly at the sky, which swirled violently overhead until suddenly the universe was there, in all its divine, cosmic glory, so close Tristan was sure she could have touched it if she had the time. The funnel transformed into a thick wall of blood red smoke, and in rapid succession the visions came next -- visions of people, of destruction, of galaxies known and unknown. Of all four elements, of heaven, of hell. Of the King, Holly and Oak, dark and light, locked forever in battle. Images of famine and plagues, of feasts and islands pregnant with resources, of organisms invisible to the eye and animals as large as skyscrapers. Everything the universe overlooked, everything it was responsible for, it was all there, offering her the truly limitless power of which Orion could only ever dream. Tristan brought her arms together, channeling it instead into the smoke wall, which descended upon Orion as swiftly as his attacks had upon Tristan.

Orion screamed -- a drawn out, most satisfying sound of the purest agony she'd ever heard -- and Tristan continued pushing the wall until all she could hear was the deafening wind it was generating. Using her scorched, burning hands, she molded and shaped the smoke into a tight ball that grew smaller and smaller, until it disappeared completely in a comically dainty *puff*, taking with it the greatest threat she and the community had ever known. Her only regret was that she hadn't been able to see Orion die.

Tristan turned toward the blue sphere that had encased the Elders. It had disappeared, and they were all getting to their feet, muffled shouts of panic barely reaching her. She took one step towards them and went down hard, everything going black once again as the ground rushed up to meet her.

CHAPTER 39

The first thing Tristan heard was a steady beeping noise. It was paced pleasantly and reliably apart -- *beep,* pause, *beep,* pause, *beep,* pause. Somewhere in her mind she knew what the noise was, what it belonged to, but she was too tired to think about it. She felt as though her brain and body had run a very, very long marathon, and now she was in her rest period. She listened to the beeping until she'd drifted back to sleep, half-wondering if she was in a crash and had stayed home from school to spend the day in bed. She snuggled into her blankets, figuring if that were the case she'd better get comfortable and enjoy it until Sol did her mini-infusion to get her through until the gathering.

The gathering. Anxiety edged into Tristan's mind, but why? What was it about the gathering that suddenly made her feel so uneasy? Her head began to hurt, just a little bit, and Tristan stopped trying to think about it. She was simply too tired.

The next time Tristan came to, it was because she felt someone sit on her bed. Rising slowly through the levels of exhaustion that continued to linger on her like smoke on skin, Tristan concentrated very hard on opening her eyes.

In her immediate line of vision was Sol, looking as angelic and youthful as ever with her long hair waving softly down her back, her face free of makeup. Tristan frowned, blinking slowly. The harsh light in the room was not her bedroom light. She looked to her left, seeing a bed rail, an IV pole, a chair, and a bank of windows running the length of a wide windowsill. She was in the hospital.

"Mom?" Tristan croaked. She sounded like she was about two thousand years old, and her throat felt like it'd been rubbed with sandpaper. Her sluggish brain tried hard to make sense of where she was and why.

"Hi honey."

Tristan shifted, pain blasting through her body, and she froze. Hands and forearms heavily bandaged, she slowly lifted the thin blue blanket that covered her to find her left leg casted. Orion. The battle. The gathering. Beckett...

Covering her face, Tristan immediately burst into tears. Sol placed her hand gently on Tristan's good leg while Tristan bawled until she gagged. The noises she was making were awful, and shockwaves of electric pain tore through her body with each sob that wracked her, but she couldn't stop. She remembered now, and she wished she hadn't. Beckett was dead. Orion was probably dead, too, and she'd happily dance on his grave when her leg healed, but Beckett... After everything that had happened, she hadn't been able to save him.

"It's OK, honey. Let it out." Sol's voice was soothing, but it did nothing for Tristan, who knew she would never be soothed again. Not in this lifetime, anyway.

When Tristan physically couldn't cry anymore, she used her blanket to wipe her face, wincing at the scratchy fabric on her raw skin, and tucked her hair behind her ears with hands that stung and burned in protest. She looked at Sol, not knowing what to say or how to start.

"We can talk, but I know you're still very weak, so if you're not up to much conversation, tell me and we will take a break, OK?"

Tristan nodded, and so did Sol.

"The first thing you need to know is that Beckett is alive."

Tristan blinked, and then blinked again. And then she tilted her head, squinting at her Mom. She *had* killed Orion, right? He wasn't here now, pretending to be Sol, trying to mentally torture her by telling her Beckett was alive when he wasn't?

Sol shook her head. "It's me. You did kill Orion. He did not kill Beckett. Beckett is on the floor above you, in the Intensive Care Unit, in bad shape but stable. If it's OK with you, Dad, Oceana, and Ember would like to come in. We can help fill in any blanks you might have."

Tristan nodded, still too shocked to speak. The news that Beckett had survived, though she hesitated to believe it still, heartened her, and she felt the all-consuming fatigue loosen its grip on her a little more. Sol floated out of the room to collect the rest of the Wallaces, and Tristan tried to remember what she could.

"Hey, badass."

Evander came in the room first, followed by Olivia, who was already in tears. Sol and Umbris pulled up the rear, and Tristan noticed immediately the wall of tension that stood between them. She looked at her family, who looked back at her. Olivia rushed to her side, taking her hand.

"How are you?"

Tristan opened her mouth, but nothing came out.

"She's a little overwhelmed right now, I think," Sol said gently, and Olivia nodded, backing off.

"How are *you?* The last I saw you, you were..." Tristan's croupy voice trailed off; she was not eager to vocalize the horrors that had taken place at the gathering.

"I'm fine," Olivia said quickly. "A little stiff, but otherwise fine. Mom worked her magic... no pun intended."

After a weak chuckle that passed around the room, everyone fell into silence, each person waiting for the other to begin *the* conversation.

"Trin, I have to apologize," Evander said finally, stepping forward. There was real anguish on his face, which Tristan felt like she should understand, but she couldn't connect why he looked that way. "Telling you that Beckett was dead was the worst thing I've ever had to do. If we hadn't thought it was the only way, I would have refused."

"We?" Tristan asked, an edge to her voice that surprised even her.

"I told him to lie to you." Sol came to stand beside Evander, looking equally as sorrowful. "I knew it was the only way you would be able to defeat Orion. The only way you could access the power you needed."

"Funny, because I think I remember you saying something like, *there's always another way* when it came to Orion." Tristan's voice was venomous, which she knew was not entirely fair, but with each memory that came back, each reminder of having touched the very bottom when she'd been told that Beckett had died in spite of every effort she'd made to protect him, anger flared higher within her.

"There might have been," Sol agreed, her voice still calm. "But not for you. You hadn't used your abilities in eight years; Orion would not have even had to lift a finger to kill you. You needed to access what has always been inside of you in order to take him down, but you couldn't do that unless you truly believed you had nothing left to lose."

Tristan understood what Sol was saying. Objectively, she could see the necessity, but subjectively? She could not quite believe how deeply her family had betrayed her. Tristan looked at Umbris. Then again, maybe she wasn't quite in a position to cry about betrayal.

"And have I lost him anyway?" Tristan asked quietly. She looked between Sol and Umbris. "When you did the memory wiping on Beckett, did you do it back to September after all?"

"No." Umbris looked at Sol, who would not look at him, and Tristan's heart contracted just a little bit. She had never known Sol and Umbris to be anything but harmonious, and that she'd caused a rift between them was making her feel things she wanted to keep being too angry to feel.

"I did the modification," Sol told Tristan. "I took him back to Friday afternoon. You agreed to go to prom with him. You were in a car accident on the way -- an elderly driver lost control of his car, going too fast on the wet road, and the car flipped. It ripped the frame around the windshield, which gouged Beckett's shoulder. The car itself crushed the front of Beckett's car, which resulted in your broken leg, and his broken ribs and concussion. We needed to be able to explain your burns, as well, so a good Samaritan had pulled you both out of the wreckage, and as you were lying in the road, the car exploded. You were burned along your right side when a piece of metal struck you, and your hands, arms, and face got something akin to a bad wind burn from the blast."

You could have heard a pin drop in the hospital room. Tristan and her siblings stared at Sol with their mouths hanging open, rendered speechless.

"Well, now we know where you get your badassery

from, Trin," Evander said finally, and Tristan smiled. Her first real smile. It made her face hurt.

Sol's eyes crinkled, but a grin never made it to her face. She looked at Tristan once again.

"Memory modification is not perfect, especially when it's this complex. There were a lot of memories we had to amend, to sync, and there is a chance that in the future Beckett will remember real events from last night. The preference is that you correct him with the falsified memories, but we won't ask that of you. Which leads me to this." Sol finally glanced at Umbris, briefly, before continuing. "The Elders will be coming to our home when you're discharged. Since everyone now knows you will not be accepting your place in the community, they believe there is no reason for you to hold onto your abilities any longer than necessary. Once you're off the map, you're out of their jurisdiction and there is nothing they can do about what you choose to share with whom."

Tristan frowned, puzzled.

"So you modified Beckett's memory, but you're giving me the OK to tell him what really happened?"

"I'm neither giving you the OK nor forbidding you from telling him. My only advice would be to wait a while before you do, if that's what you decide. It's a lot for all of us to take in and process, Trinity, which makes it ten times more confusing and overwhelming for a commoner. For now, the best thing to do is to go with the car accident story. We've given you the memory as well, since you'll need to access it, but did not touch any of your real memories from last night."

"Last night. It was only last night?" Tristan touched her forehead.

Sol nodded.

"What else do you want to know?" Evander asked, sounding both eager and impatient; the master of decorum.

A nurse came in the room then, looking startled at the Wallaces surrounding Tristan's bed.

"Tristan, hi," Nurse Meeker, per her ID badge, greeted in a voice as sweet as honey. "It's so nice to see you awake! I'm Rachel Meeker, and I've had the pleasure of taking care of you while you've been here. How are you feeling?"

"Sore."

Rachel laughed as she busied herself with the various tubes coming from Tristan's IV pole. She looked like an actual ray of sunshine, all blonde and petite with gigantic blue eyes and rosy cheeks, decked out in bright yellow scrubs and immaculate white clogs, and Tristan immediately felt some of the gloom in the room lift.

"I'm sure you are! I'd say you got off pretty lucky, considering how bad your wreck was, but most patients don't like to hear things like that."

Tristan smiled in spite of herself.

"So I take it this is your family." Rachel brushed a curl out of her eye as she checked Tristan's IV placement, and then shot a smile towards the huddled Wallaces. "Nice to meet y'all. Also I understand you have a friend up in ICU, huh?"

"Yes, this is my Mom and Dad and my sister and brother. And yes, my... Beckett is up in the ICU, yes." Tristan's heart beat a little faster, and she wondered why she was suddenly so nervous.

"I haven't had the pleasure of meeting him yet, but I

will when he gets down here. I know they're hoping for to-morrow, but if not, definitely Tuesday," Rachel beamed.

"And when will I be here until?"

Rachel pulled a clipboard off of the end of Tristan's bed and flipped up the first page.

"Probably tomorrow or Tuesday as well. It really depends on that burn on your side. It's a nasty thing; the burn unit is going to want to look at it again before you get to go anywhere."

Tristan studied the frown on Rachel's face.

"It's that bad?"

"You know, it's not even that it's that bad as in *deep*," Rachel said, her voice relentlessly chipper even though her smile had disappeared. "It's that they're having a real hard time seeing any change in it. We all know burns take forever to heal anyway, right, but usually after the immediate treatment they can see some sign of progress, and well…"

Rachel trailed off, but Tristan didn't need her to continue. The burn wasn't healing because it was a magic burn, not a car fire burn, but how did you tell the hospital staff that?

"But you're in the best place with the best care team, so I reckon they'll have you fixed up in no time. Your hands and your face, especially your cheek, are already looking better, so that's good news. How is your pain?"

As Rachel finished her assessment, Tristan felt herself growing tired once again, but she gave herself a mental shake. She would not go to sleep until the previous night had been rehashed with her family. She needed to know everything she could so she could start to process everything that had happened, and the sooner she could get started on that, the better.

"She was very cheerful," Olivia observed, once the door had closed behind Rachel.

"I think I'd like to tell you guys what I remember, and then maybe you can tell me what I'm missing. Does that work?" Tristan shifted, her tailbone aching, and gasped at the searing pain in her side. She closed her eyes for a moment, opening them again to four worried faces. "I'm fine."

"I'm going to see if I can get another chair." Umbris left the room without waiting for a response, and Tristan looked at Sol.

"I was right, wasn't I? He was going to wipe Beckett's memory back to September."

Sol nodded, fresh hurt filling her eyes.

"Unfortunately, yes."

"I'm sorry, Mom. I know he truly believed it would have been for the best."

"Yes, well." Sol cleared her throat delicately, then squared her shoulders. "You let me worry about your father. Why don't you start with when the guards brought Beckett into the clearing?"

And so Tristan did, and true to their word, her family filled in the pieces she was missing. Olivia told her about her quick thinking in getting Celes to manipulate the scene, Sol revealed that when she'd disappeared she'd gone to clear the other guards from the perimeter, and Umbris described how he'd helped camouflage Dune so he could hide in the woods and help Celes with the manipulation he'd performed -- a true manipulation, it turned out, not just a mirage. Though Tristan knew it would mean nothing to him, a small surge of pride passed through her upon hearing that Celes had finally achieved his goal. Evander confessed to filling Beckett in on everything as he'd run him through the woods, including his destiny connection with Tristan, and how apprehensive he'd been when Thera Crenshaw had appeared to help them.

"And then I ran back after I dropped Beckett off, and you were unconscious right on the edge of the clearing. I pulled you into the trees and woke you up, and that's when I told you about Beckett." Evander looked at Tristan regretfully. "I don't know what happened after that. Everything went black and I couldn't see or hear you or anyone else, so I took off running towards where I thought Oceana was. I thought if I could get to her I could get her out of there, but I guess I ran the wrong way.

As soon as I made it about a hundred yards, I could see the woods again. The clearing was totally blacked out though. I ran into Celes, literally, and it took some convincing but he got on my back and I got him away as fast as I could. I knew they'd be after him if they weren't already. Imagine my surprise, and everyone else's, when I was suddenly running down the sidewalk in the French Quarter with him on my back."

Tristan smiled again.

"And I don't remember anything but pain, and then waking up on the couch at home." There was a faraway look in Olivia's eyes, and she wrapped her arms around herself. "Everything hurt. Everything. My skin, my muscles, my bones, my organs, my *blood...*"

Sol put her arm around Olivia and kissed her temple, and then addressed Tristan.

"After Ember left, we took Beckett back to Lavelle. I did the memory wiping on him on the way. We set up the accident scene and Axis brought you to us, and he posed as the good Samaritan who found you and called the ambulance."

"I know this is the part where I tell you about what happened between me and Orion, but I don't think I'm up for it right now." Tristan rested her head back against her pillow, her eyes struggling to stay open. "I just... Can you just tell me... How many people died?"

Sol and Umbris exchanged a glance.

"Please." Tristan closed her eyes. "I need to know."

"We don't know the exact number," Sol replied eventually, her tone measured. "For instance, we don't know how many guards were killed just yet, and we may not. But if you mean outside of Orion and the guards, six."

Tristan nodded, tears escaping out from under her closed eyelids. Six deaths, at least. Seven, including Entros, who Tristan had worked out had been trying to save Beckett for some reason by bringing him to the clearing. Eleven, including Orion's personal guards she'd taken down herself. Twelve including Orion. And the number would climb. Senseless, preventable deaths, besides Orion; the worst loss the community had seen maybe ever. Try as she might, Tristan could not stop seeing Monse Telarie de Maragon reaching for her dead sister's hand. Innocent lives had been taken last night, and Tristan was partly at fault for that.

Tristan sensed her family leaving as she quietly wept, somewhere on the edge of consciousness. She felt Sol take her hand, rubbing her thumb over Tristan's knuckles the way she'd done her whole life when Tristan was upset.

"You did an incredibly brave thing, Tristan. I know it's cold comfort, but you *saved* so many lives last night. You saved the community. You rest now; I'm going to walk everyone out and then I'll be back to stay with you."

Tristan let the fatigue take over, only stirring when she

felt a firm pressure on her burned side. There was a quick, sharp burst of pain, which felt like she was being sliced by thousands of tiny razors, but within seconds Tristan felt a cooling sensation that acted as a balm on her nerve endings. She wanted to wake up, to see what was going on, but Tristan didn't know when she'd feel so painless again, especially after experiencing so much in such a short time, and so she gave up, letting the relief carry her away.

**

Tristan had a terrible night. Her nightmares, her memories, were ceaseless, and by the third time she'd woken up in the middle of a panic attack, her night nurse, Leon Sprague, brought her something that knocked her right into a blessedly dreamless sleep. To Tristan's surprise, it was Umbris who had ended up staying in her room for the night, not Sol, and he was there each time she woke up taking big, gasping breaths, smoothing back her hair until she was able to calm down.

The nightmares reminded her of after she'd been attacked by Emmeline and her friends, something that felt like child's play now, and how she'd never felt safer than when she'd fallen asleep in Beckett's lap. What she wouldn't give to do that now, to curl up beside him so they could hold each other until they'd both begun to heal on the inside.

Tristan was exhausted by morning, and the white light that filtered through her blinds made her still sore eyes hurt. She couldn't go back to sleep, however, so instead she watched Umbris sleeping in the chair beside her bed. At rest, he didn't look nearly as intimidating as usual, and she could see the fine lines that had blossomed around his mouth and between his dark eyes, the salt that peppered the black hair at his temples. Though he was dressed as he usually was in a perfectly tailored suit, he looked exhausted, tinged with gray, and Tristan was nearly overwhelmed with guilt.

In the stark hospital room with its unforgiving light and cold, endlessly beeping machines, Tristan had no choice but to face how irreparably she'd fucked things up. In her fear, her selfishness, she'd withheld a necessary honesty from her parents about the path she was going -- or rather, was not going -- to take. She'd known the right thing to do, but she'd let denial take the wheel and she'd convinced herself that the eleventh hour was an OK time to drop the bomb on them. Behind their backs, she'd applied to a multitude of colleges and universities across the states, keeping from them something they most likely would have been happy to be a part of, if only she had let them.

Now that it was over, that the truth was out and had just been one more painful part of Saturday night's horror show, Tristan was profoundly embarrassed by how silly it had been to not be forthcoming with Umbris and Sol. In her fear of disappointing them, she'd instead broken their hearts. And it didn't stop there -- she'd also embarrassed them, and the Crenshaws, and she'd deeply betrayed Celes who, despite everything else, had always been her friend, had always been a far better person than she, and had not deserved any of what Tristan had put him through.

Tristan briefly wondered if Celes would visit her, but she knew the answer; the likelihood that he'd ever even *speak* to her again was slim to none, so of course he wouldn't be visiting her. Not that she wanted him to, not really. The only visitor Tristan wanted, now that she'd seen her family, was upstairs in the Intensive Care Unit. She closed her eyes, and in seconds she saw Beckett. He was still asleep, attached to all kinds of wires. There was a bandage around his head, and most of his face was the color of eggplant. Tristan could see the edge of another bandage beneath the neckline of his gown, likely the wrapping on his shoulder, and her heart contracted as she stared at him. In her mind she took one of his broad, flat hands in hers, holding it gently, and though she was no healer, she tried anyway to give him what pure energy she could.

Tristan had forgotten that she was full of power now, however, and the surge that passed from her to Beckett was strong and soothing. So this is what it felt like to be a healer. They were common in the community -- Sol, Olivia, Celes, and Thera alone all healers themselves -- but, not being one herself, Tristan had never given much thought to what they could do or how they could do it.

Beckett began to stir, tensing up, and Tristan went still, hoping she wasn't hurting him with her inexperience. Just because her intuition seemed to know what it was doing, that didn't mean it actually did.

"Tristan?" Beckett whispered, his eyes still closed, and Tristan's eyes filled with tears as she very, very gently squeezed his hand.

She concentrated on the task at hand, though the urge to interact with him was so strong it left her breathless. When he'd settled back down, his breathing even and deep and the tension leaving his hand and arm, Tristan let go, retreating back to her own room.

Just seeing Beckett had calmed her in a way she didn't know she'd been needing -- Tristan supposed part of her worried that he would be angry with her, that he wouldn't want to see her, but then, as far as he knew, they'd been in a car accident. If he knew the truth, he might feel differently. Tristan sighed. One more thing to feel guilty about.

Umbris stirred, and Tristan watched as he woke up, looking briefly disoriented before he remembered where he was.

"Good morning." Tristan's voice still sounded metallic, like an old rusty gate scraping against a concrete floor. It was jarring, and she hoped she would sound like herself again soon.

"Good morning. How are you feeling?"

"Tired."

Umbris leaned his elbows on his knees, scrubbing his hands over his face and through his hair, leaving it standing on end. The sight was *more* jarring than Tristan had found the sound of her voice -- if Umbris was anything, he was impeccably groomed. Always.

"Dad, why don't you go home? I'm fine, and I'm sure you want to sleep in your own bed."

"Your Mom is on her way. I'll go when she gets here." Umbris sounded as exhausted as he looked, and Tristan took a deep breath, knowing the sooner they got this out of the way, the better.

"Dad, I am so sorry. I am so sorry for not telling you that I wasn't going to join the community. I'm sorry I left it go so long. I'm sorry Orion was the one to give you the news, and that I embarrassed our family and the Crenshaws." Tristan's eyes filled with tears. "I know you expected so much more of me, and I disappointed you, and that's killing me. I'm sorry."

Umbris stood, walking the short distance to Tristan's bedside and taking her hand.

"Trinity, listen to me."

Tristan braced herself.

"I am the one who should apologize, to you. What kind of mixed messages did I send you over the years that you felt you couldn't be honest with me? Your Mom and I, we've always told you and the twins that your path was your own and we'd support you no matter what you chose, but did I show that to you? Did I back up my own words over the years? I don't believe I did. Somewhere along the way, I chose for you, and in choosing for you I made a grave error with both you and Mom."

Tristan stared at him, her mouth hanging open.

"I wish you would have told me. I expected that you would have. But then, I've always had such high expectations of you, and maybe that's been part of the problem."

Tears rolling down her cheeks, Tristan shook her head.

"You haven't."

"I love you, Trinity. I don't tell you that enough. I don't tell the twins that enough, either. If you ever decide to become a parent someday, I pray you'll never know the fear that comes with the possibility of losing your child or your children. It's a fear I hope to never feel again for the remainder of my life, but it also has a way of putting things in perspective."

There was a knock on the door, and Sol entered, taking in Tristan's tearful face and Umbris holding her hand. She did a quick read, catching up, and she came to stand by Tristan's other side, taking her other hand in silence.

"I love you too. I love both of you." Tristan sniffled, looking between Umbris and Sol. "Please don't fall apart now, OK? Please don't be mad at each other."

Sol and Umbris exchanged a look Tristan couldn't read.

"We'll be fine." Sol's voice was truthful, reassuring, and Tristan nodded, letting go of the breath she'd been holding.

"There's one more thing." Tristan looked down at her lap, shame creeping back into her heart. "Last summer, out of panic and the desire to have a backup plan in case I ever got the courage to actually deflect from the community instead of just dreaming about it, I applied to a bunch of colleges."

Her parents were silent, and Tristan looked up to find them both watching her expectantly, perhaps holding their reactions until she finished her thought.

"I... I have been accepted to quite a few." Tristan's eyes darted between her parents, who looked surprised and, dare she hope?, maybe even proud. "Ward Livingston University, in Boston, was my dream choice, my longshot, long before I knew it was Beckett's top choice, too, and I got in. And I didn't just get in, I got a pretty hefty scholarship."

In unison, her parents threw their arms around her, and Tristan bit back a yell of pain, not wanting to take this away from them when she'd already taken so much.

"Trinity! We're so proud of you!" Sol's eyes were shining with tears, and even Umbris looked emotional, which set Tristan off all over again. She could feel their hurt through their excitement, but their reaction was genuine, and Tristan's heart filled to bursting.

CHAPTER 40

Tristan and her parents wept, holding each other, until Leon came in the room, looking at them awkwardly for a few beats before he cleared his throat. Sol and Umbris stepped back, Sol gently wiping Tristan's face first, and Leon recovered swiftly, smiling at the trio.

"I hope those are happy tears. It's too early for sad tears."

Tristan laughed.

"They're happy."

"Good, good. How are you feeling this morning, Miss Tristan? Had kind of a rough night last night."

"Tired," Tristan replied, nodding. "But my pain isn't as bad today as it was yesterday, actually. I don't feel like screaming every time I move."

Leon smiled.

"That's certainly an improvement. Your breakfast tray is going to be here shortly, and then a little while after that the burn team is going to come check you out. This afternoon we might try to get you up and walking somehow, but I'm not sure how that's going to pan out since I think your side and hands aren't going to allow for you to use crutches, but we'll see. We are hoping to get you out of here tomorrow. My shift is just about over, so I'm going to say goodbye to you here. Rachel will be your next nurse. Can

I get you anything before I go?"

"Do you know how Beckett is? The boy I came in with, he's up in the ICU?"

Leon smiled.

"Beckett is doing well. I believe they're going to try to move him down to our floor today."

Tristan smiled, not even caring that her face hurt.

"Anything else, Miss Tristan?"

Tristan shook her head, and Leon left, saying goodbye to Umbris and Sol as well.

"Leon mentioning the burn team reminds me. Did one of you do something to my side last night?" Tristan asked, looking between her parents.

Sol nodded.

"When Rachel said yesterday that your burn was not progressing, I realized it was because it's not a typical burn, so it won't respond to typical methods of medical care. I should have realized that sooner, but I didn't think about it. I didn't heal it entirely, but I healed it enough so the burn team should be satisfied, and I can take care of the rest once you're home."

"It was such a nice feeling." Tristan rested her head back against her pillow. "I can't remember the last time I felt so painless."

"We'll work on it more at home," Sol assured Tristan again. "Oh, speaking of home, Ivan and Ruby send their love, and so does Joe."

"Joe?" Tristan was blanking.

"Riser, your boss. I contacted him yesterday to fill him

in, and he said to tell you to come back when you're ready, and that if you try to come back before that, he's going to send you home and probably won't pay you for the day."

Tristan laughed, settling further into the bed and briefly closing her eyes.

"That sounds like Joe."

She must have drifted off, because the next time Tristan awoke, her breakfast tray was sitting on the rolling table beside her bed, and Sol and Umbris were gone. Tristan inched the table towards her, wincing at the unpleasant tingling the movement caused in her hands, and lifted the lid, revealing a surprisingly appetizing looking stack of pancakes, two pieces of crisp bacon, a small bottle of water, and a small carton of orange juice.

Tristan ate the cold but tasty meal carefully, deciding to roll up the pancakes and eat them that way instead of attempting to cut them into pieces, and was almost finished when someone again knocked on her door.

"Come in."

Gabriella Benson appeared from behind the curtain that was half-drawn beside Tristan's bed, and Tristan's eyes widened.

"Mrs. Benson, hi."

"Hi, honey. I was just up to see Beckett so I thought I'd come see you while they change his bandage. I don't have the stomach for that kind of thing."

Gabriella Benson was a petite, almost meek woman with light brown hair and eyes the same turquoise as Beckett's. She was quiet, unassuming, and Tristan had a hard time reconciling that impression with the Gabriella who apparently gave it to Raymond Benson as good as she got it. Not that it was Tristan's business.

"How is he?"

"Doing really well. He turned a corner early this morning and so they're talking about getting him out of the ICU today. They had originally said he could be in there for up to a week, so it's kind of a miracle."

Tristan smiled.

"I heard he might be moved today. That's great."

"He asked about you before his eyes even opened," Gabriella said, smiling at Tristan as she surveyed her face. "That boy is a fool for you."

Tristan blushed.

"Well... The feeling is mutual."

"I know it is." Gabriella studied Tristan for a few beats, and then smiled again. "I was gonna say something about you two being so young for being so serious, but I was your age once. How are you feeling?"

Tristan didn't let the comment bother her. She knew how the intensity of hers and Beckett's relationship must look to commoners, but there wasn't anything she could do about that and she wasn't interested in trying, anyway. They'd see for themselves eventually.

"I feel OK. Mostly tired and very sore. My whole body hurts, and while my burns hurt worse than my leg right now, I'm just thankful I didn't come out of the accident with worse."

Gabriella nodded, wide-eyed.

"Me too, honey. You and Beckett sure were lucky, all things considered."

You have no idea, Tristan thought, but she just smiled and nodded.

"I just can't believe Beckett lost so much blood so fast. To go into organ failure the--"

"Organ failure?" Tristan interrupted, alarmed.

Gabriella nodded, looking at her strangely.

"Yes, that's why he's up there in the ICU. He lost so much blood from his shoulder that his body started shutting down. He went into shock. There's a name for it, for what happened to him, but I can't remember it right now. The doctors said he got here just in time... I don't know what I would have done if that good Samaritan hadn't come along and pulled you two to safety..."

Tristan's heart was beating painfully in her chest. She knew he was doing better now, was on the mend and being prepared to move to her floor, but the knowledge that Beckett's organs had begun to fail, that he'd been *that* close to death...

"I didn't mean to upset you," Gabriella said, wringing her hands as she looked worriedly at Tristan. "I thought you knew already. I'm sorry, Tristan."

"Don't be, it's OK." Tristan tried hard to get the threatening tears under control. "I just miss him."

That had done it. She'd broken her own floodgates, and now Tristan was sobbing again as Gabriella looked on in distress. She hugged Tristan delicately, not wanting to hurt her, and shushed her while she cried.

"He's OK, honey. The doctors don't think he's going to have any lasting damage. They acted fast and got him what he needed, he's OK."

"Tristan?" Sol's voice interrupted, and Tristan looked up tearfully into Sol and Umbris's apprehensive faces.

"It's my fault," Gabriella said, her voice full of regret. "I thought Tristan knew Beckett had gone into organ failure, I didn't think anything of saying it because he's doing so well now--"

"It's OK," Tristan interrupted, waving her hand. She made a mental note to stop doing that, as it reminded her too much of Orion. "I'm OK. It just caught me off guard and I'm tired and stressed and hurting and I wish Beckett was here."

"You're in luck!"

A chipper voice blasted into the room along with Rachel, who today wore vibrant, royal blue scrubs.

"We were gonna wait to tell you until later, but I think you could use the news now." Rachel came to stand beside Tristan's bed, her smile as white as her shoes. "We're gonna move you into a double room this afternoon, and you're gonna have a very special roommate."

This made Tristan cry harder, which made everyone laugh. Things had been so awful, so beyond awful and dire, and the reminder that things were OK now and good things could still happen was just a little bit more than Tristan could process normally.

"I'm going to get back upstairs." Gabriella smiled at Tristan and her parents. "Tristan, I'm glad you're OK and on the mend. I look forward to seeing you once you're out of this place."

Tristan said goodbye to Gabriella, and Sol smoothed back Tristan's hair, handing her a tissue so she could wipe her face.

"Is there anything you can do about my leg once I'm out of here?" Tristan quietly asked Sol, as the skin beneath her cast itched terribly.

"I could, but it would look suspicious," Sol frowned as she glanced toward the open door to Tristan's room. "You won't leave here with a fractured fibula and suddenly be up walking around normally within a few days."

"A fractured fibula?" Tristan asked, surprised. "That can't be right. I'm pretty sure I felt Orion break every bone in my leg."

"We did what we could," Sol told Tristan, raising her eyebrows to impart what she didn't want to explicitly say.

"Oh," Tristan said, finally catching on. "Oh, OK. I'm sorry, I didn't realize."

"Don't be sorry. There's still a lot we have to talk about, but we will have time to do that once you're home."

Tristan nodded, in agreement with Sol. When she thought about it, Tristan was surprised that they'd already talked so much about what had really happened -- anyone could have heard anything at any time.

"The conversation last night was protected," Umbris told Tristan, hearing her thoughts. "It was something we needed to discuss immediately, so we took precautions."

***

The rest of the morning dissolved into the afternoon, and Olivia and Evander showed up as Tristan was eating lunch, having stayed home from school that day. They, along with Sol and Umbris, were asked to step out shortly after their arrival as three doctors -- well, a doctor and two residents -- from the burn unit showed up to check Tristan's wounds.

"*That's* the progress we like to see," Doctor Blanche Brown said, once one of the residents, her name Liza, unwrapped Tristan's side. "That's what we were looking for.

Just took your skin a little bit to catch up."

Tristan looked down, her stomach immediately turning at the raw, wet pink skin that covered an area of her side about nine inches wide and maybe five or six inches long, based on feel. She looked away, nausea from the sight and the pain of just the air hitting her wound nearly overwhelming her.

"I know it looks bad, but trust me when I tell you it looked a lot worse just two days ago. You have a deep second degree, almost third degree burn, and I regret to have to tell you that they are by far the most painful. This actually looks excellent compared to Saturday night, though. I don't even think we'll have to graft you." Dr. Brown sounded amazed. "OK, let's wrap this back up and look at your hands and arms."

Dr. Brown carefully applied ointment to and re-bandaged Tristan's side, apologizing the whole time as Tristan gritted her teeth in an effort to not scream. A few times a cry escaped her lips, and the doctor assured her she was almost done. They gave Tristan a minute or so to catch her breath, and then Liza and the other resident, Clint, unwrapped her hands and arms. Dr. Brown smiled once again, nodding.

"Excellent. Excellent progress, Tristan. You might have some light scarring on your palms, which seem to have taken the brunt of whatever happened to cause these, but your forearms should heal nicely and so should your cheek." Dr. Brown addressed Liza and Clint. "I think we can just wrap up her hands, leave the arms out."

"What kind of scarring am I looking at on my side?" Tristan didn't want to ask, but she had to know.

"That depends. It's hard to say with a burn like this. When all is said and done, and unfortunately that could mean a year or two from now, you could just have a slight disturbance in your skin that's the same color as the rest of you, or you could end up with discoloration and relatively noticeable scarring. It depends on what your body does as it heals and produces new tissue."

Tristan nodded, distracted by the continuing pain in her side. Tears trickled out of her eyes, and Dr. Brown looked at her sympathetically.

"I'll have Rachel get you something for the pain, OK? Hang in there, Tristan."

The doctor and residents left the room, and Tristan pressed her head back against her pillow, squeezing her eyes shut. She'd experienced more pain than this on Saturday night, but that didn't seem to matter now. Beneath the bandage it felt like someone was relentlessly rubbing ground glass against her tenderized skin.

"Trinity?" Olivia's voice was worried, and Tristan felt her come closer. "I'm going to help you, OK?"

Olivia's hand rested gently on Tristan's arm, and within seconds Tristan's pain had started to subside. Rachel flitted into the room then, and Olivia stepped away, to Tristan's chagrin.

"Having some bad pain?" Rachel asked Tristan, who nodded, wiping away her tears.

"OK. I'm going to give you some medicine that's going to help. Do me a favor and when you feel the pain starting to come back, you let me know, OK? We want to stay ahead of it instead of trying to tackle it once it's out of your control."

Tristan nodded again.

"The good news is that the burn team was really impressed by your wounds, and they've cleared you to go home tomorrow." Rachel beamed as that finally got a real smile out of Tristan. "Now, in a little while here a couple of team members from the physical therapy unit are going to come in and see if we can somehow get you up and walking; it's pretty important for your healing even though it sounds counterproductive. You rest now, and they'll be here for you soon."

Rachel left the room, and Tristan looked at her family. Before she could speak, Olivia did.

"Oh! I have something to show you."

Tristan waited while Olivia tapped her phone screen. She turned the phone around as she walked towards Tristan, holding up a photo she'd taken, a wide smile on her face.

"Now that word is out about you deciding on WLU, Joe added a new drink to the menu at Rise and Grind."

Tristan took the phone from Olivia and zoomed in on the specialty drinks. There, at the top, was The Wallace. *Limited time!* A yellow sign beside the description of the new addition proclaimed.

"Our soon-to-be famous Beantown blend, featuring a vanilla bean base and swirls of dark chocolate and caramel, crafted in the honor of Rise and Grind's newest future Ward Livingston U graduate and employee of the month. Congratulations, Tristan!" Tristan read the description aloud, touched beyond words. She was oddly choked up and her face hurt from smiling, but she couldn't stop. "Oh, Joe."

"It's good too, I tried it." Olivia smiled, taking her phone back.

"Word got out quickly about WLU, by the way. Isn't it Monday? And you guys aren't even at school. How does everyone know already?"

"Dean LeFebvre and I got to talking when I called Jamestown to let them know what was going on, and you know how news travels in Lavelle," Sol said, smiling sheep-ishly. "I didn't think you'd mind."

"I don't." Tristan smiled back at Sol, her head still spinning in an attempt to process everything. She gestured to her family. "You guys should go grab lunch or something. I'll be fine here, I'm just going to take a nap."

Reluctantly they agreed, and Tristan watched the four of them go, her heart swelling. They'd all been changed by what had happened on Saturday night, but as a family it had only brought them closer. The knowledge, once again, confirmed for Tristan how very fortunate she was to have been born to Umbris and Sol. Her smile fading, Tristan thought again of the Telarie de Maragons, and in her mind she saw a brief flash of Terminus and Noxis, Monse and Mora, their faces shattered with grief. Tristan quickly pulled back; yes, she was lucky, but there were at least eleven families who may never feel that way again, and for that Tristan was partially responsible.

Tristan fell asleep before the tears had dried on her cheeks.

CHAPTER 41

"Trinity."

Someone was saying her name, but Tristan didn't recognize the voice.

"Come on Trinity, we have to get you out of here."

Out of where? Who in the hospital was calling her Trinity if she didn't recognize the voice as one belonging to someone in her family?

"Trinity, open your eyes."

Tristan did, treetops and the night sky coming into view. *What the hell?*

Tristan blinked, looking to her right, where Axis Daddona was looking down at her with an expression of urgent concern.

"I have to get you back to Lavelle, and I need you to pay attention to what I'm about to tell you. I can't imagine the kind of pain you're in right now, but I need you to try and focus."

Pain? Tristan wasn't in any pain at all. Things started to go black, but then her eyes popped back open. She became aware of a few things, then. First, her body was on the ground at a funny angle. She wouldn't look, but she could sense that her left leg was bent unnaturally outward while her body curved in the opposite direction. She was also having trouble opening her eyes all the way -- her face and lips were tight like she hadn't had water in days, and she had that same tight feeling, in varying pressures, in her arms, hands, and along her right side. Her side was the worst -- it was so tight that she was afraid she'd rip if she moved. The rest of her body felt like it was under a weird kind of pressure, too, and it occurred to Tristan that maybe the universe took it as a challenge every time she thought that things couldn't get any more bizarre.

"Trinity," Axis said firmly. "Look at me."

Tristan looked into Axis's strange indigo eyes, and he nodded, lifting her. Tristan felt her mouth open in a scream, heard and felt the scream reverberate through the air and through her body, but that was all the sensation she experienced -- sounds and vibrations.

Axis was talking, and Tristan looked at him again.

"I'm taking you back to Lavelle. When we get there, I'll plant in your head a memory of a car accident. No matter what, this must be the memory you draw from when the ambulance arrives and they take you to the hospital. Do you understand?"

Tristan's head rolled back and forth, which was apparently good enough for Axis. With a nod, he bowed his head, and with a dull pop they were suddenly in Lavelle, at the scene of a horrific car accident. Beckett was lying on the ground some distance away from two very mangled cars, and Tristan lifted her arm only to feel it drop immediately. She was making terrible noises she'd never made before every time she moved, but she couldn't seem to stop no matter how hard she tried. Axis set her down too far from Beckett, too close to the wreckage, but Tristan knew this was how it had to be. She stared at Beckett, who was completely still in the road and a shade of gray that could mean nothing good. He was almost unrecognizable between the blood and the swelling, but Tristan didn't care. Her arm went out and she gripped the road with her fingers, feeling her arm vibrate with effort as she tried to pull herself towards him. She was screaming again now, but she had one goal in mind and it would be the last thing she ever achieved, if necessary.

To her right, Beckett's car exploded, a wall of pressure sweeping across the road and over Tristan. A large piece of metal, glowing red, clattered to a stop beside her. Tristan persisted in inching toward Beckett.

Muttering expletives to himself, Axis lifted Tristan again, moving her closer to Beckett, and then kicked the debris towards her so it would at least look believable that it'd hit her. Tristan stretched out as far as she could and took Beckett's lifeless hand in hers, closing her eyes and trying to summon energy to transfer into him. It never came.

Sol knelt beside Tristan, looking furtively over her shoulder at the lights of an ambulance in the distance. Tristan felt her leg move with a great jolt, her mouth opened in yet another agonized scream, and then Axis was shooing Sol away, taking his place by Tristan and Beckett as the ambulances screeched to a halt.

"Tristan. Come on, Tristan, open your eyes."

Her eyes were open, weren't they? There, she could see Axis, glowing orange in the light of the car fire. She could see the wet road under her back, the trees, the paramedics rushing towards her. She could feel her hand tight around Beckett's.

"Tristan!"

She was being shaken now, and Tristan closed her eyes, opening them again to find Rachel's worried face peering into hers.

"There we go. There you are. I think we might have

gone a little heavy-handed with the pain medication. I'm gonna ask you some questions now that I need you to answer, OK?"

Tristan could still see the scene of the accident, though it was fading now, being replaced with her hospital room. No wait, not her hospital room, a different one? The walls in here were pale blue; her room had lavender walls. That meant...

Tristan's head swiveled back and forth like it'd been unhinged, and there, to her right, was another hospital bed, and in it, asleep, was Beckett. The image of him in bed was overlaid by him in the road, and Tristan just stared dumbly. What was happening?

"Tristan, I need you to tell me what day it is, OK? Tristan." Rachel's voice was loud, brash, and she clapped several times, the noise sounding like gunfire next to Tristan's head. She winced.

"What day is it?" Rachel's face once again moved into her line of vision, and Tristan tried to get a grip on her scrambled egg brain.

"Monday?"

"Good. What month?" Rachel asked briskly, nodding, and Tristan wondered where her eternally sunny disposition had gone.

"Um... May?"

"Good. What's your full name?"

"Tristan. Trinity. Tristan Trinity Wallace." Tristan's mouth felt like it was full of cotton, and sounded that way, too.

"And how old are you?"

"Eighteen."

"Who's that in the bed beside you?"

"Beckett."

"Full name."

"Beckett," a weak chuckle escaped Tristan's lips, "Beauregard Benson."

The fog in her mind was lifting now, and Tristan could tell Rachel knew it, too. Rachel nodded again as she hung a bag of something on Tristan's IV pole, hooking it up to her port.

"Good. Two more questions. What's my name?"

"Rachel."

"Do you remember my last name?"

"Meeker."

"And do you know why you're here?"

"That was three questions. Car accident."

Rachel checked the bag she'd hung, checked Tristan's IV, and finally smiled at her.

"Excellent. I just gave you something that should help clear up the rest of your grogginess. PT will come for you after dinner now instead, which will give you some time for the pain medication to level off."

"Can you..." Tristan pointed lazily to Beckett's bed. "Can I be closer to him?"

Rachel gave her a kind smile.

"Let me see what I can do."

She left the room, returning not ten minutes later with three males in scrubs Tristan vaguely recognized. Quickly and efficiently, they cleared the furniture from between the beds and rolled Tristan and Beckett towards each other, until their bed rails were touching. With a grateful smile, Tristan snaked her right hand through the rail, grasping Beckett's. Though he'd stayed asleep during the action, his hand twitched in hers, and she stroked the back of his hand with her thumb.

With her other hand, Tristan raised the head of her bed so she could see Beckett over the rail. She stared at him, not wanting to look at anything or anyone else for the rest of her life.

Beckett's head moved on his pillow, and his eyes fluttered open. He looked down at his hand, following it up to Tristan's face.

"Tristan."

"Hi."

"You're here."

"I am." Tristan gave Beckett a watery smile.

"I knew you would be." Beckett smiled, and Tristan's heart quadrupled in size. "My beautiful girl."

"I love you. I'm so glad you're alive," Tristan whispered.

"There was no way I was dying without you. We were going together or we weren't going at all. I'm so sorry for the accident, though. It happened so fast, I'm still not even sure how."

"It wasn't your fault. The man lost control of his car. There was nothing you could do."

"Tristan."

"Yes?"

"I love you. Don't ever scare me like that again."

"I won't if you won't," Tristan laughed, letting out a small sob.

"I remember you holding my hand," Beckett said, slightly lifting their joined hands, and Tristan froze.

"What?"

"After the accident. Or during? Sometime after the shit hit the fan. The last thing I remember is you holding my hand."

Tristan smiled at him, and Beckett studied her face, his gaze an easement on her soul.

"I wasn't sure I was ever gonna see that smile again. It's even better than I remembered."

"You almost didn't," Tristan told him, cold fingers of fear wrapping around her heart. "I was so close to losing you. I would have never forgiven myself."

"Tristan, the accident was in no way your fault. It wasn't anyone's fault but the other driver, and hell, maybe it wasn't even his."

The accident. Right. Tristan felt a strange pang of sadness -- she knew Sol was right, that to tell and show Beckett too soon what had really happened would overwhelm him, but selfishly she couldn't imagine carrying the secret for both of them for very long. She was done with secrets, done with lying, done with evading questions and making up vague, non-excuses for things. What had happened had brought her and Beckett closer than they'd ever been, and it was a hard pill to swallow knowing that context had disappeared for Beckett.

"I wish we could share a bed," Tristan whispered, and Beckett smiled at her again.

"As soon as we get outta here. We'll have to do some maneuvering around my shoulder and ribs, but we'll figure it out."

"And my side. And my leg. We're quite a pair."

Beckett frowned.

"What's wrong?"

"My fibula is broken, in my left leg, and I have a really horrible burn on my right side. My hands were burned, too, but not too bad."

"I am so sorry." Beckett's finger traced the line of the bandage at her wrist.

"Don't be."

They lapsed into silence then, looking at each other, holding hands, needing nothing else in the world.

CHAPTER 42

The remainder of the week brought about many changes. Tristan was released from the hospital on Tuesday, and, though she was reluctant to leave Beckett, it looked like his discharge was not far behind; only by two days, in fact, if he continued progressing so well. Tristan had transferred more energy into him one last time, early Tuesday morning while he slept, and when he'd woken up he'd talked animatedly about how good he felt. Tristan had been pleased, noticing that he even looked better -- his bruising was fading quickly, and his color was nice and healthy.

Tristan could not walk because she could not bear weight on her leg and could not bear pressure on her hands or sides to utilize crutches, so the hospital released her with a wheelchair -- which Tristan knew they'd be returning as soon as Sol could work her magic on Tristan's hands -- and a pair of crutches anyway, for later use. Indeed, once Tristan had gotten settled in at home, Sol fully healed her hands, and worked some more on her side, which was proving to be incredibly stubborn; apparently a burn from a direct hit by powerful magic fire was a lot worse than a residual burn from trying to hold off a wall or two of elemental magic. As they'd agreed, Sol left Tristan's leg alone, something Tristan wanted desperately to recant once she started attempting the crutches.

Olivia brought home Tristan's school work, and Tristan spent virtually all of Wednesday and Thursday catching up. Hers and Beckett's senior English class project was thankfully well and truly complete -- drafted, proofread, finalized, community service hour sheets turned in, portfolio ready to be handed over to Ms. West. All they had left was the oral presentation, and Tristan was confident they'd handle it with ease. She thought back on their community service days at the library in the next town -- their ESL students were so young, ranging in age from six to twelve, had come so far, and were so eager to help Tristan and Beckett assemble their project in whatever ways they could. Tristan smiled. She and Beckett had agreed they'd continue tutoring "their" brilliant kids through the end of the school year, and she hoped the accident wouldn't end up setting them back too far; Tristan had come to genuinely love the work.

On Friday, the Elder committee showed up. Tristan knew they had arrived before they ever knocked on the door; she felt their presence at the end of the driveway as surely as though they were already in the room with her.

"Mom," Tristan called out calmly, from the living room couch. "The Elder committee is here."

Sol appeared from the kitchen, looking surprised before she pulled open the front door, confirming. The Elder committee -- ten of them normally, today only nine: Pele, Vitalis, Axis, Bayle, Abrus Macimier, Azure Colquitt, Perpetos Ruptis, Cimmeris Plamondon, and Iniq Botterill -- filed inside the house, greeting Sol as they passed her by. Tristan tried not to be nervous, but as the cloaked Elders lined up before her in the living room, she felt trapped, and about two inches tall. Sol came to sit beside her, and Tristan took her hand gratefully.

Just as Tristan began to wonder who would speak first, Pele stepped forward. Tristan had been afraid that would be the case.

"Trinity, presumably you know why we're here

today."

Tristan nodded, forcing herself to hold Pele's violet-eyed gaze even though she really wanted to run out the front door and keep going until her legs gave out. Not that she could, of course, but still. Pele had been closest to Orion, and Tristan didn't need her to say anything to know that Pele harbored plenty of ill-will towards her.

"We will ask first that you relay your version of the events that took place on Saturday night. Then, with your permission, we will retrieve and review your raw memories to see how the two correspond."

Tristan nodded again.

"Would you like to sit?" Sol asked, but the Elders declined in unison.

That wasn't unnerving or anything. Annoyed, Tristan set aside her schoolwork and tucked her hair behind her ears, folding her hands in her lap. She took a deep breath.

"Where would you like me to begin?"

"You can choose," Bayle responded, his voice much kinder than Pele's.

Slightly bolstered, Tristan decided to start with when the guards had brought Beckett into the clearing. She relayed the information nearly tonelessly, sticking only to facts; she did not want to involve her emotions in case they muddied up the waters of her recollection. When she'd finished with waking up in the hospital, the Elders -- minus Pele and, Tristan noticed, Perpetos -- looked equally impressed, horrified, and satisfied. Pele's face was pinched with distaste, and Perpetos looked highly suspicious.

"You don't believe me," Tristan said to Perpetos, in disbelief. It was out before she could stop herself, not that she would have really tried.

Pepetos looked offended now, his face twisted in a sneer as he looked down at her.

"Your tale is quite unbelievable. Surely someone as *intelligent* as you realizes that."

Why had he emphasized the word intelligent? Tristan's eyes narrowed, and she'd just opened her mouth to fire back at him when Pele interjected.

"Cimmeris will retrieve your raw memories now," Pele said in a raised, clipped voice. She turned to Sol. "Is there a space we can use to view the memories privately before we reconvene in here?"

"The dining room is open, or there's a patio set in the backyard you can utilize. The yard is protected, so no need to worry about a lack of privacy."

Pele gave her a short nod. She looked at Cimmeris, who approached Tristan, his blue eyes kind, but Tristan for the life of her could not relax. His eyes were far, far too close to the same color Orion's had been, and she shrank back into the couch cushions.

"I think perhaps Bayle or Axis should do this part instead," Cimmeris said after a moment, sending a not unkind look Tristan's way before turning back to Pele.

"Why?" Pele snapped, and anger flared in Tristan. She clamped her mouth shut lest she start a whole new battle with the remaining Elders.

"Trinity is more familiar with them," Cimmeris replied placatingly, and, as Pele's sharp nostrils flared, Tristan wondered why he bothered.

"Very well. Bayle." Pele looked at Bayle and jerked her

head at Tristan, and Bayle nodded, dropping to his knees in front of Tristan.

"Hi Trinity, glad to see you're well."

Tristan smiled in spite of everything.

"You too."

Bayle's hazel eyes were kind as he nodded, placing two fingers from each hand on each of her temples. It occurred to Tristan for the first time that, though he was of no relation, with his dark hair and light eyes, Bayle could be Celes's older brother. The thought of Celes made her sad.

"I just need you to close your eyes. This won't take long."

Tristan complied, unsure what to expect, but all it felt like was someone kneeling in front of her with their fingers on her temples. It probably didn't help, however, that her mind was on high-alert already, and her thoughts raced around her skull like she'd ingested speed sometime between the Elders arriving and Bayle collecting her memories.

"That sped-up feeling is from the retrieval," Bayle told her, a smile in his voice, and Tristan tried not to feel embarrassed.

A few minutes later Bayle had finished, and he stood, a medium-sized, bluish white sphere suspended between his hands. He nodded at Pele, who, wordlessly, turned on her heel. The rest of Elders followed her, filing through the house and out into the yard. Tristan exchanged a glance with Sol.

"Pele and Perpetos can't still be loyal to Orion, after everything?" Tristan asked.

"Oh, they could be, Pele especially. She stayed loyal to him after everything with Adara, somehow, so it would not come as a surprise to me." Sol's voice and face were dark as she responded.

"Then why is she allowed a seat on the Elder committee? Doesn't anyone find it dangerous or risky or anything?"

To Tristan's surprise, Sol shook her head.

"In spite of her personal feelings, Pele is an excellent and fair leader. Same with Perpetos. I am surprised at him, though -- he's usually much more level-headed than he was just now. Then again, he hates nothing more than to be embarrassed, so I'm guessing he's having some displaced anger about being frozen in time by Orion while Orion wreaked havoc on the community."

"He seemed to imply that I am not intelligent," Tristan said, miffed.

"Then he doesn't know you at all." Sol smiled at her, and Tristan wished, once again, she had even a fraction of Sol's serenity.

CHAPTER 43

Nearly an hour had passed before the Elders came back inside. Tristan had resumed doing her homework, the finish line finally in sight, and on a sigh she put her laptop down once again. When she looked up, she was truly taken aback to find *all* of the Elders looking at her with a sort of admiration or begrudging respect that definitely had not been there when they'd left the room. Tristan blinked several times, hoping one of them would speak first, because she sure couldn't.

"We have found that your raw memories of the reckoning between you and Orion were identical to your recollection," Perpetos said, his tone mildly surprised.

"The reckoning? Is that how we're referring to it now?" Tristan arched an eyebrow, and Sol subtly elbowed her.

"We don't usually obtain raw memories that perfectly match someone's recollection of events," Vitalis spoke next. "So you'll have to excuse us if we seem surprised."

Pele looked at him sharply, but Tristan ignored her.

"I have an eidetic memory."

"We know that now," Pele said brusquely. "And since we've confirmed what happened on Saturday night, we can move to the next order of business. We, as a committee, feel as though you maintaining your abilities beyond today is needless. Since it's been made clear that you will not be joining the community next month, we see no reason to delay our standard procedure, which is to strip you of your elevated connection with the universe."

She sounded genuinely regretful at that last part, and Tristan looked at Sol, who looked back at her sadly. Guilt sent a wave of heat into her cheeks, but Tristan knew, in her heart of hearts, that nothing about her decision had changed. She nodded.

The Elders all exchanged an unreadable look, and Vitalis stepped forward just slightly.

"Understand, Trinity, that we have never done what we're about to do. Anything like your circumstances -- your *reckoning,* with Orion," Vitalis shot a look at Perpetos, "Had never before occurred in the community, and we truly hope there will never be a reason for anyone to repeat it in the future. You broke so many laws that we can't even really keep track. You inadvertently introduced a commoner into a community gathering. You brought public embarrassment to your own family and to the Crenshaws, who are well-respected in the community, and you, in effect, killed one of our Elders."

"Now wait a second--" Sol stood, but Vitalis held up his hand, his expression pleading with her to let him finish. Sol crossed her arms, falling silent, but did not sit back down.

Tristan unclenched her fists, the scarred skin on her palms feeling tight and strange, and forced in a few deep breaths. How dare they, after everything they'd seen, admonish her and act like she'd done something wrong in killing Orion? How dare they--

"Because of those things, there are certain other procedures we now need to follow. Effective immediately, and decided upon on our honor as Elders, you are hereby banned from all community-related activities. This means gatherings, summer and winter solstice celebrations, festivals, seminars, you get the idea."

Tristan's mouth fell open, tears springing to her eyes, and she looked at Sol, whose face had gone white with outrage.

"Really Vitalis, is that necessary? Trinity--"

"Broke our laws. *Several.*" Pele cut Sol off contemptuously. "Sixteen people *died.* How do you think it will look to the community if there are no consequences for what happened? There was some discussion that we implement this ruling against your family as a unit, but since Trinity is deflecting anyway, we took that into consideration, which was more than fair."

Tristan's chest heaved, but she did not want to give the Elders the satisfaction of seeing her cry. Banned from solstice celebrations? Those were what she held most sacred, the days of the year she looked forward to spending with her family the most, and now she was banned because Orion had gone on a crazed, power-hungry rampage and tried to use Trinity as a pawn in his demented game?

"It's a lot to take in, we know," Vitalis's tone was soothing, maybe even holding a tinge of regret, but Tristan knew their decision was firm. "And we know it seems and feels incredibly unfair, Trinity. On our honor, we did not come to this ruling lightly. Next spring, we will reconvene and decide if the ban will continue, and we'll notify you accordingly."

Tristan just stared at him. It didn't just *feel* unfair, it *was* unfair. What was the alternative? Joining Orion the way he'd wanted her to and taking the community back to the dark ages? Tristan's anger was rising in her again, and she tried to bite her tongue, but it was no use. The repeated *"on our honor"*s -- the Elder mantra, to convey the oath they'd taken as Elders while also subtly reminding their community of who was in charge -- was her tipping point.

"Oh, well thanks so much for that courtesy," Tristan's words left her mouth in a bitter, caustic rush of sarcasm. "I'm so sorry it was such a struggle for you to decide to punish me for Orion's actions. I am sure it was incredibly difficult and not at all a decision rooted in bias."

"Excuse--" Pele started, but Tristan cut her off.

"I sure am thankful that after nearly losing my life, nearly losing my loved ones, watching innocent people die, and having no other choice but to kill not so innocent people, but fellow humans all the same, in order to make sure the community didn't fall into the grips of a *lunatic,* that your ruling is to punish *me* for his actions. That definitely is sound and fair decision-making."

There was a considerable pause, and finally it was Bayle who responded.

"I'm sorry we've laid this on you when you're already hurting. I know it is the last thing you want to hear right now, when you've had no real time to process or begin to heal from everything that happened."

Tristan clenched her jaw, fighting off an unexpected wave of sorrow brought upon by Bayle's words.

"Trinity," Azure stepped forward, and Tristan noticed that her eye color perfectly matched her name. "You must understand that while you feel like you're being punished for Orion's actions, this ruling is the very lightest we could have decided upon for you, especially as you're deflecting next month. I'm not going to have us all stand here while you develop some perspective, that wouldn't be fair to any of us, but try to keep in mind that while you'll be missing two solstice celebrations with your family, there are families in the community who will never have any solstice celebrations with their loved ones again."

"Don't do that," Sol said, her voice icy. *"Do not* put undue guilt on Trinity for the killings. *Orion* was responsible for those deaths."

Azure nodded.

"He was. And I'm not trying to gloss over that or to place undue guilt on Trinity. I am simply trying to get an eighteen year old, knowing how eighteen year olds are, to see the bigger picture, and to try to look at this from a community point of view. From our point of view."

"Trinity is smart," Axis said, studying her from across the room. "She'll come to that, I have faith. Just maybe not today, when things are still so raw."

"I don't agree with your ruling, but I accept it," Tristan said finally, loath to admit Azure had a point. "If you want to take my abilities and go, I'm ready."

"Just one more thing," Cimmaris said, and Tristan only just barely held in an eye roll. Instead, she leaned her head back against the couch, rubbing her eyes with two fingers.

"In spite of everything we just discussed, we would be remiss in our duties if we did not acknowledge the prodigious things you did on Saturday night."

Tristan's head snapped forward.

"What?"

"You saved the community. You performed incredible, advanced magic, and though Orion pulled out all the stops, your quick thinking and quicker reflexes saved you, as well. You displayed empathy beyond what anyone would have expected, under the circumstances, when you paused to protect those in the clearing from further harm, and, most importantly, you put yourself on the line for a community you had no intention of joining." Abrus was speaking this time, his voice so deep Tristan could feel it in her bones, which wasn't an altogether unpleasant sensation.

She fought the urge to wave off what felt like a bunch of heavy-handed compliments, skeptical of why the Elders had so quickly done a 180 degree turn from where they'd just been.

"As Vitalis mentioned, your situation and how we've had to respond to it is unprecedented, and there is unfortunately no guide on how to deal with the aftermath of a one-man rebellion and massacre -- not yet anyway. So while we've had to decide on consequences for you, we also had to decide if there was something we could do for you, to show our appreciation."

Tristan opened and closed her mouth, once again thrown for a loop.

"After many discussions, we've come to this. Trinity, your deflection from the community will genuinely be a great loss for us. We've known you your entire life, so we know that you are intelligent, thoughtful, and wise beyond your years. We also know your battle with Orion unlocked within you an incredible reserve of power that would open you endless doors to endless possibilities. Alas, none of that means anything if you know in your heart the community path is not the one you're meant to take. So we'll stop your abilities today, but on our honor as a committee, we have decided to allow you to keep just one thing. Just one link to the uncommon world. Your choice.

We know your deflection is not driven by malicious intent. We believe that when we leave here today, the only ones grieving the removal of your abilities will be us and your family, and therefore we have no reason to believe that leaving you one link will bring the community harm." Perpetos had taken over, and Tristan eyed him dubiously.

On an irritated sigh, he looked contritely at Tristan.

"I am sorry I implied anything negative about your intelligence earlier this afternoon. On my honor and on the honor of the committee, what I've just spoken is a truth held by myself and my fellow Elders."

Tristan looked uncertainly at each of the Elders' faces, trying to determine if there was a catch, or if they were lying. This incredible gift was unheard of, unprecedented, like Abrus had said, and she had a hard time believing what she was hearing. But if they meant it, and Tristan supposed they had no real reason to lie to her about it, what would she choose? Her first instinct was to choose ongoing telepathy with her family, but how useful would that be in the long run? Would it open doors for her, or enrich her life in any way? Ten years from now, would she be happy that was what she'd chosen?

After several minutes, Tristan looked up at Pele.

"I want to retain my ability to read people."

Everyone looked surprised by this, but none more than Sol.

"Trinity, are you sure?"

Tristan nodded, hating that she'd probably once again let her Mom down; she was sure Sol expected her to choose to leave open the connection with the family. Tristan hurried to explain.

"Oceana is my best friend, and I happen to be lucky enough that she's also my sister. I know that not being able to psychically connect with her will be a hard adjustment, but will not damage our relationship. Ember and I never communicate psychically anyway, and frankly, you and Dad don't really need to have that connection with me anymore, and maybe you never did." Tristan smiled to belie the bluntness of her words. "But if I can read people, that will also open doors for me throughout my life, in many different capacities. So it seems like the best choice."

"Smart girl," Sol murmured, looking so proud that Tristan almost wept.

"Very clever. Reminds me of how someone else used to think," Pele mused, but continued on before Tristan could react. "Bayle, if you will, then."

"Wait." Tristan knew she was pushing her luck, knew she was in yet another situation where she was given an inch and trying to take a mile, but if she never asked, she'd never know, and there were two things she still needed from the Elders.

"Yes?" Pele asked irritably.

"Two things, if I may. First, I was wondering if you can tell me why Entros brought Beckett into the clearing that night. I got the impression that he did it to save his life, but I can't make that make sense."

The Elders looked among each other for a few beats, and Tristan prepared herself for them to decline to respond. To Tristan's surprise, however, it was Iniq Botterill who answered her question. Iniq had otherwise been silent and stone-faced the whole time.

"A long time ago, Entros Janek fell for a commoner.

He joined the community anyway, obviously, but it was a relatively well-known fact that he never really got over that loss. We believe, when he became aware of the destiny connection between you and your commoner, and the fact that you were going to deflect, he developed a soft spot against his better judgment. His choices were to dispose of your commoner immediately, or to bring him before the Elders. He chose the option that would, at best, give your commoner a chance at survival, or, at worst, give you one last opportunity to see him."

Tristan was stunned. The guards were notorious for their ruthlessness, chosen carefully because the Elders believed they'd put duty before personal ethics when they were called to do so. Entros was the head guard -- it seemed beyond improbable that he would have let Tristan's connection with Beckett interfere with his job. Tristan was no one to him, and Beckett was even less of a blip on his radar.

"We're not sure why your particular situation struck a chord with him, either, Trinity," Bayle said regretfully. "And unfortunately we'll never know. Entros was a good person and an excellent head guard, so we trust that he had his reasons for doing what he did. It could have been as simple as not expecting that Orion would have reacted the way he did. Perhaps he thought he'd be facing the whole committee, not just Orion."

The Elders faces mirrored each other's pain, and Tristan was sure hers did, too. She didn't know Entros, but his decision *had* saved Beckett's life, and had needlessly cost him his own in return.

"We really must wrap this up," Pele sniffed, but her eyes were still as hard as rock as she looked at Tristan. "What's second on your list?"

Tristan took a deep breath.

"Well, first, I want to say thank you for allowing me to retain the ability to read people. I certainly did not expect that kindness, and I promise I will use it well. I know I'm pushing my luck here, asking this, but I wanted to ask if you could also please leave me the ability to restore memories, even if it's in a single-use capacity."

Tristan could see Pele getting ready to reject her request, so she quickly continued.

"Keeping secrets and telling half-truths was what led to what happened on Saturday night. Beckett knows nothing about this part of my life, and that has been on purpose. I knew if I had told him anything, that Orion would have made him a target long before he actually did. I chose wrong. Or maybe I didn't, I don't know, and I never will now. Anyway, I can't keep keeping secrets. I don't want to. I don't want to spend the rest of my life pretending we were in a horrific car accident, and he deserves to know what really happened to him. I'm not going to tell him now, not for a while, but when I do, I'd like the ability to restore his memories of that night."

"I'm not sure that's necessary," Perpetos frowned. "You telling him what happened should suffice."

"I disagree," Tristan replied calmly. "Imagine someone telling you that what you remember happening is not what happened at all, and they can't offer you any proof, but they insist, and they've never lied to you and you have no reason to believe they'd start now. Wouldn't that scare you? Wouldn't you have so many more questions than you would if they told you what really happened and then they were able to restore your memories of it happening so you could see for yourself?"

"She has a point," Bayle said, and, to Tristan's shock,

Pele reluctantly nodded in agreement.

The Elders conferred silently, and Tristan saw Perpetos, the last holdout, finally relent.

"Both inquiries are settled then," Abrus said, and Tristan nodded to confirm. "And so all I have to ask before we wrap up now is, are you *sure* you want to do this? Are you sure you want to give up your abilities and deflect from the community?"

Tristan could see the benefits to joining the community now more clearly than she ever had. The Elders were offering her the chance to keep the ever-flowing, wonderful power that had been with her since Saturday night, to join the community and maybe someday even join *them* on the Elder committee. Tristan didn't doubt she could utilize her abilities well. She didn't doubt she could carve a niche for herself in the role she accepted, maybe even have some influence and make a real difference within the community. But she also knew she could do that in the common world, if she chose, and she knew the personal cost of joining the community was still far too high, despite every opportunity it had to offer. Joining could mean incredible things for her, but it would also come with the same basic expectations it always had -- marry, reproduce, raise the children, and then *maybe* pick up an interest or a hobby, but still ultimately defer to whomever she wed. They were antiquated expectations, and Tristan knew she wouldn't be the one to change them. Therefore, Tristan also knew, as she'd always known, that her path diverged here. The common world waited for her, and while she was under no illusion that it would be easy or glamorous or always exciting, she could not ignore its siren song.

"I'm sure," Tristan nodded, and the Elders nodded at her in turn.

Sol took Tristan's hand, her eyes bright with emotion, and Tristan gave her an apologetic look.

"Don't be sorry," Sol said quietly. "I'm proud of you for choosing your own path."

Tristan squeezed her hand gratefully.

"Bayle." Pele directed Bayle over to Tristan once again and, just as before, Bayle knelt before her.

"You won't feel a thing. I am sealing off your abilities permanently now, but on our honor as Elders, we are leaving you the ability to read people, and the one-time opportunity to transfer memories. We are sorry you've chosen to deflect from the community, and we thank you for everything you've contributed over the years. We are sure you'll take the common world by storm."

Tristan smiled as Bayle once again placed his fingers on her temples. It was a quick process, and true to his word, Tristan felt nothing. When he removed his hands, Tristan noticed she felt a little more tired than she had, her side and her leg hurt a little more than they had, but otherwise she felt the same.

"This concludes our business here today," Pele announced, as Bayle resumed his place beside her. "Sol, please notify Umbris and your twins that there will be no expectation for you to appear at next month's gathering, as it will be optional for this one time only. Trinity..."

Pele trailed off, and Tristan raised her eyebrows, waiting. For a moment, Pele looked like she might say something friendly, something that would be in stark contrast to the flinty manner in which she'd regarded Tristan all afternoon, but her eyes hardened once again and the moment passed.

"Do not make us regret what we've done for you

today."

"I won't." Tristan lifted her chin.

"Use it well."

Tristan's gaze held firm to Pele's as she nodded, feeling more determined than she ever had.

"On my honor, I will."

EPILOGUE

Five Years Later

"Ready?" Tristan asked, looking across at Beckett, who was sitting in the passenger seat.

"I'm ready. I've only been waiting four years to come to one of these with you."

Tristan smiled, and they got out of the car, approaching the house. Before they had set foot on the steps, the front door opened, and Olivia came outside, dressed in a black, sleeveless turtleneck sweater dress, a wide smile, and slight panic in her eyes.

"Trinity! Beckett! Hi!"

"Hi Oceana." Tristan smiled at her, walking up the steps toward her. She tilted her head. "Is everything OK?"

"Umm, yeah. Yes," Olivia said brightly, rocking back and forth in her red heels. Her voice was unnaturally high-pitched, and Tristan raised her eyebrows. "Ah, so listen, do you know how, do you remember how I mentioned, once, at some point a while ago, that I was sort of seeing someone?"

"Yes," Tristan said slowly. "You weren't sure where it was going, because he wasn't your type. Wasn't that like a year ago?"

"Types are funny, aren't they?" Olivia laughed nervously, and Tristan just stared at her. "It turns out that he was my type after all. Surprise! Or maybe I don't even have a type, I don't know. Crazy right? Anyway, he's here, with me today, inside, so I just wanted to let you know."

Tristan fought to keep a straight face. She had seen this coming years ago, though she had never told Olivia, and she certainly wasn't going to tell her now. It wasn't often she got to see her baby sister squirm like this.

"Thanks for letting me know?" Tristan looked at Beckett, who was staring at Olivia like she'd grown another head.

"Uh, so there's just one small thing." Olivia waved her hand, her look of panic intensifying. "No big deal really, it's just th--"

The front door opened behind her, and Celes stepped out onto the porch, not looking surprised in the least to see Tristan and Beckett. Olivia looked like she wanted to die on the spot, and Tristan gave Celes a knowing smile.

"Hi Celes."

"Trinity. Beckett."

"Hey man," Beckett shook Celes's hand, but was looking at him somewhat guardedly.

Celes put his hand on Olivia's lower back, and Olivia smiled up at him faintly before turning her big, nervous eyes on Tristan.

"Your Mom was wondering where you went," Celes told Olivia, who nodded.

"I'll be right back in."

Taking his cue, Celes nodded at her and went back inside.

"Are you mad? Do you hate me? Do you want us to leave? You're not going to leave now, are you?" Olivia grabbed Tristan's hands, still looking one second away from a panic attack.

"No! No, no, and no," Tristan exclaimed, shaking her head. "Oceana, it's OK. Really."

"I don't know how it happened." Olivia shook her head, searching Tristan's face as though she was trying to make sure Tristan wasn't lying. "A few months after you deflected he and I hit it off at a gathering, but it made both of us feel really weird and I was dating Tyler Daniels at the time, so we sort of avoided each other after that. And then fast forward and I had graduated, and then joined the community, but then I was doing school and working and not really going to the gatherings too much, and then about a year and a half, maybe almost two years ago now, I went to one because Dad said I was making them look bad by not showing up, and..."

Olivia trailed off, a faraway look in her eyes as she shook her head once again.

"We started hanging out after I moved to Metairie. We went to lunch a couple of times, we'd go on runs together, we became friends. And then I went as his date to Sanguin's wedding over a year ago and..." Olivia lifted one shoulder.

"You don't need to explain any of this to me, Oceana," Tristan said gently, reaching out and squeezing Olivia's hand.

"I think he's going to ask me to marry him, Trinity," Olivia blurted, covering her mouth with both hands. Removing her hands, she added, "Well, either that or he's getting ready to break up with me, with the way he's been acting."

Tristan smiled, hugging Olivia.

"I'm so happy for you, and while I have no insider

knowledge, I'm positive he's not breaking up with you. Also, I knew this was coming long before you did."

Olivia pulled back, looking at her in amazement.

"What do you mean?"

"You wouldn't remember if I told you, but there was a moment, very quick, a long time ago between the two of you, and I just knew it would end up being relevant at some point. Plus, there was that little premonition I had of my own demise and in it Celes was in love with you."

Olivia opened and closed her mouth, not used to not being the one to know things before anyone else did.

"So you don't think it's weird?"

"I mean, it's a little weird," Tristan replied. "Considering on another path Celes would have been the one to send me to my execution, but you know. It'll be OK."

Tristan laughed then, and Olivia laughed as well, while Beckett looked on, still mystified by these strange sisters he loved so dearly.

"Let's go in before everyone comes out here instead," Olivia said, turning. She turned back. "Oh, one more thing. Ember brought someone home with him this year, too."

Tristan nodded, looking at Beckett, who raised his eyebrows.

"The fun continues. Maybe it'll be Emmeline Strandquest," Beckett said, good-naturedly, and Tristan laughed again.

They followed Olivia into the house, greeting everyone, who looked up as they entered the living room. Olivia went over to Celes, who took her hand, looking down at her in adoration, and Tristan smiled. Celes had hit the jackpot with

Olivia, and Olivia would be in good hands for the rest of her life.

"Hey Trinity, Beckett, Happy Solstice." Evander approached them, smiling, and Trinity hugged him in greeting, noticing a man lingering a few feet over his shoulder. Beckett shook Evander's hand, and Evander turned, beckoning the man over to them.

"This is Lios Fodor. Lios, this is my sister, Trinity, and her boyfriend, Beckett."

"Nice to meet you," Lios greeted, shaking their hands before smiling over at Evander. "I'm Ember's boyfriend."

His voice was pleasantly deep, his hair sandy blonde, eyes light brown. His face was friendly, but there was a wary look in his eyes that Tristan couldn't blame him for, living in the deep south and all.

"And a Yankee?" Tristan asked delightedly, grinning, and Lios nodded.

"Guilty. I'm a Rhode Island transplant."

"Well, welcome to Lavelle," Tristan replied. Then, exaggerating her accent, "And good for you! We need more'a you dem dere Yankees down here in our little ol' southern town."

"Will you ever not be embarrassing?" Evander asked, as Beckett and Lios laughed.

Tristan shook her head.

"No, probably not. What other function do I serve as your sister?"

"Trinity!" Sol approached, arms out, and Tristan hugged her. Sol turned and hugged Beckett next. "Beckett. We're so glad you could make it."

Umbris wasn't far behind with his own hugs and greetings, and Tristan looked around the room, smiling.

"The gang's all here this year, huh?"

"And we couldn't be happier," Sol replied, her face and voice as serene as they always were. "You should know that the Crenshaws will be here later."

Tristan nodded, trying not to grimace as Sol and Umbris walked off to talk to Olivia and Celes. Tristan and Celes had buried their hatchet a long time ago, and Celes had clearly moved on and was happier than ever, but Thera and Dune Crenshaw had never quite gotten over Tristan's rejection of the community and, by extension, their son.

Beckett put his arm around Tristan's waist, careful to avoid her right side, which had never fully healed. Sol had done an excellent job on the burn imparted by Orion, and fresh skin had eventually formed over the wound, but it had never progressed beyond that, and was still tender to the touch all these years later. It was better than Tristan had hoped for, once Sol had voiced her concerns that the burn was not going to get better *at all,* but it was a constant, unfortunate reminder of Orion.

Orion. Tristan couldn't believe it had been over five years since the battle of her life; couldn't believe it had been four years since she'd told Beckett the truth. She'd held out as long as she could, after, but when Bayle had contacted her in the spring to let her know they'd lifted her ban, nearly a year after the confrontation, Tristan could no longer keep silent. The next time Beckett mentioned another "strange dream" he'd had -- this one about running through the woods on Evander's back -- Tristan had used it as her opening.

In his usual fashion, Beckett had rolled easily with the news that Tristan had to tell him something important, and had not even looked concerned when she'd told him she didn't want him to say anything until she'd finished talking. As Tristan had known he would, Beckett had looked amused and highly skeptical as she had filled him in, though by the time she restored his memories he'd begun to take her seriously. Tristan would never forget the way his brow had tightly knit as his hand had gone to the jagged, dark red scar on the front of his right shoulder, his fingers tracing the uneven skin as he remembered being stabbed by the guards.

It had ended up being a weeks-long process, Beckett digesting the information and unpacking it mentally. While Tristan had been relieved that there were officially no more secrets between them, it had been incredibly hard for her to watch Beckett struggle and to know she was partly responsible for how he did. He'd been angry with her at one point, which Tristan had expected, though that hadn't made it any easier to deal with. He'd also been scared, shocked, grieved -- he'd run the gamut, and Tristan had waited patiently by his side through it all.

The turning point came when Beckett had told her, in bed one night nearly two months later, that his favorite piece of the new information he'd gotten was the part about his destiny connection with Tristan. They'd both begun breathing regularly again, after that, and Tristan had known they'd be OK.

And they were. They were more than OK. Tristan looked at Beckett, and he looked back at her, his eyes traveling down her face and body, his expression still giving her butterflies after over five years of seeing it with regularity. Beckett leaned in to whisper in her ear.

"I'm having very ill-timed and inappropriate thoughts about you in that dress."

Tristan blushed, looking down at the blood red velvet skater dress she wore. It was long-sleeved with a scooped neckline and a short, flared skirt, and around her neck was the trinity knot choker Sol and Umbris had given her so many years ago.

"You were having them earlier, too, and that's why we were the last ones to get here," Tristan whispered back, and Beckett grinned, wiggling his eyebrows at her.

Indeed, Tristan had come out of their hotel bedroom, ready to go, and Beckett had walked her right back in, kicking the door closed behind them as Tristan had half-heartedly protested. It had taken his lips on her neck, however, for her to change her mind, and they'd ended up leaving for Lavelle nearly an hour after they'd intended.

"Beckett, how is the psychiatry program coming along?" Umbris asked, strolling back over to them, and Tristan hid a grin at Beckett's brief struggle to change the direction of his thoughts.

"It's coming. People who say the first year of medical school are soul-sucking are not kidding, is what I've learned so far."

Umbris clapped him on the shoulder, a proud grin on his face.

"If anyone can do it, you can."

"I appreciate your confidence, sir." Beckett smiled back at him, and Tristan squeezed his hand.

"And Tristan, how is work?" Umbris asked, turning his gaze on her.

"Amazing," Tristan said with a smile.

For the last year, she'd been working with an author who had decided to undertake, in earnest, an in-depth project on Atlantis and its possible link to the Bimini Road in the Bahamas. Prior to beginning working with him, Tristan had thought the topic had been covered to exhaustion, but she'd quickly learned how wrong she was. It had been an endlessly fascinating year of research, including a trip to the Bahamas, and Tristan was in her element.

"It's fascinating, the work they're doing," Sol told the room at large, and Tristan quickly caught them all up.

"Can you imagine if your author blows open the lid on Atlantis? Remember us little people." Evander grinned good-naturedly, and Tristan laughed.

Olivia suggested they go decorate that year's solstice wreath, then, and she and Celes led the way to the backyard. The group sat down at the table, chatting and laughing, and Tristan felt a completeness in her soul that she'd longed for her whole life. Things had worked out in ways she had never expected, and every day confirmed she'd chosen right when she'd taken Beckett's hand and joined him in the common world.

As she added laurel leaves to the wreath, Tristan sent up a genuine offer of gratitude to the universe, and somewhere, deep inside of her, Tristan could swear she felt the very briefest stirrings of pure, golden energy.

Made in the USA
Middletown, DE
20 July 2021